Praise for Heart of a Dove

"Set just after the U.S. Civil War, this passionate opening volume of a projected series successfully melds historical narrative, women's issues, and breathless romance with horsewomanship, trailside deer-gutting, and alluring smidgeons of Celtic ESP."
— *Publishers Weekly*

"There is a lot I liked about this book. It didn't pull punches, it feels period, it was filled with memorable characters and at times lovely descriptions and language. Even though there is a sequel coming, this book feels complete."

— *Dear Author*

"With a sweet romance, good natured camaraderie, and a very real element of danger, this book is hard to put down."
— *San Francisco Book Review*

ALSO BY ABBIE WILLIAMS

 THE SHORE LEAVE CAFE SERIES

SUMMER AT THE SHORE LEAVE CAFE

SECOND CHANCES

A NOTION OF LOVE

WINTER AT THE WHITE OAKS LODGE

WILD FLOWER

THE FIRST LAW OF LOVE

UNTIL TOMORROW

THE WAY BACK

FORBIDDEN

THE DOVE SERIES

HEART OF A DOVE

SOUL OF A CROW

GRACE OF A HAWK

Soul

OF A

Crow

ABBIE WILLIAMS

central
avenue
publishing
2016

Published by Central Avenue Publishing, an imprint of Central Avenue Marketing Ltd.
www.centralavenuepublishing.com

Published in Canada
Printed in United States of America

1. FICTION/Romance - Historical

Library and Archives Canada Cataloguing in Publication

Williams, Abbie, author
    Soul of a crow / Abbie Williams.

(Dove)
Issued in print and electronic formats.
ISBN 978-1-77168-036-3 (paperback).--ISBN 978-1-77168-037-0 (epub).--
ISBN 978-1-77168-051-6 (mobipocket)

    I. Title.

PS3623.I462723S69 2016   813'.6   C2015-907436-3
                                                C2015-907437-1

NOT A DAY GOES BY WHEN I DO NOT THINK OF YOU

L EAVE IT, SAWYER, we'll not be needing a fire this night," Gus told me. "It's warm enough."

I obeyed, sitting back on my bootheels, and continued to stare fixedly at the kindling I had arranged in the shallow fire pit, freshly scraped into the earth with the blade of my knife. I blinked and attempted to refocus upon Angus Warfield's face; behind the full, unfamiliar beard, his flint-gray eyes were steady and blessedly recognizable. He was still the man I'd known in my old life, the life to which the path leading back had been obliterated. I knew that I would not ever find my way along its length again, despite the fact that the War ended.

The country was formally at peace.

Word came to us that Lee walked from the courthouse with his sword in hand; it had not been tendered in the Surrender. Eleven days later, modeling himself after Grant at Appomattox, Sherman formally accepted Johnston's surrender of the Army of Tennessee. All of the officers in attendance were allowed to keep their sidearms. Despite our lesser status in the eyes of the army, Boyd and I retained our .44 pistols, first issued to us as cavalrymen in 'sixty-two; Gus still had his Enfield rifle strapped to his horse, a solid, dappled gelding named Admiral.

Boyd and I found Gus by a stroke of sheer luck only days past; he had been riding west from Virginia, where his regiment spent its final weeks. Gus had been with Lee's army to the end; I couldn't look into his eyes for any great length of time, overwhelmed by the anguish that lingered there, just beneath the surface.

"We're going home now," Gus said, crouching near me and studying my face. He said, low, "Sawyer, by God, it is good to see you. I haven't seen a soul from home in close to two years."

Home.

Where in God's name was home anymore? I could not have answered this question had my very life depended upon a response. I was so tired. I was tired way down deep inside my bones. I could feel it sapping at me, draining me of everything but the urge to sink into slumber. I could not deny that my mind flirted, however unwillingly, with the notion of death—it seemed an entity which crawled seductively near these days, as close as my own shadow at times, whispering a promise of rest, a cessation of the nightmares which plagued the meager sleep I could claim. It was all I could do to refrain from scouring the darkening woods for a glimpse of the black-winged death specter skulking amongst the tree trunks, whose concentrated gaze I could sense with a soldier's instinct.

Go, I ordered it, though I didn't look its way. *Go, now. We have given you enough.*

But it remained unmoving, observing silently, and a distinct unease skittered along my spine.

Jesus, Sawyer, I reprimanded myself, unable to restrain a shudder at what my imagination conjured. With a sincere determination, I shut my eyes and fixed a thought of Tennessee, which I had once called home, firmly into my mind.

The dusky evening, the pile of kindling, vanished as I imagined the Bledsoe holler where I'd been raised, a captivating place of early sunsets and old-growth trees, grapevines trailing my shoulders and icy creek water around my ankles as I explored with my brothers and the Carter boys. I had at one time known every gnarled tree root that snaked along the ground, every secret hiding place that young boys neglecting their chores could seek out.

Warming to this vision, I pictured the wide front porch that ran the length of my boyhood home, upon the railings of which honeysuckle grew so thickly that its flowering limbs seemed to support the porch rather than the wooden beams beneath. I saw the adjacent two-story barn silhouetted against the breast of a pale sky, gilded by a mellow amber afterglow of sinking sun, its upper windows propped open to the sweetness of an evening breeze. I recalled long afternoons spent playing in that barn, my brothers at my side, as they had been to the last.

My brothers...

Ethan...

Jere...

Just the thought of their names was painful as a blade between the ribs, with a slow death to follow, blood draining away like wine from a tipped bottle; I had witnessed many such sluggish deaths. Despite various injuries, my body survived the War and still remained functional—all of the death was in my mind, sticky as an orb spider's web, just as difficult to brush aside. The skeins of it clung.

No.

Do not think of being too late.

Do not think of crawling through the ditch with cold red water seeping over your wrists.

Oh Jesus, please... make it stop...

My head ached and I closed my eyes even more tightly, and there, just yonder in my memory, I could see ghost mist that rose up from the ground on spring evenings, tinted a haunting blend of indigo blue and deep green. I could smell the rich earth of Cumberland County, the syrup of the honey-suckle blossoms, the dusty, hay-filled barn and the horses therein, all scents as familiar to me as my own skin. Mama and Daddy would be waiting for me at the top of the porch steps, side by side; Daddy would have an arm about Mama's waist, holding her close, as always. I'd not received a letter from my parents in many months, but post had long since ceased to move freely; it was a gamble sending correspondence anywhere these days.

Though perhaps now that the War was over...

Boyd and I had spoken those words to one another as though mired in a dream when the news first came to us, in Georgia. Our regiment had been camped there, and we'd been eventually discharged. No money was paid out, though we'd been allowed to keep our armaments; our commanding officer's exact words were, "I don't give a flying fuck. And you'll need them on the way home, poor bastards."

It was still surreal. The Confederacy, the dream of it, was dead, reduced to ash. I felt as insubstantial as ash myself, ready to scatter to pieces on the faintest breeze. If someone were to ask me why I'd fought, why I'd spent the last two and a half years as a soldier, I could not have articulated a response. I stared now at Gus without saying anything, and he gently curved a hand around my right shoulder, squeezing me the way my own father would have, had he been here in the clearing with us.

"It will be all right, Sawyer," Gus said quietly. Though he said no more on the subject, I knew he understood what I was feeling; he did not press for a response.

Boyd joined us momentarily; he'd walked into the cedars for a bit of privacy. He bore dark smudges of fatigue beneath his eyes. With a thick black beard obscuring the lower portion of his face, he closely resembled his father, Bainbridge Carter, and appeared a good decade older than his actual age. I was certain the same could be said of me; I had not scraped a razor over my jaws in months. With sincere determination I kept my thoughts upon my parents, James and Ellen Davis, and upon Bainbridge and Clairee, imagining how they would rejoice to have us home again. And little Malcolm, who was close to ten years old by now. Malcolm, the only brother left to Boyd. My brothers had been slaughtered on a battlefield strewn with rocks within two months of leaving home; Beaumont and Grafton Carter had both been dead by the following summer, of 'sixty-three.

If I closed my eyes too long when awake and not numbed by the haze of exhaustion, images sprang forth, unbidden. The specter would scuttle closer, its black-bright eyes intent. I pressed both hands over my face, catching the scents of dirt and smoke from my skin. Boyd and I slept beneath the distant stars, though close to one another, our backs nearly touching, since leaving the regiment; the warmth of another person was the only thing that offered any hope of alleviating the night terrors, for the both of us.

Boyd and I had served together for the duration of the War and had seen more than any one person should be asked to bear witness to in a single existence. I prayed that in good time we would be able to speak of it, at least to one another. Boyd was the only person on the face of the Earth with whom I felt as though I could be completely honest, could speak without having to carefully guard each word. Perhaps Gus now, as well. Gus had been a soldier. He knew. I spoke little these days as it was; Whistler was the only one I could manage more than a few sentences for. My horse, my sweet girl. She had saved my life time and again.

And you kept her safe, in return.
You couldn't manage to keep Ethan and Jeremiah alive.
Don't let Mama and Daddy blame me.

I blame myself. I will always blame myself for it.

Gus's low, strained voice penetrated my desperate thoughts. He crouched on the opposite side of the cold fire pit and said, "I figure we'll be home by end of the week, if the weather stays fair. I've not a word from my Grace in months."

It was concerning him greatly; he'd mentioned this at least three times. I tried not to let the knot of unease in my lower belly take precedence over my already-tenuous control. None of us dared to acknowledge what could await us upon returning home; I reminded myself that Sherman had not sliced so brutally through Tennessee, as he had Georgia…

Oh dear God…

Boyd held half a day-old biscuit towards me and his forehead wrinkled as he asked a silent question. I shook my head at once, not the least hungry, though we'd eaten little since mid-morning coffee and hardtack. Hunger seemed a trivial thing, food a luxury I could not bear just now.

"They've surely heard word," Gus continued. "Doubtless they're expecting us any day."

From the near-distance, perhaps a few hundred yards, came the sound of laughter, further adding to the nightmarish unreality of the evening. Men's laughter, rapidly approaching our position. We were not upon a well-traveled road and all of us tensed at once, hands lifting to the pistols strapped upon our hips.

"Shit," muttered Boyd.

We hunkered, animal-like, wary as criminals in the gathering darkness, armed but still vulnerable; despite the fact that the War was indeed over, running across a group of Federals was not an encounter any of us were eager to experience. It would be inevitable, eventually, but I would much rather it be in daylight hours. Wounds were keen-blooded and raw, and animosity would rage for a long time, I felt certain. I listened hard, but we needn't have worried in that moment. The sounds of their passage, whoever they were, soon faded to silence.

"Come, let us retire," Gus muttered.

Sleep came upon me like a heavy cloak, and so it was with an exaggerated sense of disorientation that I startled awake at some later point in the night. I blinked, confused, as though engulfed in ghost mist, the low-lying fog of home. I stared at the bare branches entwining their fingers high above me, mind reeling to full consciousness, and then heard the noise that had surely jolted me from sleep in the first place: Whistler's frantic whinny.

I moved fluidly, driven by instinct, knife in hand before I was even upon my feet. The moon was only a few nights past the new, just bright enough to lend the clearing a pale, eerie glow in which I could plainly observe two men, working swiftly to untie our horses. A third, mounted, lingered in the trees and whooped a wordless noise of alarm upon hearing me, lifting his pistol at once. Moonlight glinted off the long, slender barrel as he called over, with an almost jovial tone, "Hold up there now, Johnny Reb!"

Drunk. I could hear it in his voice. Boyd and Gus scrambled to their feet as I disobeyed the order and stalked towards the horses.

Shoot me, bastard, I thought. *You couldn't know how little I fucking care.*

"Stand down!" he yelled, and fired twice when I did not.

No matter how grim my thoughts, instinct sent me instantly into a crouch. He discharged a third round. I heard the bullet strike a trunk mere feet from my head. Gus and Boyd disappeared into the cover of the trees, where they would certainly circle in an attempt to flank the thieving bastards. I kept to ground, ducking into dense brush, and whistled to my horse; I was heartened to hear her immediate nickering response. I knew she would dig in her heels until I could get to her.

One of the Federals whistled back, in mockery, as though for an errant dog. He called from the darkness, "Where you hiding, Johnny?"

"C'mon, let's ride!" a man urged from a different direction, and I sprang into flight, towards that voice.

They had reclaimed their own mounts and were preparing to flee, not twenty paces to my left, and I charged them. They had all three of our horses by their lead lines, somewhat hampered by this burden. I heard two shots fired at a right angle to my position, and knew it was Gus or Boyd, from the trees. Two of the Federals fired back repeatedly, cursing, and I was nearly upon them, breathing hard, fury lending my limbs additional strength. I came abreast of Whistler and caught her halter, forcibly stalling their forward motion.

"Sonofa*bitch*," the man holding her line grunted, forced to rein to a halt. I didn't release my hold. He turned swiftly in his saddle, aimed directly between my eyes, and fired. The cylinder clicked on an empty chamber and he spat his frustration. Heart pulsing at this narrow escape, I saw the silver length of his blade flash seconds before the tip of it scoured my right cheek, sending trails of hot blood at once down my jaw.

Had he leaned forward even a fraction, he would have stabbed well into my face and rendered me incapable of responding; it was his misfortune that I was further enraged by this slicing of my skin. I was conscious of the surroundings only minimally behind the red haze that descended. My fingers closed around the wrist of his sword arm and before I realized I'd yanked, he was flat upon his back on the ground before me. I fell to my knees almost atop him, breathing harshly, knife already poised to kill.

Gunshots rang out directly above, but I didn't stop to see from where they were fired.

In the milky moonlight I saw how his eyes widened in surprise—the body is always surprised by death, even an expected death—just before I plunged the blade into his throat. I'd aimed true; it sank without resistance to nearly its hilt. The handle slipped in my sweating grasp as I wrenched it free and then stabbed again, and again. A madness fell over me, as blood flowed down my neck from the superficial wound on my face, coppery-scented and far more heated than my skin. His blood flew in arcs, wetly striking my lap, and still I stabbed.

"*Sawyer!*" I heard somewhere behind me, as though Boyd was shouting at the other end of a long tunnel. He fired twice in quick succession, almost over my shoulder, and then Gus's arm came around my chest and he dragged me backwards.

Hooves thundered away into the night. This was the only sound I could discern above those of my ragged breathing, my heartbeat which seemed ten times amplified. Gus released me, his own breathing fast and uneven. I staggered to the edge of the clearing and vomited repeatedly; the knife fell, striking the ground with a muted thud.

"Well, you done kilt him all right," Boyd said, though I was unable to stand straight to look over at him. Absurdly, he laughed. It was unhinged laughter, in no way acquainted with any sort of humor. He added, "He's dead as a goddamn stuck pig, that's what."

"Sawyer, your face," Gus said quietly.

I was rendered wordless, hands braced on my knees. Another round of nausea engulfed me, though surely there could be nothing left for my stomach to expel. I could smell bile, and blood.

Boyd said, "Jesus Christ, we oughta ride after an' kill them other two."

Gus shook his head, I could see from the corner of my gaze.

Boyd insisted, "We oughta, I feel it. I feel it, strong."

Gus said firmly, "No, let it go. Let us ride, boys, we cannot remain here. Jesus, we'd be hung."

Boyd came near and caught up my knife, wiping it clean on his trousers. He said, low, "Let's go, old friend. Let's go *now*."

Together we grabbed the heels of the dead Federal and dragged him through the debris of the woods and into the cover of the cedars, before we rode out.

The crow remained amid the tree trunks, watching, its sleek black wings hunched as it sat sullenly and, for that night, silently let us go.

I NARROWED MY left eye to a slit, taking careful aim; I did not intend to miss this shot. The last two rabbits I drew a bead upon were little more than startled at the echoing report of the gunfire, leaving me with a sore shoulder and ringing ears, not to mention wasted ammunition, rather than fresh meat. Merely the prospect of a spitted rabbit roasted to a juicy crisp over our cookfire was motivation enough to continue in the frustrating endeavor of hitting such a fast-darting target.

"Steady," Sawyer murmured, his voice scarcely more than a breath. Though he was armed with his squirrel rifle, he carried it loosely in the crook of his right elbow, its long barrel directed at the ground three feet before us. He could have easily taken the animal with one shot, I knew, but he refrained, patiently allowing me the practice. I released a slow breath, a trickle of sweat slipping wetly between my breasts. It was thickly overcast and had grown increasingly humid, the heavens quilted with fat-bellied clouds, promising objectionable weather before long. I scarcely formed the thought before a cold drop flicked my ear, and then several more my left cheek, tilted slightly upwards above the rifle's metal sights.

Do not be distracted. You have been practicing for this, I reminded myself, and centered all focus upon the creature. The prairie, cloaked in dour grays this day, the grasses appearing all the more vividly green against such a drear backdrop, receded to the distant horizon. The small midges that seemed to adore flying into one's nostrils and eyes, the increasing patter of rain, the restless grumble of thunder to the west—all were silenced and stilled. By contrast, the rabbit's outline grew sharp, the bunched energy of its long hind legs, the slender peaks of its ears, the single watching eye, each etched in charcoal by the intensity of my focus.

Squeeze the trigger, rather than pull, I heard Angus instruct.

And so I did.

The stock punched hard, as I anticipated, sending me quick-stepping backwards despite having braced for the impact; Sawyer reached instinctively, cupping his free hand beneath my right elbow and keeping me stable. A flock of blackbirds hidden by the tall grass were disrupted by the shot, now furiously taking wing into the pewter sky, fanning out like spread fingers. I could not hear Sawyer over the ringing in my ears, but the smile upon his face indicated that my aim proved true; it was the first time I had struck something other than a tin can, and I felt an answering smile bloom over my face.

He leaned closer to me and his mouth formed the words, *Good shot!*

Together, we hurried to claim the prize before the rain grew heavier, and Sawyer bent to catch up the creature by its ears. My hearing at least partially restored, his words were only slightly muffled as he said admiringly, "Clean through the head."

"I hit it!" I rejoiced, perhaps disproportionately pleased at this truth, but proud of myself nonetheless. The squirrel rifle in my grip once belonged to Angus, and was a heavy firearm, but I neatly shifted it to my elbow so that I could take the rabbit from Sawyer.

"It's messy," he warned, and indeed my fingers grew slick with blood as I accepted it from his grasp.

"I cannot wait to show Malcolm," I said, refusing to behave squeamishly. I had gleaned from my time in Missouri many invaluable lessons, far more demanding than any imparted upon me at my mother's knee, in the luxury of a loving home. Here in the wilds it became quickly apparent that learning required the completion of tasks at one point in my life unfathomable; the result of refusing to acknowledge this was the inability to survive, a truth as simple as that.

If there was one thing I had learned, with great humility, it was how to survive.

"He'll be in a tizzy if you bagged a rabbit and he did not," Sawyer recognized with amusement, and even in the darkening, rainy gloom of the afternoon and the shadow of his hat brim, his eyes glinted with golds and greens, captivatingly beautiful, and dearer to me than I could have put into words.

"I hope he did, as I intend to eat this one entirely myself," I said, only half in jest.

My appetite had been poor of late, and welcome hunger now grumbled in my belly, echoing the strengthening thunder. The words barely cleared my lips when Sawyer silently held out his arm, indicating that I halt, bent swiftly to one knee and raised the rifle with a movement as graceful as a heron lancing a fish. Rising just as effortlessly to his feet, he jogged to retrieve the second rabbit; upon his return, he held it aloft and said, "I was just making certain that you're able to, Lorie-love."

Whistler and Admiral were tethered in copse of cottonwoods fifty paces east, closer to the river and our camp. Sawyer and I had not ridden far, as it was still difficult for me to sit the saddle for long periods of time; in the days since we traveled at a deliberately slow pace north from Missouri, having cleared the Iowa border just yesterday, I had been content to ride on the wagon seat. Today was only my second attempt at horseback, and to my considerable relief it had not proven painful; I'd not shed any additional blood since miscarrying nearly a fortnight past, and the saddle burns welted upon my inner legs healed over remarkably well.

All of the irreparable damage was emotional, the toll exacted for my having survived when Angus and his unborn child had not. Only a wooden marker, painstakingly crafted by Sawyer and Boyd, gave a hint as to the reality of the man who lay beneath the ground, the brave and kind man who had recognized me as the daughter of a fellow solider, who had subsequently insisted I leave behind, as of that very night, the indignities of my life as a whore and accompany him and his companions on their journey north. Angus saved me from the horror of my existence at Ginny Hossiter's, and no words could effectively convey the enormity of my gratitude.

As I had dozens of times and in various incarnations since riding away from Angus's body and the wooden cross Sawyer constructed for the child, I thought, *Forgive me, dear Gus. Please, forgive me. You would have done right by me, this I know to the bottom of my heart. You did not deserve to die in such a terrible way. Please forgive me. I know that you will look after our child in the Beyond.*

"Storm's rolling in!" Sawyer said, moving closer to me as we hastened our strides, reaching the cottonwoods and their meager shelter as a towering thunderhead unleashed a torrent perhaps a half-mile to the west. Whistler and Admiral danced on their tethers, agitated by the rapidly-advancing storm, the whites of their eyes visible, indicating their unease. As we neared, Whistler nickered in clear relief, nudging at Sawyer's side as he hurried to unwind her lead line, while I tugged free Admiral's. The big dappled gray tossed his head, nervously side-stepping, but I held firmly and he stilled.

"Look there!" I cried, and could not help but pause, one boot in the stirrup, captivated by the sheeting rain; it appeared a near-solid mass of roiling silver, a sight as eerie as it was impressive. A blinding bolt of lightning erupted in a crackling pulse, striking the ground where we had only minutes before been standing, and my spine twitched.

"It's not safe beneath these trees!" Sawyer shouted, and he took the rifle from me, securing it in the saddle scabbard before replacing his own, then helped me atop Admiral; I was wearing Malcolm's trousers, and could have taken the saddle with no assistance, but Sawyer was protective, more so than ever since our ordeal in Missouri, and made certain I was settled before mounting Whistler with his usual easy grace. Together we cantered across the prairie, each clutching a rabbit, arriving just ahead of the rain. To the east of our small camp the Mississippi rolled at a clip, crested with white arrows of waves as the wind blew fitfully. Fortune and Aces High, along with Juniper, were all three staked within sight, indicating that Boyd and Malcolm were here.

"Twister?" Boyd yelled in our direction, competing with the wind to be heard as he emerged from his and Malcolm's wall tent, twenty paces away. He stood straight and shaded his vision against the gale, looking westward.

"Take these and hurry inside," Sawyer leaned near to tell me, and while I would have helped him secure the horses, I gathered the game and did as he asked instead, recognizing concern in the way his eyebrows were knit.

"We didn't catch a glimpse of one!" I called to Boyd as I neared, the ground already growing muddy beneath my boots.

"You bag them hares?" he asked, nodding at the limp creatures in my grasp.

"One of them!" I said proudly.

Malcolm's freckled face appeared in the pie-shaped opening of his and Boyd's tent, and the boy called, "I shot me a foolbird, Lorie! You shoulda seen it!"

He used the common name for prairie fowl, plump and tasty birds with less sense than chickens, and I called, earning a grin from him, "I plan to *eat* it!"

"We ain't gonna eat nothing but day-old biscuits 'less this storm clears out before nightfall!" Boyd said. He told me, "We'll skin them critters when it blows over."

I nodded agreement and ducked into the tent I shared with Sawyer, lacing all but the bottommost entrance tie. I stowed the rabbits near the edge of the canvas farthest from our bedding, laying them neatly atop the flattened grass, and then stepped on the heels of my boots, one after the other; once barefooted, I shucked free of my wet clothes and shivered into a dry shift, one of two that I possessed, next wrapping into my shawl. The wind increased in strength and the rain in tempo, thunder detonating so near our tent I pictured it hovering only an arm's length above as I knelt beside the small porcelain wash basin and scrubbed the blood from my hands. To my relief, I heard Sawyer returning after the next shattering blast of thunder; I listened as he hastily stowed our saddles beneath the awning.

"You're chilled," was the first thing he said upon entering, re-lacing the ties against the surly weather before unceremoniously stripping his boots, wet shirt, suspenders and trousers, leaving only the lower half of his union suit, a thin garment rather in need of repair. I had dried my hands but not yet lit our lantern, and reached wordlessly for him. He grinned in immediate response, catching me close and taking us at once to the rumpled bedding, where he promptly drew the quilt and snuggled me to his bare chest. Despite having just come in from the rain he was warm as an ember, and issued the low, throaty sound of contentment to which I had grown blissfully accustomed, declaring, "Much better."

"*Worlds* better," I agreed, closing my eyes, thankful beyond measure; there would never come a time, even if fortune was kind enough to allow us the rest of our lives together, that I would take for granted the feeling of being held secure in his arms.

"It was a good shot," he said again, gently stroking my hair. Though I had neatly braided its length this morning it was currently half-undone, tangled and damp with rain, but Sawyer was undeterred. I contentedly rested my nose at the juncture of his collarbones, feeling the rasp of his stubble, as he cupped the back of my head and pressed his lips to the slim, white scar near my left ear.

"I put them over there," I mumbled, drowsy with warmth; I did not manage to open my eyes as I indicated vaguely in the direction of the dead rabbits, though I flinched inadvertently as thunder sliced apart the sky. Sawyer's arms tightened in response, and I whispered, "Boyd said we'd clean them after the storm."

"You rest, darlin'," Sawyer said, his voice low and sweet, so familiar to me; the soft cadence of Tennessee lingered in his words. He said, "There are shadows beneath your eyes, and I mean to see them gone. You rest, and I'll hold you."

WHEN I woke, the air outside was utterly still, the canvas wall slanting above our heads tinted with the placid auburn tones of an evening sun; from outside, near the smoldering fire, I could hear the comforting rise and fall of Boyd and Malcolm engaged in quiet conversation. Sawyer was snoring, flat upon his back, one arm stretched outward, the other curved about my waist, and his forearm was no doubt numb, pinned as it was beneath me. I was rolled into the quilt like a sausage in a flapjack, and smiled at the sight of him asleep. Unable to resist, I smoothed my fingertips along his fair hair, trailing over the blue-striped ticking of his pillow, softly as a cottonseed alighting upon the surface of the river.

Sawyer issued a particularly loud snore, almost a snort, and I muffled a giggle, stretching to kiss the small dark mole on his neck; it was one of four on his upper body, the other three positioned in a neat row on the left side of his powerful chest. I leaned to kiss him in that exact place, my loose hair falling over his nose and chin, and he snorted again, groaning a little and then moving with purpose, engulfing me in his arms and exhaling a rush of air directly against the side of my neck, where he knew I was enormously ticklish. My breathless laughter was followed by the immediate sounds of Malcolm scrambling to our tent, curious about the racket within.

Positioned just where the entrance was laced, Malcolm demanded, "What you-all *doing* in there?"

"Never you mind, kid," Sawyer teased, while I climbed atop him and ineffectually attempted to poke his ribs. Sawyer was too quick, rolling to his front side and blocking with his elbows, preventing my jabbing fingers from making contact, and I could suddenly smell roasting meat. When I looked that way I saw that the rabbits were gone; surely Malcolm must have crept within to retrieve them for Boyd's knife. The resultant scent was rich in the air, and my stomach responded accordingly. I left off tickling him and aligned my front with Sawyer's back, hooking my chin at the juncture of his neck, so that my breath was near his ear. Face buried in the pillow, his laughter was muffled.

"We best join them," I murmured, with reluctance, and in fact found myself latching one thigh even more securely about his hip in order to keep him here a little longer, forcibly if necessary; I sensed rather than saw his grin. I shifted to rest my lips between his shoulder blades, feeling his hard muscles beneath my breasts and belly. He turned effortlessly, keeping me atop his body, stacking both forearms under his head and grinning at me in the way he had that set everything within me to quickening. I gripped his ears and rested my forehead against his for the space of several heartbeats, studying his eyes at close range. My long hair fell all around us.

"You blinked first," he murmured, teasing me further.

"I did not," I retorted in a whisper.

"What in *tarnation* is taking you-all so long? We got dinner cooking!" Malcolm informed impatiently, still directly outside our tent and no more than five feet from us.

"Goddamn, boy, leave them two alone," Boyd ordered, and I smiled to hear the customary note of affectionate irritation in his tone as he addressed his younger brother.

Hungry as I was, I was not yet ready to be pulled from my preoccupation with Sawyer; I traced my fingertips in a beloved path along his handsome face, touching his cheekbones, sunburned to a deep golden-brown, his jaws and chin, my thumbs caressing the lines of his eyebrows in passing, the shape of his sensual mouth. He shivered, catching my hands into his much larger ones and kissing each palm.

"You did blink first," he whispered, and I was unable to keep from smiling at him.

"Lorie," he murmured. Studying my eyes, he told me without words, *I am so happy to be here with you, like this.*

It is a gift, I thought in return, and knew that he heard; it had been that way between us from the first.

"I got a surprise!" Malcolm insisted, still nearby, and I could not help but giggle; Sawyer grinned, tenderly kissing the side of my neck, stroking lightly with his tongue, as I shivered and indulged in being sheltered against him for one last, sweet second.

"I wish to see you eat well," he said firmly, drawing us to our feet; standing, my nose was at a level with the center of his chest. He donned his dry muslin shirt, tucking it into his trousers and buttoning his suspenders into place with the easy motions of one not at all concerned with a fastidious dressing routine. He slipped the suspender straps over his shoulders and then swept back his thick hair, holding a leather thong he'd grabbed from the ground between his teeth, before retying it deftly into place around his hair. He knew I had been unable to eat much of late; my ribs were more prominent than they had been at the beginning of June.

"I will," I assured him, and he stroked my face, bestowing a final kiss before ducking outside. Sawyer was thoughtful to a fault, allowing me as much privacy as he could manage when we shared a space scarcely large enough for two adults, so careful to give me the chance to recover from what I had been through in Missouri; until I was fully healed and we were properly joined in marriage, he would not seek anything physical beyond kissing me and holding me close as we slept, this I knew well. It did not, however, alter for so much as an instant the intensity of awareness between us that existed from the first days we had known one another.

Outside, Malcolm immediately claimed his attention; a smile tugged at my heart as I buttoned into a skirt and then knelt to root out my comb.

"Sawyer," the boy said. There was a note of reprimand in his tone and I listened with interest as my fingers flew, re-braiding my hair. Malcolm went on, as though addressing a naughty child, "You ain't got your boots on, an' you's always harping on me for it."

I imagined Sawyer ruffling Malcolm's shaggy dark hair. He replied calmly, "That's the truth. My socks haven't finished drying, that's all. Though I do appreciate your concern."

"Where's Lorie-Lorie?" Malcolm all but demanded, referring to me by his usual nickname. Each of them had a particular way of addressing me; Boyd called me 'Lorie-girl,' and to Sawyer I was 'Lorie-love' or *mo mhuirnín milis*, one of the Irish endearments he favored. My heart swelled with love for them, all three.

"I'll be out directly," I called.

"Well, hurry!" Malcolm ordered. "I ain't had a chance to show you—"

"Hold your tongue, boy," Boyd interrupted him to chastise. "Mama, God rest her sweet soul, would strap your thoughtless hide for talkin' to a lady that way."

"Aw, Lorie knows I ain't but excited to see her," Malcolm said. He came close to the tent and attempted to rap on the canvas the way he would have a wooden door, imploring, "Ain't that so?"

Fully dressed and hair braided, I emerged into the evening light and Malcolm caught me in an exuberant hug. I smoothed Malcolm's shaggy hair, regarding him with deep fondness. He was tanned as brown as a batch of walnut-dye, his dark, long-lashed eyes merry. Freckles walked all along his nose and cheekbones, and he was in rather desperate need of a creek bath.

"It's so," I confirmed. "What did you want to show me?"

"Lookee," Malcolm enthused, tugging me towards the embers over which the iron grate was propped, and where two rabbits, in addition to two prairie hens, crackled deliciously. He pointed to the ground near the shallow fire pit Boyd dug last night, where five speckled eggs were lined in a row, smooth and pretty as rocks plucked from the river bottom.

"Eggs!" I exclaimed in joy, already imagining the cheerful sizzle of them cracked into our pan.

"Nest was yonder," Malcolm said, indicating westward; the open plains stretched as far as an eye could see in every direction around our camp, though I knew that Keokuk, Iowa waited just to the north. It would be the first we had seen of a town in some weeks, and as much as I wished to avoid most all contact with strangers, I was hopeful for the presence of a preacher.

"It's been a piece since we's had eggs," Boyd said, from his seat on the ground, where he contentedly drew on a tobacco roll. Though Boyd was much taller and far more solidly built than Malcolm, they resembled each other to a marked degree, the two of them nearly the last of their family left alive.

Before the War, the Carters had densely populated the Bledsoe holler, in Cumberland County; Boyd and Malcolm's family had numbered six, not including aunts, uncles, cousins, and other shirttail relatives; they farmed the eastern edge of the holler, while Sawyer's family resided just across, to the west. Sawyer and Boyd were of an age, both twenty-four, and had been raised as closely as any brothers. In the crisp late-autumn of 1862, they joined the Army of Tennessee under General Joseph Wheeler, in the company of four additional brothers, Ethan and Jeremiah Davis, and Beaumont and Grafton Carter—of the six of them, only Sawyer and Boyd returned to Tennessee alive. Boyd and Malcolm were the sole remaining members left to pass on the Carter name; likewise, Sawyer was the last Davis.

Boyd used a sharpened stick to poke at the meat, declaring, "Any moment now. Good work, Lorie-girl. It's right satisfying to eat what you done shot, 'specially for the first time," and I grinned at his compliment.

"The practice has proven helpful," I said.

Sawyer took his customary position to Boyd's right, sitting on a split log with one foot braced against an adjacent piece of wood. His feet were bare and dirt-smudged, as were the hems of his trousers; he held a tin cup of steaming coffee. He reached his free hand to me, angling a knee for me to sit upon. Once settled, I appropriated the cup for a sip.

"You twos are hoping for a preacher in the next town," Boyd noted, reading my thoughts. He winked at Sawyer and me, adding, "Get you two hitched up proper-like. Aw, shit, Davis, what I wouldn't give for a wedding celebration like in the old days." His dark eyebrows lifted in amusement at what he could clearly discern as my skepticism at this remark. He hurried to explain, "Lorie-girl, once upon a time, back home, a wedding was a cause for celebration the likes of no other on the ridge. Daddy would tap a whiskey barrel, Mama would dress in her finest an' make sure the lot of us was likewise spit-shined. Damn. Me an' Sawyer, here, an' the boys"—and I understood he meant their brothers—"would suffer through the ceremony, castin' our eyes about for the prettiest girls in the church, so's we could try an' talk to them later. You remember the night that Grayson Pike an' Orla Main hitched up?"

At Boyd's question Sawyer snorted a laugh and affirmed, "I could hardly forget."

Malcolm knelt near Sawyer and me, stirring at the fire with a long stick as Boyd's eyes took on a storytelling shine I knew well. Studying the horizon, gazing into the past, Boyd said, "Sawyer an' me was sixteen or so, an' fortunate enough to sneak a bottle of Daddy's apple-pie around the far side of the barn. The August moon was full as a fresh-scrubbed face, pouring light upon us near bright as day, an' the two of us was drunk as skunks."

Sawyer grinned at the memory of their past misbehavior. I watched him with pleasure, still holding the warm tin cup of coffee, letting its steam bathe over my nose. He traced a line between my shoulder blades with his knuckles as he said, "I could hardly see for the headache I had the next day."

Boyd agreed, "Same for me, old friend," before continuing the story. "Next thing we knew here come Ethan, all outta breath an' wanting t'tell us something. We figured it was to boast about how he'd been kissing on Helen Sue Gottlender –"

Malcolm interrupted Boyd to interject, with an air of all-knowing, "Ethan was *always* a-kissing on girls. An' *talking* about it, which Daddy said a gentleman wasn't never s'posed to do."

Sawyer and Boyd laughed heartily at this, while I listened in fascination.

Ethan had been Sawyer's younger brother, a twin to Jeremiah; Ethan and Jere had been born on the same day and were later killed within the same quarter-hour, both shot to death on the rocky ground at the battle of Murfreesboro, early in 1863, over five years ago. Sawyer carried their lifeless bodies from the field and brought them home to Suttonville, wrapped in blankets in the back of a flatbed wagon. The pain of this picture beat at the edges of my mind; I was grateful to hear the way Sawyer was still able to laugh at a memory of his brother in life, before the War ripped Ethan from existence.

"That he was," Boyd agreed, with relish. "Eth was a true ladies' man. An' ladies loved him right back. This one, too," he teased of Sawyer. Boyd winked companionably at me and continued, "But here come Eth, swearing that he'd spied two people..." Boyd twisted up his face in pure good humor, before finishing with a tone of deliberate delicacy, "Enjoying each other's company a *very* great deal, out in the holler."

"Meanin' what?" Malcolm demanded.

Though his eyebrows registered amusement, Boyd chose to ignore this question and said, "So, of course Sawyer an' me followed him out there, the two of us hanging onto each other like a pair of drunkards so's we didn't fall, an' low an' behold, Ethan was telling the truth, as there was Gus an' his sweet little wife, Grace..."

Boyd was referring to Angus and the woman with whom he'd been happily wed, long before the War created dust of their former lives. I was heartened to think there was a time when Angus had been so youthful and brazen that he had dared to make love to his wife out-of-doors, perhaps inspired by the romance of a summer wedding held on the night of a full moon.

"We ought to have been ashamed of ourselves," Sawyer said, sighing a little, with both good-natured humor at the memory and the ache of loss that would never be fully absent from any of us, now that Angus was gone.

"But we hid in the trees like the young scoundrels we was, an' watched them twos, thinkin' we was getting a few lessons," Boyd laughed. "Shit, we deserved our hides strapped raw. Never told Gus about that, though I think he mighta found a bit of humor in it, I truly do."

"He would have," Sawyer agreed, and I rested my head upon him; he smoothed the base of his palm gently down my back, caressing me.

"Angus was happy with Grace," I murmured, and I knew this for certain. The thought of Angus, whose deep-gray eyes held such kindness, who had been willing to make me his wife to give our child a name, tangled around my heart with an aching guilt. Before Angus realized that he'd known my father in the War, he paid for my services at Ginny's whorehouse—by the next morning, having fled Ginny's and St. Louis in the company of Angus, Sawyer, Boyd and Malcolm, it was too late. In the backlash of resultant shock at what I had finally done—abandoning the misery of my existence as a prostitute—I neglected to remember to cleanse my insides with the usual butter mixture, which contained potash and subsequently aided in the prevention of unwanted pregnancy.

"He was," Sawyer agreed softly. He well understood the painful thoughts that circled my mind as crows would a carcass. He added, comforting me with his words, "Before the War, Gus was happy as a man could be, I well remember. He and Grace were married for many a good year before he left home as a soldier."

"But *what* was they doin' out in the holler?" Malcolm pressed, still caught up in this portion of the tale.

"Ask me again when you's a piece older," Boyd told him.

Malcolm turned his inquisitive eyes to Sawyer, sensing he would receive no satisfactory answer from his brother. Dark eyebrows knitted, the boy speculated with certainty, "It's got to do with why you an' Lorie's in such a hurry to find a preacher, don't it?"

Before either of us could respond, the boy went on, "You seem wed already, anyhow." His coffee-brown eyes twinkled, moving between Sawyer and me. "An' you already share a tent, so why does it −"

"Kid, I know it isn't the proper order of things, as two people should first be wed. But Lorie and I dearly love each other, and besides, I cannot sleep unless she is tucked near to me," Sawyer interrupted to quietly explain, and, as they were prone to of late, tears blurred my vision at the sweetness of his words.

"I know, I know, I was just sayin'," Malcolm insisted. Attuned as he was to my feelings, the expression in the boy's eyes instantly became one of concern and he insisted gently, "No cryin' no more, Lorie-Lorie."

At these words Sawyer's left arm came immediately around me, joining the right. Malcolm reached and politely took the tin cup from my grasp, depositing it on the ground, then wrapped about me from the front, and I was effectively cradled between him and Sawyer. It had not been long ago that I thought them gone from me forever, and I heaved with a sob I could not contain. I caught Malcolm's elbows, clinging tightly to him, and the two of them held me between them. Even Boyd, who normally pretended to shun such displays of affection, gamely moved behind Malcolm and bear-hugged all of us; though tears streaked my face, their tender, combined comfort effectively kept full-fledged weeping at bay. I could not imagine facing another day without the three of them.

Yet because of me, we were all without Angus.

"It's all right, Lorie-Lorie," Malcolm soothed as he stood straight. He patted my cheeks and said, "We won't let you go again."

Boyd echoed this sentiment in his usual gruff fashion, saying, "Damn right."

I scrubbed away the wetness on my cheeks and then clutched Sawyer's strong forearms, still locked about me.

"Thank you," I tried to say, but it emerged as a hoarse whisper.

Our horses were grazing to the west, their hides still damp from the earlier violent rainfall; my eyes sought Whistler first, the beautiful red-and-cream calico mare, Sawyer's horse who loved him dearly and was equally loved in return, by both of us. She had tirelessly carried Sawyer over the prairie to me, across the endless miles; I knew if not for Whistler, I would currently be lying in the ground alongside Angus and the grave marker for our child, in a freshly-dug hole and with rocks piled over my body, one of thousands left forever behind on the trails.

You fought back. You wouldn't let Sam kill you without a fight. Sam is dead now. Jack and Dixon are dead.

A shudder trembled over me before I could quell, with tremendous effort, the thought of those three men sprawled in the camp in which I had been a prisoner, one with his eye punctured out. My fist clenched in a spasm of remembrance, as though I still clutched the stone arrowhead.

"Lorie-Lorie, let's fry up these here eggs," Malcolm said, neatly collecting them into his palms, drawing me from the dark swamp of my thoughts.

"Let's," I agreed, glad for the distraction.

We ate around the fire as the sun slowly sank, sitting in our usual places just as we would have at a household table, balancing plates on our knees, disregarding forks. The evening light was splendid as it spilled over us, so windless in the wake of the storm that the leaves of the cottonwoods near our camp remained silent, not whispering with their usual companionable rustle. The stillness created the sense that words spoken miles from our position could perhaps be discerned.

The muted coo of mourning doves, so common to fine evenings, met our ears, along with the warbling trill of a red-winged blackbird; in the distance, a crow rasped its rusty call. The birdsong blended with the ever-present, low-pitched buzz of insects amid the prairie grasses, enormous dragonflies that darted erratically through the air, tiny yellow butterflies whose flight patterns were slow and gentle by contrast; a shiny-green locust a good two inches long startled me as it sprang with heart-stopping suddenness upon the edge of my skirt, much to Malcolm's delight.

"Aw, it ain't but a hopper," he cajoled, neatly catching the creature and dangling it near my hair.

"But its feet are so sticky," I said, shying away from the frantically-struggling insect. I had never sounded more like an older sister as I nagged, "Stop that!"

"You two planning to join the boy an' me in town, come morning?" Boyd asked. To Malcolm he added, "Leave off or Sawyer'll strap your hide for tormenting his woman."

Sawyer laughed at this, while Malcolm immediately fired back, "Lorie's *my* sister."

"I'd like to see the day either of you could strap Malcolm," I said, and just as I spoke, the locust wriggled free and fell directly into the gaping collar of the boy's shirt. He yelped and sprang to his feet, springing from bare foot to bare foot in what amounted to a wild jig as he attempted to dislodge it.

He cried indignantly, "It's *sticking* to me!"

I said, with no small amount of satisfaction, "I *told* you."

D EEP IN THE night, I woke from a strange dream.

Cold and unsettled, I blinked into absolute darkness; the moon had long since set, our lantern extinguished for the night hours. My hands were clenched into fists, as though poised to do battle, my heart erratic even as all evidence suggested that nothing was amiss, that indeed I lay safely within our tent.

And yet a breath of icy apprehension lingered at my nape.

It was only a dream, I thought, willing myself to believe this. *You have been through an ordeal. It will take time to recover from the shadow cast in Missouri.*

I became suddenly aware that Sawyer was awake, sitting beside me with his face buried in both hands. My heart jolted and immediately I threaded my arms about his waist, pressing my cheek to his naked back. He grasped my forearms and a shudder trembled through him.

"What is it, what's wrong?" I demanded in a whisper.

He whispered, "I'm sorry to wake you, I didn't intend to." His voice emerged low, and harsh with emotion, as he explained his distress, "I dreamed I couldn't find you, I was riding hard and couldn't find you."

I rose to my knees to bring him closer, cradling his head to my breasts. He wrapped both arms around my waist, and I stroked the hair back from his temple, kissing him there. His skin was heated, damp and salty with sweat.

"What if I hadn't gotten there...*you were in such danger...*"

"Sawyer," I soothed, my heart splitting with concern and tenderness.

His hands moved slowly over my back, fingers spread wide; he nodded and I could tell he was too choked to allow for response.

"Let me get my legs around you," I insisted, and he shifted to allow this, keeping me near as I resettled upon his lap, my thighs spreading to curve about his hips. I knew he was resolute in his decision that we would be wed before we fully joined, as he wished to follow the proper order of things according to his sensibilities. I knew he worried so about how I was healing, both physically and emotionally, and if I would even welcome any sort of carnal indulgence. Though in this moment, it was not about such things.

"There," I murmured with quiet satisfaction, holding him tightly.

He curled his fingers into my hair, his cheek against my temple, until he had calmed. I kissed his jaw, letting my lips linger, imbibing the scent of him, until he exhaled a slow breath and softly kissed my shoulder. Taking us back to the bedding, he whispered, "I did not mean to wake you."

"You did not wake me, love. I dreamed of something that frightened me," I admitted. "But I cannot exactly recall it."

"There is an odd sense in the air," Sawyer whispered. "It seems a night fit for disturbing dreams. But only dreams, nothing more. It is all right, Lorie-love."

And held securely in his arms, I felt the essence of the nightmare retreating, the tension within me ebbing away. I allowed his words to comfort; within minutes, the sound of his breathing had evened, indicating sleep, and I pressed my face to him, wishing for the countless time that I could as easily will away all such darkness.

Heaven knew I harbored my fair share. It seemed in some ways as though an entire lifetime had come and gone, whispering its fingertips fleetingly over my cheek to acknowledge its passage, in the last three years. I had been subsequently released from both of my old lives—the first, my idyllic childhood in eastern Tennessee, the youngest in a family of five, longing to be a boy so that I would be granted the daily privilege of working with horses alongside my father and two older brothers.

As a little girl I spent countless hours hanging on the corral fence, as attracted to the horses as a divining rod is to groundwater; Daddy indulged me, his only daughter, and from him and my brothers I learned the ways of horses, and to ride, despite the mild shock to my mother's delicate sensibilities. Mama had deigned to allow these less refined elements of my education, but took it upon herself to ensure a thorough tutelage in more sophisticated subject matters.

I often wondered, with considerable writhing of spirit, what my dear, faultlessly proper mother would say if she knew that at times I kept myself sane by reciting Shakespeare in my mind as yet another man rammed his whiskey-tainted tongue into my mouth and squeezed my breasts with hands both rough and unconcerned. How I would study the water-stained ceiling above my loathsome narrow bed at Ginny's place, dim in the lamplight, and upon which the shadows of man after man's frantic rutting atop my body was cast like flickering demons come to mock me as I lay beneath each in turn, clenching my jaws to keep from uttering what would surely become an unending scream.

Even now, though years had elapsed since I beheld the last of my family still living, the wealth of their love remained in my heart as a token held over from the sweetness of that young and innocent existence. The memories of my parents, my brothers, sufficed to sustain me through the horror of what I faced after the War came crawling and blotted out the sun, casting instead a light with a muddy, blood-tinged tone. William Blake, my father, and my brothers, Dalton and Jesse, left to fight for the Confederacy in 1861, never to return to our home in Cumberland County. The boys died in battle at Sharpsburg in 1862, while Daddy survived until 1864. Upon his death, my mother withdrew even more deeply into herself and expired from illness a year later, in the July of 1865.

Left utterly alone at age fifteen, in the war-torn Southern land of my birth, I had no possible opportunity to choose my own destiny; I was eventually sent northwest in a canvas-topped wagon with a family named Foster. In my memory, it remains a rather benign journey, though of course I had no notion then as to what would become of me only months later. The Fosters and I traveled placidly beneath the late-summer sunshine, through the heart of a country now at tentative peace; though by the time the wagon rolled into St. Louis, Missouri, Mrs. Foster had died of a lung ailment, leaving Mr. Foster floundering at what to do with a young girl not his kin. Hardly two days passed before his dilemma was solved: he bet me in a card game and lost, and I was summarily deposited on the doorstep of a clapboard building that housed a bustling, ground-floor saloon and a thriving, second-floor whorehouse, only a few blocks from the overpopulated river district.

My virginity ensured a heavy profit for the owner and operator of the place, a grim-faced and calculating opium addict by the name of Ginny Hossiter, who put me to work the very next night, despite my status as a terrified novice, ignorant to all but the most basic facts concerning physical consummation. Out of the necessity born from the will to survive, I learned quickly the tricks of my new trade, that of disguising my choking fear and subsequent lashing shame, and feigning pleasure for countless male customers, whose sole desire had been to spill their sticky-hot seed between my legs.

If asked now, I would not willingly estimate how many men had thrust their bodies inside mine, night after horrific night during that period, leaving me drained of all desire to live, all sense of true self, by morning's tepid light. In the confines of my room at the whorehouse, the sun had appeared indifferent, weak and insubstantial, a sharp contrast to the way I regarded its light as a girl, as something joyous and beautiful, a benediction upon my shoulders. At Ginny's, where I had been forced to change my name to Lila, I internally retreated to a degree that I believed myself incapable of ever feeling genuine emotion again; I had long speculated that death would come leaping far too early for me, whether through the brutality of a drunken customer or my own desperate hand wielding a knife to lay open a vein on the underside of my wrist.

Stop, I commanded. *Enough for tonight.*
It is done. You will never be Lila again.
Never, Lorie. It is all right.
It is all right...

MID-MORNING FOUND Sawyer and me together on the wagon seat, Boyd and Malcolm mounted on their horses, Fortune and Aces High, respectively, and yards ahead on the trail. Juniper and Admiral worked as a team to pull us along, while Whistler politely kept pace alongside. We left our tents staked out near the fire pit, intending to return by late afternoon.

"We needn't accompany them, if you'd rather wait in camp," Sawyer reminded me; he knew I had little desire to visit a town. "I'll stay with you. If Boyd rustles up a preacher, he'll ride back here before we can say 'I do.'"

I reached to tuck a wayward strand of golden hair behind his ear, as it tended to slip free from its moorings throughout the day. He grinned at the gesture and bent to kiss the side of my forehead, angling so that his hat brim did not bump my head. I said softly, "Imagine if the sun set upon us as husband and wife, this very evening."

"I have in mind a gift for you, and I need a town to have a hope of finding it," Sawyer said, releasing his grip on the reins with his right hand to catch my left. He held it and used his thumb to gently touch each of my fingers in turn. He said, "I would like very much to place a ring just here," and so saying, pressed his thumb to my third finger.

Though the sun was already casting us in heated beams, I felt a similar bloom at the idea of wearing a betrothal ring. I admitted, with quiet joy, "I have been letting myself imagine our home. I picture us building it together, and our barn. A large one, for all of our horses."

Sawyer enfolded my hand within his, saying, "Our home won't be grand in scale—not just yet—but we will live together within it, which is the grandest notion I can conjure."

"Truly, if we continued to roam the prairie and reside in our tent until the end of time, I would be content," I said, letting my gaze rove to the northwest, the direction in which we traveled, where the blue edge of the sky blended together with the rippling prairie; from our vantage point on the wagon seat, the horizon appeared as unreachable as stars in the heavens.

"There is a certain satisfaction in being on the trail," Sawyer acknowledged. When we lay close at night, before sleep claimed us, we often spoke quietly of such things. There was a simple, sensual pleasure in living day by day so close to nature, a sensory absorption of the outdoors; I had discovered that I enjoyed the sense of freedom that daily travel occasioned, of not being bound to a certain plot of land. Sawyer felt the same and believed it meant that we were beginning to heal from the loss of our old lives, those which we had known when we were deeply rooted in Tennessee.

"No matter where we settle, even when we are no longer traveling, I want for us to always watch the sun set," I said. We had determined that evening was the time of day we collectively favored, when a stillness descended over the land and lifted from the earth rich scents that seemed stifled by the sun. When jewel-beads of dew formed, and the air held its breath, when the western rim of the world was decorated by the warmer tints of its spectrum, scarlet and rose and saffron, by turns. I added, "I have found such solace in the outdoors, and I want us to remember what it meant to travel such a great distance, seeing the country in this fashion. Many years from now, I want to remember these days, here with you."

"For certain," Sawyer agreed. "When I soldiered there was such little comfort, but sometimes, on a fair evening, or during a quiet sunrise, I could find a measure of calm. Dreams seem possible again, for the first time in so very long. I admit I fall asleep imagining all of the horses we will breed."

As though she understood, Whistler nickered.

"You're in agreement, aren't you, sweet girl?" Sawyer asked her, companionably. He spoke to her always with such affection; even the very first night we met, despite the animosity otherwise bristling from him, I noticed his connection with Whistler, their mutual trust.

"Dozens of little paint foals," I said, delighted by this picture.

"I recall the afternoon Whistler was born as if it was yesterday," Sawyer said, sounding just like a proud daddy; he had related this story to me many times already, but it remained one I cherished. "I was late for the picnic at the Carters' but I couldn't leave before she was delivered. I went back to the stable before nightfall, as it was, just so I could see her again. She was such a dear little thing, wobbling around."

I smiled at his tender description, supplying the final detail, "And then you whistled for her, and knew what her name was to be."

He joked, "You have heard this story before?"

I rested my cheek briefly to his upper arm, whispering, "A time or two," and then said, "Daddy let me watch whenever our mares foaled, if it was in the daylight hours, even though Mama always disapproved. She considered it far too 'earthy' a lesson for a girl."

Sawyer's gaze lifted up and to the left, back into time, as he speculated, "I believe my own mama would have taken a similar position, had Eth and Jere and I been daughters instead of sons. Mama midwifed, after all. She knew firsthand that birthing *is* an indelicate business all around."

"Well, *our* daughters will be allowed to watch any foaling they choose, with no compunctions from me," I declared, and Sawyer laughed, shying away when I pinched at his ribs for laughing.

He used his elbow to defend against my fingers, and hastily explained, "I'm in agreement, darlin'. Don't be cross. It's your tone that makes me smile. You sound as though I was about to contradict you. There may be *times* when I contradict you, but not regarding that."

I relinquished my hope of pinching him and instead poked into his side, pleased when he yelped at my tickling. I said primly, "A true gentleman never contradicts his lady."

Sawyer winked at me and said wickedly, "Then I ain't a *true* gentleman."

An inexorable beat of desire pulsed within me and he recognized that I was rendered momentarily speechless. I elbowed him, pretending irritation, and his grin deepened; well he knew the need for him that burned inside of me, even without my speaking it aloud.

"Might we grow morning glories along the southern wall of our barn?" I asked, attempting nonchalance. I needn't close my eyes to picture my childhood home, but I did. The sun created shifting golden patterns against the backsides of my eyelids but I saw only the rolling valley in which Daddy's ranch had been tucked as dearly as a beloved child to a warm bed. Mama loved flowers in all shades of blue, from richest indigo to palest cerulean. The small, joyous trumpets of the morning glories and true-hued gentian salvia had been among my favorite of the blossoms.

"Of course. Morning glories grew along the livery stable," Sawyer remembered. His father had run the Suttonville livery all of Sawyer's life—he, Ethan, and Jeremiah had learned the trade, and that of smithing, from their youths. The business had been looted and subsequently burned to the ground over the course of the War; only Sawyer had been left to claim the meager leavings upon returning home in 1865.

In the years between then and now, he sold the remaining equipment in order to provision himself for the journey north from Tennessee; I knew he kept the horseshoe his grandfather, the elder Sawyer Davis, had carried with from England and that subsequently always hung over any bellows upon which he conducted his smithing. In addition to this, Sawyer retained his father James's iron tongs and hammer. He'd told me he could not bear to part with these vestiges of his old life, which he so dearly associated with the menfolk who taught him his craft, who instilled within him a sense of appreciation for their work. Sawyer, like his father and grandsire before him, loved horses especially, and I had yet to see any horse that did not respond to his voice.

"I know the basics of birthing foals, but I would that you teach me to properly shoe a horse," I said, as I thought of his family's trade.

"I will teach you whatever you wish, though that is heavy work, and you are so slightly built, however brave, *mo mhuirnín mhilis*," he said. With quiet vehemence, he added, "I despise the thought of bruises on your body."

"I know," I acknowledged softly; not long ago, my body had borne severe bruising. "Though, occasional injury is inevitable, eventually. I mean to ride Whistler every day, now that I feel up to it. I've missed it so."

"I mean to ride with you," he said. "It is such a pleasure. I am thinking of that first afternoon."

I recalled the unexpected beauty of that day, when Sawyer allowed me the privilege of riding his horse; he had joined me, on Juniper, and together we'd cantered them over the prairie, talking and racing, by turns. I admitted, "I realized I was finally seeing the Sawyer about whom Gus spoke so fondly."

He said, "I was not bold enough to tell you, not that day, that I felt such joy simply having you at my side."

"I mean to stay by your side," I whispered, tears prickling at the edges of my eyes.

Reading my thoughts, as he was so inclined to do, he said tenderly, "I pray that in time we will have a house overrun with our children, and a corral with our horses."

I repeated his words, "For certain."

"My childhood would have been a different thing without Eth and Jere," Sawyer said. "And without the Carters. I mean for our children to know the love of family, of friends and siblings. God willing, our sons will never leave home as soldiers."

"Wouldn't it be lovely if Boyd found a wife within the year? His children would be raised with ours," I mused. I speculated, teasingly, "She would need to be possessed of a *very* good-natured spirit, to put up with his."

"Boyd spoke often of a wife when we were soldiers, though in our youth he was fickle," Sawyer remembered. "Back home, before the War, he favored a new girl every other week or so. But he's much changed now, and I know he longs for a family to call his own." He grinned as he added another detail to my description, "A patient wife for him."

"Patient, yes," I agreed, and then, unable to deny the ages-old habit, I added dutifully, "Synonyms include: *tolerant, serene, unflappable.*"

"*Forbearing,*" he finished with a scholarly intonation, teasingly nudging my shoulder; I had told him of the way Mama favored the thesaurus for my daily lessons.

"Oh, that's a particularly good one. I hadn't thought of that," I said.

"I find myself imagining our little ones at your knee, darlin', learning from you," he said softly.

"A journal," I said, on sudden inspiration. "I should very much like a journal, if there is one to be had. And someday I will read it aloud to them."

"I will do my best to find you one," Sawyer promised.

The scattering of buildings on the central street came into view on the horizon, dust swirling beneath the passage of feet, booted and shod alike, rising lazily into the hot air and creating a thin haze. The river glinted like polished cobalt along the eastern edge of the town; I knew that two rivers converged here, the Des Moines and the Mississippi. We would shortly discontinue our course along the Mississippi and for a time leave behind the giant, swiftly-flowing river we had traveled alongside since Missouri, to follow the Iowa River instead. We would cross the northern border of Iowa and travel well into Minnesota before rejoining the Mississippi again, when it hooked back in a westerly direction to lead us to our eventual destination, the homestead of Boyd and Malcolm's uncle, Jacob Miller.

I spied Malcolm racing Aces our way, dust lifting in clouds behind them as Malcolm let his horse run, bowed low over the animal's sleek brown neck. Whistler nickered and snorted as they drew near, dancing on her tether—I knew she longed to gallop as badly as I longed to be atop her back, clinging to her mane and feeling the wind scrape my hair into a tangled mess, the ground a blur alongside her flying hooves.

"Preacher's on circuit! He ain't in town!" the boy informed in a shout as Aces flashed past the wagon; yards behind us, Malcolm slowed him to a walk and then trotted back to us, flushed and breathless with the exertion of riding so fast. He brought Aces to my side of the wagon and kept pace as disappointment at this news flooded my heart.

"Next town," Sawyer murmured into my ear.

Malcolm was wide-eyed with excitement, all but bouncing on the saddle. Aces was tall and high-strung; like most of the horses I had ever known, he responded to his rider's moods instinctively, and snorted at Malcolm's antics.

"They's got berry pie an' bags of marbles, an' a tobacconist sells outta the dry-goods store," the boy prattled, and I smiled at him with love. Sawyer regarded him with a similar expression.

"For having recently arrived, you surely seem to know a great deal about the place," he remarked to Malcolm, teasing him, though Malcolm did possess an uncanny ability at unearthing both gossip and secrets. Presumably this was because he was equal parts observant and earnest; people grew loose-jawed around him.

"I done rode its length three times aw'ready," Malcolm explained cheerfully. He withdrew a slim wooden stick topped with crystalized sugar from the pocket of his trousers, blew dust from it, frowned when this did not prove enough, and then rubbed it briskly on his thigh before popping it into his mouth. His left cheek bulged like a pocket gopher's. His eyes went wide and he informed me, "I got you one, too, Lorie-Lorie!"

So saying, he dug into the leather haversack looped over his torso, its pouch dangling near his waist, extracting a bundled handkerchief. He unrolled this and produced another stick, which he leaned to place into my hands. It looked a little worse for the wear, but I could hardly refuse this offering. To Sawyer he explained, "I only had me the one penny, or I woulda got you one. You wanna lick of mine?" and he held it out with utter sincerity.

Sawyer said, "Thank you kindly, but I'll have a taste of Lorie's instead."

"Thank you, sweetheart," I told Malcolm and gamely took a lick. It was sarsaparilla flavored, sticky-sweet on my tongue; I nearly drooled. I informed Sawyer, "I *did* intend to share with you."

Sawyer leaned over to collect, using his teeth to anchor the stick and then sitting straight. He crunched a loud bite and subsequently broke off over half the candy. He said, "Much obliged."

"Give it back!" I ordered, laughing as he ducked away from my reaching hands.

"Oh, no," he teased, his words distorted by the mouthful. He added, "Sweet Jesus, it's been a long time since I've tasted rock candy."

"You ain't being no gentleman!" Malcolm yelped, but these words had scarcely been uttered before he heeled Aces, too excited to ride at a steady pace for long. Over his shoulder, he called, "Hurry along, you twos!"

Sawyer pulled the stick from his mouth and said, "I know exactly, now that I think of it. Fourth of July, 1858, ten years ago this summer. Just a boy of fourteen years I was."

"It's been every bit as long for me," I nagged, reclaiming the treat and tucking it into my cheek, reminded of the way men plugged their lower lips with tobacco.

"You eat it, darlin'," Sawyer said, with teasing magnanimity. "I'll content myself with your kisses, which are far sweeter."

"Flatterer," I muttered, elbowing his side again, though I truly loved the way he complimented me; I had never known that words could cause my stomach to feel so buoyant, as a flower petal carried on a gentle evening breeze.

The wagon rumbled into town, which was predictably quiet on a cloudless weekday; likely most of the people within many miles farmed for their living. We saw horses tethered to hitching posts and several buckboards, whose drivers lifted hands in what seemed to be friendly greetings. Still, I shifted uncomfortably on the hard wooden seat, my tension increasing as we passed two small saloons to our right. Despite their peaceful outward appearance, I recalled all too well what occurred behind those batwing-style doors and up a flight of stairs. Sawyer's observant gaze noted the proximity of these places and he intertwined our fingers, reassuring me.

In Missouri, when Angus was still alive, we agreed it would make the most sense to let people believe that Boyd and Malcolm were my brothers; this arrangement would allow a respectable, reasonable explanation for why an unmarried woman was traveling with four single men. Angus rightly assumed that rumors would abound at even the slightest notion of the truth (that of my former existence as a whore), and so concocted this relationship between Boyd, Malcolm, and me; we decided before reaching Iowa that we would continue relying upon this fabrication until Sawyer and I could be properly married.

"There's Boyd," Sawyer said, nodding towards the hitching rail before the dry-goods store. Fortune was tethered there, appearing to doze in the sun; Boyd was surely inside, making purchases. The words *National Union Republican Candidates* caught my eye, from a large red and blue campaign poster tacked near the window frame, along with the images of General Grant and his stern-faced running mate, Schuyler Colfax. It would be the first election in which former Confederates would be allowed, conditionally, to vote. I had overheard many such discussions, even during my time at Ginny's; after all, it had been scarcely two months since Johnson's near-impeachment in May and the autumn election was on everyone's mind.

"Do you think Grant will become President?" I asked, nodding at the poster.

Sawyer followed my gaze and fell momentarily still; conversely, I sensed the fast-moving flow of his thoughts, as a springtime creek over rocks, deceptively smooth beneath the surface—one wrong step, and a sharp, hidden edge could open a gash deep and painful, blood to tint the clear water red. As such were his memories of the War, most of which he had not yet spoken, and I understood well the urge, however futile, to bury away the darkness.

"It is likely," he said. "He has restored the Union. I cannot speak from experience, but I understand he is a commanding presence, and a strong leader. This country could benefit from both qualities."

"You do not believe a new Congress will join forces against him, as they did with Johnson?" I asked, thinking of the daily circular in St. Louis, *The Missouri Democrat*, a copy of which was often tucked behind the bar at Ginny's.

"I believe Congress would welcome Grant," Sawyer said. "And as much as it pains me to say, I am ever more grateful to be leaving behind Tennessee altogether."

"I have not been there in almost three years," I acknowledged, on a sigh.

"Someday we will return there together, Lorie-love. We will bring our grandchildren, and show them where we began."

I leaned my cheek again upon his upper arm.

A few dozen yards down the dusty road, I could see Malcolm on Aces, leaning forward over the saddle horn and talking to a boy close to his own age, who stood on the ground in front of a small wooden building with a jutting overhang; hooks anchored to its underside were burdened with hanging baskets of blooming flowers, and I was charmed.

Sawyer parked the wagon in the small alleyway between buildings and said, "Let us see what they have in the way of heavy material, fit for the cold."

"My clothing is not well-provisioned for winter," I agreed. We had many times marveled at the descriptions of the winter months in the Northern states that Jacob Miller included in his letters. Though Tennessee was often cold, the winter of 1863 into 1864 being the coldest in the last decade, there was never significant snowfall in the county in which we had been raised. Jacob wrote of crafting snowshoes, of sleighs with runners and long, dark nights, their cabin insulated by thick, blanketing drifts of snow. I thought of something else lacking in my wardrobe, and said, "And a corset. I am not well-provisioned in that regard, either."

Sawyer squeezed my hand, held in his. He said, "I have grown so used to you wearing trousers."

"Truly, I am not anxious to be strapped again within one," I said, but it was improper to appear in public lacking appropriate undergarments, well I knew. And propriety was something to which I found a great deal of joy in adhering, after so long neglecting the notion. I admitted, "I *like* wearing trousers, as you know. And corsets are terribly uncomfortable."

"And all that lacing along the back *is* a hindrance," Sawyer said, eyes glinting with teasing devilment, and I could not help but blush, this time succeeding in my endeavor to pinch him.

The sun crept over the town and was angling decidedly westward by the time I found myself in the small bathhouse, certainly a luxury I would do well to appreciate now; chilly creek baths were the norm, and would continue to be so in the foreseeable future. Sawyer, Boyd, and I spent the day listening to advice concerning what garments and supplies would be necessary in the forests of the Northland; we lingered unexpectedly over a pleasant conversation in the modest hotel abreast of the post office, as the owners were both friendly and informative. Their son was the boy with whom Malcolm had been chatting earlier, and his mother made a gift of a delectable spice cake and subsequently the tin pan in which she had baked it, telling me to make plentiful use of the pan; it was now wrapped in a linen and tucked carefully into the wagon bed.

In the narrow wooden tub in the quiet, damp, musky-scented bathhouse, I washed my hair and scrubbed my body with a cake of lilac-scented soap, exploring tentatively between my legs with gentle fingertips. I could discern no further damage, and no longer felt as tender there, or within my abdomen. My skin was moon-pale beneath the water. I submerged entirely, keeping my eyes open and letting my hair drift around me in the water, like a slow-moving creature intent upon touching my face. I remained there until my lungs burned, lifting slowly back to air and then inhaling deeply. I was so very thankful to be alive.

The warm, soaking water felt good against my limbs, such a contrast to the usual rushing chill and muddy shallows of the river; I smoothed my hands upwards over my belly and breasts, full and still achingly tender. As often occurred when I was naked, my thoughts inadvertently coiled back around to my time at Ginny's, when I bared my body repeatedly, for stranger and regular customer alike, learning swiftly to bury the accompanying shame. Sawyer had refrained from asking me directly about my time there, allowing me to offer information as I chose instead, though I knew him well enough to understand that he would listen to whatever I revealed. I thought of what he had spoken in Missouri, about husbands and wives keeping no secrets from one another; though I agreed, I knew it would be a long time before I would be strong enough to reveal all of the horrors I kept hidden away.

Deirdre, I thought at last, holding my old friend in my mind, as carefully as I would have cupped a baby bird. *How I wish I could still see you, even from time to time. I would be content with that. You were one of the few people who knew what it meant to live as a prisoner there.*

What about that fellow called Slim? I heard her ask, in my memory, and she giggled relating the story. *He's awfully proud of his pecker, and it's nothing to brag about, let me tell you. All of them are so proud of the damn things, as though we should be privileged to take them into ourselves. Men are either the most deluded, arrogant lot in existence, or the stupidest.*

At Ginny's, I had grown accustomed to the finger-shaped bruises on my thighs from the continuous assault of gripping hands, night after long night. My insides would ache if I forgot to ease the way with butter; by contrast, the morning's potash always stung. Most all men reeked of tobacco and whiskey, unwashed hair and sweat. Some were heavyset and fumbling, others lean as bullwhips and just as unkind. Men with bristling, graying whiskers, older than my father. There was the young man who spilled his seed before I even took him into my body, so nervous was he at the prospect of being with a woman. There had been the regular who preferred to bind my wrists to the bed posts before he lay with me; though he never physically hurt me, I had been so frightened, so vulnerable in that position, that bile would rise as he went about his business. I'd clenched my jaw in order not to vomit. Thankfully, like most of them, he never lasted long.

With sincere effort, I sent those memories scattering and focused upon the image of my dear friend Deirdre that always appeared first, she with her dark hair hanging soft and loose, clad in her pale-yellow dressing gown, delicate face free of any artificial adornments. I had known her face in many guises in the years we lived at Hossiter's, but always in my memory I saw her as I had the afternoon of our first meeting. She had been widowed prior to her time as a whore, young, and as dear to me as any sister; her husband had been killed in the War, like so many other good men, leaving her abandoned and with no resource other than that of earning money the one way always available to women, rich or poor, in sickness and in health. Instead of forsaking all others, we forsook no one in our old profession.

I found meager comfort in addressing her, choosing to believe that she was able to hear me, wherever it was that her soul now lingered, and thought, *Deirdre, I pray that you have found your Joshua in the Beyond. I miss you so. And do you know what, dear one? I am going to be married. His name is Sawyer Davis. All those nights you and I sat on the side balcony staring up at the stars and hearing the coyotes yipping, he was moving towards me. I hope you know this. I pray it. I love him so, Deirdre, I could never explain in words.*

Though in my mind Deirdre seemed to smile at me, a gentle and familiar expression that brightened her dark eyes, a sudden seizure of need to see Sawyer rose in my body, insistent as a late-winter wind, as though something may have caused him harm as I lingered in this wooden tub. I sat in haste, water sloshing over the sides, scrubbing damp strands of hair back from my forehead with both hands. Wet, it hung nearly to my waist, heavy and inhibiting as a woolen cloak.

Don't fret, I told myself, though my heart was erratic as I hurried to dress and braid my hair, my unease as pointed as a needle. *Sawyer is safe, he's close and he's safe, just at the wagon. He is more than able to take care of himself.*

Still, last night's dream sought a handhold in my mind, and I shivered. My hair was damp as I all but ran from the bathhouse, into the gathering grays of twilight in the small Iowa town; at once I saw Sawyer, heading my way from where the wagon was parked at the side of the dusty street. Relief flowed as palpably through my body as blood, displacing the chill. He sensed that something was amiss, perhaps my posture or just a feeling, as he jogged the last few strides to meet me, catching me against him. I held fast, possessively gripping the material of his shirt and cradling my cheek to his heartbeat. Death had come so close to picking me utterly clean of those I loved.

"I'm here," he whispered, understanding without words. "Come, Lorie-love, let us go. Boyd has promised something to eat, back at camp."

Once free of the town the light subtly shifted, reaching us with no manmade structures to block its radiance, and promptly I felt restored; upon the open ground of the prairie the sun shone with soft yellow tones, beaming long and low from the west to touch us as we rode the short distance south to our camp. Sawyer drove the wagon, Whistler following alongside, as she had this morning, and I turned to look back at her. In the sunset light, her hide gleamed rust-red and cream. Her intelligent brown eyes acknowledged my attention as much as her quiet whicker.

"We'll ride tomorrow, how's that?" Sawyer said to our horse, and she snorted as though in agreement. There were times, as now, when I was certain she truly understood our words.

"Whistler," I murmured. "You good girl. You kept him safe in the War, didn't you? You brought Sawyer to me."

Sawyer said, "She loves you, too, you know. She raced to get to you. We knew you were in danger, and she ran as she never has before."

Boyd had a side of beef grilling over the fire, the rich aroma causing saliva to dart into my mouth. Malcolm whooped at the sight of us, springing up from where he sat polishing his saddle in the last of the light, and deep within I felt a sense of coming home, strange as it might seem to feel such stirrings for a place with no permanent structure, a camp we would vacate at dawn. Sawyer drew the wagon near before surrendering me to Malcolm's enthusiasm; immediately the boy asked, "You wanna play some marbles, Lorie-Lorie? I smoothed me out a big circle in the dust, yonder."

"Of course I do," I said happily, and reflected for the countless time how fortunate I was to have this family, my Sawyer and Boyd, my sweet little Malcolm, to call my own.

T HE FOUR OF us lingered for a long time around the fire that evening, in our usual places. The sky was clear and without end, the stars cold and glittering, somewhere far distant from us. Boyd brought his fiddle from the wagon and bowed out notes here and there, quietly, in keeping with the mood of the night. I studied the orange flames as they licked the wood, drifting somewhere between wakefulness and sleep; I let my eyes close, and Malcolm whispered, "Lorie's sleeping."

"Don't fall asleep yet, I still have your present," Sawyer murmured into my ear, and then to Boyd and Malcolm, "I believe we'll retire, you two. Goodnight."

"'Night, Sawyer, 'night, Lorie-Lorie," Malcolm said, kissing my cheek as I reached to hug him.

Boyd played us Byerley's Waltz as Sawyer helped me to my feet and into our tent. The music was so sweet that I shivered, as Sawyer hung our lantern upon its hook, staked into the ground close to our bedding. When I reached to unbraid my hair, he stilled my motions, requesting, "Let me."

Without a word, I nodded; his gentle touch sent immediate shivers fluttering down my spine. I pressed both palms lightly to my belly as he worked efficiently and tenderly, freeing the last twist so that my clean hair fell loose in a heavy sweep, which he entwined in his fingers.

"My beautiful woman," he murmured. His strong, supple hands moved to my waist and drew me closer as I tried to recall how to breathe, heat flowing freely from his skin to mine. He studied my eyes, his own somber, before bending to one knee. Reaching into the leather bag tied to his trousers, the small one in which he kept coins, he extracted something that he held between his index finger and thumb. His eyes were steadfast upon mine as he procured the fingertips of my left hand, kissed my knuckles, and then slipped a ring upon my third finger.

With quiet satisfaction he said, "I knew it would fit." His joyous eyes lifted to mine, alight with anticipation and joy. "I bought it while you were bathing. I wanted you to have a betrothal ring and this one was so delicate and lovely, just like you. I know it is not fancy—"

"I could not love it more," I whispered, bringing my hand near to examine the ring in the lantern light. It was a smooth golden band, detailed with engravings of roses, and it fit snugly at the base of my finger. I knelt as well, so that I could get my arms about him. We had come so close to losing one another forever, and I held him as hard as I could. I whispered against his warm skin, "Thank you."

He whispered, "You are so very welcome." He kissed the side of my forehead and said, "I looked for a journal, but there were none to be found. I would that you were able to write your thoughts. I know well the comfort of that, as I wrote to my parents often during the War."

These letters were kept treasured in a small leather trunk bearing his surname; when we had been forced from each other in Missouri, I took from this trunk several of the letters written in his hand, and his picture, the framed tintype made just days before he left Suttonville as a soldier, back in 1862.

Although he already knew it, I whispered, "I read those letters nearly to pieces. I felt I had a part of you still with me, and not just in my memory."

"Lorie," he whispered. "It hurt so unbearably to be apart from you."

"I would have kept your picture for always," I said. "I would have cradled it to my heart, every night."

"We will never be apart again," he promised.

I drew back enough to see his eyes, and said, "I wish I could have known your family."

Sawyer's voice was tender with remembrance as he said, "They watch over us, as does your kin, and they understand that you are my family now. My mama always wanted a daughter. She would have taken one look at you and known you for mine. Daddy would have kissed your hands and entertained you with stories, and my brothers..." Here he laughed a little, before he explained, "Jere would have blushed and been too tongue-tied to speak to you, for days no doubt, but Ethan would have shoved me to the side and flirted for all he was worth," and I smiled at this description of the twins.

Outside, Boyd was still fiddling the soft, sweet waltz.

Sawyer whispered, "They would have loved you so," and the air between us subtly shifted, a potent beat of desire taking up an insistent rhythm as our gazes held; there came now the necessity of removing our clothes. Low and husky, he whispered, "May I?" and indicated the buttons of my blouse.

I nodded and his fingers moved to the fastenings that ran in an evenly-spaced length between my breasts, slowly unbuttoning each. Once undone, he drew the material carefully down my waist, leaving only my shift. Though one had been purchased this afternoon, I wore no inhibiting corset, and Sawyer's eyes were so intense that I began to tremble, my blood a hectic spring-time stream, bound to overflow its banks.

"Now you," I whispered, and I reached to slide the suspenders over his wide shoulders, then tugged free the shirt from his trousers; as his skin was subsequently slowly bared, heat absolutely leaped between us. I made a small, inadvertent sound, letting his shirt join the soft pile of clothing on the ground, moving my fingertips to the planes of his face. I traced along the high cheekbones that created such angles, before letting my hands slide down to caress his bare chest, firm with muscle. Once in my life, I would not have believed myself capable of speaking the words, certain the ability to experience desire had been eradicated from my soul; I whispered sincerely, "You are beautiful, Sawyer, truly."

He smiled, radiantly, shaking his head at me, taking us both to the bedding. Bracing just above me, he said, "You flatter me, darlin'." A heartbeat later, he murmured, "Your skirt."

With my eyes, I told him what I wanted.

"Very well," he whispered, and his fingers moved to the back of my waist. He took my hips fully into his grasp, bracketing my body, before sliding just beneath me to unfasten the pair of buttons, slowly and deliberately.

I love you so very much, he said without words, letting his thoughts penetrate mine, his eyes intent with purpose; my heart thrust with such vigor that I was lightheaded, drunk upon his presence, his touch, his eyes and his scent. He told me, *I wish to bring you pleasure as you have never known.*

Yes, I responded in kind, flush and feverish with need for him. *Oh Sawyer, yes.*

"Once we are wed," he whispered, softly kissing my lips, tasting just lightly with his tongue. "I know you are still hurting, Lorie-darlin', and I won't ask anything more than you're ready for, you know that, even after. We will wait until you are ready." He tucked hair behind my ear, fingertips lingering on my jaw.

I couldn't help but smile at these gallant words, even as my limbs trembled at his touch. I whispered, "I know."

"Lift your hips," and his voice was a throaty murmur. "So that I may remove this skirt." He slipped the material down my legs, freeing me from it, and then said, "Come here to me."

"I love when you say that," I whispered, as he gathered me close. His eyes asked me to explain what I meant, and so I did. "You said those words just after we kissed for the first time, in the thunderstorm."

He said softly, "All I want in the world is for you to come to me."

I bent my right leg around his hips, lifting my chin so that I could kiss the juncture of his collarbones, where his pulse throbbed hectically, matching mine. Through his trousers and my shift, our lower bodies pressed intimately close. Despite his promise, which I knew to the depths of me he meant sincerely, and would honor, he was rigid as the trunk of a hardwood tree. I swallowed and begged softly, holding his gaze in mine, "May I at least touch you?"

At my words a tremor passed through him and he sounded strangled as he whispered, "I do not expect—"

"I want to," I implored in a whisper, interrupting him. "Please, let me touch you."

Without waiting for his acquiescence, I slid my left palm down his belly, flat as a knife blade, and then over his solid length. He moaned, deeply, as a shiver jolted through him, tipping his forehead to my shoulder, hand gripping my thigh. I held my touch steady against him, blood thundering through me, not daring to free him from his trousers, though instinct was demanding heatedly that I do so. My entire soul was afire.

"Lorie," he groaned. There was such repressed passion in his eyes that everything within me flashed and sizzled in immediate response, as if struck with bolt lightning. "You don't know how incredible your touch..."

He briefly closed his eyes, as if gathering strength, and then determinedly caught my hand into his, kissing my knuckles before bringing it to his cheek.

His voice shook as he whispered, "I am attempting to be a gentleman, truly. A gentleman," he repeated firmly, as though I'd contradicted him.

My hand still burning, I murmured, "I know, I do. I'm sorry."

"Never be sorry for touching me," he said passionately, kissing the neckline of my shift, where my skin was bared, and I shivered. He said, "Never be sorry for that. I would beg you to touch me, all the time. But you are not fully healed, and I would despise myself for making love to you at present. I will wait."

I pressed even closer to him.

"I love taking down your hair," he whispered, stroking its length. "And letting it fall all along your shoulders. You are so very soft. And so lovely I can hardly breathe for wanting you." He drew slightly away and ran his fingertips slowly between my breasts, my nipples round and swollen against my shift, craving his mouth; his touch moved to my belly, over which he spread his hand in a wide, warm length. His eyes were ember-dark with desire as they moved slowly back to my face.

I told him, "As soon as we are wed, you will have to fight me away from you."

He laughed, low, and said, "Now that's a fight I will gladly lose."

It seemed as though I had scarcely closed my eyes when Sawyer said in my ear, "Lorie, stay here and don't make a sound."

Mired in the deep black bowels of night, our tent was encased in smothering darkness. His words conveyed such seriousness that I did not dare ask what was the matter, though clearly something was—having delivered this order, he moved swiftly, and I sensed more than saw him crouching at the entrance to our tent. I lifted to one elbow, unable to continue lying flat, and as my eyes adjusted, I saw that Sawyer held his pistol at the ready; my heart seized and began thrashing, but I remained obediently silent. Sawyer bent his head, as one listening fixedly, and I threw my senses immediately outward, hearing nothing at first other than the ferocity of my blood.

What is it? I begged him.

Someone's out there, he responded. *The horses are restless.*

And then I could hear exactly what he meant—from the direction of their tethers came the agitated rustlings of our animals, whickers and whooshes, a stomping of hooves, quiet sounds that would go unnoticed by day's light, but nonetheless those indicating that someone approached their position. Sawyer whistled two quiet notes, those of a bobwhite quail, which was his and Boyd's customary call for each other's attention when words could not be used. Seconds later, to my relief, I heard Boyd stir within his tent.

Sawyer told me, *I will return shortly.*

I knew it was useless to beg him to be careful; he was cautious and well-trained, a former soldier whose Company had engaged in countless brutal conflicts during the War, but it stabbed at me to remain behind as he silently undid two of the entrance ties, taking a moment to retie each behind him before slipping into the night. I rolled immediately to all fours, crawling to the edge of the canvas nearest the horses, and listened with all of my effort, hearing little but the continual flow of the river, just to the east. Time inched rather than passed. I heard Boyd emerge, his footfalls barely perceptible; I imagined him joining Sawyer, the two communicating with gestures as they determined their next move. Malcolm was also awake in the adjacent tent, and though the boy did not share the ability to hear my thoughts, I sent a message his way, *Be still, please, dear one. Be silent.*

I waited, finding it nearly unbearable, more excruciating as seconds ticked by with no indication of what was occurring outside. My eyes roved over the canvas mere inches from my nose as I crouched, pale even in the pitch-dark night.

Malcolm whispered fervently, "*Lorie.*"

I jerked in fright at the sudden sound, and could tell he was right outside; my lips compressed into a tight, angry line at this certain disobeying of Boyd's orders. I opened my mouth to respond when a woman screamed, a high-pitched, blood-curdling yowl that set every hair on the back of my neck rigid. I choked on a gasp, scrambling to the entrance, fingers shaking almost too much to free myself from the tent.

Malcolm cried shrilly, "What is it?"

In the same instant, perhaps two dozen paces distant, Sawyer shouted, "Just there!"

Boyd yelped and there was the shock of gunfire at close range, three shots in rapid sequence; Boyd roared, "They's headed for the river!"

I fumbled to my feet and raced around the side of the tent, frantic to know what was happening. A supple blur of movement from the direction of the horses caught me unaware; something formidably large bounded so close to me as I stood there, unsheltered, that I nearly toppled over. Before I could make sense of what I had just seen, Sawyer bellowed, "*Lorie!*"

A second creature leaped through our camp on the heels of the first, lithe and enormous, a courier of death as surely as a bullet to the heart. The wailing screech again shattered the night; my blood went to ice—and then Sawyer was there, ascertaining that I was safe before charging after what I belatedly realized was a pair of catamounts. Though utterly unharmed, I sank quite involuntarily to the cold ground. Near the riverbank, Sawyer fired twice after the fleeing animals, just as Boyd ran from around the far side of the tents. Catching sight of Sawyer loping back to us, Boyd stopped short, tipping forward to catch his breath; both of them were almost visibly sparking with energy.

For the fourth or fifth time, Boyd sputtered, "*Jesus H. Christ.*"

Malcolm fell to his knees beside me and I caught him in my arms; the boy's heart fired rapidly. Sawyer paced around us, putting his free hand on my hair, my shoulder, reassuring himself that I was indeed all right; he was, however, unable to cease moving, far too riled up.

"Are the horses safe?" I asked, terrified anew.

Boyd, having regained a sliver of composure, responded, "They's fine, though they was close to being dinner for them big cats. *Shee-it.* My heart just about quit beatin' when the one screamed. I never *seen* such big critters."

Sawyer finally came to a standstill, drawing a fortifying breath and staring in the direction of the river. He said, somewhat hoarsely, "Me, neither."

Boyd focused on his little brother, and his tone promptly changed into that of a disciplinarian, stern with warning as he said, "Boy, I oughta strap your hide within an inch of your life. Did I or did I not tell you to stay in that goddamn tent?"

Malcolm did not so much as attempt to offer an excuse, though his slender arms tightened their grip on my waist; I almost smiled at this gesture, which surely indicated that the boy would have to be pried forcibly from me in order to receive a whipping. Malcolm said meekly, "You did."

"You's goddamn lucky I have to piss just now," Boyd carried on, irascibly. "When I get back, you best be outta my sight."

"You mind watching your mouth in front of Lorie?" Sawyer asked sharply.

Boyd huffed a surprised laugh, and we were all laughing then, the tension of the past quarter-hour taking abrupt wing. Boyd said, "I apologize, Lorie-girl, I truly do. I had me a shock to the system, you see. An' I *do* have to piss, something fierce."

"Then *get*," Sawyer ordered. He was laughing nearly too hard to say, "But watch out...*for panthers*..."

"Jesus *Christ*," Boyd uttered again, clutched in hilarity. He declared, "Davis, you's gonna accompany me...an' then you's gonna watch my back while I water them cottonwoods..."

By the time we retired to our tent, dawn was perhaps an hour away, at most. The night had lost its clutch on the air, giving way to tones of gray; beyond the river, a faint stripe of pale peach heralded the advancing day.

"I'm just as guilty as Malcolm," I admitted, my cheek resting upon Sawyer's heartbeat as he stroked my back, up and down in a gentle rhythm; it felt so good that most of the tension in my body had fled. I explained, "You told me to stay in the tent, too."

"I did," he agreed in a whisper. "It was a dangerous situation and I suppose I should be angry, but you're safe in my arms, and I can't muster up any anger just now."

"Were they stalking the horses?" I whispered, horrified at the prospect; I had never considered that a horse could be a prey animal.

"They must have been," Sawyer replied. He cupped my shoulder blade, gently stroking his thumb along the hollow created by it, which he knew I loved. He murmured, "I recall Mama worrying over panther tracks near our well a few times when I was a boy, but I never saw the size of such creatures back home."

"Do you think your shots hit them?"

"No, I don't believe so. They were moving too fast."

"I aim to keep practicing with the rifle," I said, snuggling nearer to his warmth.

"Yes," Sawyer murmured in agreement. He kissed my ear and whispered, "Sleep for a spell before dawn, *mo mhuirnín milis*, the danger's moved on now."

W E TRAVELED ON into the prairies of Iowa. According to our route, I knew that we would shortly catch the Iowa River, which angled northwest, and would guide us nearly into Minnesota, where we would continue to travel due north before retaking the much-larger Mississippi, which had unfailingly led the way from Tennessee. Boyd posted a letter to Jacob, back in Keokuk, letting Jacob and his wife, Hannah, know that we were only a little behind their predicted schedule.

"Gus figured that by August we would be in central Minnesota and pick up the Mississippi again, and follow it all the way to Jacob's homestead. When we were plotting a route last winter, we determined that if we veered northwest in Iowa, it would cut weeks from the journey. With luck, we'll arrive by early autumn," Sawyer said.

He rode Whistler near the wagon, which I drove, sweating under the long afternoon sunshine despite my wide-brimmed hat. The air was warm and bright, and I had rolled the sleeves of my blouse above both elbows. I was barefoot and wearing Malcolm's trousers, belted now with a length of satin ribbon. Malcolm and Boyd rode just ahead, and I reflected anew how much I appreciated the freedom to wear boy's clothing; here on the prairie, the strict rules of conduct which had been instilled in me from my earliest days did not apply as exactly. I allowed myself room to speculate that perhaps in Minnesota I would be allowed to retain this independence, however sparingly. What an unexpected luxury it would be if no one in the north woods objected to my unladylike mode of dressing.

Besides, I reflected, with an acknowledgment of the bitterness coloring the thought, *You are no longer exactly a lady. No matter how dearly Sawyer treats you, how much he loves you, it can never fully absolve you of the truth.*

And the truth was, like it or no, and I hated it to the blackest depths of my soul, I'd been a whore.

Forgive me, Mama, I found myself thinking, as I did time and again, though somehow I knew in my heart that even my lovely, decorous mother would find it in hers to accept my plea.

"I am eager to see the North country," Sawyer said; we spoke often in this conversational vein. "To read Jacob's letters is to picture a sort of heaven on earth. Lakes as you've never imagined, forests so deep it would take days to walk from under the tree limbs. The winters, though, I've trouble imagining as Jacob describes them."

"Drifts higher than the windows," I said, recalling the phrasing of one such letter. Inevitably we circled back to the idea of winter; Jacob was a descriptive writer, prone to excessive detail. For the countless time, I found myself anxiety-ridden, speculating just what Jacob Miller would think of my unexpected presence; Boyd kept his uncle well informed, and he was insistent that Jacob and Hannah would welcome all of us with open arms, but I was still apprehensive to meet them. As I told Sawyer, I would be content to forgo homesteading and roam the prairie for the rest of our days, as long as he was at my side.

Malcolm declared, "I aim to throw a snowball, that's what."

"And catch a fish bigger than you," Sawyer teased the boy. "Boyd, you recall the catfish in Sutter's Creek that was known to eat boys in one gulp?"

Boyd laughed, reining Fortune so that they could ride alongside Sawyer and Whistler. A smoke dangled between his lips; he spoke around it to reply, "For certain. Goddamn thing. Tried to snatch itself a piece of my foot, on occasion."

"Daddy said it might snatch itself our winks, if we didn't stop swimming bare-naked," Malcolm giggled, prompting everyone's laughter.

"Shit, I believe I just been insulted," Boyd said, still grinning. "My wink's big enough that no catfish would ever mistake it for food, *thank* you kindly."

Sawyer said with mock solemnity, "I'd like to think the same, of mine."

"You-all *wish!* I seen you twos in your nothings-on," Malcolm cried, taking great joy in teasing them, and Boyd reached and flicked a finger beneath the brim of his little brother's hat, setting it sailing; the boy had not latched his chin strap, as it was a windless day. I could not stop laughing.

Malcolm yelped and halted Aces to retrieve it; as he rejoined us he said, with an air of slight disdain, "Besides, that catfish was just a legend, Uncle Malcolm told me."

I teased affectionately, "This from the boy who believes in hoop snakes with all his heart."

"Lorie! I can't tell you again, them things are real!" the boy insisted, dark eyebrows lofted high. He peered at me from beneath the brim of his newly-resettled hat.

"But not a man-eating catfish?" I pestered, smiling at him.

He pursed his lips and squinted one eye at me in the way he had, replying, "No, but I done heard of a bird in the North that eats children. Flies down an' swoops 'em up in his talons."

"Perhaps like those?" Sawyer asked in all seriousness, though I caught the note of teasing in his voice. We all looked upwards, where he was indicating, at a pair of wide-winged birds gliding on an updraft, crisp and black against the deep blue backdrop of the sky.

Malcolm whooped, and both Aces and Juniper shied at the unexpected sound, snorting and stomping. He yelped, "Run for cover! Lorie, *get down!*" He heeled Aces and cantered ahead, still shouting for all he was worth, as though in pursuit of the birds; he took aim with an imaginary pistol, and I could see the bunching of the horse's muscular flanks as he flowed smoothly into a gallop. Malcolm's already-lively imagination had been much stimulated since the night the catamounts bounded through our camp.

I changed the subject, taking up an earlier conversation, "Do you believe we'll be able to purchase land upon arrival?"

"We'll apply immediately," Sawyer said. "The purchase will be determined upon approval of our application. And that's where it becomes a fair amount sketchy for us, as former soldiers. We've taken up arms against the United States government, officially, and therefore might not be granted permission by the Act of 'sixty-two, though Gus was certain that it wouldn't be so strictly enforced any longer."

"We'll pray that's so," Boyd agreed. "Uncle Jacob was never a soldier himself. We may just be guests upon his homestead for the rest of our livin' lives."

Winking at me, he said, "Y'all don't mind living your golden years in a hay-mow, do you?"

Sawyer assured me, "We'll make our own home, I promise you. Even if I have to clear every acre with my bare hands."

I knew he would, too, if it came to that. I assured, "I will help you."

"Yes, an' gripping your sharpest saw," Boyd snorted in retort. "You may be strong, Davis, but I've yet to see you uproot a tree all alone. In fact, I recall the time me an' Beau beat you an' Ethan in the tug o' war competition, July the fourth, 1858. Exactly ten years ago this very day, if I don't mistake the date."

Sawyer laughed and Whistler tossed her head and high-stepped at the sound, happy to hear the joy in his voice. He countered, "Not by much, if you'll recall."

"Don't listen to him," Boyd warned me. "*Shee-it.* Me an' Sawyer was four-teen years old that summer, more fulla piss an' hot air than you's ever seen. Christ."

"Where was I?" Malcolm demanded breathlessly, rejoining us. Sweat trickled over his temples and created fine rivulets in the dust on his face.

"You was just a babe, still on the breast," Boyd gleefully informed him, and Malcolm's lips went into an immediate pout.

"I done missed all the fun," the boy muttered.

Boyd explained to me, "It was the Suttonville celebration, the one in which Ethan usually won the blue ribbon in the horse race. He rode Buck that year, did he not?" Sawyer nodded with amused agreement and Boyd continued, "You shoulda seen Ethan, strutting around with that ribbon on his shirt. Remember how we all tried to get Emily Ingram's attention that summer? Lord, that girl. She was pretty as a starlit night, but such a nag. Not that we noticed, nor even cared. We just wanted to get her around the corner of a barn for a kiss or two." Boyd grinned impishly. "But she had her eye on Sawyer, an' oh was I jealous."

"Emily Ingram," Sawyer said, laughing. He shook his head and said, "Just the thought of her voice makes me cringe, yet. She always said my name in two parts, *Saw-yer*, all singsong-like."

"I notice that didn't stop you from stealing a kiss, yourself," Boyd remarked.

"She was the first girl I'd ever tried to kiss," Sawyer told me. "I was so ner-vous I was sweating buckets, and hardly had I touched her when she started giggling, and then ran away. I never knew if I had done something wrong, or what."

I laughed at this description, unable to imagine any girl who didn't near die with pleasure at being kissed by him. I tried to form a picture of Sawyer at fourteen years of age. And Boyd, surely even more incorrigible than he was now, a decade later. They were each so solidly-built, strong and broad and capable, intimidatingly formidable when the need arose, and adorned by various scars from battle; I had difficulty envisioning them as slim and gangly boys, full of mischief but innocent to what they would someday be forced to know.

"Well, you musta done something right, as she bragged about it to all the girls in attendance that day. I wanted to wring your gullet," Boyd said good-naturedly, his eyes merry with remembrance. "I just knew I had to beat you at something if I wanted her attention."

Like my own, their memories of the idyllic days before the War were as precious as gold, though even in 1858 the conflict was already on the horizon, an all-encompassing shadow, its approach inescapable. I did not wish to dwell on that thought, and so I prompted, "What of the tug of war?"

"Oh yes," Boyd said, resettling his hat. "Well, Beau an' me thought there was no better way to get the ladies to notice us than to challenge the Davis boys to a little friendly competition. Beau had his eye on Sara Lynn LeMoyne, you'll recall, an' we figured the girls would pay attention if we tugged you twos into the mud. There was a right big crowd gathered to watch, as it had been goin' strong since afternoon. I recall that both Emily an' Sara Lynn was in the crowd."

"It was an outright battle," Sawyer said. "I remember you and me faced off in the front, Boyd. And Ethan behind me, yelling in my ear at the top of his voice, 'Pull, goddammit, pull!'"

"The determination in your eyes was right frightening, old friend," Boyd said. "At the last moment I looked away an' saw Emily watching, cheerin' an' clappin', an' I knew that we just had to win."

"Carters *always* win in tug o' war," Malcolm said, sounding affronted. "Daddy said it's since we got such strong arms, that's why."

I was laughing so hard I could hardly catch a breath, and Sawyer's eyes were warm upon me.

Boyd said, "An' I was rewarded. Beau an' me let the rope go slack just long enough to fool the two of you, an' then hauled for all we was worth. There went Sawyer an' Eth right into the mud-slick, all churned up from the boots of near every man in Suttonville. Oh, it was a ripe victory. We basked in glory until I felt a sudden cold chill an' looked to see the glint in Ethan's eye. See, Lorie, his blue ribbon was covered in mud. I barely had time to move before he launched at me, swingin' for all he was worth."

"I was sitting right in the middle of it," Sawyer informed me. "Ethan went near over my head and socked Boyd square in the nose."

"I then had to defend myself," Boyd added, as Malcolm laughed and nodded in approval.

"Beau tried to grab for the two of you and fell, and I couldn't get to my feet as the mud was so slippery," Sawyer said. "Then I got an elbow in the face."

"Before you could slap a tick, the four of us was all-out wrestling like a bunch of boars in spring," Boyd laughed. "Jesus, our poor mamas was downright ashamed. Big boys like us shoulda known better."

"Your daddy waded in and near cracked our heads together," Sawyer remembered. "And for all that trouble, Emily ended up on Nash Gandy's arm anyway."

"Lord, that's right, I'd forgotten," Boyd said. He sobered and said softly, "Gandy didn't make it past the summer of 'sixty-three, not so's I know of."

"It's a wonder we did," Sawyer said quietly, his gaze on the far horizon before coming back to me. He saw the concern in my eyes and sent me a smile of reassurance, asking, "You feel up to a ride? I'll mind the wagon."

"I think I would," I said, shifting and drawing back on the reins, halting the team. Sawyer pulled off his riding gloves and I slipped them into place, loving the warmth of the leather that had just been touching him. I hugged Whistler's neck before climbing neatly atop her back; Sawyer shortened the stirrups for me, then straightened to his full height and curved both hands around my lower leg.

"Don't ride out of sight, I can't bear it," he told me, and I promised I would not.

Malcolm doubled back and appropriated my attention immediately, coaxing me to canter.

"Please, Lorie-Lorie," he begged. "Aces wants to race."

"Let's ride ahead a bit, instead," I told him.

Malcolm shrugged agreeably.

I heeled Whistler and she pranced forward eagerly, following after Aces. Malcolm led us out at a trot; I overtook him easily and for a time we rode abreast while Boyd stayed back near the wagon.

"You look right healed up," Malcolm said, our knees no more than two feet apart. "You's feeling better, ain't you? I been awful worried."

"I am," I assured. Wishing to compliment him, I specified, "The three of you take such marvelous care of me."

"We aim to," he said. "Ladies need someone to care for them."

"Boys, too," I couldn't help but tease.

"I'll be a man right soon," he contradicted. "Right soon." He scrunched up his face and mused, "Do you think my uncle will care for us?"

"He's your family," I said; it was so like Malcolm to express a similar sentiment, to echo what I had been wondering about, only earlier this day. I reassured, "Of course he'll care for you."

"He's your kin now, too," the boy said. "You's our sister now, recall?"

I said solemnly, "Yes, I recall. Though I don't know if your uncle will share that opinion."

"He will," Malcolm said with all the confidence of a child. He added, a wistful note softening his voice, "I hope he looks like Mama. He is her kid brother, after all. I hope he reminds me of her. Lord, I do miss her. Sometimes I can't quite see her face or hear her voice no more. It's been near four years since she passed." He released a little half-sigh, looking towards the horizon. He whispered, "I miss her, even still."

I reached and squeezed his forearm, and he tenderly patted me, brightening a little.

"Did she sing?" I asked.

He nodded vigorous affirmation. "She did, all the time."

"What did she sing?"

"From the hymnal, mostly. When the boys was gone to War, she sang from the hymnal every night. Daddy would play his fiddle an' we'd sing, real quiet-like. She loved 'My Old Kentucky Home,' though we did live in Tennessee. An' songs of Christmastide. Her favorite was 'It Came Upon a Midnight Clear.'"

"Perhaps if we sang for a spell, you'd hear her voice more clearly in your memory," I said.

His dark eyes lit with anticipation and he said, "Let's sing the midnight one, do you know it, Lorie?"

"I know that one well," I said, and together we sang through all its verses. Malcolm's voice was sweet and true. He loved to sing, or whistle, while he accomplished his chores, sometimes almost unconsciously; I had grown so accustomed to hearing him, and felt there were few things more cheerful than a whistled tune.

"Let's sing 'Silent Night, Holy Night' next!" he said upon finishing the first song, bouncing on the saddle.

We worked our way through every Yuletide hymn we could recollect, until Boyd yelled from some distance behind, "Guess I best hang out my stocking tonight! An' make up a mince pie or two!"

"Oh Lordy, mince pies," Malcolm said. He begged, "You'll bake up pies for us, won't you?"

"It has been a long time since I baked anything," I admitted, and another small burst of angst shivered across my belly; I lacked so many of the skills that a woman my age, nearly eighteen, would normally possess. My existence at Ginny's required no work in the kitchen or lower household; my services, like all of the other women's, had been expected exclusively in the rooms upstairs.

And as he was so often wont to do, the boy lifted my spirits without even realizing, as he chirped, "Well, you's a fast learner."

I looked his way, immeasurably touched at this observation.

Malcolm's eyebrows lifted abruptly and he indicated with an extended finger, noting, "There's smoke up there!"

"Looks more like dust," I contradicted, squinting against the brilliant sun. We traveled along a beaten path upon which rain had not fallen for many days; a smoke-cloud of powder-fine dust rose in the wake of our passage, as well. I said decisively, "Come along, let's ride back."

We circled the horses. Sawyer and Boyd had already noticed the disturbance on the trail; Boyd asked, "You three in the mood for a bit a company?"

I was most assuredly not, but refrained from voicing the thought.

From the wagon seat Sawyer asked, "Are you longing a bit for Christmas, you two?"

I smiled up at him, replying, "We were remembering songs that Clairee used to sing."

"Then you shoulda been singing 'Twinkling Stars Are Laughing, Love,' as that was her favorite," Boyd said.

"Aw, Mama used to sing that, too," Sawyer said. "That is such a lovely tune."

"Let's!" Malcolm said, and so it was that all four of us were singing the lullaby as a pair of horses appeared distantly on the trail, trotting our way at a leisurely pace. As we finished the final verse, Boyd stood in his stirrups and called, "Hello there!"

One of the approaching riders waved and called a greeting. Despite the friendly exchange thus far, I could sense both Sawyer and Boyd grow wary, their eyes calculating and noting details, surely far beyond that which mine would observe. Boyd and Malcolm maneuvered in front of me, and I was no more than a few feet from Sawyer, and so I let my shoulders relax. I noticed the horses first as they neared, one a lovely, showy sorrel with an amber mane that caught and threw the sunlight, the other a tall chestnut. The men mounted upon them were not traveling far, as they rode with no saddle bags or bedrolls. They were most certainly a father and son, and halted near us.

The father spoke affably, greeting us, "Good day, fellows," before he caught sight of me. He swept off his hat and amended, "And ma'am. Begging your pardon. Charley Rawley, and my boy, Grant."

The son also removed his hat, nodding politely; curly hair flopped at once over his forehead, and he quickly replaced his headwear.

"That's Lorie an' she *is* actually a girl, even if she wears trousers," Malcolm said importantly, and I blushed hotly at this well-meaning explanation.

Sawyer took charge and said in his deep voice, "Pleased to meet you, Mr. Rawley. I am Sawyer Davis. This is my wife, Lorissa, and Boyd and Malcolm Carter. The four of us are bound for Minnesota."

He spoke the word *wife* with such pride and my heart swelled, overjoyed that he would introduce me so, despite our decidedly unmarried status according to the laws and expectations of society. I knew Sawyer wished to honor me with a proper wedding service, but in our hearts we were already wed; no words spoken by a reverend could make this any more true, at least not in mine or Sawyer's eyes.

"Tennessee?" asked Charley Rawley, surprising all of us. He sensed this and hurried to explain, "My wife is of Tennessee, originally. I can always recognize that particular lilt."

"We are, at that," Boyd said, and I could hear his good humor though he faced away from me. "That's a fine ear you have. Whereabouts is your wife from?"

"Crossville, in the Cumberland County," Charley replied, resettling his hat.

"*Shucks*, we was raised not but a stone's throw from there, in Suttonville," Boyd said.

"As it is the Fourth of July, we are bound at the moment for the neighboring homestead, to invite them for an afternoon celebration," Charley said. "We would surely appreciate your company for dinner, as well. My wife isn't often able to converse with folks from her home state."

"Have you firecrackers?" Malcolm asked, with such eagerness that Charley laughed.

He said, "We've a few, son."

Sawyer looked to me.

Do you wish to join them?

I think that would be all right, I responded.

Boyd turned in the saddle to regard the both of us.

"We could spare an evening," he murmured. He turned back to Charley and said, "We would be most delighted to join your family."

Charley tipped his hat brim and then said, "I'll continue to the Yancys' homestead, and Grant shall show you the way to ours, if that suits? We're but two miles northwest of here."

Charley heeled his chestnut and waved farewell, as Boyd and Malcolm rode forward to speak with his son. I heard Malcolm say, "That's a fine sorrel you got there. Does she like to race?"

I murmured to Sawyer, "I cannot pay a call dressed this way."

"I like how you look," he said, grinning at me.

"Mrs. Rawley would be horrified, as you well know," I said, with absolute certainty. I could not under any circumstances meet a Tennessee woman while clad in Malcolm's trousers. In my memory I heard the sound of my mama's shocked, indrawn breath, the kind she always held just before releasing a deluge of critique. I had to presume that Mrs. Rawley's sensibilities would be similarly delicate.

"Thank you for introducing me as your wife," I added softly, reaching up to rest my hand upon his knee.

"I won't have folks talking of that which isn't their business. And you are my wife, Lorie-love, no matter if a preacher has spoken over us or not," Sawyer said, echoing my thoughts exactly, and lifted my knuckles to his lips.

T HE RAWLEYS' FARMHOUSE was set near the road, constructed of logs, square-cut and sturdy. The barn was nearly twice the size of the house, a looming structure with an oblong corral, a chicken coop, and a pig pen adjacent to its foundation. Stately pines guarded the northern edge of the dooryard, while chickens roamed in their enclosure; it appeared a tidy and pleasant place, similar to what I envisioned when imagining Jacob and Hannah's homestead. There were three boys climbing on the corral beams as we entered the yard, but they all ceased playing with amusing suddenness, jumping from the fence to watch with open curiosity. It was probably coincidental that they stood in descending height order, like risers on a staircase.

Grant proved to be a conversational fellow, only months older than Malcolm. He grew more animated as we neared his home, explaining that his family had farmed in Iowa for the past decade, after relocating from Ohio, saving the time his father served in the War.

"Pa was discharged early on, as he was shot in the hip," Grant said. "He was lucky, though, gone scarce a year from us. Mama said it was a heaven-sent bullet."

Grant had four younger brothers and confessed that his mother longed for female company.

"All we got for womenfolk other than Ma is the milking cow," he joked, then immediately asked Malcolm, "Guess what?"

"What's that?" Malcolm responded gamely.

"Ma's making ice cream!"

I caught Sawyer's eye as he smiled, both of us thinking that Malcolm had found a kindred soul.

The lady of the house came outside into the sunny day before Sawyer halted the wagon. I elected to ride beside him on the wagon seat, dressed properly, as so to avoid shocking her, though my initial impression suggested that she was not one easily shocked; she clapped her hands and smiled with welcome, calling, "Visitors! I knew it, I had a feeling this morning, did I not, Grantley?"

Her voice held the soft, familiar lilt of home, and I was certain that, like me, Sawyer, Boyd, and Malcolm each pictured their own mothers. Mrs. Rawley was a slim, angular woman with dark hair in a braided bun, untying and removing her apron as she walked. Sawyer and Boyd swiftly removed their hats, almost in unison.

"Who have we here?" she asked, regarding us with genuine warmth.

Boyd dismounted, hat held to his chest, and bowed formally. I could tell she was charmed.

"Boyd Brandon Carter, ma'am, of Suttonville, Tennessee," he said, in his most gentlemanly cadence. "Your good man invited us to dinner, if that suits you. An' your boy escorted us, forthwith. This here is my dearest friend, Sawyer Davis, his wife an' my sister, Lorissa, an' my brother, Malcolm."

"Suttonville!" she cried. "Oh, I could have heard it in your voice. My mama was from Suttonville herself, young man." She offered her hand to Boyd, which he took and lifted politely to his lips. She said, "I am Frances Eugenia Rawley, but you may call me Fannie. How pleased I am to meet you."

Malcolm mimicked Boyd, bowing politely, hardly able to contain his exhilaration. He was nearly beside himself at the promise of ice cream and firecrackers, not to mention the troupe of rambunctious-looking boys eager to play. He enthused, "Ma'am, I hear tell that you's making ice cream!"

Fannie patted his cheeks and said, "Bless you, son, we are."

Any concerns we may have harbored about a less-than-enthusiastic welcome were swept away as quickly as dust by a broom. Fannie Rawley proved as gracious as any Southern hostess from my childhood, hugging each of us as though we were relatives expected for a much-anticipated visit.

"Newlyweds, I can tell," she said to Sawyer and me. "May I say, Mr. Davis, I have never beheld such a beauty as your wife. You are indeed a lucky man."

Sawyer grinned widely, saying, "Thank you kindly, ma'am. I couldn't agree more."

Fannie appropriated my arm and sent a sharp tone in the direction of the boys, calling, "Come here and meet our guests, for pity's sake!" To me she clucked, "You'd think they were raised along with the pigs. Boys, all I have are boys!" Indicating Grant, she said, "You've met my eldest, named for my daddy, Grantley Belford Catton, God rest him. This young scoundrel here is Miles, and this fellow is my best troublemaker, Silas. There's my bashful Quinlan yonder, he shan't venture near just yet, and inside at the window is my youngest, Willie. He's turning the crank, as you'll shortly notice. How old are you, son?"

This question was directed at Malcolm, who replied, "Thirteen, this month."

"You shall fit right in with these boys. We may have to keep you here with us. Mrs. Davis, do join me inside. Boys," and she addressed Boyd and Sawyer with this word, while I bit back a smile, "If you would be so kind as to set out the table and chairs from the barn under the poplar trees, just there? And then do be seated. Miles, fetch two jugs of tea from the root cellar. Silas, fetch Quin and spread out the quilts near the table. We'll have us a proper picnic once the Yancys arrive."

Upon the narrow table in her living space sat a small wooden barrel with a hand-crank, which she explained was the ice cream maker. A boy of perhaps a half-dozen years sat working the handle; he watched with bright-eyed interest as his mother entered with a stranger. A nearby sideboard bulged with food. I saw sliced ham and boiled eggs, two loaves of bread, a crock of creamy butter, jars of preserves, and best of all, two fruit crumbles with crusts so golden and tempting Malcolm's eyes would undoubtedly grow tear-filled with happiness; mine nearly did.

"Willie, this is Mrs. Lorissa Davis. She, her good man, and her two brothers have only just arrived to celebrate the Fourth with us," Fannie said, while I beamed with pleasure at being referred to with Sawyer's last name attached to my first. She invited, "Mrs. Davis, do have a seat."

"I am pleased to meet you," I told the boy, settling upon a chair near him, offering a smile.

Willie was possessed of curly hair and lively brown eyes, and explained importantly, "I gotta keep cranking this here handle, Mrs. Davis."

My smile broadened at his earnest words; I earned one from him, in return. He perched a little closer to me, on the edge of his chair. He could have been Malcolm's kid brother.

Fannie lifted the cover on the barrel, peered within, and informed her son, "Your work is well done, sweetheart. Introduce yourself to the men, yonder, and then you may find your brothers and meet young Malcolm," and Willie burst outside with no further encouragement, while his mother smiled after him.

"You have fine boys," I said.

"Thank you kindly. I wish I could tell you that there shall be more womenfolk to chat with once the Yancys arrive, as they're our closest neighbors, but Thomas Yancy is a widower. I tell you, I have been attempting to find him a wife for over a year now. He's two sons, Fallon and Dredd - named for his mother's family, that one - and they need a woman's influence. They are as wild as you may imagine." She did not cease moving as she spoke, gathering a tray of tin cups. "There are few marriageable women in this area, unfortunately for Thomas. The homestead north of ours is also owned by a widower. Crawford is his name, Zeb Crawford. He too lost his wife before he returned from the War, and his boys were killed in action, the entire lot of them. It was a terrible misfortune."

I opened my mouth, on the brink of admitting to having lost my own brothers, before frantically stifling this error in judgment; I could not admit, even indirectly, that Boyd and Malcolm were not truly my kin. Instead, I asked the first question that scrambled to mind, "Will Mr. Crawford join us, as well?"

I did not believe I was imagining the suggestion of a shadow that flitted over her features. Unknowingly confirming this, Fannie heaved a small sigh and admitted, "He shall not. I do not much care for the man. Please do not think me an unconscionable gossip, Mrs. Davis, though it has been months since I've conversed with another woman. The truth of the matter is, I consider myself a solid judge of character and I do not wish my boys near him. The few occasions we have met, there was something about Zeb I found unpleasant. And there was the rumor, last autumn, that he had…"

My eyebrows lifted in alarm at her tone and the implication of such a pause; though I was not certain I wanted to hear the answer, I asked quietly, "Had what?"

Fannie lowered her voice and finished, "Burned a dog alive."

I had been privy, in my time at Ginny's, to all manner of despicable tales featuring unscrupulous men, capable of any number of immoral acts, and I was less shocked than she would have known, though the idea of any man treating a living creature with such cruelty turned my stomach.

"To this day I am not certain if that was simply a tall tale," she said, saving me from responding. "I would like to believe so. Thomas Yancy served with Zeb in the Fifty-First, and has never expressed undue concerns about him. My own Charley does not share my excessive dislike of the man, and so it may be that I am simply reading too much into the situation." She offered me a sudden smile and admitted, "It would not be the first time my imagination has captured my senses." She rolled her eyes at herself, apologizing, "And here I am, chattering up a windstorm at you. Forgive me. Tell me, how long have you been on the trail?"

She has no idea you used to be a whore. No idea at all. Do not fret.

I faltered for the faintest flicker before lying, "Since April." It was a half-truth at best; Sawyer, Boyd, Malcolm, and Angus had begun their journey from Tennessee then, while I joined them, however unexpectedly, later that spring.

"Oh, how well I remember the spring in Cumberland County. How wonderful that the four of you are from that area. I've not been able to successfully grow honeysuckle here, no matter how I try."

"It is the best scent in the world," I agreed, and allowed myself the luxury of relaxing enough to enjoy conversing with a proper woman. It had been so long.

"Here's Miles with the tea," Fannie said, as her son clomped inside bearing two corked, earthenware jugs, the kind in which people back home kept moonshine. "We have plenty of food, do not you worry. Even with the addition of three strapping young men." She winked at me and directed Miles, "Take those to the table. Mrs. Davis, why don't you join them and bring these cups, and I shall finish my tasks."

"Please, do call me Lorie," I told her, accepting the tray.

Sawyer and Boyd were hatless, elbowed up to the table, which was surrounded by four chairs. Silas and Quinlan had spread the quilts, though the boys were not in sight. Miles, after depositing the jugs, scampered off in search of them. I set the tray on the table, moving just beside Sawyer's chair to do so, and he curled an arm around my hips and drew me briefly against his side. I smiled at this husbandly gesture, bending to kiss his temple. His hairline was damp with sweat.

"What have you there, Lorie-girl?" Boyd asked. "I'm a-thinking we stumbled onto the best dinner we's had in a month of Sundays." With his usual drama, he added, "This makes up for them panthers attacking our camp, wouldn't y'all agree?"

"There *is* fruit crumble within the house," I confirmed in a whisper, and laughed as this comment elicited small groans from Sawyer and Boyd.

I poured cups of tea for each of us; the smell of mint rose pleasantly from the liquid. I had just settled into a chair when Fannie appeared in the doorway and called, "Lorie, I do apologize, but would you mind spreading this cloth on the table?"

"Of course not," I responded, and hastened to her.

"Thank you," she said. "As soon as Charley has returned we shall have our dinner."

Boyd lifted the tray and Sawyer the tea while I spread the linen and straightened it with care. No more than a half-hour later Charley returned with two riders, and I helped Fannie cart food to the table; the boys materialized as though conjured by magic once dinner appeared. It turned out that the neighbor's sons had accompanied Charley; their father would be along later in the evening.

"Oh, it is so lovely to have a woman here," Fannie said as we collected dessert from the sideboard. "Any chance you folks would be willing to settle near? I do not speak lightly," she insisted, as I smiled, almost shyly, at her. "I am so starved for a woman's company. And now Thomas has put an idea in Charley's head, that of taking a marshal position. Thomas works as a marshal himself, between Cedar Falls and Iowa City. Both of them served in the Federal Army, so it makes sense, I suppose. I've been fretting over it, I'll not deny."

"Iowa City is along our route," I said, feeling an old twinge of discomfort at the mere word *Federal*, but I would never dream of letting that show; I was her guest. Following her outside, cradling a delectable-looking blackberry crumble, I said, "I'm given to understand that it's one of the larger settlements we'll come across for some time. Perhaps until St. Paul, in Minnesota."

"Iowa City is a good five dozen miles northwest, half a week's ride in the wagon, considerably less on horseback," Fannie said. "I've never been farther north than that. You are on an adventure, my dear, but if I thought for a moment that I could convince you and your good men to settle near, I would," and I was sincerely heartened at her words.

Charley carried an additional chair to the table and the five of us chatted as a magenta sun melted downwards along the western curve of the sky. Again I relished the satisfaction of conversing with respectable people, at a dinner table no less, able to draw upon my intellect and education, as I had not in so very long. We spoke of travels, the upcoming election, the Homestead Act; Charley felt certain, as had Angus, that Sawyer and Boyd would be granted eligibility as homesteaders.

"They are anxious to settle the Northern and Western lands," Charley said. "The two of you are able-bodied, willing to work and start families, and as such are ideal candidates."

"Malcolm may very well be in possession of a great deal of acreage, if they deny us," Sawyer said, though only half in jest. "He can sign the deeds for us, as he was never a soldier."

Boyd snorted a laugh, and Charley said, "Despite the current climate in Washington, there are those in Congress who wish to leave the shadow of War behind, for good."

"Such a long shadow was cast," I said, before considering the depressive nature of the statement; after all, we were here to celebrate the nation's original independence. I added hastily, "I do not mean to be morbid, but I fear it will take some time to escape its reach."

Charley said, "You are correct, but let us allow for the possibility of sun. Perhaps with a change in administration, the escape shall be swifter."

"Iowa and Minnesota shall lean towards General Grant this autumn, I am thinking," Fannie said.

"I believe Tennessee will give her electoral votes to Grant, as well," Sawyer acknowledged.

"He could hardly do worse than Johnson," Charley said. "Ulysses is no politician, but he is one hell of a leader, which is what this country needs. We shall exist only tentatively at peace without strong leadership."

"I fear you's right," Boyd said.

"And certainly part of why you are choosing to relocate," Fannie acknowledged. "I understand the sentiment."

"Tennessee will be the home of our youth, for always," Boyd said quietly.

"An' my memories of them days'll always be sweet. But it ain't home, no more."

"Home is where your family resides, and no other," Fannie said, patting Boyd's forearm, just to her right, a gesture both tender and maternal; Boyd nodded in half-bashful agreement and I smiled to myself at the sight of such an uncharacteristic flush upon his features.

"That is the truth," Sawyer said, laying a hand briefly against my back.

"I am even tempted to think of the prairie as home, at times," I admitted. "I have found journeying across it unexpectedly pleasant."

Charley said, "When the sun lifts over the fields, come an early morning, there is not a much prettier sight. Especially this time of year."

"An adventure," Fannie said again, and her gaze moved to encompass her boys. She murmured, "Soon enough the wanderlust shall strike them."

"The country is expanding westward, in leaps and bounds," Charley said, with a sigh. "I expect they shall not be easily corralled, give or take five years."

The boys, eight in all, ate their fill and began kicking up trouble with one another. I was put in mind of Clairee Carter minding her four sons, plus Sawyer and the twins, once upon a time. Though, Fannie seemed unconcerned at their antics. She and I relocated once dessert was served, claiming a spot to ourselves upon a quilt spread beneath the shade of a sprawling poplar. The mahogany-tinted evening light dusted the sun-warmed earth, arousing in me memories of Tennessee; it was the lilt of a woman's soft voice, the sounds of horses in the background, and boys roughhousing with one another. If I squinted, letting my vision haze, I could almost imagine I was back at my daddy's ranch.

"I haven't had ice cream since I was a little girl," I said, as we spooned the treat from small porcelain bowls. I sat with my feet tucked beneath me, my indigo skirt belling and both sleeves rolled to the elbow. My hair had come down from where I'd neatly pinned it, but despite her status a Southern-bred woman, Fannie did not strike me as the sort to be unduly bothered with such details. Her hair also escaped its confines and curled around her face.

"It is delicious, is it not?" she agreed.

"And I do thank you for letting us share your celebration so unexpectedly," I added. "Truly. It's very generous of you."

"I appreciate the company, do not fret yourself a moment," she said. "I love to hear your Tennessee voices and recall my youth."

"My childhood home lay just outside Lafayette, in the valley near Lake Royal," I told her. "Before the War."

"Lafayette, such pretty country there. You'll find the North beautiful in its own way, though I do long for the red dirt roads and the pawpaw trees. There's nothing like that here. But I've grown fond of it, after all these years." She licked her spoon. "Though you must be prepared for the winters. Into Minnesota, even more so."

I nodded. As we conversed, I'd told her of our plans to eventually retake the northernmost branch of the Mississippi, and how we planned to follow the Iowa River for a spell, which Fannie said was just miles from their homestead. As for our final destination, I knew only the name of the lake near which Jacob Miller homesteaded; Flickertail, it was called.

She insisted, "Of course you shall set up your tents in the yard for the night. I wish I had a spare bed to offer to at least you and your husband, but we haven't a spare inch! We are so glad of the company, I would offer you the barn if I thought perhaps you would stay another few nights."

And I spared another moment, however unspoken, to be grateful for the many ways in which my life had changed since last spring.

A FTER DINNER, I helped Fannie as the boys played tag and the men remained around the table in the last of the day's long light, Charley with a pipe and Boyd with a tobacco roll. The sky stretched vast and satin-smooth, tinted a rich rose. The Rawleys' dooryard was cheerfully pleasant in the still air, replete with the sense of a close-knit family fortunate enough to remain intact. Chickens clucked as they roosted for the night; a band of crickets commenced their comforting nightly refrain. As I emptied the washbasin out to the side of the house, smiling at the lightning bugs' sporadic sparking in the ditch across the way, Malcolm caught sight of me and hollered, "C'mon, Lorie-Lorie, it's time for the firecrackers!"

Though I politely waited for Fannie, every male in sight gathered hastily into a semi-circle around Charley, who crouched at the far edge of the yard with a small brush torch in hand, poised to start the show. He had made two rows of tin cups, upside-down, each covering the pay end of a short fuse.

"Charles Rawley, you mind those boys!" Fannie hollered to her husband, removing her apron and waving it in frustration as her words were either unheard or unheeded; there was a great deal of excited chatter from that part of the yard. She muttered, "Boys and their 'fun.' You'll learn soon enough, my dear," and her smile grew teasingly impertinent as she said, "The way that handsome man of yours looks at you, you'll have a wagonful of your own sons in no time, mark my words."

"Ready now!" Charley heralded, making a half-hearted attempt to shoo the boys away; I saw Boyd clamp ahold of the back of Malcolm's shirt as Charley yelled, "And, *fire!*"

Charley lit a fuse and jumped to the side, rather theatrically, as powder exploded beneath the first of the tin cups, sending it sailing with a bang that made the horses startle in the corral and the boys cheer wildly. I watched them, Malcolm especially, without approaching any closer. Did he realize how blessed he was? That, at his age, the boys I had known would soon be soldiers and engaged in warfare on an unimaginable scale? Could any boy be expected to comprehend how strange it must be for former soldiers to hear the sound of a detonation and know it for celebration rather than grave danger?

"Happy Fourth!" some of them yelled, as Charley sent more tin cups bursting into the darkening air.

I did not venture near, preferring to keep a bit of distance from the explosions, controlled though they were, and it was then that a rider approached at a leisurely trot up the road; he drew his mount to a walk and entered the Rawleys' dooryard with an easy sense of informality. Clearly this was their widowed neighbor. Fannie affirmed my notion, calling brightly, "Thomas! We are glad you could find the time to join us this fine evening."

"Fannie," he returned in polite greeting, tipping his hat brim, sending me a curious second glance as he tied his horse to the hitching rail. I watched him performing the mundane task; it was just as he shooed a fly from his face that a small mouse of discomfort skittered along my back. He called, "I heard that powder from a half-mile out. Are the boys behaving?"

"As well as expected. Come and meet our guests," Fannie invited.

Obediently he walked in our direction, removing his hat on the way. I studied him with the faintest sense of unease clinging to my spine, though I could not have pinpointed what it was that triggered this perception. Thomas Yancy appeared agreeable enough, a man of perhaps five and thirty years, with intimidating shoulders. His mustached face was baked a dark red-brown from the sun, his hair receding from a high forehead with a white strip near the top where his hat kept him in shade; pale eyes with prominent squint lines unobtrusively scrutinized me.

"We have been joined unexpectedly but most delightfully by a family traveling north to Minnesota," Fannie explained. "This is Mrs. Lorissa Davis, whose good man and two brothers are accompanying her. Lorie, this is Thomas Yancy."

"Mrs. Davis," he said, taking my proffered fingers into his grasp and bowing slightly.

"Pleased to meet you," I responded, withdrawing my hand as quickly and discreetly as possible.

"Heading north, you say?" he asked, in the manner of someone accustomed to making gracious small talk.

I nodded, impolite but unwilling to further elaborate.

"Then let me wish you a safe journey," he said. He was correct and courteous to a fault. Why then did a hint of something not quite right hover about him, an aura I felt certain I could visualize, if only I had the ability?

This man is not Sam, I thought, suddenly certain I was unjustly comparing the two men; Yancy's voice had a faintly similar timbre. *Stop this. Sam Rainey is dead. He can never hurt you again.*

"Lorie, if you would show Thomas to the table? I shall be out directly with a plate," Fannie said.

"No need, ma'am, I know the way," Thomas Yancy assured me, resettling his hat. I lingered in the door, peering after him, observing as he neared the corral and then abruptly halted, ceasing movement as suddenly as one having come up against an unseen fence. I stepped forward, propelled by an urgency I could not explain, to see his eyes fixed on Whistler as she nosed the top beam of the split rail, the only horse in sight. Yancy stood still enough to resemble a wooden carving, a likeness of a human; hardly a breath seemed to escape him in the graying twilight. I found I could hardly swallow.

Dear God, what is it...

What is it...

As though mired in mud, almost painfully slowly, I saw his gaze turn towards the menfolk.

Behind me within the house, Fannie dropped a dish and exclaimed in aggravation; I startled and turned immediately to help her.

You are being ridiculous, Lorie, I scolded. *There is nothing wrong.*

"Lorie, I've gifts for you to take north," Fannie said, as we collected broken crockery from the floor. "What have you for medicine stores, or herbs?"

"We haven't much in the way of medicines," I admitted. I knew, as I had begun an informal inventory of our supplies. I was hesitant to root through Angus's trunk, feeling as though it was a violation; Boyd had finally pointed out, with reasonable logic, that Gus would have considered it sentimental hogwash to treat his belongings as though enshrined.

"We was his only kin," Boyd said, a few nights past. "He would want us to make use of what we could," and Sawyer had agreed.

"I shall prepare for you a basket," Fannie insisted, and would not be diverted from this plan, lighting a lantern and then rooting in a cupboard.

The firecrackers had all been spent, the darkening air dominated now by the scent of black powder, the boys' laughter, and the deep murmur of men's voices. By the time I made my way back outside, I was relieved to observe that the earlier sense of strangeness had evaporated. I went to the wagon, parked around the far side of the barn, and dug about until I found my shawl; as I wrapped it over my shoulders I noticed Sawyer headed my way across the yard.

"Are you cold?" he asked, gathering me near and tucking the shawl more closely about my body. Satisfied that I was sufficiently garbed for the rapidly-cooling evening, he murmured, "There."

I said, "I'll help you lay out the tents."

"We'll just set up ours," he said. "Malcolm elected to sleep in the haymow with the boys, and Boyd said he'll curl in the wagon for tonight. I'll grab the poles. We'll pitch it out here."

We worked together as dusk fully descended, the western sky a lovely rich purple, stars beginning to spangle its breast like diamonds upon a wealthy woman's gown. Or, in my own experience, paste brilliants edging a whore's cheap velvet costume. I was concentrating on holding an edge for Sawyer to stake out when he paused and caught his breath. He said, "Lorie, look there."

I followed his gaze upwards and was rendered both speechless and immobile as I beheld the rising moon to the east, spectacularly full, brass-tinted as a trumpet and appearing twice its usual size.

"I love seeing it with no buildings, no window frames to block my view," I said at last. With no whorehouse looming behind me from where I sat on the side balcony during the nights of my monthly bleeding, feet tucked under the edge of my petticoat; how I despised such memories, which ambushed me if I wasn't on guard. As though to reassure myself, however irrationally, that he was indeed still near me, I looked at Sawyer.

"It is a gorgeous sight. Near to magical," he agreed, and I studied his profile as he studied the sky.

"I think of you watching the moon when you were soldiering," I whispered. The night of the last full, which we had witnessed together, Sawyer told me of the way he found moments to appreciate the moon's presence even during the midst of the War, allowing himself to see it as a sign of a world beyond the ferocious fighting. A world in which an end to the conflict was perhaps possible.

"By the next full moon we will be properly wed," he said, and in the celestial light his eyes were steady upon my own, and very beautiful, rich with promise. "I swear to you, Lorie. From now forth, we'll watch it rise in each other's arms."

I nodded, quite unable to speak past the emotion lodged behind my breastbone. With the fingers of the opposite hand, I caressed the gold ring Sawyer had placed upon me.

"Ain't that a sight?" Boyd said suddenly, from behind us, coming to root in the back of the wagon for his fiddle case. He said, "I aim to play for a spell."

"You met Thomas Yancy?" I asked Sawyer; having finished erecting the tent, we followed Boyd, who skipped the bow expertly over the strings as he walked, listening for discordant notes. Though I kept a carefully neutral tone asking the question, I was more than curious to learn Sawyer's opinion of the man. I hoped he would put to rest my concerns, however inadvertently; I had not yet mentioned my strange qualms about Yancy, determined to believe that any sense of the negative was a result of my overactive mind.

"I did," Sawyer said, gently swinging our joined hands as we walked. He did not instantly elaborate, and I felt momentary relief, but then he continued, "He isn't the friendliest of fellows."

"We's just grown used to Charley in the course of the day," Boyd said. "Now *there's* an amiable man, if I ever met one."

Charley lit a fire in a stone-ringed pit near the edge of the yard and I could see Fannie busy spreading quilts around its leaping warmth. Malcolm was indistinguishable in the pack of boys. Yancy had already taken a seat, staring into the growing flames as he sipped from a tin cup. He did not acknowledge us as we neared, scarcely glanced upwards, but I did not believe I should disregard my apprehension as false.

I do not understand. Yancy has never met us before this very evening.

But we are of the South. Yancy was a Federal. And for many, that is more than enough reason to form an instant dislike. This I know.

And though I desperately wished I would never be forced to think of him again, I could not help but acknowledge, *It was reason enough for Sam Rainey.*

When I blinked, Sam's face appeared against the darkness of my eyelids, his sole remaining eye fixed on me with all of his burning hatred. I gritted my teeth, willing away the vision.

Sawyer instantly sensed my agitation and slowed our pace. He asked quietly, "What is it, Lorie? You went so still."

I drew forth all of my resolve and whispered, "It is only my imagination."

"We needn't join them," he said quietly, and I heard his hesitation to let me avoid explaining what truly troubled me.

"No—I would like to sit at the fire, at least for a spell," I said, sincerely enough. I did wish to listen to the music, and to be near Fannie. I enjoyed her company, and it would be discourteous to retire early when we were here for a celebration. I added, willing my words into his mind, *I will explain later, I promise,* and Sawyer nodded his understanding.

The space upon the blankets around the fire was limited, the overall mood raucous, and I was happy to claim a spot upon Sawyer's lap to create additional room. He sat with his legs folded so that I fit neatly against him, his chin at my left temple; he rested both hands briefly against the outsides of my thighs, squeezing lightly, a gesture both tender and intimate; it struck me afresh how dearly I treasured these touches, and that Sawyer wholeheartedly understood my need for them. He patted my legs with two gentle motions, and then enfolded my left hand in his, linking our fingers.

"Lorie-*Lorie,*" Malcolm said in his best wheedling tone, finagling his way to our side like a pup. He complained with a sigh, "It's been *ever so long* since you combed my hair," and so saying, he neatly displaced Sawyer's right arm and leaned one elbow comfortably over my lap, his slim legs sticking out behind us. I curled a hand into the boy's shaggy mane, petting him as though he was indeed a beloved animal come to seek affection.

"Kid, you are something else," Sawyer observed, roughing up Malcolm's hair before I shooed away his teasing hand. "You count your every blessing to have Lorie touching you like that."

"Oh, I do," Malcolm muttered, his voice drowsy, with perhaps just a hint of smugness. "I do, indeed."

I was abruptly reminded of our proximity to Thomas Yancy, around the fire to our right, as I unwittingly caught his eye; perhaps the sound of my laughter at Malcolm's words had tugged Yancy's attention my direction, over the other noise. I resumed stroking Malcolm's hair; I had frozen for the space of a breath. Sawyer rested his jaw gently against my temple and I let my spine relax; in the spirit of fairness, there was nothing overtly untoward about Yancy. Surely nothing I could use to provide evidence for my wariness of him, other than a feeling. I knew Sawyer would not disregard such, but I would tell him later, as I had promised, in the privacy of our tent.

Boyd skipped out a few notes to whet the whistle; Fannie clapped along, and the boys, with the exception of now-languid Malcolm, cheered and hooted, still vying and elbowing one another for better seats at the fire. Charley saluted with his tin cup and Boyd proceeded to make the fiddle sing. I studied the leaping, ever-changing flames as Boyd bowed familiar tunes, mesmerized by the beauty both corporeal and abstract, until I was coaxed into a warm and dreamlike state. I was safe in Sawyer's arms, Malcolm's hair was soft as down beneath my fingers, and my eyelids seemed leaded, growing heavier. Each blink lasted longer than the next and so I did not at first realize that Thomas Yancy's gaze was fixed upon me.

My hand in Malcolm's hair jerked in surprise as I came fully awake, and Yancy's eyes darted away. I reeled a little, my mind attempting to reconcile past life with present, to interpret the speculative look upon his face, one that men had worn every night at Ginny's. Though I was far from any whorehouse at present, I longed instantly to cringe away from such an expression—one with which I was all too detestably familiar.

You're safe here, in this place. You are no longer forced to do what Ginny Hossiter demands.

I recognized these truths, but they were not exactly what troubled me. It was the essence of Lila that still existed within me, the persona of the whore I had been, a woman whose services could be purchased for a dollar a minute, monetary amounts kept precisely with the aid of an egg timer. I knew there was no way that Yancy could possibly know what I had been, but I imagined he could. However unwittingly, I pictured myself upon the main floor at Hossiter's, circulating the crowd, leading man after man up the ornate staircase and along the carpeted hallway to that narrow brass bed in my old room.

Let me forget being called Lila, please, let me forget what I have been. Oh Jesus, please let me forget those things.

But I knew it was an empty request, at best, and my soul writhed in agony; there were so many dark parts of me that Sawyer willingly accepted.

He shifted just slightly, cupping my knee.

Tell me what's wrong, sweetheart.

Nothing, it's nothing. I'm well, I responded, and though I knew he did not fully believe this, he only nodded incrementally.

Charley passed around a small, earthenware jug of whiskey when Boyd took a break from fiddling; Fannie declined, as well as Sawyer and I, though Malcolm shifted to sit up and asked pleadingly, "Boyd, might I have me a taste? Daddy always let me have a taste, just."

"A nip," Boyd agreed. "I may have myself a snort as well. Ain't had a good hooch in ages."

Malcolm tipped the jug for a swig and backhanded the resultant drips from his chin. The whiskey made the rounds and Boyd resumed playing, with gusto. When Malcolm tried to sneak another drink, Sawyer leaned and caught it away from him.

"No more, kid," he said, low, but firmly enough for Malcolm to discern his seriousness.

"*Aw,*" Malcolm complained, but then he caught sight of Sawyer's stern gaze and sighed, relinquishing the jug.

"I'll take it," Thomas Yancy said. He, who had not yet directed a word our way, plucked the drink from Malcolm and consumed a long pull before studying me again, perhaps emboldened by the alcohol. Behind me, Sawyer's posture became discreetly threatening; I couldn't see Sawyer's eyes, but he clearly communicated something, because Yancy leaned slightly away from us. There was something undeniably dark in Yancy's gaze, I knew to my bones I was not imagining it; furtive and quickly veiled, but enough that my eyes, long observant to such nuances, caught the flicker. A ball of ice formed anew at the juncture of my ribcage. As though to make an excuse for himself, Yancy said casually, "No mistake, Mr. Davis, your wife is the prettiest thing I've ever seen."

No one could possibly know that this sentiment was nearly the exact one the man called Dixon had spoken to me in Missouri, only minutes before he killed Angus; I had not even told Sawyer. Nausea rippled through my center. Not for the first time, I despised that men found me beautiful, utterly loathed the unwanted attention this had garnered time and again. And, just like Dixon, there was a faintly insulting tinge to Yancy's voice that contradicted what should have been a compliment.

"Perhaps you should keep such opinions to yourself," Sawyer said quietly, without overt challenge, but even I shivered at his tone.

The song ended, Boyd laughing and swiping his sweating face with the back of one wrist. He had been playing wholeheartedly, oblivious to anything but the flow of notes from his strings, and most everyone was clapping.

Yancy held Sawyer's gaze in the relative silence that followed the absence of music and I tensed, but then Yancy looked over at Boyd. I could hardly believe the next words he dared utter, again with an air of calculated joviality that did not quite succeed in masking the venom in his tone, "How about 'Dixie,' son? Or perhaps a little 'Bonnie Blue?' You surely know how to fiddle *that* one."

Boyd's black eyebrows drew together; I sensed more than saw Charley give his neighbor a hard look.

Yancy tried for a smile, gesturing with the whiskey. He asked, "Hasn't anyone a goddamn sense of humor?"

The edge of tension was softened by the boys, who were unaware of any undertones whatsoever, all them still roughhousing. Boyd's eyes met Sawyer's, the two of them exchanging a message, before Boyd took up the bow and began a Tennessee waltz. I could not tell if this was somehow an unspoken jab at Yancy's provocative comment; I hoped not. The Rawleys had been so kind to us, had welcomed us into their evening of festivities. I would not have that ruined because of a few words spoken by their neighbor. However, I could no longer sit at the fire. I kept my movements unhurried as I rose, bending near Fannie to murmur, "I am to bed. Thank you ever so much for this evening."

She turned and caught my hands in hers. "You are ever so welcome. Goodnight to you, dear Lorie."

I KNEW THAT of course Sawyer would not let me go alone; I counted on it, and paused as he caught up with me in the darkness, well away from the noise and glow of the fire.

"Come with me," he whispered, taking my hand and leading us to the corral. At first I did not understand, but then he whistled and our horse came walking, her hooves striking the ground with comforting clomps.

"There's a sweet girl," Sawyer said to her, as Whistler lifted her nose over the topmost beam and nuzzled him. I climbed upon the bottom rung and hugged her, clinging, breathing her familiar scent. I murmured nonsense to her, letting my cheek rest upon her hide, and at last began to calm.

"I saw you kiss her nose, and embrace her, that second night," Sawyer said after a time.

I turned to look at him in light as bright as midday, spilling silver-white over us as the moon lifted towards its zenith. I whispered, "You did?"

He nodded. "I intended to brush her and I saw you, already there. You touched her so tenderly, and I wanted so much to take you into my arms it was near physical pain."

I encircled him with both arms, and said softly, "Gus had told me that afternoon how much you loved your horse. I didn't fully understand at the time, but I sought her out, I hugged her close, simply because she was yours."

"My Lorie," he whispered. "*Mo mhuirnín milis.*"

"I am sorry I left the fire just now, but—" I said, though Sawyer cut short my explanation.

"You needn't apologize," he told me, almost severe in his sincerity. "You needn't apologize to me for anything. Please know this."

I confessed, "I despise…that men look at me in a certain way. I feel near ill with guilt."

"No," he said at once. "You've nothing to be guilty for. Perhaps I should have bitten my tongue as Yancy seems the sort to welcome a fight. I was on edge, as it was."

"I despise most all men," I admitted.

"I can understand that," he said, and gently kissed my closed eyelids, one after the other. He whispered, "Darlin', never be ashamed of what you feel," and I opened my eyes to the intensity of his.

"Thank you," I whispered.

"Not ever," he repeated.

"Might we look in the trunk before we sleep?" I asked, as its contents also comforted me.

Sawyer knew exactly what I meant, and nodded before leading us to our tent. I lit a lantern to carry inside after fetching our bedding, creating for us a cozy, insular space, while Sawyer found his trunk in the back of the wagon and then joined me, kneeling to unbuckle the strap. I traced my fingers over his surname, carved upon the leather. As he opened the lid, I lifted the small, framed pictures of his brothers, taken upon their enlistment into the Army of Tennessee in late 1862; I had been correct in my guess at which twin was Ethan and which Jeremiah.

"I imagine them so well from your stories," I said, studying their silent faces in the candle's warm, wavering glint.

Sawyer stretched comfortably at my side, propping on an elbow, while I sat with legs folded beneath me; I had kicked off my boots. He said, "Not a day goes by when I don't think of them, somehow. I never considered a life without them as part of it. I reckoned we would always live close and our children would play together. That Daddy would set on the porch and hold his grandchildren on his knee, and Mama would spoil the daylights out of them."

"Even if you and Boyd hadn't told me so, I'd guess that Ethan was mischievous," I said, heart aching at the scene he described—that which should have been, but never would.

Sawyer laughed a little, reaching to trace a fingertip over the image of his brother. He said, "Aw, Eth got me into a fair amount of trouble. He even… we even…"

His deep voice trailed away and I saw that he was staring up at the canvas above us, back into time. His gaze came back to me and he said softly, "Scarce a week before Ethan, Jere, and I left home as recruits, I accompanied Eth..." He paused, before whispering, "Boyd and Jere were the only ones who ever knew."

"Knew what?" I whispered, tracing my fingertips over his cheekbone.

He cupped my knee, stroking with his thumb, and said, "I was nineteen, Eth eighteen. We were about to head to war, and Ethan didn't want...he didn't want to die without knowing what it meant to be with a woman." His eyes held mine steadily, though I could sense his hesitancy to tell me such things and risk my offense. At last he said, "Ethan somehow arranged to call upon a woman from Suttonville, who was widowed. Mary Douglas was her name, and her husband was killed in action the summer of 'sixty-two. Eth had it in mind that he would sweet-talk Mary and then she would...well, that she would let him..."

I blinked and several questions wanted to leap forth, but I restrained these as he continued, somberly, "I rode with Ethan to her house that night. I thought he was plumb crazy, but Mary let us in and was clearly expecting company. Ethan took her hands and kissed them, and I could tell he was smitten with her, more than he'd let on. She had coffee boiling, I remember that. We sat at her table and she asked after our parents, and Jeremiah, as though we'd come to pay a polite social call, when all the while her eyes kept lingering on my brother, speaking far more than her words. Even I could see it." He paused to sigh. "I had known Mary most of my youth but I'd never noticed how pretty she was, and not terribly much older than us, when it came to it. I sat there mute while she and Ethan spoke, wondering why my brother had even wished for me to accompany him in the first place. Now that I look back, I can understand how lonely Mary must have been, how she longed for company, even ours. I figured that once she understood what Ethan wanted she would throw him out like dishwater. But she was charmed by him, it was obvious, and the next thing I knew, I was riding Whistler home while my brother stayed behind, with Mary."

"And they..."

Sawyer nodded before saying somberly, "Even that night I wanted to ask Mary forgiveness for my brother's brashness, for wishing to use her body in such a fashion, simply to satisfy a curiosity. Ethan and I were not raised that way. Daddy would have skinned us alive. But then, there were nights after we'd left home and lived as soldiers that my brother would speak of her. I believe he loved her. After the War, in 'sixty-five, I went to her home, not exactly certain why, perhaps just to see another person who had known my brother, maybe even loved him. But poor Mary had died months past, as it was." He lifted his face and the concern in his eyes leaped into mine. "Should I have told you this?"

"Yes," I said firmly, stroking the side of his face, letting my fingertips linger. I clarified, "I am not upset. Just as you once told me, there is nothing you could say that would shock, or offend, me. I wish to know everything about you, Sawyer James Davis."

He rolled from leaning on his elbow and moved swiftly, pinning me beneath him on the bedding, bracing on his forearms and studying me at close range, his fair hair falling over one shoulder and his eyes so full of love that my heart beat wildly. I held his shirt, curling my fingers into the material of it, feeling his heart thrusting just as strongly as we studied one another.

He murmured, "You blinked first," and kissed my nose, then my eyes, one at a time, closing them momentarily; he said quietly, "For me, there haven't been many women, no matter how Malcolm teases me about..."

"About women running their fingers through your hair?" I supplied. Malcolm was known to poke fun at Sawyer for this comment, which he had supposedly once made.

Sawyer grinned, admitting, "I told Malcolm that, mostly in jest, near last Christmas."

"Well, I aim to run my fingers through it, and often," I said with a proprietary air, doing so. His grin deepened and he rolled us so that I lay atop him.

You may do anything you like, as long as you're touching me, he said silently, his eyes taking on heat.

"How gracious of you," I murmured, and shifted so that I could gently kiss his face, soft little kitten-kisses. We were unable to keep from touching and I considered how different our circumstances would be, in our old lives; the idea of an unmarried man and woman, even two who were promised, sharing a tent, let alone a bed, was so far beyond etiquette that it was unimaginable. Neither of our families would have fathomed allowing such; there would have been absolutely no question. And yet here we lay in this place, far removed from Tennessee and wrapped in one another's embrace.

Sensing my thoughts, Sawyer said, "Had there been no War, I would have come every evening to your daddy's house to pay a call, and properly court you. I am able to picture that so well, Lorie, it seems almost within reach." He caressed my jaws with his fingertips, and his eyes were deep with feeling as he continued, "But I would not wish for things to be different than they are right now. The two of us, here together on the prairie—I feel with my entire being that this is how it was meant to be. If there had been no War, I would have lived out my days in the quiet peace of Suttonville, would probably have married a feather-headed girl like Emily Ingram, and I would have never known what it meant to love a woman the way I love you."

Tears blurred my vision and a husk impaired my voice as I whispered, "But you would have your family, your brothers...*they would all be alive...*"

"I loved them all dearly, and I will never stop missing them to the day I die. But this is the only place I am supposed to be," he said intently, and my tears streaked forth and spilled onto him, as he lay beneath me.

"Sawyer," I whispered, and moved so that I could hold his head to my breasts. His arms went around my waist and we clung as closely as new leaves drenched with springtime rain. He pressed his mouth to my heart, just above the fullest part of my left breast, kissing me through the fabric of my clothing, before speaking.

"I have lain with other women, I have felt fondness for them, and desire, but never have I come near what I feel for you. I have never been promised to a woman, nor asked for a woman to promise herself to me. Not until you, Lorissa Blake. War changed so many things, caused me to consider that which I would never have dreamed of considering in my old life, and yet I would not ask for that old life to return, even had I the power, because this life led me to you," he said. Our eyes held fast. The candle encased us in its warm intimacy; the soft light, cast through small holes punched into the sides of the lantern, tinted our skin with a ruddy glow. He whispered, "It is such a weight from my soul, to know that I may speak freely to you, and hide nothing."

"I will always listen. And I long to tell you everything, in return," I whispered. I thought of sitting in the warmth of the bathwater in the small border town days ago, of the thoughts that had plagued me. I admitted, "But it is not easy for me."

"Your heart is beating so fast," Sawyer whispered, his face resting just there as he held me close. "I will listen to you, to anything you choose to tell me, *mo mhuirnín milis,* please know this."

I nodded. I knew he meant this, sincerely, but I imagined all of the secrets I kept so tightly bound within the dark corners of my mind and heart, pictured them as resembling snakes, creatures poised to spring and sink their fangs into the unsuspecting. I would not let Sawyer be savagely bitten in this fashion, not ever.

At last I spoke the foremost of my terrible thoughts.

"I try not to think about what happened the night Sam took me, Sawyer, I try to keep it from my mind, but it comes back. His face comes back to me. I suppose Yancy reminded me a little of Sam, however unfairly," I said, and shuddered, unable to restrain it.

"Tell me," he whispered. "And in telling, let it go from you."

"I…" I faltered, unsure where to begin. I thought of the way I felt just earlier at the fire, as though Lila, the most sought-after whore at Ginny Hossiter's, was still alive within me. I longed for the ability to rip her forever from my memory, fling her soiled body into a raging fire, reduce her to ash. How could I confess to the man I loved the sheer amount of strangers that had requested Lila's services, above those of the other whores? How long would she cling to her hateful handhold in my soul? At last, quietly and without drama, I said, "When I lived at Ginny's, I buried my real self deeply inside. You know that Ginny called me…Lila." I could barely speak the hated name. "When Sam took me, I felt her coming back inside of me. The way they treated me, as though I was worthless, nothing more than a whore, and would never be anything more."

Sawyer shifted our position again, so that I was cradled protectively.

I said faintly, "When I found an arrowhead on the grass that morning, it seemed like a sign I must heed. I knew what I had to do with it from the moment I saw it. I thought that even if they killed me after, I would do my best to hurt one of them first."

Sawyer's arms were like bands of iron about me. He whispered, "It breaks my heart that you had to consider such a thing. Oh God, that thought will plague me always, knowing that I might have been too late."

"But there's a part of me that wanted to kill them, especially Sam, a part of me that found joy in the prospect. I have no regret for harming him," I confessed. "It seems wrong that I do not."

"No, it is not wrong," Sawyer said, decisively. "It's not wrong to defend yourself. Those bastards that took you deserved everything they had coming to them. I only wish I could have made them suffer instead of killing them so quickly, for hurting you, for intending to kill you." He asked somberly, "You do not think less of me for wishing this, do you?"

I whispered, "When I heard your voice, when I knew you had come for me, I have never known such relief. Oh, Sawyer…"

"If they had taken you from me, my heart would have shattered apart for good." He drew a slow breath before he continued quietly, "For years after the War I felt the guilt of what I'd done as a soldier. Those I killed, Lorie, they were men just like me. They weren't my enemy. Someone had told them they must fight, just as we'd been ordered, and so we fought. It was an unforgiveable waste of human life."

He drew a second deep, sighing breath and then said, "Gus helped me to see that. He was so calm, so reasonable. He would come to find me in the Suttonville graveyard where I drank myself into a stupor, night after night, and it was he who convinced me to keep living. He said that those who died perhaps had the easier task, though I didn't understand what he meant for a long time. Living takes courage. Gus showed me that. Living with what you've been through. It's not an easy task for anyone." I listened with my whole heart as his quiet words continued. He whispered, "The night Whistler and I rode away from you I thought I would die from the pain of it, but I told myself that you were with Gus, that he would care for you as he'd once cared for me."

Tears leaked across my face, wetting his shirt.

He whispered, "Your memories are full of pain, but always know I will listen, and understand. You are an incredibly brave woman, Lorie-love, brave and strong. Know that, I would that you know that."

I kissed his neck and let my lips rest there, and my tears no longer flowed. His words gifted me with a fleeting peace. I whispered, "Thank you. I do know it, deep down."

He said, "Together we will make new memories, and they will be sweet. Slowly the terrible ones will fade away. I promise you."

He saw the tenderness in my eyes and smiled softly, sliding his hands along my ribs to anchor around my waist. At the fire, Boyd continued wielding the bow, sweet and haunting.

"Do you wish to go back outside?" I asked, hoping he did not.

"No, I would that you stay in my arms right now," he said.

And so I did.

F ANNIE RAWLEY PREPARED a breakfast spread the likes of which I had not seen since my childhood in Cumberland County. As the morning was so calm and fair we dined outside as we had yesterday afternoon, the men claiming the table while Fannie and I enjoyed the relative privacy of our own quilt, spread beneath the sweeping shade of a pine tree. Thomas Yancy, to my considerable relief, had long since returned home, though his two sons spent the night hours in the barn loft with Malcolm and the Rawley boys; all of them bore sleep-smudged eyes and had bits of hay stuck in their hair.

"I am already regretting your absence," Fannie said. Her dark eyes were warm upon me, and I found myself realizing I would miss her a great deal, too.

I said, "It has been so good to talk with a woman." Especially one who would never know that I had spent years as a whore, who would only know me as a properly-wedded lady.

"Perhaps someday you shall brave the journey back south, and we'll meet again," she said, with affection.

I thought of what Sawyer and I spoke of last night, about what our lives would be today, had there been no War—and I would not, despite the abject horrors of the past three years, ask for my old life to be restored. I looked towards the horizon for which we were bound, lit so angelically by the amber light of early day, and imagined my former existence; surely, in that life, I would currently be wed to one of the Howell brothers from the neighboring homestead, living placidly day to day. Had that been my fate, would I ever have experienced an inkling of *this* one—would my gaze, compelled by a feeling I would never have been able to fully articulate, at times have drifted northwest, accompanied by a pulse of regret for the life I was meant to live?

"Ma, I decided something," said one of the boys, dropping abruptly to his knees beside Fannie. Other than Grant and little Willie, I could not distinguish the Rawley brothers from one another; they were so close in age and all resembled each other to a marked degree, favoring Charley. This boy possessed hair and brows of ebony, and striking dark eyes.

"What's that, son?" Fannie asked gamely.

"I aim to go north with Malcolm," he said, nodding vigorously, his voice taking on a pleading tone. He was perhaps ten or eleven. He urged, "Malcolm says it's a right adventure, Ma, and I have my new horse I could ride. I won't slow anyone down," and he looked to me with black eyebrows lofted high, as though I had suggested otherwise. I couldn't help but smile at his eagerness. He added, anticipation ripe in his youthful voice, "I want to see Minnesota. I'm close to twelve years now. Near to being a man!"

Fannie listened with patience. When he paused for breath, she said, "Son, what would we do without you? *I* couldn't do without you, you realize. You're my Miles. I haven't another Miles in all the world."

The boy's shoulders sagged and his lips took on a disappointed droop despite his mother's loving words. He begged, "*Please*, Ma. I'd be back to visit, I swear I would. Please, can't I go?"

"Malcolm's uncle would be hard pressed to find room for another boy," I said, only realizing my blunder after I had spoken; Jacob should be my uncle as well, as I was pretending to be Boyd and Malcolm's sister. I kept my gaze on Miles and said quickly, "Besides, your family would miss you far too much."

"Aw, shucks," Miles said, rocking back on his heels, seeming to concede defeat, but then his eyes brightened and he said, "I aim to ask Pa, then."

"Your pa will say the same," Fannie told her son.

"But, Ma…" he said.

"But, nothing," she replied, not without affection.

He rose to his feet and shuffled towards Malcolm and the other boys, presumably to relay the disappointing news, and Fannie said, "He was born with the need of adventure, that one. Just like his daddy, though thankfully the War cured Charley of that particular trait."

"He will come to visit us when he is older," I said, with certainty.

A sudden commotion arose from the direction Miles had just walked, and we all looked that way to see Malcolm engaged in a wrestling match. Despite all the boys' nearly-constant physicality with one another, this encounter had the feel of actual antagonism. Boyd had already discerned this and rose swiftly from the table, marching unceremoniously into the mess of floundering arms and legs, plucking the two apart with no effort. Malcolm had been tussling with the eldest Yancy brother, the boy named Fallon. Boyd held them at arm's length and ordered in a voice that brooked no disagreement, "Enough." Through it all, his smoke remained anchored in the right side of his lips.

"Cheater!" snarled Fallon, referring to Malcolm; he struggled against Boyd's firm grip, though when Boyd gave him a shake, he stilled instantly.

"He didn't cheat!" Grant countered angrily. The rest of the boys were arranged in a messy semi-circle around the two combatants, as breathless and ready to jump into the fray as much as any boys.

"I *ain't* a cheater, you dang polecat!" Malcolm shouted, his fists bunched and arms bent, still quite obviously raring to have at his opponent. Boyd sent his little brother a single look and Malcolm visibly paled and relaxed his angry stance.

I knew boys often fought, and no one seemed especially upset at this disturbance to our breakfast; still, Boyd made them apologize to Fannie and me. Malcolm's cheek was decorated with a raw, red scrape, but I knew better than to concede to my first instinct and make a fuss. I caught Malcolm's eyes and offered him a small, encouraging smile; he was uncharacteristically sullen and though he politely asked our forgiveness, which I could tell he meant, there was an edge in him as he regarded the Yancy boy. I made up my mind to question Malcolm later.

"Now you," Boyd ordered, nudging Fallon with perhaps a tad more force than required.

"Sorry," Fallon said, and the slightest smirk danced over his upper lip. He and Malcolm were both dirt-smudged.

"Thank you, boys," Fannie said formally, nodding at them while I remained silent, studying this eldest son of Thomas Yancy. I knew the boy was motherless and for that I was saddened, experiencing a beat of empathy, wondering how and when his mother had died; had she been lost during the War, like so many others left behind without their menfolk?

Certainly aware of the way I watched him, the boy's eyes lifted from the ground, and any fellow-feeling I harbored was subsequently and straightaway destroyed. My throat went dry as Fallon's gaze ensnared mine; he had pale eyes, an almost translucent blue, which would have been quite captivating if not for the emptiness that his irises only thinly masked. He stared at me, unblinking as a buzzard, and abruptly I tasted vomit.

I turned away, pretending to be preoccupied with collecting dishes.

Stop this, I chastised myself, as the boys went their separate ways. *He is just a boy. You are imagining terrible things where there are none. That is all.*

But as my gaze flickered again to the retreating figure of Fallon Yancy, I felt cold.

WE LEFT the Rawleys' homestead with the warmth of longtime friends, parting with hugs and well-wishes and promises that our paths would cross again. Fannie gifted us with a side of bacon, a crock of maple syrup, a half-pound of ground coffee, and a loaf of wheaten bread laced with dates and cinnamon, in addition to several packets of medicinal herbs and another of tea. Malcolm had already torn a large hunk from the bread, and was contentedly munching.

Grant and Miles rode their horses along the trail with us for a good two miles, flanking Malcolm and Aces on either side with their own mounts, Dallas, the gorgeous sorrel, and Blade, Miles' liver-chestnut gelding.

"Y'all will ride north come a few years, won't you?" I heard Malcolm ask, for perhaps the third or fourth time. The boys rode abreast, their hats settled low, all three with the slender bone structures indicative of their youth, though they each handled their horses with the ease of grown men. Malcolm's face was in profile as he spoke, and a strange flicker of knowing struck my awareness, rippling outward as rings cast by a disturbance to the surface of a lake. I knew, even before Grant spoke, that his promise would be fulfilled.

"Of course we will," Grant said.

"Just as soon as Pa can spare us!" Miles added.

"I'm a-countin' on it," Malcolm said. "I'm *holding* you to it."

"And he don't forget a damn thing," Boyd, riding closer to the wagon, muttered to Sawyer and me.

"He does have an uncommon keen memory, that's God's truth," Sawyer agreed.

Grant eyed the blue sky, into which the sun was lifting with the promise of another hot day, and his movements spoke of the fact that they had dallied long enough. He said to his brother, "Miles, we best…"

Miles nodded, and with obvious reluctance the two Rawley brothers drew their horses to the side, prepared to let us ride on without them.

"You boys thank your dear mama for us," Boyd said. "We ain't had such good food or hospitality in many a month."

"We will," Grant promised, tipping his hat brim.

Malcolm turned in his saddle to wave farewell; alongside Sawyer on the wagon seat, I looked back as well, watching as the boys grew smaller with each revolution of the wheels. Just before we were out of earshot, Miles waved one arm and yodeled, "So long, Crow Feather!"

Malcolm giggled, waving back, and Boyd asked, "What in tarnation is he talking about?"

"It's my name," Malcolm said, lifting his hat to swipe hair from his eyes. He settled it back in place and his eyes were merry with excitement. He said, "We all picked us a new name. Grant said his pa trades some with the Sauk people. In'juns," he clarified. "An' them Sauk boys get to choose their own names when they's of an age, an' don't have to keep the ones their mamas give 'em. Ain't that grand?"

Boyd scrutinized his brother, at last acknowledging, "Well, it suits you. Charley spoke some of trading with the local folk. I suspect we'll learn to do much the same in Minnesota. Seeing as how Jacob is wed to Hannah, an' she is a Winnebago woman."

"What were you and that boy fighting about?" I asked Malcolm, unduly troubled by the memory of Fallon Yancy's empty eyes.

"Jesus, boy, I woulda thought you'd have more respect than to scrap when we was guests," Boyd muttered. He looked a little peaked this morning, beneath the deep brown of his sunbaked skin, and I surmised he had imbibed more whiskey than intended.

Malcolm's grin dissipated like smoke in a sudden breeze. His dark eyes narrowed and he said vehemently, "He's a rotten turd. I got me a bad feeling about him."

"I felt the same," I said, and Sawyer looked from Malcolm to me, at once.

"His father is a bad apple, too, I'd stake my claim on that," Sawyer said.

"Yancy's a veteran," Boyd said, pinching the bridge of his nose and squeezing his eyes tightly shut. "An' as such he bears a bone-deep dislike with us, as Southerners. Though I didn't get the same sense from Charley, an' he fought as a Federal."

"Some are affected that way, won't ever get over it. On both sides," Sawyer said, arching his back to stretch it, shifting position on the seat before reclaiming my left hand into his right, linking our fingers. He mused, thinking aloud, "There was a time, during the first year home, I could hardly let my eyes rest on anyone wearing a shade of blue."

Boyd took a second to light a smoke before muttering, "How many times we aim straight into a field of that color? Shootin' for our lives."

"Too many to count," Sawyer murmured, and I tightened my fingers around his.

Malcolm remained silent, absorbing their words. I waited quietly as well; rarely did they discuss specifics regarding their soldiering days around anyone but each other.

"Yancy ain't seen no worse than what we seen," Boyd said, with certainty. "But he lost his wife in the meantime, while he was gone. Might be that set him over the edge."

"Gus never forgave himself for the fact that Grace died while he was away," I said. Angus had told me this himself, during the days when we traveled alone together on the trail in Missouri.

"He tortured himself with it," Sawyer acknowledged softly. He added, "Though Yancy is not one-tenth the man Gus was, and I refuse to believe that his wife's death is the reason for Yancy's foul attitude. Even an unfortunate hour spent in the man's company is enough to recognize this."

"There was a bad look in his eyes," Boyd agreed. "It weren't until he asked for 'Dixie' that I saw it, but there it was. He was hoping to provoke something, I could see that, too." Almost unconsciously, he began whistling the tune through his teeth.

A sudden memory caught me unawares; I flinched, watching again as Dalton and Jesse raced into the parlor, nearly atop one another in their excitement to tell Mama and me that they had enlisted, blue eyes avid and grins overtaking their earnest faces. They scarcely delivered this news before darting outdoors, the both of them whistling merrily, their naïve anticipation superseding all else, failing to acknowledge the horror in Mama's eyes, the way it tightened her features. I had been eleven years old, and only peripherally aware of my mother's agony; what I felt most strongly that June afternoon, less than a week since news had reached us of Tennessee's secession on the heels of Arkansas and North Carolina in May, was a flush of pride as I continued to watch my brave brothers out the window, while they roughhoused under the summer sunlight.

Look away, look away, look away...

I could not suppress a shudder, tasting vomit for the second time since sunrise.

Malcolm said, "Last night Dredd was a-telling us that his pa sometimes knocks 'em black an' blue, an' that they hide their bruises from Mrs. Rawley, as she'd go after their pa, maybe try an' take 'em away from him. An' he said that Fallon is meaner'n a weasel. When we was sleepin' in the haymow, Fallon fell asleep early an' Dredd told us some tricks he done pulled." Malcolm ran a thumb over the scrape on his face and added, "He even fights dirty. Ain't no boy I know'd claw like a girl."

"Their father beats them?" I asked, and a spurt of anger flared to life.

"They ain't the first or the last boys to take a lickin' from their daddy," Boyd said, not without sympathy.

"But, even so..." I let my voice trail away, realizing there was nothing to be done. Sawyer squeezed my hand, stroking his thumb over the back of it.

"They have good neighbors in the Rawleys, at least," Sawyer said. "Fannie cares for them."

"That's the truth," Boyd said, then shifted in his saddle, inviting Malcolm, "What do you say, boy, should we ride on a spell?"

Malcolm heartily agreed, and Boyd concluded, "Besides, we ain't like to run across the Yancys again," before the two of them heeled their mounts and cantered north, the sun glinting on their stirrups.

I was to think back many times in my life on those words.

WE CAMPED in the late afternoon, near the banks of the Iowa River. While Sawyer and Boyd cared for the horses, Malcolm and I worked to set up the tents and hang the clothes line, and then I gathered the laundry and carried it down to the shore, spending an hour scrubbing it in the shallows. It wasn't unpleasant work, as the day was so fine. I watched spindly-legged water bugs skate over the surface of the water, which was decorated with a rippling patchwork quilt of sunbursts, observing minnows that swam in shiny clouds just under the surface. Water lilies grew in profusion to my left, flat green lily pads so thick it appeared I could step atop them and walk along as though on a carpet. Dragonflies skimmed the lily pads, their tails incredible tints of glinting blue, and golden-green to rival Sawyer's eyes.

A few yards up the bank, Boyd whistled under his breath as he fried bacon and Sawyer came to help me, gathering the clean clothes and hanging them on the line as the sun angled towards evening. As he took the first armful of them, I could not help but watch him walk in his effortlessly graceful way up the low-pitched bank, caressing his wide shoulders with my heated gaze, his trousers that fit the shape of him so well, and I had sudden difficulty drawing a full breath.

"We should try fishing again," I said on his second trip, having regained my composure. I used the back of my wrist to wipe away sweat, my hat abandoned on the sandy bank. My hair hung in an inelegant braid and I had changed into a pair of Malcolm's trousers, though I wore them often enough that they were mostly mine anyway; I had decided, stubbornly, that I would continue to wear them until forced by necessity into more feminine clothing.

"We could this evening, but it will be raining by then," Sawyer said, crouching alongside me. He was hatless, the gold in his eyes highlighted by the sun. His lashes nearly cast shadows over his cheekbones.

I tore my eyes from the beauty of him and searched the cloudless blue heavens.

"If you say so," I allowed. A pair of dragonflies alighted on my wrist and I went motionless, admiring them at close range.

Sawyer rested his hand on my back and rubbed gently, sending warmth all along my limbs. He observed quietly, "They're mating."

Just that quickly the warmth became heat that flared upwards from my thighs and downwards from my belly, simultaneously, and I studied him with everything I felt pouring directly into his eyes. He swallowed and moved to cup my jaw.

"Soup's on!" Boyd called from the fire. "Boy, where'd you get to? If you done et all of that bread, I will pitch a hissy fit the likes you ain't *never* seen!"

The heel of the cinnamon bread was all that was left, as Malcolm had been snitching it all day; Boyd sat on his brother and threatened to rub his face in the dust, while Malcolm struggled and pleaded. It was Boyd's turn for the dishes, though he ordered Malcolm to fill the wash basin after we ate, while he smoked. Coming up from the river toting the basin minutes later, Malcolm pleaded, "Might we swim just a bit? Please, Sawyer? It's so pretty here, an' it seems ages since I had me a good swim."

Sawyer regarded the sky. There was still no trace of clouds, but if he said it was going to rain, I believed him. At last he decided, "Perhaps for a bit."

Malcolm whooped and shucked his shirt, suspenders, and trousers as he raced back to the river, bounding in with a tremendous splash; the lower half of his union suit, all he was still wearing, became immediately transparent, and I giggled. Sawyer rose more slowly and helped me to my feet. He asked, "Would you care to swim?"

"I think I'll just watch," I said. "I haven't any dry clothes, if I get these wet."

"Boyd?"

"*Hell* no, I'm not about to get wet before bed. I'll just wash up these dishes for y'all ungrateful wretches."

I sat on the bank with Fannie's basket situated upon my lap, rummaging within the small linen bags of herbs that she'd labeled with neatly-penciled tags, prepared to continue my sorting. But I watched, absorbedly, as Sawyer stripped his shirt and boots. He directed a smile over his shoulder, surely sensing the ardor of my thoughts, as he waded out to his hips, the sun tinting his skin golden, each muscle along his powerful torso sharply defined in its light. He dove under, surfacing with a roar, and Malcolm jumped immediately upon his back, trying to dunk him under the water. They wrestled and Malcolm coaxed Sawyer into throwing him; Sawyer made a brace with both hands, upon which Malcolm stepped and was subsequently chucked into the air. Malcolm hollered and wind-milled his arms, flying farther each time.

"Well, if there's any snakes the boy'll scare 'em away," Boyd said, finished with the dishes, coming to squat beside me, smoke dangling between his teeth. "What you got there, Lorie-girl?"

"Herbs that Fannie sent along," I told him. "I wish I knew more about each. They're labeled so well, but I don't know the uses of all of them. Ground willowbark, that's for pain. Chamomile, that's to encourage good sleep. But what about comfrey?"

"That's to aid a healing bone," Boyd said, rooting in the basket, blowing smoke from both nostrils. He lifted out another packet. "Garlic. Mama used it for poultices, bruises an' the like. Mint tea, as well?"

I nodded. "Fannie made such a fine gift for us."

Boyd eventually ambled down the bank to smoke and skip rocks across the surface of the water. I set aside the basket after a time, thinking I might bathe in our tent while everyone else was occupied and our clothes were clean, fluttering in a soft breeze as though touched by gentle fingers; an unbidden memory came creeping as I knelt, of Mama straightening a damp, snowy-white underskirt that hung on the clothes line, twitching the material so that it would not dry in a mess of wrinkles.

Lorissa, little one, go and fetch your brothers, I heard her call, just at the edges of my consciousness. I shivered and nearly rose to my feet to do her bidding.

Instead I caught the basin on my hip and dipped it full at the edge of the water, smiling at Sawyer and Malcolm playing in deeper territory. Inside our tent, I stripped my clothes in the dusky glow of late evening and washed my body in increments, all the tub would allow. I reflected that as a child I had hardly bathed more than once a week; it was living at Ginny's which altered this practice—there, I could scarcely bathe enough to scrub the scent of men from my body.

No, I told myself, with determination. *No thoughts of that, not tonight.*

I combed out my hair until it was soft as the hide of a newborn foal, and did not bother rebraiding its length. I slipped into my clean shift and wrapped into my shawl, ducking back outside to see Sawyer and Malcolm climbing the bank, both soaked to the skin.

"I'm gonna freeze!" Malcolm gasped, and indeed I could hear his teeth chattering.

"Fire's hot," Boyd said. "Boy, get in dry clothes an' go sit near, before you catch a chill."

"Thanks, Mama," Malcolm teased, scurrying into their tent.

"Goddammit, don't get that bedding wet!" Boyd yelped after him.

"You need to get warm, too," I told Sawyer, who was wet and shirtless, toweling his hair. He grinned at me, almost devilishly; as though responding to the expression in his eyes, thunder rumbled to the west. There was a sharply-delineated cloud ridge there, pewter-gray, silhouetted against a sky gone nearly ruby with the sunset.

"That I do," Sawyer said, disappearing into our tent.

Boyd perused the eerie array of clouds. He grumbled, "Let's hope it runs outta steam before morning. I don't relish traveling in the rain."

Lightning sizzled across the western sky, appearing to take giant, crooked-legged leaps along the edge of the massing storm. By the next brilliant pulse, raindrops spattered the ground with a sound like frying bacon, and Boyd hurried to bank the fire.

"I'll check the horses!" he called. "G'night, Lorie-girl."

"'Night, Boyd," I responded.

Within our tent and clad in the bottom half of his dry union suit, Sawyer was shivering a little, his loose hair damp down his naked back. Almost before I realized I had moved I was in his arms, holding him close.

"I'll warm you," I whispered, running urgent palms along his chilled skin, gripped by an overpowering urge to grasp his hands and cup them over my breasts. My nipples pushed brazenly outward against the thin fabric of the shift, needing to be touched.

"You're so warm, sweetheart," he murmured against my hair. "And so soft."

Rain sheeted over the canvas and Sawyer moved quickly to secure the laces. We heard Boyd running back, though the driving storm summarily drowned out all sound. Once the entrance was secure Sawyer turned to me and saw something that would not be denied, burning in my eyes. He ordered, low, "Come here."

We came together at once, kissing deeply, and he lowered me to the bedding. This was more fervency than he had yet allowed, and there was a sense of abandon in these kisses that eradicated any notions I harbored of waiting to be wed before we made love. I shivered as though fevered and bent one leg around his hip, the edge of my shift bunched high upon my legs; I wore no garments beneath. His kisses destroyed all reason, his lips and taste, his stroking tongue that claimed mine as I held fast to his shoulders.

"Lorie," he whispered, resting his forehead against me, eyes closed as he attempted to catch his breath. He said intently, "I mean to wait..."

I made a sound of immediate disagreement, moving my touch to his collarbones, drawing his lower lip into my mouth, suckling gently, skimming my tongue over the fullness of it. He cupped my breasts, thumbs stroking my nipples, which he had not yet dared, and I moaned, lifting into his broad palms. His hands went heatedly to my thighs, bringing me closer, and I opened my lips upon the planes of his chest, tasting him, our movements urgent and reverent, at once. Thunder exploded amid the restless rain and

Sawyer moved suddenly to his back and covered his eyes with a forearm. He said hoarsely, "I promised myself I would wait until we were properly wed."

He was so honorable; it only served to increase my want, but I drew forth the wherewithal to whisper, "I know…"

"You deserve *no less*," he said firmly. I curled my arms tightly around my bent knees; my heart throbbed frantically. The way he was lying flat only served to highlight the evidence of his desire, and it took all of my resolve not to climb atop him and simply put the decision behind us, once and for all. But then I recalled Sawyer's face as it had looked the night he and Whistler came for me, the night he found me in Sam Rainey's camp, bruised and bloody, and how I'd been so close to dying without realizing that he was still alive and desperately searching for me. Tenderness flooded my soul, replacing a fraction of the heat, and I lay carefully beside him and rested my head upon his shoulder.

At once he curved protectively, sweetly aligning our bodies. Echoing my thoughts, he said, "I am thinking of how I found you that night, Lorie. I have never known such fear as I rode towards that camp and heard you scream." His eyes drove into mine as he spoke. "I cannot bear the thought of you hurting. I will cradle you in my arms and protect you, always. And yet here I lay, wanting you so much I feel like an animal. My daddy would strap my hide raw for taking such advantage of you, for letting my own needs overpower me so."

"Sawyer," I scolded, touched to my core at his words. "You mustn't punish yourself." I implored, "You are not taking advantage. You don't think I want you just as fiercely? I can think of nothing else, truly." Thunder detonated in the sky directly above us, as though in response to my words. I repeated in a whisper, "Truly."

His lips curved into a half-smile and he said, "I do know that for truth. Your thoughts are so clear to me. That night I pulled the splinter from your foot…"

I smiled, slipping my left leg between both of his, cautiously. He allowed this and I remembered, "You spoke my name for the first time that night, when I crawled over you."

"I had been lying there dreaming of you and you were suddenly on top of me. Your hair was loose…"

So saying, he reached and curled his fingers into a long strand of my hair, which fell all over the both of us.

"For the first time in my life, I feel whole," he whispered.

"Sawyer," I whispered, my ring catching the flicker from the candle flame as I held his face, and in that moment I refused to leave our lives to chance, to wait until we happened to come across a preacher to speak the words over us. The notion struck me so strongly I could not believe I hadn't considered it before.

I said, "We will handfast."

His eyes burned into mine.

"I will wait no longer," I said, quiet and adamant. "In my heart, I am already yours. Nothing else matters to me, not a document, or the words of a stranger."

Tears glinted in his eyes as he whispered, "I've told you of how my grandparents were handfast."

"You have, love. And that they chose to be wed that way is more meaningful than any wedding in any church."

"Tomorrow," he said, taking my hands and kissing them, and there was such anticipation in his voice that I laughed, even as tears streaked over my cheeks. He said, "I would join our hands and bind us, this very second, but there is ceremony to the process. And I believe I can say with certainty that Boyd and Malcolm would be out of sorts if they were not allowed involvement."

"Tomorrow," I agreed, and I would not fear my abounding happiness.

But Sawyer was far too sharp-eyed, far too adept at reading my thoughts, and he caught the flicker, asking at once, "What is it?"

I whispered, "There is such joy within me, but I won't fear it. I will not."

His eyes were deep with understanding, though I thought of something else then.

"Tell me," he said.

Recalling how he had so carefully cleaned the blood from my thighs that night on the prairie in Missouri, in that miserable camp, I whispered, "I wish your first sight of my body could have been less…gruesome."

"Never think that," Sawyer insisted, almost severely. "Lorie, never. You couldn't be more precious to me, or know how it feels for me to look upon you." His eyes flashed with determination and he said, "I would look upon you now, *mo mhuirnín milis*. Let me," he whispered, shifting us so that he knelt before me. Lightning backlit the walls of the tent as he took my knees into his warm, strong hands. "I love you so, let me look upon you. I would see for myself that you are no longer hurting."

I trembled with emotion as I nodded, and he kept his eyes upon mine. His bare chest rose and fell as he drew my knees carefully around his hips. The lantern light danced golden over us as he smoothed the shift slowly upwards; I lifted to my elbows to watch him, overcome at the sight of him between my legs. His lashes swept low as he trailed his touch deliberately and with utmost gentleness to the skin between my legs, my lower body bared before him.

He said, "You are the most beautiful sight I have ever beheld. Jesus, Lorie, sweet Jesus, *you are beautiful*."

He touched me, his face stern in its emotional intensity, fingertips resting upon the center of me. I could not help the small sounds that escaped my lips, closing my eyes, head falling back as he traced along my flesh. He groaned softly, his hand stilling its tender motion, cupping me.

I opened my eyes. Sweat was trickling over his temples, his eyes blazing so intensely with heat that every nerve between my legs tightened, sensation jolting swiftly enough to startle me.

"I would that no one had ever touched me there but you," I whispered.

"No one will, ever again. You are mine," he said, and bent forward between my legs, palms curving under my backside as he kissed me just where his hand had been.

No one had ever before put their lips upon me so; it was the Frenchy sex that Ginny had always disdained and would not allow in her whorehouse. Though in the next second the shock of it was swept away, Sawyer banishing all else from my senses but him, his kisses and his stroking tongue, the immediacy and intensity of him. My neck arched and I cried out as he opened his lips upon me, holding me close. Within my body was a river, suddenly undammed, a flowing heat that burst amidst my blood, my nerves. I had never experienced such a thing. The force of it overtook me, shook me in its jaws, so that gasping cries broke free from my throat. It built, and built, as he continued his passionate ministrations, with each thrust of my throbbing heart, and swelled until the final pulsation shattered over me.

Afterwards I lay wilted and replete, my cheek turned to the rumpled bedding. I was too spent to allow for movement; Sawyer was breathing as though he'd just run miles upon miles, unabatedly. He collapsed against me, grasping my hips. He rested his forehead on my belly, his shoulders arched over my thighs. I wanted to touch his hair, his mouth, convey to him that he had brought me more physical pleasure than I'd even known existed, but my hands rested limply on either side of my face, the undersides of my wrists tinted a pale cream in the lantern light. The skin between my legs pulsed, slippery with warmth.

"Thank you," I managed to whisper. "Thank you...for that."

"Lorie," he murmured, his voice muffled against my flesh. It tickled but I had not the energy to move. He placed a tender kiss upon my pelvis and whispered, "My beautiful, beautiful woman. You are so very welcome."

"I've never...no one has ever..." I desperately wanted him to know what was in my heart.

He trailed warm kisses upward along my belly. As his nose encountered the material that still covered my breasts, he paused and grinned at me, asking sweetly in his husky voice, "May I, darlin'?"

At my breathless nod, he bared them and opened his lips over my nipple, which swelled against his tongue; I should have known that of course he would call forth such unfathomable and blissful response. I clutched his hair and held him. He groaned and cradled my other breast, full and heavy in his tender grasp, before shifting his mouth there, taking me into its incredible warmth. He caressed gently between my legs, gliding his knowing fingers over the sensitive flesh, sparking afresh the quivering sensation that lingered in the wake of his kisses.

"Sawyer," I gasped repeatedly, my breath emerging in bursts, as though I was being pummeled. It seemed I could only call forth his name; I could scarcely recall my own. I felt him smile against my skin, tongue still upon me; my nipples gleamed wetly. I begged, "Don't stop, please...*don't stop...*"

Rain pelted our small shelter, thunder colliding upon itself in the sky just above. A small, rational part of my mind was grateful for this noise, as perhaps it muffled my cries; I was not being particularly quiet. Sawyer gently rubbed his chin, prickly from two days without shaving, between my breasts, simultaneously pressing the base of his palm against the juncture of my legs; I shivered delightedly. He murmured, "I will never stop loving you and never stop bringing you pleasure." He grinned, almost wickedly, so handsome that my entire body seemed to hum, as strings would when skimmed by a bow. He said, "I do so hope to bring you pleasure, my Lorie."

My every nerve sparked as the ends of matches when struck to life. A flush bloomed all along my bare skin. I whispered, "You bring me pleasure as I have never known." I smiled almost shyly as I borrowed his words, "In case you hadn't gathered."

His grin broadened and he said, his deep voice soft, "I gathered."

Y OU TWO HAVE that look about you," Boyd said in the fair morning light, squinting one eye at us, before concentrating on lighting his first smoke of the day. The storm had passed over, leaving the world refreshed in its wake.

My cheeks grew hot. Sawyer told Boyd, "Perhaps it's because Lorie and I are to be wed today."

Boyd crouched beside the fire and at his knowing smile, my cheeks blazed even hotter; I could not deny there was an insistent, driving ache within me by dawn's fairy light that I found rather alarming. I wanted more of what Sawyer had shown me last night. So much more that I felt moon-eyed and faint, by turns, my stomach light as a boll of cotton.

"Well, that explains them stars in your eyes, Lorie-girl," Boyd teased. "Though, I don't recall seeing a preacher in these parts. You got one hog-tied in your tent? Not that I'd blame y'all."

"No, we'll be handfast," Sawyer explained, just the slightest catch in his voice, reflecting the depth of his feelings.

Boyd said, "Just like your grandfolks. I'll be."

"We hoped that you'd play us a waltz or two," I said.

Boyd's eyes grew soft with fondness as he said, "Of course I shall."

Malcolm bounded from their tent, crying, "Can we have us a wedding feast an' the like?" He dropped to his knees near where I sat and his countenance changed markedly. He uttered, "Lorie, wait!"

I lifted my eyebrows at the alarm in his tone.

"You ain't got a wedding dress," he said, so clearly dismayed that I couldn't help but smile.

"No matter," I assured him. "I don't need—"

"Now, hold up," Boyd said, lifting one hand. "That ain't so."

"Mama's!" Malcolm realized joyfully. "Mama's dress is in the trunk." He bounced with glee. "You'll wear it, of course. Mama wouldn't have it no other way."

"Oh Malcolm, I couldn't possibly—"

But the Carters were up and rooting in the wagon before I'd finished my protest. I looked at Sawyer and found him smiling. He lifted our joined hands and kissed mine, saying, "I knew their mama well, and she would be overjoyed to lend you her dress."

My eyes filled with tears. Sawyer said softly, "She would, don't spend one second thinking otherwise."

Behind us, Malcolm crowed in triumph, "Here it is!"

Boyd called, "Lorie-girl, get over here on the far side of the wagon! Sawyer ain't allowed to see this 'til it's on you."

Clairee Carter's wedding dress was sewn from ivory silk. Watered silk, with a fitted waist and draped sleeves that flowed delicately to the elbow. Seed pearls glistened on the neckline. Neither passing decades nor having been stored in a cedar trunk had diminished its delicate beauty. Boyd held it aloft in the morning sun and I clasped both hands beneath my chin.

"It's exquisite," I whispered, reaching to touch the material. The sun gleamed over the pearls, throwing fire. My eyes were likewise dazzled at this gift.

Exquisite. Synonyms include: elegant, impeccable, gorgeous, striking.

"You look about of a size with Mama," Boyd said. "I do believe that this'll fit you right nice."

"I can't thank you enough," I said, tears blurring the sight of the silk.

Boyd said, "There wasn't much my sweet mama loved more'n a wedding, an' fancies. How I wish she could be here to get you ready, Mama and Ellen Davis, both. You'll just have to trust me an' the boy, Jesus help us."

After breakfast, at Boyd and Malcolm's insistence, Sawyer was not allowed to set eyes upon me until what Malcolm referred to as 'the service.'

"Don't worry, we'll get your betrothed cleaned up right nice," Boyd assured me.

"You gotta wash your hair, Lorie-Lorie," Malcolm ordered, insistent as any lady's maid. "I feel that oughta be the first thing, ain't that right?"

In my shift, I ducked, shivering, into the river as the sun rose and sparkled over the water in ever-shifting golden coins; we had indeed happened upon a lovely spot to camp, near a small, rocky beach alongside the indigo rush of the Iowa. The shallows, where I bathed, were blessedly warmer than the deeper center of the waterway, in which Malcolm, who had stripped to his skin, swam delightedly while I soaked; when my fingers skimmed over the flesh between my legs, hidden beneath the water, I let my fingertips linger a heartbeat longer, closing my eyes and recalling every blessed second of last night. Though his hands and mouth left no part of me untouched, Sawyer had refrained from fully joining our bodies—that would be for tonight. And a giddy anticipation rendered me weak-kneed; I ducked beneath the surface, pressing both hands to the fluttering joy centered in my stomach.

A half-hour later I was scrubbed within an inch of my life, dressed in a dry shift while Malcolm proceeded to brush out my hair; I sat on the bedding in the tent I shared with Sawyer, knees drawn up and chin resting upon them, while Malcolm knelt behind me.

"I am ever so happy that you twos are hitchin' up," Malcolm said, smoothing the fingers of one hand within my loose hair; his touch was so gentle, almost worshipful, his familiar voice with a note of winsomeness not normally present. "When we rode away from you an' Gus, I was scared, I tell you. Sawyer couldn't eat, an' hardly spoke. At night he curled over an' wept like his world was ending. It was right terrible."

I had known this, and still Malcolm's words tore at my heart. I whispered, "Thank you for taking care of him."

Malcolm said guilelessly, "I wish *I* could marry you, Lorie-Lorie, I ain't gonna lie, but I can't imagine you or Sawyer without the other, not no more."

"You are such a dear heart," I told the boy, turning to look at him as he frowned with the concentration of working gingerly through a tangle; he knew to start at the bottom, combing the ends before the roots. The scratch on his face appeared raw and sore. I said, "Someday you will make a fine and loving husband."

Malcolm rested one hand flat against my skull, the brush poised in his other. I studied his brown eyes with their long lashes, the dusting of freckles over his nose and cheekbones. He held very still and his gaze was fixed distantly, somewhere other than this moment.

"What is it?" I asked quietly.

He blinked and refocused upon the here and now, meeting my eyes and imploring, "Will I ever meet a girl I love as Sawyer loves you?"

"Oh, Malcolm," I whispered at this heartfelt question. "For certain you will meet a girl you love with all of your heart. You're so young yet. Wait until you've lived a little longer."

He resumed stroking the brush along my hair. "I do hope so. I aim to have me a passel of young'uns an' make sure that there are more Carters than anyone ever did see."

"Then you will," I promised, and his face lit with a smile, eradicating the winsome yearning present just moments ago.

"Me an' Boyd got lots more planned for you, but it's a secret," Malcolm informed with a wink, reminiscent of his elder brother, and somehow, I was certain, their father. He said, "You's a bride today an' it's your wedding, even if we ain't got no cake."

"I am a bride," I marveled softly, biting back a smile at Malcolm's lamentation regarding the decided lack of victuals available here on the prairie. My mama would have swooned, probably fainted outright, at the notion of such an ill-prepared and hasty service, requiring smelling salts to revive her sensibilities. But material things mattered not a whit to me; I was content beyond reasoning, I who had spent years accepting that I would never marry, that I would die alone and likely of unnatural causes. I looked at my ring, bringing it to my lips. I begged Malcolm, "Tell me of the surprises. What have you done with Sawyer?"

But the boy only grinned like an imp.

"You'll see, Lorie-Lorie," was all he would say.

I EMERGED from the tent in the late afternoon; I had slept for a long time, waking on my side to behold a canvas wall glowing with soft afternoon light, and rested my cheek to Sawyer's pillow. I thought of him telling me about his paternal grandparents, about Sawyer and Alice Davis, who handfasted long ago, against the wishes of her family in their homeland of England, before bravely journeying to a new continent to begin their lives together. I thought of my own parents, William and Felicity Blake; under other circumstances, my daddy would be walking with me on his arm to place my hand within Sawyer's. Mama would arrange my dress, tucking and tidying to her satisfaction, before standing back to admire me, her beloved only daughter. Although I was not one for praying, I brought my folded hands to my lips and closed my eyes. I saw them each in my memory, and that was enough.

Mama, Daddy. Dalton, Jesse. I will never forget you, not so long as I live. I hope you are able to see that I am at last happy, that I am marrying the man I love.

I whispered, "Amen."

"Lorie, come eat!" Boyd called from outside. "Just a bit longer now," he said as I joined him, and then he immediately groused, "This is one sorry wedding feast. Dammit, if the two of you woulda give me some warning." But as I sat and accepted a plate of food, his teasing tone changed markedly. He fixed his dark eyes upon me, as somber as Malcolm had been earlier, when brushing my hair. Boyd said softly, "I was scairt, Lorie, when he thought he'd lost you. I can't tell you. I've never seen him suffer so."

I whispered, "Thank you for being there with him, Boyd, when I could not."

"Lorie-girl, I love him, too. Him an' me are brothers to each other. He knows my life an' I know his, an' to see him so happy does my heart a good turn, I tell you."

"May I see him soon?" I begged.

Boyd said, "Soon enough, little bride. Come, eat an' we'll get you into your dress."

Within my tent, I shed my garments and slipped into Clairee's gown; it was wrinkled, as there was no helping that, but its silken length fell softly over my skin. I couldn't manage the delicate fastenings that laced closed the back of the gown; Malcolm had returned, I heard him whispering with Boyd, and I called, "May I have a bit of help?"

"C'mon out," Boyd said.

I ducked from the entrance, clasping the dress together behind my back, to observe that Malcolm was carrying an armload of wildflowers so large it nearly obscured his face.

"Me an' Sawyer spent all afternoon picking these for you," he announced.

Boyd moved behind me and without compunction began hooking the small loops over each subsequent pearl button. His face near the back of my neck as he bent close to work, he muttered, "I gotta admit that I'm a bit more familiar with this process in reverse."

"You ain't gotta talk like that. It's Lorie's wedding day," Malcolm scolded, depositing the flowers gently near my feet. He said, "Here, let's get some a-these in your hair."

At last Boyd successfully secured me into Clairee's lovely gown and then I choked on a restrained laugh as Malcolm observed, concerned, "It's a bit tight, just there." Adding to the unconscious hilarity of this statement, he poked a finger in the direction of my breasts, as though I did not take his meaning.

Boyd snorted in surprised exasperation, though he could not help but laugh, his eyes almost inadvertently detouring to briefly regard the material that did fit a touch too snugly across my front side. Boyd winked at me and said, "I doubt that Sawyer will complain."

He and Malcolm arranged flowers next, and I marveled as I watched them at close range, the Carter brothers with their dark eyes serious and contemplative as they threaded more than a dozen blossoms into my hair. I was at once overcome with love for them and with the urge to giggle as they worked over me, as attentive to detail as any two handmaidens. Malcolm gathered up the rest of the flowers, which smelled of the green tang of freshly-plucked stems.

He said, "This here is your bouquet, an' Sawyer done give me this for you."

Malcolm passed the flowers to my waiting hands and reached into his trouser pocket, withdrawing Sawyer's mother's lace handkerchief.

He said, "This here is to bind your wrist to Sawyer's, Lorie-Lorie. You're to tuck it against your heart, Sawyer told me. I'll be back directly!"

So saying, he darted away, fleet-footed. I held Ellen's handkerchief to my lips before tucking it, as instructed, near my heart.

Boyd stepped back and surveyed me with lips pursed. He pronounced, "You are the prettiest bride I ever seen, savin' the woman that I shall wed someday, God an' good fortune willing."

"Oh, Boyd," I said, catching him into a hug, my bouquet brushing his ear with petals. "Thank you, for everything."

He hugged me close and kissed my temple, then drew away to regard me again, with a critical eye, straightening a flower in my hair. Clairee's dress *was* snug against my hips and breasts, which contributed to my increasing breathlessness, though otherwise fit well. The silken sleeves left my arms bared from elbow to wrist, the neckline dipping gracefully beneath my collarbones. My hair, decorated with blossoms, hung loose.

"Let me grab my fiddle," Boyd said. "An' then I will be pleased as a daddy to escort you to your betrothed."

I saw Malcolm leading Whistler. The long evening sunbeams struck the two of them, edging them each with a halo of golden radiance; my throat ached at the beauty of it.

"Sawyer's a-waiting for us!" the boy called, anticipation ripe in his tone. He chirped, "What do you think of Whistler-girl, huh, Lorie-Lorie? Don't she look pretty, too?"

He had woven flowers into her mane and tucked them in her bridle.

"Thank you, sweet boy, for all of this," I whispered, hugging him tightly. "I couldn't possibly love you more."

Malcolm blushed and twinkled. He said gruffly, "I love you, too." He added, with a tone of quite flattering awe, "Lordy, you's a sight. I can't wait 'til Sawyer sees you, I tell you."

"Whistler," I murmured to her, and she nickered in gentle acknowledgment. I kissed her nose and whispered, "You look so pretty."

"Now let's get you atop this here horse," Boyd said. He was dressed in his black trousers and had combed back his hair, carrying his bow and his fiddle, though he set it gently to the ground to assist me upon Whistler's unsaddled back; there, I sat as though using a side-saddle, both legs on the left, gently clasping her mane in one hand and my flowers in the other. Boyd, fussy as any mother-in-law, arranged the silk train to his liking over Whistler's hide. He said, "Mind them bare feet now."

"I will," I whispered, breathless and fluttering as Malcolm took Whistler's reins and Boyd retrieved his fiddle. They both looked up at me, their dark eyes catching the sunset light.

Malcolm said, "C'mon, girl," to Whistler.

The prairie was splendid under the low-lying beams of evening sun. I let my senses imbibe every last detail, the slant of the saffron light, the violet tint of the clouds on the western horizon, the purple-hued rising moon, adorned with a glinting star just near its left curve. The air was still, Whistler's feet making muted cupping sounds against the earth as she walked. As Boyd began to play, tears spilled from my cheeks onto Clairee's dress. I was almost unbearably happy, but I had promised that I would not fear it. I lifted my eyes to the sweep of sky and thought again of my long-lost family, imagining what they would be feeling just now, before I looked back to Earth and smiled at the sight of Malcolm's shaggy hair. And then just ahead I saw Sawyer, waiting for us.

Everything within me flowed towards him as I beheld his resplendent expression. Upon his face I saw the intensity of his love and the incredible strength of his spirit, the overwhelming awe of this moment and the near inability to bear all of these gifts at once. The hawk eyes I knew so well flashed into mine, sparking with tears as Whistler and I drew near. He was clad in black trousers and his white muslin shirt. I saw that someone, surely Malcolm, had stuck a flower into the second-to-top buttonhole.

Malcolm halted and bowed formally to Sawyer, though we did not remove our eyes from one another. Boyd kept playing as Sawyer stepped to Whistler's side and rested a hand on her hide, placing his other upon my thigh, warm and strong against the silk of the dress, my blood leaping at the touch. He blinked, the sun catching his eyes and refracting from his lashes. At last he said softly, "Lorie, look at you. I could never explain in words what this moment means to me." His voice was husky with emotion as he lifted me from her back, his hands about my waist, mine upon his shoulders.

Boyd, with a showman's timing, let a last note waver and fade, and Malcolm was waiting to take the bouquet of flowers, which he set carefully on the ground, a courteous attendant.

"Come," Sawyer said, his eyes intense upon me. He took my hands in his and kissed them, one after the other, before leading me a few feet away from Whistler.

Malcolm, clearly having rehearsed his part, stepped forward and addressed me, intoning ceremoniously, "Have you the cloth for binding?"

I nodded, and with utmost care, reached and drew the handkerchief from the dress, warm from being cradled to my skin. Malcolm asked, "Who shall bind this man and this woman?"

Boyd said, "I shall," and took the cloth from me with great dignity.

Sawyer gathered my left hand decisively into his right, threading his fingers amid mine and lifting our joined hands to his heart. Boyd tied the lace kerchief about our wrists, tightly linking us. The sun dipped below the horizon; its last rays created a spectacular light show, had we been willing to look away from one another and into that direction. Boyd stepped back and joined Malcolm, who sat quietly upon the ground.

His eyes bearing into mine and with a lilt of incantation in his deep voice,

Sawyer said, "Lorissa Anne Blake, under this sky on this night, I take you to be my wife. I love you with my heart and soul, and I will protect you, and cherish you, until my last breath. You are mine, and I am yours. By this hand-fast, from this moment forth, we shall remain bound for all time."

I had been unsure about the exact proceedings, but I trusted Sawyer's knowledge. His solemn words filled my heart and as he paused I began, re-peating the vows as he had spoken them, "Sawyer James Davis, under this sky on this night, I take you to be my husband." I tightened my fingers even more securely around his. "I love you more than my own life, and I will care for you, and cherish you, until I die." Tears brimmed as I whispered, "I am yours, with my whole heart, and you are mine. From this moment forth, and by this handfast, we shall remain bound for all time."

The air around our bodies seemed to swirl and sigh, settling upon us as our vows drifted up and into the night, into the endless sky, the unchanging heavens that would exist long after both of us. And somewhere within it, our words would survive, too.

Sawyer drew me instantly close. I curled into his embrace, momentarily forgetting our audience of two, and kissed him as though this was perhaps our last night upon an earthly realm. Though I wasn't fatalistic enough to think it truly was, there was a dark and aching part of my soul that would always fear the dawn and what it might bring, how it might work to separate me from those I loved.

Our wrists remained bound, hampering my ability to get my arms around him the way I desired, and he drew back enough to slip free the binding, keeping the knot intact. He scooped me up and into his arms, holding me close to his heart as he reclaimed my mouth; all about us, the light leached from the prairie and twilight sprang to dusky life.

Boyd and Malcolm were applauding with vigor.

"I now pronounce you *man an' wife*!" Malcolm whooped. "I remember Reverend Wheeler sayin' that!"

Sawyer laughed at these exuberant words, against my lips as we were still kissing, and Boyd added, "To Mr. and Mrs. Davis!"

Sawyer whispered, "My wife."

"My husband," I whispered in return, twining my fingers into his silken hair.

The fiddle sang joyously for us.

Malcolm ordered, "Sawyer, set down your bride so's I can dance with her."

Sawyer let me back to Earth and I waltzed with Malcolm, mindful of my long hem. Flower petals scattered everywhere, falling at our feet as Malcolm spun me with his usual enthusiasm.

"Who's gonna catch the flowers?" Malcolm worried between songs, nodding at the bouquet. "There ain't no ladies!" He yelped gleefully at Boyd, "Me an' you's gotta fight for it!"

Boyd laughed, plucking a string with his right thumb while turning a peg on the instrument's neck. He said, "I'd give an eye tooth for a pretty little woman of my own just now, that's God's truth." He winked at Sawyer and said, "You best claim your bride for a dance before Malcolm wears her out. Soon as I sweeten this note, I got a waltz all set for you twos."

"Lorissa Davis, come be in my arms," Sawyer invited, and Malcolm surrendered me to my new husband.

The fiddle sang for us as we danced, and I understood that I would not trade this ceremony for the fanciest church wedding on Earth. I well knew what waited out beyond the prairie—sprawling towns and thriving cities, hundreds of thousands of people in the Eastern lands; the vast, wild, and far less populated territories loomed in the West, but at this moment it seemed unfathomable that any of that wide, exuberant, and dangerous world even existed. There was this place, there was right now, and nothing else mattered.

I implored, "Say it once more…"

"Lorissa Davis," he repeated, knowing exactly what I meant. The joyous satisfaction in his eyes was mirrored in my own. And then I realized something else.

"You're a good dancer," I marveled, my voice with a note of teasing accusation, and he grinned, both of us thinking of our evening with the Spicer family in Missouri, before we had admitted our feelings to one another.

"I said I didn't dance *much*," he reminded me. "Not that I couldn't."

"Sawyer James Davis," I chastised, and his full name was sweet on my tongue, as always. "Whatever will I do with you? Perhaps I will address you thusly when I am angered with you."

He lowered his eyelids just slightly and at once I saw him braced over my naked belly as he had been during last night's thunderstorm. He said with honey in his tone, "I won't give you cause to be angered at me, darlin'. You are so beautiful, Lorie-love, that my knees are outright weak. You think I'm teasing, but I am not."

I looked deeply into his eyes and sent forth a clear and detailed picture of what I wanted to do with him, as soon as possible, and then I was the one smiling so knowingly as he swallowed hard and cast a glance at Boyd and Malcolm.

"Remember…" Sawyer said to Malcolm, and that was all it took for the boy to nod importantly, scoop my flowers from the ground, and race without a word in the direction of our camp, clutching the wilting bundle.

"Lorie-girl, give me one more hug," Boyd ordered, drawing out a final note on the strings. "I am the least romantic fella that ever lived an' here I am with tears in my damn eyes."

I hugged Boyd tightly and then he bear-hugged Sawyer, who murmured, "Thank you, *cara d'aois*."

"You are most welcome, old friend," Boyd replied, clapping Sawyer's back with two energetic thumps. "Lorie, the boy an' I have elected to give you two a bit of privacy this evening. We moved our tent a goodly distance." He kicked Sawyer's ankle with these words, and Sawyer grinned and flushed, I could tell even in the twilight.

The sky had given over to darkness, star-spangled and magnificent. Malcolm raced back, out of breath, and informed us, "All set."

"We'll see you two by daylight, then," Sawyer said formally, and swept me neatly into his arms.

"G'night, you lovebirds!" Malcolm yelped.

Boyd collected up his fiddle and resumed playing "Sweet Liza Jane" as Sawyer carried me to Whistler, who waited patiently for us. We paused at her nose and Sawyer leaned to kiss her between the eyes. He whispered, "Lorie and I are handfast now. She's my wife. What do you think of that?"

Whistler nickered, bumping her nose against him. Held in Sawyer's arms, I lay my cheek upon her warm hide, absorbing the familiar scent and feel of horse. It was a smell as dear to me as any I knew, made fathoms more precious by the fact that this horse loved my husband and had kept him safe for years, had carried him to me.

Sensing my thoughts, Sawyer whispered to her, "Thank you for bringing me to this night, *mo chapall daor*. For bringing me to my Lorie."

"Oh, Sawyer," I whispered. His eyes glinted with tears. Whistler nudged my side with her long nose, and I laughed, even as tears fell upon my cheeks.

"Come," he whispered, softly kissing my lips. "Let me help you up."

He lifted me to her back before bracing his hips and climbing behind me. Once settled, he gathered me close, rocking his hips to set Whistler in motion, while I shivered as his touch glided around my waist to the warm silk covering my belly. Our horse turned smoothly for the camp, as the Carters called heartfelt good wishes, and Sawyer gently swept the hair from my temple and kissed me there, setting ablaze my skin.

I leaned against the broad strength of him, running both hands over the length of his strong thighs, braced around me. I felt a trembling within him as I continued stroking along his legs, thrilling me. He closed his teeth gently over my earlobe and murmured, "This dress is so soft, and yet your skin beneath it is softer still, and so warm…"

I grasped his right hand, lifting it to my lips before transferring it to my breast. He exhaled in a rush and caressed me through the silk, my nipple swelling against the material. The campsite came into view, lanterns lighted; our tent shone with welcome. Sawyer nudged Whistler into a canter, dismounting almost before she halted, collecting me into his arms. I opened my lips to take deeper his sweet, stroking kisses, more inviting than anything previously known to me. We broke apart long enough to duck into our tent; Sawyer entered just behind me and cupped my upper arms, whispering against my temple, "I wish I had a feather bed in which to place you just now, darlin'."

"No," I insisted, turning to bring my throbbing heart to his. "I want this moment exactly as it is, here on the prairie. This is just how it should be, truly."

He nodded acknowledgment of this truth, slipping his hands over my ribs, anchoring about my waist. He kissed my lips and chin, my jaw, lingering, sensuous kisses that stole my breath. I clung to him. He studied my face, whispering, "I've dreamed of making love to you so many times."

"Don't make us wait any longer," I begged.

He took us immediately to our knees upon the bedding, where I curled my fingers into his loose hair, spreading it over his shoulders. His eyes were dark with passion, his palms gliding down my arms, fire flaring along my limbs in the path of his touch. He whispered, "If you only knew how you look just now. The way your cheeks are blooming, and the love and wanting in your eyes."

"Hurry," I moaned in response, caressing him firmly through his trousers. "Help me from this dress…"

Sawyer began unbuttoning at once. I tried to assist, impatient with urgency, though we both laughed, between deep kisses, at the maddeningly slow process. The moment the dress was open enough to slip forward, Sawyer gently freed me from it. My head tipped back, exposing my throat, which he bent to kiss, my shoulders and collarbones, each by turn, suckling kisses that made me moan and lift against him, though he moved lower with deliberate slowness, inhaling against the skin between my breasts, his thumbs caressing my nipples, which were round as pearls, aching for his touch.

"You smell so good," he said, cradling his cheek to my heartbeat, breathing hard, his arms around my waist. "You taste so good, Lorie-love," and his tongue was upon the peaks of my breasts, calling forth deep pulsing sensations lower down, waves of tightening that made me gasp. Sawyer straightened just long enough to tear the shirt roughly from his body. He was so strong, so solid, his skin taking on a golden cast in the lantern's glow to match his eyes and his hair, as though I was about to make love with a gorgeous creature not quite of this earth.

"*Sawyer*," I demanded in a gasp, the silk dress spreading to a puddle around my knees as I reached to yank open his trousers.

He kicked free of them and caught me against his naked body at last, taking me to my back, where I twisted and writhed in attempt to be closer to him, running my calves along his waist, along the sides of his hips, trembling beneath him as he caressed me, shallowly and then at last within. Soft cries of pleasure and love, the sweetness and heat of him as he stroked me, his teeth closing lightly over my earlobes, my lower lip, my chin. He claimed my mouth, his tongue delving deep, as were his fingers below. His hard length urged at the juncture of my legs and he begged, "*Touch me*."

I reached fervently to take him in hand, my body convulsing to feel him against my skin at long last.

"Now, please, *now*," I ordered, and he groaned as though I'd caused him physical pain as he linked our bodies and surged fully within me.

"Lorie," he gasped, remaining perfectly still, reverent, for the space of a heartbeat, our foreheads lightly touching, before my insistent urging propelled him into motion. His voice was low, hoarse with emotion, as he breathed, "How I love you."

I kissed his neck, his chest, my legs spread beneath him, hips thrusting to meet his deep strokes. I clung to him and was soon beyond all sense, wild, wordless sounds of joy flowing between us. His body called forth responses from mine that no one had before. Love transformed the act into something glorious, its true nature laid bare to me at last in those moments with my new husband.

Just the thought caused my body to spill over, tightening around him as he groaned and I tilted my hips to take him even deeper. He twined my loose hair in his fingers, our kisses lush and deep, wet and sensual, as though we could never give or take enough of one another. Our souls meshed between us, crackling together in bursts like heat lightning, and though it was just beyond the limited ability of our eyes, I could sense that he felt it, too, the joining that leaped far beyond the physical. Time ceased to mean anything as our bodies intertwined and curled and plunged as one, carrying us somewhere unexplainable, past all words.

I only knew that it was as it should be; it was right.

Much later, as dawn cast its first light into our tent, we lay still, sweating and exhausted, our limbs tangled together. I understood that if the world somehow ceased to exist today, or if we were meant to die this very afternoon, then the hours of last night would make everything worth it. I rested, warm and blissfully sated, as he stroked soft patterns between my shoulder blades. Just as I was about to surrender to sleep, I spied for the first time the bouquet from our handfasting, neatly arranged into a tin cup of water and positioned near the bedding, surely by sweet Malcolm.

Love could pierce a heart in a thousand places at once.

Sawyer murmured and shifted his left leg gently between both of mine, his eyes closed, arms locked around me. My nerves were still feverish with the intensity of our loving and though he had just left my body, in spite of the tenderness, I craved him back within. I reached to draw his leg flush between mine, closing my thighs around it, sending small surges of pleasure through me. He smiled sleepily and I rocked my hips against him. He opened one eye and the right side of his mouth lifted higher into a lopsided grin.

"Come here, darlin'," he said, low and soft, but with determination. "Come here to me."

So saying, he drew me under him, my arms winding around his neck as his beautiful hawk eyes smiled down into mine. It hurt a little as his solid hardness, his length, filled me again. But I would have him, he was now mine in every way, and I wanted nothing more on earth. He claimed my body with utter sweetness and moved slowly, drawing out with deliberate strokes before gliding back within, as we kissed without end. When he shuddered in release and then fell still, tears of joy for everything we had found together trickled over my temples. He licked them away, before kissing me one last time. And then we slept.

P ROBABLY WE SHOULD get up," I said much later that day, though everything within me rebelled against the thought of leaving our warm cocoon. We were both naked as the days we'd been born, sprawled together on the bedding. So far neither Boyd nor Malcolm had returned to camp; Sawyer explained that they were hunting, allowing us the remarkable privilege of a brief honeymoon.

"You will stay right here with me," he ordered, his eyes glinting with warm teasing, yet imploring me at the same time. He confessed, "There's a part of me that's terrified this will all be a beautiful dream. I'll wake up and then I'll die from longing to get back to the same dream."

I rolled atop him, my hair spilling all over us, and regarded his dear, handsome face. He lounged on his back, both pillows and one forearm braced beneath his head. His eyelids were at half-mast, content and lazy, and he looked so good that perhaps he was being conjured by my fancy. Between us there existed an ever-increasing sense of wonder—a discovery of one another on levels previously unimaginable to either of us. The strength of our loving, the joy that surged so freely between us, only served to heighten this awareness, this intimate intensity and keen-edged delight, born of the knowledge that we were now allowed to touch and join with no inhibitions, with no restrictions. And, oh—how we had joined. The magnitude of our joy cast aside all worries, all fears—at least for this day.

Much better than any dream, I told him with my eyes.

He grinned and slipped a warm hand around my backside, adding, "It's very realistic, I'll concede that."

"Sawyer James," I scolded, curving into his touch. I pressed my breasts more firmly to his chest and asked demurely, "Will you kiss my nipples again, please?"

His grip tightened and his grin deepened. He blinked once, and then replied in a voice sweet as clover honey fresh from the comb, "Well, since you said 'please.'"

I giggled, squirming as he pinned me flat on my back, kissing me just as I'd asked, as softly as though skimming a feather over my flesh. I shivered and moaned, "That tickles."

In response he bent lower and ran his tongue lightly along my belly, teasing my navel, as I laughed helplessly and twisted beneath him, before moving back to my breasts, opening his lips as my laughter became soft moans.

"Please," I begged, lifting my hips in adamant invitation. "Please, *please…*"

"That I should make you beg," he marveled, my fingers buried in his golden hair. He lamented, "I am no gentleman," stroking softly between my legs.

"*Sawyer,*" I demanded, breathless, and his half-wicked grin, the one to which I had rapidly grown accustomed, ignited fire anew in my soul. He licked a path upwards between my breasts, at last claiming my mouth. I reached down and clutched him none too gently, impaling myself as he groaned against my lips. I rolled him to his back, which he allowed, his hands gliding over my hips as I straddled him, letting my hair surround us in this beautiful world we had created with just us two.

We had made love countless times since last night, but my craving of him, my intense preoccupation with him, saturated me past all reason. There was, within me, an impassioned desire for the absorption of all details relating to him, those large and those seemingly insignificant, each mattering equally to me because I loved him, body and soul.

The shape of his strong hands and long, capable fingers, the pale half-moons at the base of each of his nails, the lines etched into his palms, which I explored by the lantern light, teasing him that I could follow the path of his destiny, there scribed.

The bones that contoured his handsome face, and the way it took on a fierce, almost stern, expression before he spilled over inside me.

The soft, husky sound of his voice, murmuring to me in love, and passionate desire; the caress of my name upon his lips.

The shape of his long nose and firm chin, jaws stubbled with a day's growth of beard.

The arch of his wide shoulders, to which I repeatedly clung, as the hours of the day melted past.

His strong, muscular legs, the curve of his buttocks beneath my grasping hands.

The salty taste of his sweat, licked from his chest and his neck, the texture of his skin beneath my fingertips and tongue, where he was scarred from battle—the rough puckering of a healed musket wound on the outer edge of his left thigh, the imprint of the blades that had once opened his flesh—one upon his lower right ribcage, the other his jaw.

The dark hair that moved in a slim, straight line down the center of his lower belly, the darker hair between his legs, and the musky scent of him there.

The rigid firmness of his cock in my mouth, smooth and yet hard as a buckeye, sleek against my tongue.

The way he cradled me close time and again, whispering, "That's it, darlin', my sweet, sweet darlin'," as I gasped and held fast to him, pelted by sensation, the cresting waves that shuddered over me at his powerful, unceasing motion.

"Don't stop," I heard myself beg many times, and his answering smile, his assurance that he would never stop.

Much later, the long afternoon sun stretched through the translucent canvas, tinting the interior the mellow shade of old whiskey; we had not eaten a bite all day, sated completely upon our loving. It had been nearly twenty-four hours since we bound our hands. Happiness of such enormity was also a terrifying thing, but I had allowed myself to bathe within it since last night, held it greedily and without let-up to my heart. No matter what happened from here forward, life could not rob me of today.

Tomorrow I could not control.

Oh dear God...

A snagging in my heart, a clenching in my gut—surely I was imagining the sense of time running out that chose to beat at my thoughts just now. Sawyer slept on his back, snoring lightly, but at the sound of my distress he turned to me, eyes still closed, bringing me closer. I was afraid, after all of our easy teasing and laughter, the intensity of our repeated lovemaking, that I was about to cry. He stroked my hair as I'd seen him stroke Whistler's hide; he was a man who loved with complete devotion, with his whole heart.

He thought, *I am here. We are safe, and I am here.*

"Sawyer," I whispered, words fleeing like frightened birds from my lips as I tried to explain, "I want us to stay here, and I know we cannot." Because the time would come creeping, all too soon, when we would be forced to leave this space, bid farewell to these beautiful first hours we had existed as man and wife, and move forward into the unknown. My breath came faster, in short, erratic gasps. My heart seemed to want to hurl itself free of my body.

"It's all right," he soothed, encasing me even more securely into his arms. He said quietly, "I know, *mo mhuirnín milis*, I know."

"I cannot bear to be apart from you. Even the thought is beyond bearing. Please never leave me alone. Never leave me alone, Sawyer." I knew it was unfair to speak this way, when he had as much control over life as did I, but my words rushed out in panicked and passionate bursts; I was unable to stop them.

"Lorie," he said firmly. He drew back and said with quiet resolve, "Look at my eyes, darlin', look at me." I obeyed, and his gaze was somber upon mine as he said, "I will do everything in my power to keep us safe. I will never leave you. You know this."

At his words, the roiling waters of panic at last subsided, ebbing back to a place where I could control them, refusing to consider the many horrible ways in which life could rip us apart.

"You are overtired," he acknowledged, tenderly kissing my cheek. "Your eyes are shadowed. You sleep, my sweet love, and I'll get us something to eat."

He lifted my chin and kissed my lips, before tucking the blanket about me. His touch lingered upon my jaw, and I managed a smile.

"I'll be back directly," he said, rising and stretching, his powerful naked body such a sight to behold in the sunset light. I went up on my elbow to admire him, and he winked at me as he donned his trousers and ducked outside. I heard Whistler nickering at him in welcome, and his affectionate, teasing response, "Did you wonder where we were all day, my girl?"

I pictured him petting her face and kissing her nose, and with those comforting thoughts in mind, I slept.

WHEN NEXT I woke the night was deep and our campfire burned outside with a cheerful crackle. I was naked, tucked neatly into the blankets. I sat and ran my fingers along the heavy length of my hair, rife with snarls. I could hear Boyd and Malcolm chattering with Sawyer, and my heart swelled with gladness.

"Lorie-love, we're out here," Sawyer called, as he surely heard me rustling around.

"Thank you for filling the basin," I returned, noticing the reflected gleam of the fire's glow upon the fresh water within it, an arm's length from the bed.

"Heya, Lorie-Lorie!" Malcolm called exuberantly. The boy went on, "Boyd said you an' Sawyer'd be tuckered out after last night, so's—" Malcolm's words were interrupted by the sounds of scuffling and his issuing of a squeak, and then Boyd uttered, "*Jesus Christ*, boy!"

I smothered my laughter.

Sawyer ducked inside, retying the entrance and squatting at the foot of the bed in the dimness of the firelight filtering through the canvas, smiling at me in the way he had that set my heart to throbbing rather than simply beating. His voice was even more throaty than usual as he said tenderly, "I love how you look, all warm and tumbled from sleeping. Are you hungry, my wife?"

I kicked free of the covers and moved swiftly into his arms, where he caught me close, laughing a little. My arms laced around him, my breasts flattened against the muslin of his shirt. He smelled of the fire and of roasting meat, his hair loose down his back. I whispered into his ear, "Just for you."

He rocked me side to side and kissed my neck, whispering, "I must be in a dream. And I must be the most selfish bastard who ever lived, to keep taking advantage of the gift of you this way."

I murmured in his ear, "I won't hear any such nonsense. You are anything but selfish and unless you mean to fight me away from you –"

In response, he kissed me quite absolutely. He whispered, "All evening, while you slept, your scent was upon my skin, I could very nearly taste you, and I love it so. I had not thought it possible to need you more than I already do." His thumbs stroked my lips, my cheekbones. He clasped my right hand and brought it to his thrusting heart.

I pulled him immediately closer, thrilling to his words, working to open the fastening on his trousers. He shivered and sank his fingers into my hair, tipping me into his kiss. I tugged the shirt over his arms, caressing the ridges of muscle there, and those across his chest.

"Hurry," I begged in a whisper, as he quickly freed himself from the last of his clothing. I added, "I'll be quiet, I promise."

He laughed at that, lavishing my neck with kisses as his hand moved swiftly downward over my belly. He whispered, "I'll try to promise the same."

I curled my fingers around his length and he groaned, taking me instantly to the bedding, studying my face as he held himself poised above, just at the point of entry. I urged insistently closer, lifting my hips, and he groaned a second time, prompting my hushed giggles. He grinned and gently took my chin between his teeth, linking our fingers as he joined our bodies, sliding at once deeply within; my subsequent moans were caught between us and again we were so willingly lost to the rest of the world, wrapped in each other.

"LORISSA DAVIS, that has a fine ring to it," Boyd said later, as the four of us sat around the fire feasting on delicious venison, roasted to a perfect crackling turn. "Sounds right nice."

I smiled at his words, my mouth too full to respond. In all my life, food had never tasted better than this night's.

Sawyer leaned and kissed my cheek, agreeing, "It does, at that."

"Lorie, did you love all of your surprises, did you?" Malcolm demanded, his lips decorated with bits of char; one of his teeth was also inadvertently blackened, giving him a comical appearance, and I grinned, with complete love, as he went on lauding his work, "I lit all the lanterns, an' picked the flowers, an' decorated Whistler-girl."

"I loved every bit, it was all so wonderful," I told him. "You are surely the sweetest boy who ever lived."

Boyd made a *tut-tut* sound of disapproval, raising his eyebrows at me and indicating himself with one thumb.

"And you as well," I told him, smiling.

Malcolm explained, "We stayed away all night an' all day as so the two of you could –"

Boyd yelped, "Boy!" and leaned to kick at Malcolm's ankle. Malcolm giggled and kicked back at his brother. Boyd rolled his eyes at us and said, "I understand now why Daddy was so damn hesitant to talk to us boys about... certain things. Christ, I recall he took Beau an' me aside an' stumbled over an explanation that had more to do with horses…" and he snorted a laugh before finishing, "Horses mating."

We were all laughing then. Enjoying our amusement, Boyd went on, with relish, "Here was me an' Beau, thinking of all the times we'd watched the horses being bred, an' the impressive an' sobering size of a horse's pecker— beg pardon, Lorie—both of us imagining all manner of indecent things. Then Daddy threw us into another tizzy when he said somethin' about making sure that a woman was…" He was almost laughing too hard to continue, but he managed, saying, "About making sure a woman was pleasured during lovemaking, as well."

"I can just see him," Sawyer said; he agreed, "*And* sound advice."

Boyd continued, "Beau whispered to me, 'But we ain't *near* the size,' an' then we figured we'd never be able to bring a woman pleasure."

"Mine sure ain't near big as a horse's," Malcolm said seriously, the only one of us not swept away in mirth, provoking further hilarity.

"No one's is, kid," Sawyer managed to say, though I gave him a saucy look at those words.

"What woman would *want* a man with a wink the size of a horse's, any-way?" Malcolm demanded, a slightly horrified angle to his eyebrows; he appeared further distressed at our increased laughter.

"Oh Jesus," Boyd finally muttered, wiping his eyes with the knuckles of both thumbs. "So, being the responsible fella I am, I tried to explain to the boy here about –"

"Womenfolk an' what they may expect of me, someday," Malcolm finished dutifully, his eyes on the flames. It seemed that Boyd's lesson had been taken to heart.

Sawyer said to Boyd, "I can only just imagine what you had to say on the matter."

"It sounds right *embarrassing*, that's what," Malcolm said, looking to me with his dark eyes wide and sincere. I thought of the talk we had shared while he brushed my hair, and with effort I stifled my laughter, though Boyd and Sawyer were almost on their sides at his words. Malcolm disregarded them and said innocently, "I don't understand how it all begins, Lorie, Boyd weren't clear on that. Do I tell a woman it's time an' then it's *time?* She'll let me… *do* that to her?"

"I tried…I tried…to draw a picture…in the dirt…" Boyd wheezed, attempting to speak amidst his laughter. "I never...knew a picture in the dirt... could be so...*lewd*..."

Sawyer could hardly breathe.

"Hush, you two," I scolded. I said to Malcolm, "When you meet the right woman, as we spoke of, it won't be embarrassing. It will be beautiful. You'll see. It will all make sense."

The boy's dark eyebrows knitted together, but he nodded. I slapped at Sawyer's shoulder; he was choking on laughter, bent forward, same as Boyd. I added, "Don't pay attention to these two. You ask me, Malcolm."

And that was enough for the boy, for tonight. He smiled and said agreeably, "Aw right." His trust for me was apparent in his tone, and my heart hitched.

"You are in *trouble*," I informed Sawyer, poking him to emphasize my words.

"Ha, that's right, Lorie-girl, you tell him. I feel strongly that a proper wife oughta be a good nag," Boyd teased, at last able to draw a decent breath, though he looked at Malcolm and his shoulders shook once more. He finally concluded, "Aw, boy, you's a Carter. Ladies ain't ever been able to resist us. You'll be right as *rain*."

"Lorie-honey, don't be mad," Sawyer said, wiping tears of laughter from his eyes. "Malcolm knows we understand."

Malcolm's eyes twinkled. He moved closer to my side and rested his head endearingly upon me. He said, "No, I don't. They was being mean to me."

"Oh, so that's the way of it," Sawyer teased. He rose slowly and backed away from the fire, then curled forward menacingly and beckoned to Malcolm. "C'mon, kid, let's wrestle."

Malcolm whooped and bounded for Sawyer, dropping into a crouch and feinting with his fists. They circled while Boyd squinted one eye and lit a smoke, saying, "Money's on the boy, old friend. You *do* appear right wore out after last night an' all day today."

At that Sawyer was laughing again and Malcolm, seeing his advantage, dove for him. Sawyer sidestepped neatly.

"Get him, Malcolm!" I encouraged, laughing.

Malcolm leaped to grab one of Sawyer's forearms, clinging for all he was worth. Sawyer flipped the boy over his shoulder and held him upside-down, while Malcolm struggled and yelped, "Ain't fair! Let me down!"

Sawyer spun him instead, while Malcolm shrieked with laughter.

"All right, that's enough, I can't see straight," my husband yielded at last. He let Malcolm to the ground where they both collapsed and lay flat, staring up at the stars.

"Oh, the world is a-spinning an' spinning," Malcolm groaned.

"I remember now why I don't do this," Sawyer said, closing his eyes before deciding, "No, that's worse."

"Lorie, more venison?" Boyd asked, and I nodded eagerly. "We'll just let them two sleep out here under the sky."

I went to stand between them, still eating, poking my bare toes against Sawyer's ribs. He looked up at me and grinned, tucking both wrists beneath his head. I told him, "I used to spin like that."

He invited, "Come here, sweetheart. The stars are shining just for you."

I sat and arranged my skirt, then lay down and snuggled close to him upon the ground; my fingers were greasy with the venison I held, and Sawyer appropriated it for a bite. Malcolm moved at once to my far side and nestled against me.

"Lorie, you was my girl first," the boy murmured.

Boyd sighed as though much put-upon and at last joined us, blowing a trail of most remarkable smoke rings up at the glittering sky; he had tried a few nights back to teach Malcolm the delicate technique, at the boy's incessant begging, all without success; Malcolm had gone into an instant coughing fit after the first drag. The air tonight was completely static, clear as creek water in the springtime. Boyd removed his tobacco roll and whispered, in keeping with the quiet of the empty prairie, "By God, I'm excited to start over."

"Me, too," Malcolm whispered, and my heart clenched as he said softly, "Even if we ain't got Gus with us no more. I surely miss him."

Sawyer held me closer at once. He said softly, "I miss the stories he'd tell. He knew so many. He knew what we'd been like as boys."

"There ain't many can claim that," Boyd agreed.

"Lookee there!" Malcolm cried, pointing.

We looked in time to see the white streak of light across the heavens, sudden as a lightning flash and gone almost as instantly.

Boyd said, low, "Mama used to say that stars were souls, an' when you saw a shooting star it meant a new soul was bound for the earth, for another go-round at life. I suppose Reverend Wheeler woulda disagreed, but Mama always claimed that."

"I recall her saying so," Sawyer said. "I remember looking up at them during the War and thinking that there were so many souls becoming stars, all around us. It seemed unending and my thoughts would run so dark."

"Mine as well, old friend," Boyd said. "I thought that there surely couldn't be enough stars to go around back in them bleak days."

"Which ones belong to our family's souls?" Malcolm whispered. In his voice was a sense of awe, magic inspired by the solitude of the night and the majesty of the heavens sprawling above our four bodies. He snuggled closer to me.

"I think," Boyd began, pausing to consider. He continued in all seriousness, "I think perhaps that group right yonder." He indicated with the burning tip of his smoke. "That bunch of stars in the northwest there, all crowded together. That reminds me of our family at a picnic, everyone in someone's business. Mama would be that bright one, near the front, an' look, Sawyer, them two close together, like twins. That's Eth an' Jere, for certain."

"I see 'em," Malcolm said reverently. "Just so. They's all together, ain't they? You s'pose they wonder what's a-going on down here?"

Boyd said, with calm certainty, "'Course they's together. Gus is with them now, too, look yonder," and tears filled my eyes for the second time. I pressed my face to Sawyer as Boyd whispered, "When the night is so clear an' fine, like it is right now, I'd wager they gather an' maybe look back to the Earth for a spell."

"I hope Mama an' Daddy's proud of me," Malcolm said softly.

Sawyer leaned carefully over me and patted Malcolm. He said, "No doubt of that, kid."

"Daddy's surely laughing about what I tried to teach you today," Boyd said. He concluded, with sweet sincerity, "Just wait, boy, we'll find us fine, pretty wives in Minnesota. We'll have stars shooting to Earth every year, more young'uns than you could shake a stick at."

Sawyer moved his hand from Malcolm to gently cup my belly. He softly kissed my temple and whispered, "For us, as well," and my tears overspilled, one part pain, all other parts love.

H OLD UP THERE."

Boyd's voice, laced with concern, roused me from sleep. I blinked, requiring a moment to regain my bearings; I did not usually doze in the back of the wagon. A half dozen feet above my gaze was the wagon's ribcage, the slender, curving wooden arches over which the canvas cover stretched, peacefully backlit with late-day sunshine, and there was nothing to suggest overt trouble, but I rolled to one elbow, attempting to determine what had caused Boyd to issue such an abrupt order.

On the wagon seat and only a few feet from where I lay, Sawyer drew back on the reins, halting the team, and called, "What is it?"

"Juney's limping," Malcolm explained, flanking the wagon to the right, where Juniper was tethered and had been following alongside. I heard Boyd and Malcolm dismount; seconds later, Sawyer jumped nimbly to the ground.

I had woken at dawn, a few mornings past, with the return of my monthly cycle, cramped and bleeding, and subsequently rooted out the cloth bindings I used specifically for such purposes, wearing them now beneath my shift. As I was tired and uncomfortable, Sawyer fashioned a makeshift pallet, thick with quilts, and I had indulged in stealing afternoon naps, allowing myself the luxury; despite the intermittent ruts and bumps of the trail, I was quite content in the back of the wagon, studying the sunlit patterns on the translucent, if dirt-smudged, ivory canvas, lulled by the rise and fall of the men's voices as they chatted.

"What's the matter with him, blacksmith?" Boyd asked Sawyer as I climbed down to join them. Malcolm, who had been riding Whistler, held her lead line in a loop around his elbow and cupped Juniper's big square jaws, patting him, murmuring endearments.

Sawyer ran his hand down Juniper's right front foreleg, which the animal was favoring, lifting the hoof and balancing it against his thighs. He examined it minutely and said, "It isn't any wonder he was limping. There's swelling in the fetlock and pastern, both, and his leg is warmer than the day should warrant."

"An abscess," I understood, and Sawyer nodded immediate agreement. He murmured, "You've a good eye."

"Poor fella," Malcolm said, kissing the animal's nose; Juniper grunted and swished his tail, clearly communicating his displeasure. Malcolm murmured, "You's hurting, huh, fella?"

"I am outright ashamed of myself for not noticing this sooner," Sawyer said, gently letting the hoof back to earth, rising to his full height and patting Juniper's neck. Addressing the animal, he said, "Sorry, boy. We'll take care of it, don't you worry."

"Iowa City ain't more'n a few miles, at best," Boyd mused, pursing his lips and gazing speculatively northward. We had not planned to spend any length of time there, as we had resupplied well in Keokuk, and would come across St. Paul within the month; our intent was to pass through Iowa City this evening and cover another mile or so north before making camp for the night.

Sawyer considered this; at last he said decisively, "We'll have to stop for tonight, and make camp near that stand of willows, yonder." He nodded in the direction of the river, and then said, "We'll drain and poultice the hoof, and Juniper should be well enough to push on in the morning."

"You want me to fetch the nippers?" Malcolm asked.

Sawyer nodded, reaching to draw me momentarily to his side. He said, "Well, you did wish to learn proper shoeing technique."

Within minutes we reassembled closer to the river; Boyd and Malcolm worked together to set up camp while Sawyer gathered the necessary implements and led Juniper to the leeward side of the wagon, where shade fell in a long, slanted rectangle.

"Retie him, will you, love?" Sawyer asked, passing me the lead line, while he knelt and carefully unrolled a strip of thick flannel, in which his shoeing tools were wrapped for their passage in a trunk. He laid out the iron nippers, the crease-nail puller, a hoof pick, a nail rasp, and a hoof knife.

Juniper grunted and shifted, lifting his front leg; the hoof dangled piti-fully, indicating the level of pain, and I kissed his long nose, assuring him, "Sawyer will take care of you," and the man in question looked up at me and grinned at the confidence in my tone, nudging an itch on his jaw with one shoulder.

He said, "I haven't treated an abscess since the War, but I will do my best. Come here by me to watch, but stand well clear of those back hooves."

I was touched at his concern, though I well knew to stand clear, and poked the side of his leg with my foot. I said, "I learned that lesson long ago, thank you kindly."

Sawyer's grin broadened as he stood, the rasping tool in his grip, and firm-ly patted Juniper's flank, letting the animal know he was approaching. He said, "Steady, boy, you'll be feeling a mite better, directly."

I watched as Sawyer bent and skillfully lifted Juniper's foreleg, bringing the hoof between his knees so that he could work unencumbered. He ex-amined the shoe, brushing his thumb over the dirt, a frown creating a small crease of concentration between his brows. He said, "It does not appear too deep, thankfully. I'll have a better view once the shoe is off," and with those words, applied the rasp neatly to each clinch in turn, using the fine side of the tool to smooth the nail covers until they were even with the hoof wall, explaining each action for my benefit, beginning with the proper stance.

"Stand with your toes inward, like this, for stability, and never let your shoulders tilt below your hips. I would use the hammer in most other circum-stances, but it would be too painful for his hoof, just now," Sawyer said, his right arm shifting rhythmically with the rasping motion. He acknowledged, "This method takes a fair amount longer, but won't hurt him. One thing to remember is that you must never let your thumb or finger beneath a partially-pulled shoe. If the animal jerks away, it could get caught." He looked my way and said, "I've had many a jammed finger."

"Did your grandfather teach you these things?" I asked, picturing this scene; Sawyer had described the elder Sawyer Davis so often, and so well, that I fancied I could very nearly discern the man's spirit, leaning over his forearms on Juniper's opposite side, observing the process he had passed on to his namesake many a long year ago.

"He did," Sawyer said, finished with the rasping; thin rivulets of sweat trickled down his temples and over his jaws. In the relative quiet, he remembered, "I wasn't but six or seven the first time he showed me the process. Granddaddy put his hands around mine to guide the motions. He was patient as a church mouse. I aim to possess one-tenth his patience." He smiled as he said, "Hand me those nail pullers, please, darlin'.".

I did, and he proceeded to explain, "I'll pull out each individually, rather than use the nippers to rock free the shoe. You clamp the nail's head, right here in the crease like this, and free it by pushing the handle away from your body." He demonstrated. "See here? Just like this. Next time I'll let you practice, Lorie-love. Once all the nails are free, the shoe should come off with little resistance."

"It *appears* an easy process," I said, covertly admiring the ease with which he completed each step, so strong and nimble. His fingers were long, sure in their movements and so very capable, his forearms bared by rolled-back shirtsleeves, and taut with muscle. I did not wish to distract his industrious work, but an incessant, desirous heat throbbed in my belly, just watching him.

The shoe slipped free, and Sawyer tossed it to the ground, where it landed with a muted thud. He inspected Juniper's hoof; the horse whooshed a loud breath and shied away.

"Steady," I soothed, moving to pat Juniper's neck on either side of his warm, dark-brown hide. "There's a good boy."

"How's Juney?" Malcolm called, running up the river bank, grasping his dripping canteen. He slowed his pace as he neared, as so not to startle Juniper, and passed the canteen to me; I stole a long sip.

"Well, I can see the trouble," Sawyer said, applying the hoof pick now, freeing remaining debris from Juniper's hoof. "See the swelling, just here, in the hoof as well as his foreleg? There's a small crack leading to it, but it does not appear too deep, as I thought. We'll drain the pus, see if we can't clean out that infection. Honey, hand me the hoof knife."

"You meanin' me, or Lorie?" Malcolm giggled.

Sawyer asked the boy, "Since when do I call you 'honey?'"

"Do you suppose a rock or a stick was wedged in there?" I asked, collecting the knife from the row of tools on the flannel.

Sawyer let the hoof back to ground, stood and then swiped at the moisture on his face, lifting his hat and resettling it before saying, "Most likely. We have crossed so many creeks, which is not ideal for the integrity of a hoof, and

Juniper is the eldest of our horses. Poor fellow probably never figured he'd be asked to walk thousands of miles to Minnesota in his middle age."

"Juney-*per*," Malcolm singsonged, patting the horse's face. "Sawyer'll make you feel lots better."

"I'd like you two to hold his head steady, well away from his hooves –" Sawyer caught my eye and cut himself short, allowing, "I know you realize. I apologize. I must open a small wound to allow for drainage, and he won't be any too happy with me."

Sawyer collected the knife, assuming the same stance, and with a deft, precise motion, sliced a slit on the frog of the hoof, where the swelling was centered. Juniper shied and snorted, stamping his back hooves one after the other, but between us, Malcolm and I held him steady.

"There's good seepage, already," Sawyer said, sounding victorious as he held the hoof and pressed firmly with both thumbs, calmly aiding the flow of brownish, blood-tinged foam from the wound. "He'll be ready for travel by midmorning, I do believe. We'll poultice him with some Epsom salt, tonight."

"I could use me a soak in the stuff, as well," Boyd said, joining us. He was sweating and disheveled; the evening air was hotly immobile, and I allowed that we could all use a bath.

"We'll fashion a poultice, and then perhaps a swim for a spell?" I suggested.

THE IOWA was calm under the setting sun. I floated on my back near the center of the river, no more than a stone's throw across at its widest, submerging my ears in the ongoing rush of water. The river was pleasantly cool on my sweating skin, though I wore a shift for the sake of modesty; Sawyer and Boyd were clad in the lower halves of their union suits, while Malcolm was bare as a newborn, giggling when his pale little buttocks broke the water's surface as he played in the shallows.

"Lorie-girl, I gotta make a request of you," Boyd said, his dark hair slicked back from his sunburned forehead; he hunkered to his chin in flowing water, a dozen or so feet away. He grinned and explained, "When I dare to run to shore, you ain't to watch."

I laughed, and Sawyer kicked a splash in Boyd's direction.

"I will turn my eyes," I promised Boyd.

"Boy, if a trout nips at you, *you know where*, it is duly noted just now that I offered a warning," Boyd called over to his brother, inspiring more laughter, before Boyd ducked under, blowing energetic bubbles to the surface.

The sky was spectacular and I breathed a sigh of speechless pleasure at the sight of the entire western heaven ablaze with sunset. Slender purple clouds rippled in opaque waves, catching the day's last light and throwing it back in scattered beams of fiery gold. The horses, grazing yards away, were starkly silhouetted against the yellow sky in ink-black, the tall prairie grass appearing as a solid mass of mauve in the tranquil evening air.

"That sky is a beautiful sight," Sawyer said, floating upon his back near me, our fingers lightly intertwined. "In the holler, the sun set so early. It's such a different experience out here, where you can see everything for miles."

I nodded agreement; the press of water in my ears muffled my voice as I said, "Even the air seems distinctive in this place, wilder somehow."

"Thank you for helping with Juniper," Sawyer said. "You did well, and have a steady hand, *mo mhuirnín milis*."

"I told you I mean to learn," I said. "You are quite welcome." And then I could not resist requesting, "Say something," and he grinned, knowing exactly what I meant. I loved hearing him speak in his mother's native language, that of Ireland, which he had learned at her knee.

Sawyer clutched my fingers more tightly, in response, and said softly, "*Is é an spéir anocht álainn, ach rud ar bith ar domhan, nó neamh thuas d'fhéadfadh, a bheith álainn sin, nó daor dom, mar atá tú.*"

Though he had been teaching me basic words and phrases, this sentence was spoken too fluidly for my untutored ears to distinguish any sense, and I demanded, "What did you say?"

He murmured, "I will *show* you, I promise."

"Tell me, Sawyer James," I insisted. I dearly loved speaking both his given names; it seemed an intimacy particular to a wife addressing her husband. "Tell me *at once*."

He moved with his swift, lithe grace, catching me into his arms beneath the water; my legs slipped wetly about his waist as he crouched on the rocky bottom, our faces no more than a few inches apart, a sweet satisfaction upon Sawyer's as he grinned at me. His skin was warm against the chill of mine, his arms enfolding my waist as the river flowed gently around us, creating small eddies in its wake. He had not been shaving as readily in the mornings, simply because I refused to let him leave my embrace to do so; I would rather he remain stubbled with beard, allowing us extra time so we could make love when we woke.

He repeated, in a whisper, "I promise," and I clutched his jaws and kissed him heatedly, briefly forgetting that we were not exactly alone.

"*Jesus Christ*, you two! Morning, noon, an' night ain't enough for you?" Boyd groused, surfacing nearer to us and sending arcs of water splashing our direction. "I swear, if we gotta share a cabin all winter…"

"Aw, Boyd, they's just kissin'," Malcolm called.

I ducked to evade the splashing while Sawyer went after Boyd, who whooped in challenge; they wrestled, appearing to be attempting to cause one another grievous bodily harm, but their roughhousing did not this time attract Malcolm. Instead, he called, "Come see, Lorie-Lorie!"

The boy hunkered chin to knees on the muddy bank, having gathered a row of river snails, each scarcely larger than his thumbnail, their shells forming perfect curls. I squeezed out my hair, drawing it over one shoulder as I squatted, dripping, to examine them.

"Ain't they pretty?" he asked, poking gently. "Think I could keep 'em in a jar?"

"No, sweetheart, just as you cannot keep butterflies in a jar. It is a cruelty, as they would only die."

"I'd like me a pet of my own," he said.

"You have Aces," I reminded him, biting my lower lip to restrain a smile; his bare bottom hovered an inch above the ground and it was only a matter of time before he would grow far too modest to appear naked in front of me. But this evening he was still my sweet boy, unconcerned, his concentration directed at his snail-collecting efforts. The sun had drawn most of the light, and its subsequent warmth, to the far edge of the prairie, leaving behind a dusky twilight.

Malcolm's eyes brightened, and he agreed, "I do. But I mean a small critter, one I could haul about with me."

"We'll do our best," I promised. "Now come, let's get you dried off before you catch a chill."

Malcolm nodded, scooping the snails into his palm and tracing a fingertip over them before releasing them back to the river.

RED DIRT was warm beneath my bare feet.

What should have buoyed my heart with simple gladness—the sight of a Tennessee road, the one which led in an unhurried, winding fashion to my childhood home—instead caused the breath to solidify, painfully, in my lungs. The air was quiet and motionless, laden with scents long familiar to me, honeysuckle and sweetgrass, the loamy earth from which grew abundant wildflowers, the powder-fine dust that swirled familiarly over my toes. Sunlight cut translucent paths between the oak limbs reaching outward from towering trees in the ditch, and sifted over my loose hair.

The scene all about me was one of peaceful summertime beauty and so at first it was not entirely apparent what invited the shadow of threat to hover near...

Laughter, from somewhere nearby, filtered to my ears amid the ancient trees that guarded the right side of the road. My feet instinctively followed the sound, the grass growing tall off the beaten path and subsequently catching at my skirt, so that I lifted my hem in order to navigate the way. I found as I walked that something lurked tauntingly at the edges of my vision—a dark silhouette, hunched and silent, but when I looked in its direction, there was nothing but emptiness. I squinted, straining to spy whatever it was that observed so sinisterly, when a peal of happy sound floated to my ears, that of boys at play, and spurred my feet on their original course. People were nearby and I stepped forward, stooping to peer between two tree trunks, the bark rough and immediate under my touch.

Oh, I whispered painfully, sun flashing suddenly in my eyes, blinking against this radiance with eyelids that felt weighted. Likewise, my ankles seemed turned to iron, anchoring me to the ground when I ached to run forward.

Mama...

My mother stood no more than yards away, the delicate contours of her form so recognizable to me—but her head was angled so that I could see only the curve of her elegant jaw, not her clear green eyes or her welcoming smile. She held a little boy, perched close on her hip; one of his plump hands tugged at a strand of her honey-brown hair. My brothers, Dalton and Jesse, were playing in the chicory field that grew behind Daddy's stable—*I could see the stable, just there across the way*—chasing one another and laughing, and the boy wriggled on Mama's arm, wanting to clamber down and join them.

The sun, hovering at the edge of evening, struck all of them from behind, creating perfect haloes about their bodies, and simultaneously gilded my vision. Half-blinded as I was, I burned with the need to move towards them—and yet I could not will myself even a step that direction.

I begged, *Look at me, Mama, look this way…*

Let me see my son…

Please, let me see him…

But my pleading words did not reach her ears. Instead, a new voice echoed within mine.

Lorie, Angus said, speaking my name with affection, just as he had in life. I tore my eyes from Mama and the boy in attempt to find him in the thickening dusk, scraping at sudden pine boughs closing in near my face, the small, sharp needles prickling my skin. I thrashed with both arms, feeling as though the forest grew smaller, encroaching upon my very body. I could not see Angus anywhere near, but still I called, *Gus! Where are you? I am so sorry…I pray that you know this…*

There is danger, my dear. Danger both ahead and behind. Tell Sawyer. Do you hear me? Though I could not see him, Angus's voice had grown urgent. Somewhere beyond my field of view Jesse called out to Dalton. Mama spoke then, heralding them to return to her, and the sky grew suddenly hazy with approaching darkness. My heart clamped into a tight fist of fear. Angus spoke close to my ear, insistent as he ordered, *Tell him, Lorie. We could not have known, not that night. Boyd was right…he was right…*

I don't understand, I implored. I shoved aside branches, looking desperately for Mama and the boy, and my dear brothers, but they had all disappeared. The chicory field was empty in the silent silver air of twilight, no hint of their presence or passage out of it, oddly menacing in the gloaming. I heard a low, frightened moan and understood that it was mine.

Gus! I cried, but all sense of him had vanished.

There was a distinct skittering in the branches directly above me and I felt certain something was poised to swoop. I turned, blindly, and stumbled amongst thick undergrowth and grasping branches, making pitiful progress—and then I tripped over a toppled tree and fell hard to both knees.

Momentarily dazed, I hung my head until the dizzy ache passed. My eyes had adjusted to the dark and as I lifted my face I caught sight of...

My mind faltered, attempting to process the sight.

What I had thought was the trunk of a tree was instead...

Was instead...

No, I whispered—then shrieked—one shriek atop another, a wailing cry—

The gathering grays of night were not enough to obscure the face of the man on the ground, a lined visage grown cold and dead—the coldness seeped from him and into the fingertips of my right hand, moving insidiously upwards—branches scraped along my flesh as I tried to scrabble away from the punctured left eye, the gaping wound which had leaked dark blood down his neck and long since dried upon his collar.

He is dead—Sam Rainey is dead—oh Jesus—he is dead and cannot harm you —

Breathing harshly, I raked my fingers through fallen leaves in attempt to gain purchase and continue crawling frantically away. The air grew ever colder and it was then that I encountered a second body, that of the man I had known briefly as Dixon, the man who murdered Angus. How I realized it was Dixon, I could not have articulated, as his head was misplaced—my disbelieving eyes roved across the ground, coming to rest upon a distorted skull roughly arm's length from my nose, utterly stove in on one side.

The sight of Dixon and Sam Rainey here amongst the debris of a forest floor, far from the Missouri prairie where they had each met their end, made no sense, and I scrambled away from them as best I could, sticks and small rocks cutting into my palms. I seemed mired in molasses, moving weakly, slow as a slug.

Two bodies.

But where is—

Shouldn't there be—

Some crucial detail was escaping me—it was just at the outer edge of my memory.

You must understand, Lorie.

Lorie...

"Lorie, wake up," and Sawyer's voice, low and rife with distress, jolted me to consciousness.

I lay sweating in the darkness of our tent, flat on my back; Sawyer's outline was etched against the pale glow of canvas as he leaned over me, his warm hands bracketing my face. I reached at once and clasped his wrists, at first unable to draw a breath past the sensation of smothering. Nor could I speak, and Sawyer said again, urgently, "Lorie!"

"It's..." I rasped over the word, parched by lingering terror, and wet my lips with my tongue before able to finish speaking. I whispered, "I dreamed of...*I dreamed of...*"

I could not recall exactly and bared my teeth in a frustrated rush of breath. My heart would not cease its agitated clanking. Sawyer gently thumbed aside the strands of hair that clung to my damp temples. I held fast to his wrists.

"I'm here," he whispered. "It was only a dream."

"No," I whispered, insistent. My eyes had grown accustomed to the darkness enough to see his, mere inches away. "No...it was more than that..." I was certain of this, despite being unable to bring forth exact details.

"What do you mean?" he asked seriously, easing me up and into a sitting position, resting his hands against the outer curve of my thighs, one on either side. His hair hung loose and he was bare-chested. I sensed his desire to listen to whatever it was I felt I must say, and was grateful for the countless time that such a man was my husband, that he would not discredit any words I spoke to him, even those based entirely upon speculation.

"Something is wrong," I said with quiet certainty.

"Are you hurting?" he asked at once, his grip on my legs tightening, and I could sense his thoughts racing backwards to the days when I was ill, unresponsive with fever back in Missouri, and he had cared for me day and night.

"No," I assured immediately. "I am well."

His shoulders had tensed and now relaxed. I reached and touched my fingertips to his lips, tracing the sensual outline of his mouth.

"I am well," I whispered again, moving my hand to his cheek, overcome with tenderness.

He explained, "You were crying out in your sleep. I was in the midst of a strange dream of my own, I won't deny. I could swear that Ethan was here, with us, just before I woke."

No sooner did he speak the words when a flash of what Sawyer had dreamed blazed suddenly into my mind—I saw Ethan Davis as plainly as a thunderhead rolling in at a clip, crouched near Sawyer's sleeping body, determinedly shaking his brother's arm. I shivered at this description, a jitter that rapidly struck each individual bone of my spine.

"He was worried for us," Sawyer said, taking my elbows into his grasp, and I shivered, more violently this time. "I understand it was a dream, but it seems to me if I had woken only seconds earlier, Lorie, I would have truly *seen* him, here with us."

There was a quiet aching present in his tone, barely discernible, but I heard it nonetheless. Our bedding was jumbled, more so as I scooted forward and threaded my legs about his waist; I rested my face against him, taking soft pleasure in his scent, so familiar and beloved, the rasp of his unshaven jaw, the hard muscle of his thighs under my own.

"Did he tell you anything else?" I whispered, bringing my nose to the juncture of his collarbones.

"I do not remember more," Sawyer whispered. "I dream of my brothers from time to time, but the feel of this was different, Lorie, I tell you. Crazy I may be, but Ethan was *here*, his spirit was with us, somehow."

I resisted the urge to cast my eyes about the interior of our tent, feeling a ripple of discomfort at the notion of a spirit, even a benevolent one related to my husband, occupying the same space. I whispered, "What do you think he meant?"

"I wish I knew," Sawyer said, cupping the back of my head.

"I am fearful," I whispered, clutching him more tightly, not wanting to pretend otherwise.

"I felt a stir of fear, myself," Sawyer admitted. He sat facing the direction of the entrance and though I could not see his eyes directly, I imagined the look in them, hawk-like, keeping continual and unflagging watch over us. I knew he would never fail to protect us—but even Sawyer must sleep, must occasionally let down his guard. He placed his hands over my shoulder blades, gently rubbing me, and we held one another in silence for a long spell.

When, from Boyd and Malcolm's tent, an especially loud, grunting snore caused me to twitch, I couldn't help but laugh, quietly, at my own reaction. Sawyer made a sound of amusement and shifted position, curving both arms around my waist. My thighs spread further around his hips at this motion and I could feel the hardness of him through his trousers as our bodies pressed flush; we had not made love for several days, as a result of my monthly bleeding. He inhaled a slow breath, his lips at my temple. On the exhale, he whispered, "I apologize," so politely that I smiled.

"Such a gentleman," I teased in a whisper, grasping his face as I softly kissed his upper lip, pleased to feel the resultant tremble that skimmed over him. His eyes, now directed upon me, blazed with heat, discernible even in the darkness.

"My beautiful woman," he whispered, gliding both hands around my backside, as though in preparation to take me to the bedding beneath him, as he had done so many times now.

"Sawyer," I said, low and unrelenting, caressing downward, opening his trousers even as he protested—however weakly—that I should not.

"Darlin', it's your time...I will not take advantage of you that way..."

"It's nearly done," I whispered.

"We should not..." But he skimmed the shift from my body, making the deep sound of pleasure that I knew so very well.

"We should," I insisted, breathing ever faster. I demanded, "Help me with these..."

Sawyer worked swiftly, freeing me from the binding about my lower body, hardly breaking the contact of our mouths as we kissed. I remained astride his lap and he lifted me without effort, settling my now-naked body atop his, groaning softly as I took him deep, both of us remaining still, reveling in the moment of joining.

His hands spread wide upon my back as he whispered, "The feel of you..."

I stroked his hair, suckling his lower lip with soft insistence, shaken by the force of my love for him, the desire to be this near to him, always and always, sharply contrasted by the fear that coiled inside of me, the essence of my dream crawling forth. I rebelled against any such thoughts, determinedly rocking my hips, flesh overpowering mind. I said, "I want to give you plea-sure...*Sawyer*..."

He bent me gently backwards, bringing his mouth to my breasts as if worshiping at an altar, opening his lips over my flesh and tasting of me, as I sank my fingers into his hair. In time I moved swiftly over him, taking up a steady rhythm, his heart thundering against mine as we moved of one accord. The bedding churned to a pinwheel of material beneath us.

"I have never known such pleasure," he whispered. "The moment I leave your body, I only want to be within you again...and again..."

"Yes," I begged him. "Oh Sawyer, *yes*..."

He took me to my back upon the rumpled blankets, there able to thrust as deeply as possible, and together we tumbled off the edge of the Earth and then further, clinging to each other. Much later, in the quiet, predawn darkness, we drifted slowly back to the unyielding ground, both of us slick with sweat. I hadn't the strength to do more than smile sleepily at him, my eyes closed and my limbs limp with exhaustion.

"Lorie," he murmured, his deep voice tender. "Sleep, sweetheart, I'll hold you. In my arms and in my heart."

Iowa City was a sprawling town situated near the Iowa River, a gleaming expanse over which the sun glinted. Sawyer deemed Juniper fit for travel, and by the noon hour we traversed a wide bridge, one of two leading north into town, to cross the Iowa—Malcolm could hardly resist the temptation to draw Aces to the railing and lean over the bridgeworks, peering into the dark-blue depths far below. The wagon and foot traffic into town was fairly heavy, but we joined Malcolm and spent a few minutes leaning over the railing and marveling, comparing this river to the Mississippi, and Lake Royal back home in Tennessee, speculating how quickly one would be swept downstream in the event of leaping from the bridge. Malcolm exclaimed in dismay as he inadvertently dropped the single penny Boyd had allowed him, which winked in a copper flash as it fell, earning a smack on the back of the skull from his brother.

The town itself, a webbed network of roads, bustled with activity, far beyond what a mid-week day warranted; it did not take more than a minute outside the post office, on a busy downtown avenue, to realize the activity was because of a double hanging that was set to take place in the center of town, come one o'clock this afternoon. Apparently a gallows had been newly constructed for this rare occasion of capital offense.

"Plenty of folks are eager to see these two at the end of a rope, for robbing the stage and shooting a local fella," said the man whom Boyd inquired about the crowds, a self-proclaimed journalist that introduced himself as Horace Parmley. "Idea Wright's the one who shot Ned McGiver. Though I doubt Wright actually *aimed* for McGiver's head. Folks figure poor Ned just moved the wrong direction and caught a fatal bullet in the cheek. Always was an unlucky bastard, God rest him." Parmley interrupted this detailed explanation to tip his hat at me, from where he stood near Sawyer's side of the wagon in the bright sun. His age was perhaps mid-twenties; he wore thick side whiskers and a mustache that entirely obscured his upper lip. Using forefinger and thumb, he fastidiously smoothed it, inviting, "Spectacle's outside the courthouse, an hour past noon, if you folks have a mind to see the show."

"We'll pass an' be on our way, thank you kindly," Boyd replied, a note of dark humor woven into his ironic tone; it was not lost on him that Malcolm's shoulders drooped just a hair, in disappointment, though the boy wisely held his tongue. I supposed that were I a lad of twelve years, a double hanging might stimulate my imagination with a similarly macabre and irresistible fascination.

Not to be so easily dismissed, Parmley said, "Idea Wright wore the gray back in the War and folks around these parts are predisposed to disliking him, on account." He continued, conversationally, "Rebs, even former Rebs, get what they got coming to 'em, is my opinion. Wouldn't you say, fellas?"

There was a beat of strained silence—the journalist, who could not have known with any sort of certainty that he stood in the presence of two former soldiers—did not seem discomfited by the pause. He bore the subtle mien of a man who enjoys any negative stir occasioned by his words. Sawyer shifted position on the seat beside me. He and Boyd, still mounted on Fortune, exchanged a brief glance, conveying depths of information, in the way of longtime friends.

"If you'll excuse us," Sawyer said, jumping nimbly from the wagon and consequently almost into Parmley's space. Sawyer did not appear overtly threatening, and in fact even offered what appeared a pleasant smile, but Parmley, a goodly amount shorter, tipped his hat and was in a sudden flurry to depart.

"Five blocks east, if you change your minds!" he could not seem to resist informing us.

Boyd adjusted his hat and cast a dark glance after the retreating figure. I surmised that if Boyd had been chewing tobacco, rather than inhaling it, he would have spit a plug in the same direction. He muttered, "Goddamn pencil-necked son of a bitch."

Sawyer made a fist and tapped it once, lightly, against Boyd's bent left knee, closest to him as Boyd sat the saddle. He said, "We must expect some of that."

"Don't mean I gotta like it," Boyd grumbled, dismounting in one smooth motion, patting Fortune's neck. He ordered, "Boy, you mind the wagon while—"

"Aw, Boyd, I wanna ride the town, like I done back south," Malcolm interrupted with a wheedling tone, thumbing over his shoulder in the general direction of Keokuk.

"This is a far bigger an' busier place, an' I ain't got time to accompany you," Boyd said, in a voice that brooked absolutely no disagreement. Boyd had woken with a headache and sounded unusually cantankerous as a result; he narrowed his dark eyes at his little brother when Malcolm's mouth opened in what was surely intended to be a protest.

"Here, love," Sawyer murmured, reaching to help me down and simultaneously giving Boyd a moment to regroup; Boyd, however, seemed determined to provoke an argument of some kind. On the opposite side of the wagon, Malcolm's bottom lip protruded in a stubborn half-pout. He was still astride Aces and appeared in no hurry to relent to his older brother's orders.

Though he never sassed Boyd, there was a faint edge in his tone as Malcolm insisted, "I can ride me the town alone."

The very air seemed clogged with tension, visible as a cloud of smoke. Though Sawyer did not seem unduly concerned at the gathering storm between the Carters, I felt this rare animosity only contributed to the vague uneasiness that had plagued me for some time now, and even more strongly since last night, when Ethan Davis's spirit inexplicably visited our tent.

Boyd impatiently cracked his knuckles and said tersely, "You'll do as I say, an' there ain't no two shakes about it, boy. Now, git down from that horse afore I yank you down."

Malcolm posture squared and his jaw bulged, but before he could speak I burst into their exchange, offering, "Why don't you and I walk the avenue, dear one?"

My words had the immediate effect of pacifying Malcolm—some of the angry sparkle fled his eyes, replaced by earnestness. He turned his gaze back to Boyd, clearly asking wordless permission, and though he still radiated ill-temper, Boyd grudgingly nodded. Malcolm dismounted and tied Aces' halter to the hitching post.

"You'll be back shortly," Sawyer said quietly, not so much an order as a need for assurance. He spread his fingers over my ribs, rubbing lightly; my heart hitched on a beat and I stood on tiptoe to get my arms around his neck.

"Of course," I whispered.

"Boyd and I won't be but a few minutes, just yonder," he said. "I need a handful of horseshoe nails, and I mean to find you a journal."

I smiled at this, tugging him down so that I could kiss his chin.

Malcolm came to collect my arm, looping it around his. Having regained his customary cheerful temperament, Malcolm said, "Don't you worry none, Sawyer. Me an' Lorie's gonna be back straightaway."

If only he had been right.

EVERYWHERE WE walked, people spoke of the hanging—men, womenfolk, children running loose as stray dogs. I had grown accustomed to the peace and relative solitude of traveling the prairie and so the cacophony of voices, the clink of wagon chains and passage of hooves over the hard-packed ground, common noises which usually receded into the background, seemed too sharp, absurdly loud within my unsettled mind. If I closed my eyes too long I was unwittingly returned to St. Louis, and Ginny's, where this exact slurry of sound played continually. Display windows caught Malcolm's attention time and again—he was a great one for marveling, and had there not been a cold spot clinging to the back of my neck, I would have been able to better enjoy the sights.

We reached a cross-section of street, pausing to consider in which direction to continue, and my skin crawled as though suddenly inhabited by biting fleas; our position put us catty-corner to a grouping of saloons. A pair of women, heavily rouged, watched the lively action of their town from a storey up, leaning their hips against a decorative finial on the porch railing above an establishment called the Forked Hoof. I was uncomfortable to the point of sickness at the sight of them and the memories they unintentionally provoked, and was about to insist that we return to the wagon when Malcolm tugged my arm and exclaimed, "Kittens!"

I looked where he was pointing, perhaps twenty paces down a side street, and felt a sharp blow land solidly upon my heart; Deirdre sat on an overturned washtub, her dark hair shining with scarlet glints in the sun, smiling as she listened to two little boys. She held three tiny kittens in the hammock of her skirt, stroking their fur. The sun shone in my eyes and I squinted in stunned confusion, belatedly realizing that of course the woman upon whom I gazed was not Deirdre but instead a stranger who resembled her greatly. The sight of the girls who worked in the saloon, coupled with memories of my old friend, sent distress prickling along my scalp.

"What's wrong, Lorie-Lorie?" Malcolm questioned. As usual, despite his brimming energy he was finely tuned to my feelings; he regarded me with somber eyes, gently patting my elbow.

"I'm well," I assured, though I had to force a calm tone. I nodded towards her and explained, "The woman there reminds me a bit of a girl I used to know, that is all."

"Let's say good day!" Malcolm pleaded, not pressing for answers as he would have if older than twelve years. "Might we, Lorie?"

A beat of indecision struck at me, but then I thought of our conversation last night at the riverbank, and nodded allowance.

"But only for a moment's time," I said.

The woman acknowledged us with curious eyes as we approached, further increasing her resemblance to Deirdre; I thought of the way I used to envy my old friend's ability to express excitement and anticipation, even in the midst of life in a whorehouse, and how observing those feelings, even secondarily, gave me comfort. I thought of Deirdre brushing my hair and holding me close in the room of horrors which had been mine at Ginny's, how her friendship had been the only thing to sustain me during those years. I faltered a little, at first letting Malcolm do the talking so that I could catch my breath past the bruising ache in my breastbone.

"Howdy, ma'am, we spied these here kittens," Malcolm explained. The two boys, perhaps ages five and seven, fell silent and watched him with keen-eyed interest; I elbowed Malcolm as discreetly as possible and he swept off his hat, tucking it beneath his left arm. His dark hair was flattened with sweat, and the woman smiled indulgently at him.

"Perhaps you should like to hold one?" she invited. She was about the age Deirdre would be now, had she lived, twenty-five or thereabouts, slim and delicately built, with glinting dark hair pinned into two low rolls on her nape. She was fine-featured, her eyes a lovely, multi-colored hazel, decorated by predominantly brown tones, but rather than the pale, nearly translucent skin that Deirdre had possessed, rarely venturing out of doors, this woman's hands and face were brown with the sun; a sunburned vee of skin was visible on her chest where her collar buttons were undone two past the top in concession to the heat of the day. Whereas my old friend had been ethereal, I sensed that this woman was possessed of an opposite mettle.

"Thank you kindly, ma'am!" Malcolm enthused, accepting a small gray ball of fur; the kitten mewled and Malcolm cuddled it close, murmuring endearments.

"Rebecca Krage," the woman said in introduction, shading her eyes with her left hand and offering her right. Our eyes met and held as we shook, and I felt a knowing pass between us, even without words. In other circumstances, my instinct suggested, we might have grown to be friends. She indicated the boys and added, "And my sons, Cort and Nathaniel."

"I am pleased to meet you, Mrs. Krage," I said. "I am Lorissa Davis, and this is my brother, Malcolm Carter."

"Does the hanging bring you to town?" she asked; as though guilty for taking pleasure in gossiping, she explained immediately, "Excuse my appalling lack of manners. I must confess, I live in a household with no other womenfolk to keep me company." Adopting a conspiratorial tone she said, "My uncle, Edward Tilson, doctors for the town and surrounding areas, so I know everyone hereabouts, and nearly all of their secrets, unpleasant or otherwise. Please, do call me Rebecca."

"We are not here for the hanging. We are bound for Minnesota," I explained, charmed by her. "Sawyer, my husband, and my elder brother Boyd are at the dry-goods store at present. We knew nothing of the hanging but were quite well informed by a man named Parmley."

"Parmley," she repeated, disdain in her tone. "The man is a sore nuisance, that's what. Excuse my speaking so freely, but I have been acquainted with Horace most of my life, and he has not improved greatly with the years. He no doubt relished delivering all the unsavory details."

I found her forthright speech unexpected and admirable—as well as accurate.

"What's this little fella's name?" Malcolm interrupted to ask of the kitten; he was clearly smitten.

"Dear boy, I haven't named a one. Uncle Edward's cat very recently produced this litter and the kittens were promised to households long before they were birthed. There isn't a better way to rid a barn of varmints." Rebecca invited, "Why don't you choose a name for that one? In fact, I would be happy to gift you with the animal, if you've a mind to allow it, Mrs. Davis. No better mouser in the county than its mother."

Malcolm's face was wreathed in sudden hopeful joy, dark eyebrows lifting as his lips fell open. Staving off what was sure to become a begging campaign, I asked, "But aren't all of them promised to other families?"

Rebecca lowered her voice and confessed, "Uncle Edward wanted to keep one for himself, which I shall instead give you. I'll weather his temper, never you fear." She saw my surprise at her words, and said, "I am only teasing. Uncle Edward is soft-hearted as a dove, for all his blustering. He shan't be angered. He is more than able to keep a kitten from the next litter."

"Oh please, Lorie-Lorie?" Malcolm gushed. "*Please?*"

I reached and stroked the small creature, unable to resist. It was soft as a bird's wing, its eyes round and bright, tail sticking straight into the air. I said, "It'll be Boyd who needs convincing, not me." And to Rebecca, "Are you certain?"

"More than certain," she said. "How long shall you be in town? Might I invite you and your menfolk to dinner? Oh, I would be delighted to continue chatting."

"Thank you kindly," I told her, touched at this invitation. "But we've planned to stay no longer than it takes to make purchases."

"Our pa is dead," one of Rebecca's boys, the younger, suddenly told Malcolm.

All of us looked his way at this unexpected pronouncement, Malcolm and I with mild alarm, though Malcolm empathized at once, informing the boy, "My daddy, too. He died three years ago now."

"My pa never come home from the War," the boy explained, and Rebecca's lips twisted. She smoothed a strand of dark hair behind her ear in the manner of someone who does not wish to elaborate on a particular subject.

"My Elijah was one of far too many," she said softly. "I live now with Uncle Edward and my brother, Clint Clemens. Clint is a deputy sheriff, but he'd make a far better schoolteacher, as I've told him too many times to count."

"I am most sorry for your loss," I said.

"But now the marshal is courting Mama," the other boy said, with enthusiasm. "He pays calls whenever he's in town. Uncle Edward says –"

"Heavens, Cort, bite your tongue," Rebecca scolded. "What proclamations."

"Your mouth's as big as mine," Malcolm told Cort, companionably.

"You shall think me impudent, but may I guess your state of origin, the two of you?" Rebecca asked; I sensed she wished to change the subject, forthwith, and did not wait for an answer before saying with certainty, "Tennessee."

"That's correct," I told her, thinking of Charley Rawley's ear for accents. I wagered, "You are not from there yourself—someone you know, perhaps?"

Rebecca said, "Yes, Uncle Edward was born and raised there. He served as a field doctor in the Confederacy for the duration. His wife passed while he was serving and he relocated north to live with my mama, his little sister, after he was mustered out. He didn't realize Mama had also passed during the War."

So many lives claimed by it, whether directly or otherwise, no small amount a result of the starvation and abject poverty in the wake of years of fighting, subjugated soldiers straggling home to places that were often no more than dust and a handful of carefully-guarded sacred memories—well I knew these truths. There could never be an entirely accurate count of the overall death toll.

The sun was well past its noon zenith; Sawyer and Boyd would be expecting us, and even though I had enjoyed conversing with Rebecca Krage, the unease that was determinedly stalking me seemed nearer than ever. I shooed a fly from buzzing near my nose, wishing I could as easily shove aside the sensation of threat; I was barely able to restrain the urge to look over my shoulder. Though it was unreasonable, it seemed to me an inordinate amount of time had passed since I had seen Sawyer.

"I hate to be discourteous, but my brother and I must continue on our way," I said.

Rebecca's eyebrows drew together just slightly, as if a hint of my agitation transferred to her, though she said only, "Well, I must say that I am disappointed you are only in town the day. Take care, the both of you. It was lovely to make your acquaintances!" Winking at Malcolm, she said, "And mind that kitten!"

"Thank you, ma'am, I will," he said dutifully, cuddling the small bundle close.

"Good-day," I said, in haste to be away.

Malcolm scampered beside me, too busy lavishing love on his new pet to notice that I walked at a much brisker pace than usual; Sawyer and Boyd had likely made their intended purchases and were loading the wagon just now. The dry-goods store was only a few blocks west—wasn't it? I fell still, looking this way and that, the crowd swirling together as eggs stirred in a pan, slippery colors mixing and blending. A man with only one leg, his pants trimmed and tied off at mid-thigh to accommodate this misfortune, hobbled past us on crutches, casting a curious glance at the kitten. Sweat slid down my temples.

"Lorie, can't we just peek at them hanging ropes, just take a peek?" Malcolm cajoled, craning his neck for a better view; his voice reached me from a distance, as though he stood on the opposite side of a holler.

"No," I said, as firmly as I could manage. I forced myself to draw a deep breath, to gather my bearings, deciding, however unfairly, that I vehemently despised this busy town. The telegraph office, a small wooden structure, loomed to our right, adjacent to a whitewashed hotel with fancy gold lettering adorning the front window. A dipper rested against the rim of a water bucket being used to prop open a side door of the hotel, perhaps one leading into its kitchen; just down the alleyway beyond the door, tucked behind the building, I could see the very edge of an outhouse.

"Please, I just want me a peek," Malcolm begged, draping the kitten over a shoulder. His earnest eyes pleaded with me. "I reckon it's just yonder, where all them folks is headed. I only aim to see what it looks like, that's all. I ain't ever seen a real hanging rope, or them trapdoors they fall from, in all my livin' life! *Please*, Lorie?"

"*No*," I said decisively, tugging his elbow for emphasis; the hanging would no doubt shortly commence and the idea of him running that way and inadvertently observing two men fall to their deaths made my stomach turn. I told him, "You wait here while I use the necessary, and then we are going to find Sawyer and Boyd and leave this detestable place."

Detestable, I thought, conjuring the familiar image of the thesaurus open over my mother's lap. *Synonyms include: vile, revolting, loathsome, hateful, abominable.*

Malcolm's face registered clear disappointment, though he nodded without another word of protest. But his eyes followed the crowd.

"I'll return directly," I said, and hurried along the alley to the outhouse, determined to stop allowing my imagination to clench me in a chokehold. There was a hand pump around the back corner of the hotel, under which a clump of rangy daisies grew, long-stemmed and thriving beneath the dripping handle, and I bent to splash my face, letting the cool liquid trickle into the collar of my blouse. It felt good and helped somewhat to ease the sense of unreality that hovered too near. My sleeves were rolled back, my skirt limp with the humidity, my booted toes dusty. I drank from my cupped palm and then made haste using the outhouse.

No more than five minutes had passed, perhaps even less, but Malcolm was not in sight when I returned, and dread swooped in with wings spread.

"Malcolm!" I called sharply, earning a few glances, but no one paused to speak to me, or to inquire if I needed assistance. A pulsing jolt of concern nearly took me to my knees, and I shouted, "*Malcolm Carter!*"

He was not within hearing distance, as no response met my ears. Heart gouging a hole into my ribs, I peered frantically at the strangers passing by, hoping beyond reason that Malcolm's familiar freckled face would pop into view and he would apologize for worrying me—and then I would summarily bend him over my knee and apply the nearest convenient switch to his behind.

Surely he had gone to spy the gallows, without permission.

I knew that Sawyer and Boyd would grow increasingly concerned at our continued absence, Sawyer especially, but there was no way in hell that I could return to them without Malcolm in tow. The thought made my stomach clench around a ball of solid ice. I lifted my hem and ran east across the dusty streets, following the crowd, unceremoniously displacing people. More than one voice protested or cursed me, but I cared not a fig.

Bodies were packed elbows to ribs as I neared the town's center square, the site of the hanging—absurdly, the journalist Parmley caught my eye amongst hundreds of others, conversing with another man only a few yards away in the shade afforded by the overhanging rafters of an adjacent business—my gaze flashed upwards, to the hand-lettered sign attached to a rafter, which read G. SCRUGGS, UNDERTAKER.

Jesus, oh Jesus, let me find Malcolm.

Parmley held an open timepiece and used his free hand to tip his hat my direction. I felt my upper lip curl in distaste, immediately turning the other way, standing on tiptoe to peer beyond shoulders and around hats. It was maddening; I could have spat my frustration upon the ground like a bite from an overripe apple, as I vacillated between anger and agonized concern.

"Malcolm!" I shouted again, but my voice was lost in the buzzing of dozens of others in immediate proximity. I implored those I passed, "Have you seen a boy with a kitten?"

Some people eyed me with tepid interest, but most ignored my words, preoccupied with the proceedings atop the gallows. I spared a glance that direction to see two men in dark suits, with dark hats, ascending the narrow wooden staircase, their knees lifting in a similar rhythm as they climbed. The badges on their vests refracted the sunlight; these were not the prisoners, then, but instead the law. A third man, a few steps behind them, followed carrying two black hoods, currently limp in his grasp; shortly they would encase the heads of the condemned, blocking out their earthly last sight—that of a teeming crowd, comprised of men, women, and dozens of youngsters, assembled on the street to witness their necks break.

A rank horror enveloped my senses.

What sort of people are we? I thought, sickened. I spun away, blindly, and would not have noticed the marshal if he hadn't stepped directly into my path; I skidded to a halt to avoid crashing into the man, the five-pointed star attached to his black vest just inches from my nose. The sun glinted from its polished surface and I blinked, and then blinked again, slowly, my eyes lifting to his face.

"Mr. Yancy," I said in confusion, startled by his appearance here, when we'd left him far behind at the Rawleys' farm.

"Mrs. Davis," he returned in what should have been polite acknowledgment of our acquaintance; something in his tone was just slightly off, which I could sense if not articulate. He added, "This is a rare piece of luck, if I do say so."

Before I could guess what he meant by those words, a second man appeared beside him.

N o," I BREATHED, and faltered, my vision blurring as completely as if I'd just submerged my open eyes beneath muddy creek water. Yancy reached and appropriated my elbow as I tried desperately to reconcile what I knew to be true with what was happening.

Union Jack stood before me.

The man Sawyer had shot at close range with his Winchester and left for dead upon the northern Missouri prairie.

"Lila," Jack greeted almost gaily, his eyes gleaming with triumph, the satisfaction of witnessing my staggering disbelief. "You look like you seen a ghost, girlie."

He was a small, gnarled, bearded man, surely not as old as his appearance suggested. His skin was the brown of well-used leather and just as textured; when last in his company, I had been a prisoner, and had lost a child literally before the eyes of he and his companions, Sam Rainey and the man known as Dixon. Back in St. Louis, Jack had long frequented Ginny's place and was someone I knew from my time at the whorehouse, though he had never been a customer of mine.

He was supposed to be dead, I could not conceive of any other truth, and I read the play of thoughts across his mind as clearly as though he'd written them with chalk pencil upon a slate; he was delighted to observe my speechless, swelling distress at the sight of him, and what it could potentially mean to me—and to Sawyer—

You have to find Sawyer before they do, Lorie, oh Jesus . . .

Yancy's grip remained clenched around my elbow, for all the world as though he was politely assisting me; from all outward appearances, I was simply a woman overcome by the event of a double hanging and he was acting the gentleman. I jerked free of his fist, my gut full of ice shards, my face stiff and bloodless, and moved around them with determination. When Yancy clamped hold again, he drew me immediately closer, without drama, bringing his mouth to my ear, the better to impress upon me the seriousness of his question. In the hubbub of the excited crowd, no one paid us particular attention.

"Has Billings approached you?" he demanded, low, his voice conveying distinct menace, as I clearly discerned. I could smell the strong scents of him, sweat and hair tonic, which were at once too close to my face, foreign to my nostrils and simultaneously nauseating; his fingers were hard, his mustache brushing the top of my left ear as he quietly insisted, "Tell me."

Though I did not recognize the name he had spoken, I whispered quite truthfully, "No."

Yancy asked next, "Where is your husband? Where is Davis?"

My vision narrowed but I refused to lose focus now. Sweat erupted all along my skin. I kept my voice steady with effort and said, "He is not here."

"That is a bald lie," Yancy said, and my spine ached at his tone. "I do not suffer lying women."

Jack stood in my immediate line of sight, watching raptly from beneath the brim of his hat. My fingernails scraped over my palms, grinding into the flesh there, fists clenched with the desperate desire to strike out at the both of them, knowing I could not; so swiftly I had been rendered helpless.

"Tell me," Yancy said once more.

"Let me go," I said, gritting my teeth without realizing.

Yancy's fingers tightened. Absurdly, his mustache tickled my ear as he leaned an inch closer and murmured, "You will come with me. You will not make a scene. I would take great pleasure in shooting your husband like a bitch hound, do you hear me? Come with me, now."

As we walked, edging around those assembled, in the opposite direction from the gallows, an image of a wooden puppet overtook my mind—I felt as though I resembled one of these, my knees jerking my feet unwittingly forward, clumsy with Yancy's unyielding grip upon my arm. Voices trailed over my head like unwelcome fingers, snarling into my hair and obscuring my vision, but these receded as we left the crowd behind. I did not understand where we were bound until we cleared the masses of people and Yancy angled towards the local sheriff's office, which Malcolm and I had passed earlier, on our walk; my eyes swept the street, searching for any sign of the boy, any sign of Sawyer, or Boyd…

But there was no one.

Once at the small wooden building, Yancy released my arm to produce a key, which he used to unlock the door. Jack stepped close to my left side, clearly intending to impede any attempt I might have made to escape. Yancy ushered the three of us within the space, occupied by nothing more than the dust motes that drifted lazily in the single sunbeam slicing into the room through the south-facing window, its view impeded by iron slats. There was a desk, its surface containing a kerosene lamp and a leather-bound ledger, two ladder-backed chairs and two prisoner cells, both currently empty.

Keen-edged fear sharpened my senses—my blood trickled like heated metal as it moved along the paths in my body; Yancy's voice in the quiet room caused me to startle. He said, "Billings and Clemens are at the hanging. They've their plates full with local business, and won't have received word of Davis, nor seen us."

"That bastard Davis ain't far, I'm certain, not if this one's here," Jack said, indicating me with a tilt of his chin before dropping his sorry bones atop the nearest chair. He was dirty, his trousers stained by food and travel, and simple hard living, small eyes red-rimmed beneath his hat. Like Yancy, he wore a pistol strapped into a worn leather cross-halter on his scrawny hips, and sat nervously, eyes leaping about the space, from Yancy to me, to the window and back again, in an endless loop.

Yancy remained coolly standing, by contrast, and went to peer out the single pane at the dusty, unoccupied street—all of the residents were gathered for the hanging. I eyed the thick wooden door which had thumped closed behind us and wondered how far I could manage to run if I bolted outside, before they overtook me.

As though sensing the intention, Yancy turned to study me from a distance of perhaps a dozen feet, nearly the length of the room.

"Your husband is a wanted man in Missouri, *Mrs.* Davis," he said, with a deceptively conversational tone; the emphasis on the title confirming my married status suggested insult. "He is a fugitive from the law."

"No," I contradicted at once.

"I assure you I am speaking the truth," Yancy said, offering a smile. Though it was a false smile, as none of it reached his eyes—despite carrying himself like a gentleman, a man of the law, he exuded pure, calculated intimidation. He elaborated, "Sawyer James Davis, formerly of the Army of Tennessee, is wanted for the murder of one Samuel Rainey, of Missouri, and one Gerald Dixon, also of Missouri." The formal words were tinged with unmistakable notes of triumph.

I found the wherewithal to keep my gaze upon Yancy's. Fear stalked my face—this could not be helped; Yancy only continued smiling, just slightly. I had not an inkling of a notion how to respond—Sawyer had indeed killed both of those men, to save my life. Sam and Dixon had been criminals a hundred times over, Sam a known murderer of women, and yet in the eyes of the law, bound to blindness, I realized that Sawyer could be found guilty for dispatching them, however deservedly, from life.

A world in which this possibility existed—*only this morning, this very morning, I had been secure in his arms*—became sharply altered, growing murky and unreal all about my body; I felt a shift in my gut, a flicker of the old, familiar feeling that had encased me in its sticky skeins, without relief, at the whorehouse, the taste of despair rippling over my tongue.

No. No, oh please, no.

This cannot be.

I studied Yancy, wordless for the time being, and knew that I would do whatever required of me to prevent him, or Jack, from finding Sawyer here in this town. I would risk my own life a thousand times over before letting them have at him.

Sawyer would never let you do any such thing to save him, you understand this.

I did, but my resolve did not waver.

Yancy returned my gaze with the intensity of a predator, but even when the air around me narrowed to slim, dark tunnels, I kept my eyes steady.

Jack smirked, "Lucky little whore to find yourself a husband, Lila," and that particular word was enough to draw my attention to him, unwittingly; agony and nausea buzzed as hornets ensnared within my skull, but I could not let them see that the use of this hateful name so affected me. And it was imperative that I learn their exact objective.

"My husband is not here," I said, wishing my voice had emerged with more strength. My thoughts darted this way and that, wildly, as deer from a hunter.

They will go after Sawyer—and he will be looking for you at any moment—
He could be found guilty by a judge—they could hang him—
They have evidence, they believe they have cause –
Oh God…

Jack snorted and scoffed, emphasizing the words, "*Your husband* left me for dead and he's here now, I'd stake my claim on that, you lying whore." His face took on a maroon cast, anger bubbling to the surface of his skin as he said, "He shot clean through my side, after I done my best to help you. Smashed Dixon's skull into goddamn pulp. Stabbed Sam's eye out."

"*I* stabbed him," I interrupted, too overcome with fury to hold my tongue. I seethed, "You bastard, you *son of a bitch*—"

Yancy appeared mildly stunned at this pronouncement, though he quickly concealed any such crack in the foundation of his composure. He said, instead, "It was good fortune, running across your party at Charley Rawley's place, getting such a fine glimpse of each of you. Of course, I did not then possess the information that I do at this moment. Just over a week later I received a wire from Marshal Nelson Dobbs, on circuit in Hannibal, having taken the testimony of this man," and Yancy nodded at Jack, who shifted on his seat and was eager to pick up the tale.

"Your Reb husband left me for dead," Jack repeated, and I wished with all of my heart that he was truly dead. He elaborated, "Wasn't until a day later that I come to, with a goddamn buzzard tugging at my hair, and found Sam and Dixon, poor bastards. Ain't a sign of horseflesh on the horizon. Goddamn Reb stole 'em."

"He did no such thing!" I raged at Jack. "*You* stole *me*. Dixon shot and killed Angus Warfield and then the three of you took me forcibly from his company." I directed my fury at Yancy. "You are the law! *This* man is the criminal, not my husband!"

Yancy was gallingly unmoved. Instead of replying, he blinked. A picture of his eldest son, Fallon, entered into my mind, the boy with empty eyes. Yancy's eyes were also light in color, and likewise conniving. Determining the best course of action to improve his position.

"That's *real* devoted, Lila," Jack commented, when Yancy did not reply. Jack taunted, "Ginny'll get you back in the end, just you wait. You was the most prized whore she ever had and she aims to put you back to work. 'Course, she ain't too pleased that her brother was murdered and left to rot under the sun."

"How did you find us?" I whispered, my heart a razor, my ribs its strop. I knew I must accept what was happening; I knew I must focus.

Yancy said, "Charley Rawley kindly let me know that Iowa City was on your route. Just so happens I routinely visit this town in my marshal's circuit, along with Marshal Leverett Quade. Jack and I only just arrived here ourselves, and Quade is not far behind, west while I was south. Mark my words, I would have caught you on the trail, had you passed by. It's another piece of fine fortune that you were kind enough to present yourself to me this day."

"What do you want?" I whispered.

"Does Davis know that you're a whore?" Yancy asked, his tone a mingling of amusement and true curiosity. Before I could respond, he mused, "Seems a fitting combination, a Reb and a whore."

I swallowed away the furious words I longed to speak, my hands balled in fists. I repeated, "What do you want?"

Yancy shifted position, smoothing the tips of his fingers over the pistol in his cross-holster. Looking straight into my eyes, he said, "To see Davis hang." Abruptly he ceased all contact with the pistol and swiped a thumb over his mustache. Still eyeing me, he said, with speculation in his tone, "Though you may impede that." He narrowed his eyes and mused, "I'd not figured as such."

Jack ran his knuckles briskly over the tops of his thighs, as though to scrub at an itch, and complained, "This one's worth cash money, back in Missouri. I ain't letting you kill her before I get my share of it from Ginny."

Yancy sent a look of scalding disgust at Jack and said, "You haven't the sense of a polecat. You realize this here whore can testify against you, don't you?"

Jack shifted restlessly, regarding me with a new sense of distrust. His voice rasped in the manner of a saw blade over fresh-cut wood as he said, "Ain't nobody gonna believe the testimony of a goddamn whore. Whores lie as plain as the nose on their faces. I aim to bring her to Missouri. Ginny's right eager to get Lila back. She'll line my pocket."

You are not Lila. You will never be Lila again.

There is no way Jack can force you back to Missouri, back to Ginny.

You will never be Lila again...

And yet, no matter how I willed it to be untrue, Lila would always be part of me—dark, twisted, vulnerable to the insidious onslaught of three years' worth of memories. What recourse would I possibly have if Jack was unrelenting?

You thought before that Sawyer deserves better than a former whore.

No—he does not believe this—he sees beyond what you were.

I pictured Sawyer's eyes, the blending of golden and green in their depths, drawing thusly upon a reserve of strength. I said as calmly as I could manage, "You will not hang Sawyer, and I will *never* return to Missouri."

"You will if I say," Jack insisted, thrusting his chin my direction.

"That I will *not*," I whispered, nearly choking on the bitterness of rage. I glared at Jack with unrelieved abhorrence.

"Perhaps, rather, you'd enjoy watching Davis hang this *very afternoon.* The gallows will accommodate another Reb bastard before the afternoon's washed away, I'd say," Yancy said, and my gaze leaped at once to him.

I sensed he was bluffing and challenged, with no small amount of asperity, "You cannot hang a man without a conviction."

Yancy glared blackly, as though encountering a specimen with which he was unfamiliar—and perhaps he truly was unused to a woman who contradicted his words; the sudden, odd glittering in his eyes suggested there was truth to this presumption. Still, he would not allow me to discompose him. He said levelly, "All I need is a wire from the circuit judge, which can be swiftly arranged. Or perhaps you would prefer witnessing what a bullet aimed *just so* will do to a man. Resisting arrest requires no conviction and achieves the intended result much more quickly, truth be told."

I heard the crackling of the fire beneath me, as an animal rotating upon a spit. Metaphorically cornered, I whispered, "Why do you bear us such animosity?"

Yancy studied me in silence for the space of a heartbeat, finally muttering, "For a whore, you *are* somewhat perceptive." He concluded, "You mean something to that Johnny Reb bastard, of this I am certain. Perhaps for even more than what's between your legs." He angled Jack another look of scarcely-concealed contempt, and said, "I've a new plan, just conjured up. I'm doing you far more of a favor than you'd realize, Barrow."

"How you figure?" Jack asked grimly.

"I know you aimed to bring this whore back to Missouri, but she's a danger to you. She'll speak out against you, her and Davis, both." Yancy studied Jack as though attempting to impart upon the scrawny man a further sense of the situation; it was a monumentally worthless effort. Realizing this as well, Yancy released a frustrated breath through his nose and instead directed his next words at me, "You will accompany us. No words, no struggling, and we leave now. Let Davis wonder what became of his whore wife. Let him think you abandoned him for the next peckerwood that happened along. Marshal Quade'll be this way before dawn, I'd stake my goddamn claim. He can bring in your Reb husband and I'll watch him hang, regardless. Wondering all the while what happened to his little *wife*." Yancy aimed his words as small darts, explaining with mocking humor in his voice, "It is an agony, not knowing. Questioning what actually became of someone. Davis won't know if you were killed…or if you left him to fuck another man…"

Blood flowed from my skull—I could feel its downward progression in my body. But then my heart was dealt a sudden fierce blow, leaving splinters like small pikes in its wake.

Lorie! Where are you?

Where are you?!

A rush of breath escaped before I could prevent any such weakness from emerging. I dug both fists into my stomach, working hard not to bend forward, as though to center and therefore contain the anguish.

Sawyer's voice, riddled with desperate concern, called to me in my mind. It took everything I had, hurt my very bones, to refrain from responding to him. Instantly I hardened my thoughts against any such wayward contact. If I called back he would know where to find me, and then Yancy would apprehend him.

And I would give my life to prevent that.

My lips were nearly too numb to form words as I whispered my inescapable assent, "I will come with you."

THE WIDE BRIDGE, which I had crossed into Iowa City only this morning, then choked with wagons and foot traffic, bore not a soul upon its wooden length now, complacent by contrast in the mellow afternoon light. I thought, absurdly, of Malcolm's lost penny, which had disappeared with scarcely a splash beneath the river's surface. I rode south this time, away from the town, looking desperately back as it receded into the distance. My thoughts were so tightly corralled that my temples ached with sharp pain, images striking me rapidly now. Sawyer was frantic—Malcolm had returned to them, as I could plainly sense; their combined agony served to stab through flesh and bone, plunging directly into my heart.

I could not ease this pain, for them or myself, I could not offer reassurance, because Sawyer would know where to follow. Lumps of stone settled behind my breastbone, heavy as death, as I imagined Whistler's galloping hooves striking the earth as Sawyer rode her in pursuit, closing the hateful distance between us. The intensity of my yearning for this burned away all else, momentarily overpowering me, so my vision hazed and my palms grew slick, imperiling my hold on the reins of the dark pony with white blaze markings adorning his nose which they had procured for me to ride. I was placed strategically between the two men, Yancy in the lead, Jack a dozen paces to the rear.

"Keep up!" Yancy ordered, shifting his hips and taking his gelding into a canter as we cleared the bridge and came upon the open prairie south of town, which I so naïvely believed, only hours ago, I would never traverse again; at this moment I should have been northbound upon the wagon seat beside Sawyer, or Malcolm, while Boyd rode near, the four of us commenting on the beauty of the approaching evening, discussing the day's events in Iowa City. Sawyer's arm would be around me…holding me close to him…and all would be right in the world.

A high-pitched keening, the sound of a teakettle at full steam, of a person past all limits of endurance, rose from my soul. I saw Sawyer in the strange, wavering eye of my mind; despite the illogic of it, I knew this vision was real, a sensing within my abilities but beyond my control. He had Malcolm by the upper arms, yelling at the boy, demanding to know what had happened; Sawyer was wild with fear, his voice strained and frantic.

I could not bear this anguish, and yet I would. I must.

Malcolm's freckled face was miserable with tears as he choked out his fervent response, *I don't know where Lorie-Lorie is…Sawyer, I swear I don't know…*

The tiny gray kitten remained draped over his shoulder.

Sawyer released his hold upon Malcolm and turned away in a panic, blind and desperate. All of this was my fault; there was no denying, as much as I wished otherwise. Jack had come for me, and none other, back in Missouri, at Ginny's wishes, creating a series of events that led to Gus's death—Gus had been doomed to ill luck from the moment he took me from Ginny's place. And now I had endangered them again, these men who wanted only to complete the journey to Minnesota, where we would have homesteaded—where Sawyer and I would have begun our family. I bent forward over the pony's sleek, shiny-dark head, resting my face against the scent of horseflesh, my sobs lost in the wind of our passage away from Iowa City, away from the life that I had been foolish enough to believe would be mine.

I SAT in stiff silence at their fire, with no inkling what Yancy's plan for me entailed; I refused to ask. I would not have remained near them, I would have chosen to lie apart, to avoid all sight of their faces, but I was tethered like an animal, bound by a length of rope secured painfully about my ankles. To my right, Yancy unknotted a handkerchief and ate the sausage in a roll contained therein, with apparent relish, ignoring me completely. Jack intermittently sipped from a flask and gnawed a piece of jerky, gazing into the fire as though it contained a message he must decipher. Yancy allowed me water and a piece of hardtack, tossing it on my lap, into the hammock of my wilted skirt; it crumbled in my fingers. I ate it with all of the joy of someone consuming hot ashes, the crumbs bitter on my dry tongue.

Oddly, I did not overtly fear that either of them would attempt to force me into the act of sex; Jack was too nervous and jittery this night, and I further considered that despite numerous opportunities, he had never purchased my services at Ginny's. Though I felt Yancy's gaze rake over my breasts and hips a time or two, I sensed he was too businesslike to attempt to force himself upon a woman in his "custody"—even a former whore, certainly lesser in his eyes than a woman who had never been so employed. The knowledge that I would be safe from that sort of brutality did not in any way diminish my loathing of them, but it offered a shard of comfort, as did what I had spied earlier.

There was a knife in Yancy's right boot.

I noticed the tip of the protruding hilt as we rode hard miles south over the course of the long July evening. In addition to this weaponry he carried a .44 pistol, similar to Sawyer's Colt, and a repeating rifle in a saddle scabbard; Jack was similarly armed. I kept my eyes from the knife just now, unwittingly close to Yancy, the rope hobbling my ankles a bristly discomfort against the bare skin of my calves. This evening's ride had not chafed my flesh too badly, as I'd been able to tuck my skirt as meager protection; when I was Sam Rainey's prisoner, my wrists had been bound, even less attention paid to my state of wellbeing.

At the moment I sat quietly, damp with fearful sweat; the sour smell rose from my clothing and beat at my nose. So different was this fire than that to which I had grown so happily accustomed, the fire where I longed with my entire soul to be this night—tucked near Sawyer, listening with joy to Malcolm's chatter, and Boyd's jokes, the four of us watching the stars rise. Tonight the moon was waning, its face grim and cold. Pain wrenched my heart, leaving weakness in its wake, and aching despair, which would swallow me whole if I allowed it—and I could not allow it yet. Yancy's words plagued me—his calm assurance that another marshal would apprehend Sawyer sooner than later.

They are going to kill you, Lorie, my mind intruded, whispering with a rattle as of dead leaves. *You must realize this. You are unable to prevent a thing.*

I hardened my thoughts against what was surely the truth and instead entertained a picture in my mind of slipping to Yancy's side as he slept and sneaking the knife from his possession; a part of me realized that even imagining such a thing was a wasted endeavor, a study in the vain, but I clung to the thought regardless, pretending that perhaps I would be fortunate, that Yancy slept soundly. Clinging to this hope of escape assisted me in utilizing every dram of willpower in my possession to stop from reaching out to Sawyer. He, Boyd, and Malcolm remained in Iowa City, searching the town for any word, of this I was certain, and Sawyer's pain was equal only to my own. My heart had shrunk, wrinkled upon itself into a small, tight knot of self-preservation as I battled my deepest instinct, that of the desire to reach out to him in my mind; even still, his voice breached my defenses.

Lorie, where are you?

I know you hear me!

So plainly could I sense his tortured words, his anguish, that I brought both hands to my face, squeezing brutally against my temples, displacing the sounds, the images.

You cannot call out to him, Lorie. You cannot.

You cannot.

Think of the knife…

Think of cutting loose these bindings…

My gaze flickered to the blade, without my intending; Yancy removed it to slice a chunk of hard cheese, just earlier, and it lay now on the ground near his hip.

Look away—quickly—

Before I could obey my own order, Yancy invited, "Take it." With effort, I kept my gaze lowered, angling it back to the fire; my heart thrust in fright. He said, low, "Go on," the challenge in his voice laced with taunting. Jack looked our way with a certain amount of interest.

Yancy caught up the knife and held it directly beneath my nose, mere inches away, offering it hilt first, in a mockery of politeness. The contents of my stomach, meager though it was, curdled. The old scar on my face, where Sam Rainey's blade once sliced a jagged line, seemed to burn; only for a second, less than that, did I envision the lunacy of curling the proffered weapon into my grip and stabbing at whichever part of him I could manage to strike. Instead, I kept my eyes upon the flames. Yancy's face loomed to my right and I could not restrain a sharp gasp. The smell of my fear was more potent than ever. He touched the hilt to my cheek and I closed my eyes. He forced the handle inward until I could feel it making contact with the sides of my teeth;

I sat unmoving, the firelight burning upon the backs of my eyelids with a nightmarish flicker.

"Take it," he said again, his voice rough. "Take a stab at me, you pretty little *whore*, and see what happens."

No, I tried to say, but the word seemed stitched into the flesh of my throat.

The pressure was removed from my face, but I did not open my eyes. Just before Yancy continued speaking, I knew, somehow, the essence of what he was about to say. The memory of the night Sawyer and Boyd constructed wooden crosses for Angus and the child stirred within my mind; later, just before the dawn, Sawyer told me a story...

Yancy's spoke only inches from my face. I imagined how close he was leaning; I could smell his stale breath as he said, "Funny thing is, Corbin pulled that saber off a dead Reb soldier. Would have killed Davis with a Confederate blade if he'd leaned forward in the saddle just a cunt hair farther."

Everything within me went still as a corpse, dreading what I was about to hear.

"Goddamn Reb dragged Corbin from horseback and stabbed him," Yancy continued, low and yet somehow gaining momentum. "A half-dozen times, maybe more. I still recall that moment as though it was yesterday. It will be with me until the day I die. I served with Corbin in the Fifty-First. He was my elder brother, my *blood*, for Christ's sake. And Davis butchered him like a hog."

I opened my eyes and the fire's light was too intense, as though my face was being forced into its heat. I squinted at the sudden brightness, my mind galloping as would a spooked horse, attempting to process Yancy's revelation. Sawyer had not a hope of realizing Yancy's personal stake in all of this; he had no way of knowing I was with Yancy now, or that Jack remained alive. Yancy's animosity at the Rawleys' homestead—he had recognized Whistler the instant he saw her in the corral, the very horse he had once attempted to steal—made sense now. Beyond the fire, where our three mounts were staked out for the night, the pony I had ridden all afternoon and into the evening gave a low, snorting whicker.

"Thief," I said, without intending it, and could have bitten out my tongue.

"Come again?" Yancy responded in a hiss, crouched close to my side, the knife still backwards in his grasp. Neither he nor Jack had removed their hats, leaving their eyes in shadow while the lower halves of their faces were cast in scarlet by the flames.

"You are a lawman, and you were a soldier then," I said, speaking around a husk. But I wanted him to know that his words did not have absolute power over me, and forced myself to look at him. The fire lit flames in his pupils. I whispered, "And yet you've stolen horses."

"I've done no such thing." He spoke through clenched teeth.

"You attempted to steal horses from the clearing outside Chattanooga, in the days after the Surrender," I insisted; I was foolish to assume that anything I said would alter his point of view, make him question his culpability. Jack angled his body away from the fire to spat, and then fixed his eyes on my face. I maintained, "You came upon them in the dark of night and would have stolen their mounts. And when they resisted, you and your men attempted to kill them."

"Listen to Lila paint a picture," Jack said, hiccupping a laugh. He belched and laughed again, then drew a long pull from his flask.

Yancy's upper lip curled, as though unconsciously, but he regained control of his emotions, however tentative. Refusing to confirm or deny, he said, "Nothing changes the fact that your husband is a murdering wretch, and I aim to see him hang. I would have taken great pleasure in shooting him dead this very afternoon, as I told you, but I believe this will be more entertaining in the end. No more chance for suffering, once dead."

"He killed them to save me," I whispered, pleading now. My heart felt raw as a gaping wound. Nothing I said would be sufficient to persuade Yancy or Jack from their unanimous mindset. Sawyer was their enemy, flesh and blood, the three of them horribly connected by the undead past. By a War that refused to stay buried, that had perhaps never truly been put to rest at all. More than three years had passed, but surely decades from now the old hatreds would yet boil, requiring only the smallest provocation for ancient recriminations to flare, straightaway burning any good sense that had sprung up in the wake of the conflict.

Yancy studied me, unblinking, and I dared to hope—but then he dashed all such, confirming my initial inkling, that of wishing us only harm, as he said softly, "I hope he thinks you left him for another fella that came along."

I whispered, "Sawyer would never believe that."

Unmoved, Yancy returned the knife to its sheath in his boot, saying, "Don't be too certain of that."

Jack belched again and muttered his agreement, "After all, whores'll be whores."

THE EMBERS burned to a dull glow; I lay in bitter sleeplessness, wrists now bound in addition to my ankles. Jack snored lightly and I had just enough reach to tug the single blanket I had been given around my ears, in attempt to simultaneously muffle the sound and collect close my faint warmth. I fantasized briefly about crawling on my belly to Jack's side and winding the blanket about his face, assuming I possessed the physical strength to smother him before he could fight me away.

You should be dead, you bastard, I thought viciously, aiming my black thoughts Jack's way. *You should be dead.*

The waning moon hung low on the western horizon and I rolled that direction to study its pale face. In my current state of mind, it bore a maddeningly smug countenance, cast in partial shadow by its brighter cousin, reproaching me with a vengeful, unwavering gaze.

I hate you, I thought, inane with irrationality, screaming the words in my mind. *You've watched me every night of my life, always silent. You watched the War unfold beneath you. All that suffering, years' worth. You care nothing for anyone. Fall from the sky and crash to the earth. Burn to pieces and see who here would care for your fate!*

My skull ached with the pain of blocking out Sawyer's voice. The minutes ticked away with increasing agony—he was miles from me, stalemated in Iowa City, floundering with the lack of any clues left to him. There was no appreciable reason for my disappearance and I knew my sweet Malcolm was wracked with guilt for having disobeyed me, when in truth his minor rebellion had likely saved Sawyer from Yancy's grasp. If I had not alone blundered into Yancy at the hanging, he would have found the four of us shortly thereafter, and Sawyer would be currently in his custody. Had that occurred, I would be even more helpless than I was at this moment. Yancy apprehending me instead bought a few days, at the very least.

Lorie, answer me, I suddenly heard Sawyer whisper, his determination destroying my defenses, the strength of his plea driving into my mind. Surely if

I turned the other way, he would be there; my heart felt clamped between the two halves of a hot iron. I closed my eyes on the moon and was subsequently pelted with an image of him, kneeling on the prairie and clasping his hands, as one praying. Each breath I took became a struggle. I curled inward around my belly.

It's the strength of what binds us, I had said, back in Missouri, the night he saved me from sure death at the strangling hands of the man called Dixon.

It's stronger than anything I have ever known, he had said in return.

I knew if I called to Sawyer, he would find me. He would come to me.

Tell me where you are, he whispered now, tears streaming his face in the glow of the hateful moon. *Please, darlin', please answer. I feel like I am dying and I do not know where you are.*

I clenched my teeth, his quiet desperation scouring me as would knife points.

Lorie...

I released a strangled gasp before I could stop the sound. I could not risk calling back to him, not even in my thoughts.

Behind me, Yancy shifted, also awake. His footfalls were nearly silent as he strode perhaps a dozen paces away to make water, the sound unmistakable. I covered my ears, revulsion and hatred grappling for the upper hand. When he returned to his blankets with a grunt, I had a question for him.

"Why not at the Rawleys' farm?"

Because I was facing away, my whispered words startled him; he took a moment to reply, and I thought perhaps he had not understood the nature of what I was asking, but at last he explained in a low voice, "My boys. I wanted to slip into your tent and slit Davis's worthless throat that very night. I even doubled back and watched it for a spell in the moonlight, after everyone was asleep, considering. I came so goddamn close to killing you both. But in the end I couldn't jeopardize my boys that way. If I got carted to jail they'd starve. They haven't anyone else, for Christ's sake, and if they passed, there would be no Yancys alive but for me. Not a soul to carry on our family name. I don't intend to leave them alone for more than a week or two."

He grunted, as I sat in cold stupefaction at his words, and then said, "And I've enough sense to realize I couldn't pin Corbin's murder on Davis. It would be my word against his, and Davis has a witness in that fiddle-playing son of a bitch." Yancy paused briefly, before concluding, "But now I do believe that God is giving me a second chance, putting you and your murdering Reb husband into my path. It's Providence, I tell you, goddamn Providence. Davis was gracious enough to kill two more men in cold blood and is now a fugitive in my territory. Of course I volunteered to apprehend him." He laughed, low and with little humor, commenting, "Still riding that very same paint mare, I'll be *damned*. And now I'm in possession of his wife. Jesus, life's a funny thing."

"Please," I begged, hoarse with desperation. "Please understand. Sawyer killed them to save me. Sam Rainey meant me nothing but harm. Dixon would have—"

"Save your breath," Yancy interrupted. "Your words aren't worth a goddamn brass farthing to me. Jack can ride you back to St. Louis and claim his prize from the Hossiter woman once he testifies against Davis. She sounds a rather rough character, but nonetheless one who pays in gold. Or he can ride you all the way to Old Mexico, for all I have an interest in it." He let these words sink into my skin before saying, "Jack wanted to trade Davis to a man I served with, Zeb Crawford, lives not a dozen miles from my homestead. Zeb offered us gold, no less, which is tempting, I'll admit. We spoke of it not two nights past. And you know what Zeb had planned for a murdering Reb?"

I rolled his way, unwillingly, rising clumsily to one elbow, a chill of sweat erupting as slick moisture along my hairline and down my nape. Yancy sat with one leg bent, watching me. When I didn't respond, he answered his own cruel query. "Zeb aimed to burn him alive, that's what. I don't usually condone such barbarism, but Zeb's a changed man since the War. Lost all four of his boys to battle. Claims a band of Rebs pinned down his two eldest sons in a shanty cabin and set fire to it, not long after Shiloh. He's rabid as a hound. S'pose he'll have to be satisfied watching Davis hang."

I heard Fannie Rawley's voice saying, *To this day I am not certain if that was a tall tale.*

Jack spoke up from behind me, his voice dry, as one who is recently disturbed from sleep, muttering, "Zeb'll be angered that we ain't got the Reb. And he ain't gonna like being stuck with this here whore."

Yancy made a dismissive sound and replied, "His anger is hardly my concern." He ran a thumb over his mustache and mused, as though thinking aloud, "Though there mighta been a bit of satisfaction in watching a Reb burn like a heretic in the days of old."

My lips were too numb to respond. Yancy could have been bluffing, terrifying me with lies for the sport of it, but I believed his every word. I was weak with the knowledge of what Sawyer may have faced, were he here with Yancy—who was to say that Yancy would not have changed his vengeful, fickle mind and allowed Jack to trade Sawyer to this Zeb Crawford? And what had Jack meant, *stuck with this here whore?*

Sounding more fully awake, Jack repeated, "He'll be angered. He'll want to burn up Lila, in exchange. And she's worth money to me, goddammit."

"As you've mentioned without let-up," Yancy said irritably, as I sat with a hollow gut. "Zeb will keep this whore outta sight until after Davis hangs. He owes me a favor or two. Then she's no longer my concern."

"Davis shot me. I still ache across my goddamn guts. I aimed to see him burn," Jack complained, with a tone of petulant irritation.

"We never agreed to the burning," Yancy said, studying Jack with hard eyes. "You take orders from me, not the other way around."

"What's it matter how the bastard dies, long as he's dead?" Jack fired back.

"Because *I* would have to answer for his disappearance, that's why. He's a wanted man," Yancy said acidly. "A shooting, a hanging, I can justify in the eyes of the law."

Jack's mouth distorted into a sneer but he abandoned the argument, turning his back on Yancy and me with a snort of disgust.

"We'll see Davis dead one way or another, sooner than later," Yancy said to Jack's now-prostrate form. "Think on how he's suffering just now, to have his little whore wife gone with no word."

Jack grunted.

Yancy stretched to his full length, turning away and scraping close his single blanket. He muttered, "You think on that, too, whore."

DUSK HAD COME, crowding against the window in the sheriff's office in a way that reminded me of a smothering hand.

"I will not leave this room until you agree to search every building in town again," I said to the lawman, Billings, for the second time, speaking through my teeth. With only the slightest provocation, I felt capable of ripping the sheriff limb from limb.

"I haven't the manpower to do such a thing," Billings said, clinging by only a slim margin to his composure. He bore unflinching eyes with deep strain lines between them and wanted me gone from this space, I understood plainly, but that would not happen. Not when Lorie was missing. If I had to kick down each and every door in this horseshit fucking town, I would.

"Then find more men," I demanded. My sanity seemed to evaporate more with each hammer of my heart. I was in terror, had been so since Malcolm returned to us with the news that he could not find Lorie, only hours ago. Time seemed suspended in molasses, each moment sickeningly slow and allowing for no forward progress, in the way of a nightmare. I relied now upon the mentality I learned to adopt as a soldier. If I kept moving, remained focused, I would not lose all control.

The sheriff and his deputy, a hesitant man named Clemens, were difficult to track down, both occupied with this afternoon's double hanging, and neither had proven helpful. I recalled Malcolm appearing from the crowd just earlier this afternoon, breathless and hampered by this, bending forward at the waist. A foreboding lingered in the back of my mind and exploded as would a deadly shell even before Malcolm gasped, "I can't...find Lorie..."

And hours later I knew nothing more than I had then, when the ground fell away from under my boots and left me helpless as a newborn foal.

"Sawyer."

Boyd suddenly entered the sheriff's office. My eyes flew to his and he saw that I prayed he brought good news. Boyd, who I loved as much as my own kin, and who had seen me beyond a fair amount of the worst moments in my life; I recognized immediately he was still strung with tension and this knowledge served to strike me across the face. I hurt as badly as though relentlessly beaten—and I would welcome any beating to ease this pain—to have Lorie appear before me, explaining that all of this was a dreadful mistake, that she had fallen asleep and was therefore heedless of the passing hours...

Oh Jesus, I cannot bear this. You took her from me before. Please, not again.

There was only silence when I called to Lorie in my mind and I understood deep within and apart from her unfathomable disappearance that this indicated she was in danger. A thousand times worse was the unknown—having no knowledge of the sort of danger, I could not combat it; I felt blinded, sunk as surely as a boulder beneath the surface of a lake. The unseen cord that connected me to her was intact; as real as it was inexplicable, I could sense it even though Lorie remained silent and I was afforded a small measure of comfort in this, as I knew she was alive.

Alive, and unable to respond.

I knew this—but not why, and squeezed my fingers inward to quell the urge to take a chair to the wall. Or better yet, Billings' head.

"Sawyer," Boyd said again, more sharply. Just the use of my given name rather than his typical way of addressing me belied the depth of his concern. I knew he loved Lorie as well as he would any sister of his own, just as did Malcolm, but they could not fully comprehend my love for her. I belonged to Lorie; it was as simple as that. My soul recognized this the first moment I laid eyes upon her, poised as though about to take flight from the bottommost step of a staircase, there in a Missouri saloon.

Boyd came near and put a hand on my arm. He wasn't quite my height, but strong as a bull calf; I had tangled with him on plenty of occasions during our growing years and been bruised for days as a result. He approached tentatively, so worried that shadows appeared like charcoal slashes beneath his eyes. He said, "Deputy Clemens requested another word. He sent the boy to tell me. He's a bite for us, just yonder, Malcolm said."

"I cannot eat," I said roughly, stunned that he would think otherwise.

"I know," Boyd said, and I knew he would not risk disagreeing with anything I said, not this day. He added, "His sister's the one gave Malcolm the critter. Spoke with Lorie, too."

"Why didn't Clemens tell me this?" I demanded.

"Clemens only just spoke to his sister," Boyd explained, retaining calm. He said, more quietly, "The boy's riddled as a worm-ridden apple. He's blaming himself."

I knew that my anger towards Malcolm was utterly unjustified. I had shaken him, desperate for answers, bellowing at him. And yet, I entrusted Lorie into his care...

He's only a boy, I reminded myself. *You should have been there, no one else.*

Billings, having retreated behind his writing desk, encouraged, "Clemens will be at his uncle's, Doc Tilson's place, two blocks east," and indicated out the window with his quill pen extended. "I will make the evening rounds within the hour, Mr. Davis, and I assure you I will inquire everyone I see of your wife's whereabouts. The town has quieted now that Wright and Gibbs are hung. Show's over for everyone but the undertaker today. If your wife is within town limits, we'll find her."

Billings was placating me; beneath his veneer of professionalism, I had already ascertained a sense of dismissal. Perhaps Billings thought Lorie had run away, that her continued absence was of her own choice. I closed my eyes and reassured her as best I could, *I think no such thing, darlin', know this. I will find you, this I swear.*

"Come," Boyd said. "Please, Sawyer."

Malcolm waited for us just outside, drooping against Aces, the small gray kitten tucked into one of the boy's shirts atop the wagon seat. Malcolm's desolation was as evident as his freckles and a part of me wanted to offer him comfort—but I could not muster the requisite strength. Malcolm's eyes followed us; Boyd went to him and curled the boy against his side; both were uncharacteristically silent.

Whistler nickered at me and I tugged free her halter. Admiral and Fortune were likewise tethered to the back of the wagon, drawn by Aces and Juniper, whose limp was nearly imperceptible today. Whistler nudged me and stepped closer, her brown eyes casting about in search of the woman she had come to love, and expected at my side. My heart delivered a series of forceful blows, reminiscent of those dealt by my father's blacksmithing hammer to iron he was shaping.

"Lorie can't be here just now, *mo capall maith*," I whispered, leaning my forehead against her rust-red neck, as I had countless times before. Whistler had been mine from the moment of her birth, a tiny foal born nearly into my arms. Upon her back I first marched to War, an inexperienced and prideful boy of nineteen years, and over two years and more than a hundred lifetimes later, she dutifully carried my ragged form home. She had saved my life in battle, and had once saved Lorie's. If not for Whistler, Lorie would have been killed at the whim of Sam Rainey, and the men I knew only as Dixon and Jack. Whistler had broken free from the attempt to steal her, and subsequently my only means of rapid mobility, and then carried me over the prairie to find Lorie.

Recalling that night was akin to a blade being wedged into my back—hearing Lorie screaming for me, for help, was branded into my memory—I had been nearly too late. I held fast to Whistler in the dwindling light of this hellish town, the thought of Lorie again in danger rendering me incapable of moving. Only this morning she was safe in my arms, the soft sweetness of her bare skin against my own, the sighing breath she took before coming fully awake and burrowing closer to me. The intensity of our love, the pleasure that we had shared since our handfasting, was a force stronger than my senses could comprehend. Surely I had not forgotten myself and dared to take such a sacred gift for granted.

I thought of the words I spoke so earnestly, as we lay together in our tent at the Rawleys' farm.

Together we will make new memories, Lorie, and they will be sweet. And slowly the terrible ones will fade away. I promise you.

I intended to honor this promise. Whistler nudged my ribs with her long nose, which I cupped, stroking with my thumb, pressing it to the white snip between her nostrils, where Lorie loved to kiss her.

"I will bring her back to us," I whispered to my horse. "I swear this on my life."

A small voice at my left side inquired, "Sawyer?"

It was Malcolm, leery as a hen eyeing a fox, his attitude of abject misery mirroring my own. I saw that he had taken Lorie's shawl from the wagon and draped it over his shoulders—and my heart felt split, sure as an ax to kindling. Without a word I turned and extended my left arm, inviting him close; he dove against my side, his skinny arms wrapping about my waist like two bands of baling wire.

"It smells like her," Malcolm whispered, bringing the edge of the shawl up and over his nose, and tears shrouded my eyes, falling to the boy's soft hair. He was right—I could catch the scent of my wife within the folds of the wool. I held fast to Malcolm, cupping the back of his neck, an unconscious gesture of tenderness that brought my father instantly to mind. How I longed for my father, *mo dhaidí*, whose voice had not graced my ears since the January of 1863, when I returned from battle bearing the slain bodies of Ethan and Jeremiah, delivering them home for the last time.

"I'm so terrible sorry," the boy whispered. His tears created a damp patch against my shirt. I tightened my grip about him.

Boyd gently squeezed his brother's shoulder. He said, "Come, you twos. Let us see what this Clemens fellow has to say. He struck me as a reasonable sort."

Malcolm studied my eyes, his own bearing an adult's burden, before handing me the shawl, which I held to my face; the scent of Lorie nearly buckled my knees. Malcolm leaped nimbly atop the wagon, taking up the reins draped over its edge. Wiping his nose on the back of one wrist, he muttered, "*Gidd*-up there, boys," to Aces and Juniper; I carefully replaced Lorie's shawl in the wagon, and Boyd and I mounted our horses, following behind, the few blocks over dusty streets to the shingle announcing *Edw. Tilson, Physician.*

"Here's the place," Malcolm announced, halting the wagon, hopping down to secure the horses to the hitching post. He reached to fetch his kitten, tucking the tiny bundle close. Boyd and I followed more slowly, sizing up the small wooden building with oiled canvas in the windows instead of glass, a sensible and cheaper alternative. Lantern light backlit the canvas, creating an auburn glow.

The deputy opened the door before we reached it, inviting, "Come inside, please do." Clemens appeared younger than Boyd and me, and unlike Billings, had not served as a solider. He was slim as a wax bean, with spectacles and a studious demeanor; both his appearance and quiet way of speaking brought Reverend Wheeler, from my youth in Suttonville, to my mind; by the same token, Clemens exuded intelligence but absolutely no threat, a poor quality in a lawman.

Malcolm entered first, Boyd behind him; I brought up the rear and found my gaze roving about a small area in which a doctor practiced his trade, though no doctor appeared present. The structure was comprised of two rooms connected by a narrow door, the front being the examination room. I was at once clouted by scents that reminded me of the field tents in which I had been an unwilling and temporary patient on more than one occasion, most usually in miserable, sweltering Georgia heat. Boyd's nostrils flared, indicating better than any words that he experienced a similar swell of nausea at such an unwelcome reminder of those days.

"I apologize. I would open my home to you but I typically reside here on weekdays, as our homestead is some three miles beyond the town limits. Please, do sit," Clemens said, indicating a small wooden table and four mismatched chairs. Plates were neatly arranged upon its surface, in addition to forks and tin cups; I was far too restless to do anything but remain standing, though Boyd and Malcolm obliged with murmured thanks.

"Gentlemen, this is my sister, Mrs. Rebecca Krage," Clemens said, as a woman came from the adjacent room bearing a platter of food. Boyd, only just seated, hastily rose and removed his hat.

I had no time for such pleasantries and inquired instantly, "You spoke with my wife today?"

The woman's eyes were direct, simultaneously curious and sympathetic. She said, "I did. I am in distress. I do not mean to be impertinent, but I have been terribly troubled since Clint told me of this misfortune. Please know I shall help in any way I am able."

"What did you speak of?" I demanded.

"You are most pale, Mr. Davis," Mrs. Krage said, setting down the food and approaching me in the manner of a field nurse. She indicated an empty chair and ordered, not without kindness, "Sit, please, and rest a moment. I shall tell you everything I am able." Turning her gaze to Malcolm as I reluctantly followed her orders, she went on, "I see you've taken good care of that kitten. Have you named him yet?"

Malcolm remained silent, as though not comprehending her question. His eyes appeared haunted and Mrs. Krage reached to brush hair from his forehead, as would a mother. Boyd stood just to her right, watching her in similar silence, his hat held to his belly. She was slim, like her brother, but her forthright attitude lent her a sense of height, and authority. She addressed Boyd next, saying, "I found your sister's company most enjoyable. I took an immediate liking to her. She spoke of you…Mr. Carter, is it? As my brother has forgotten to offer me *your* names."

Clemens murmured an apology, while Boyd nodded, finally affirming quietly, "It is, yes, ma'am. Boyd Carter."

"I wish the circumstances of our meeting were of a better nature," she replied. "But I am pleased to meet you, nonetheless. You may feel free to call me Rebecca."

I leaned over the table on both elbows; I had neglected to remove my hat. I asked again, forcing myself to remain steady, "What did you speak of with my wife?"

Rebecca said, "We talked of her origins in Tennessee." She worked efficiently, catching up a serving spoon and dishing out stewed potatoes and carrots. She nudged Boyd with her elbow and murmured, "Sit, please do."

I refused the offer of food, sliding my plate to the side. I said, "We are from there, yes. What else?"

"Lorie-Lorie said you reminded her of a girl she used to know," Malcolm said, addressing Rebecca. His eyes were red-rimmed and his voice husky, but he spoke with the attitude of someone attempting to be as helpful as possible. He continued, "She was upset, Sawyer, I could tell, but she tried to hide it." He gulped a little, new tears winking into his dark eyes; he did not let them fall, instead saying softly, "She wanted to get back to you. She was in an all-fired hurry."

What Malcolm spoke of was just minutes before Lorie disappeared. He had told me everything he knew at least a dozen times, at my insistence, but I persisted, "Then what?"

Malcolm clutched his kitten. Clemens was quietly and politely eating, napkin upon his lap, though he appeared to be listening with concentration, his bespectacled gaze lighting upon each of our faces by turns. Boyd could not seem to remember how to handle utensils, as he sat holding both fork and knife, but made no move to apply either to his food.

"We talked of your uncle, the doc, an' how he's from Tennessee like us, an' then you invited us to dinner. Lorie-Lorie said we didn't plan to stay that long in town," Malcolm remembered.

"Our Uncle Edward was born and raised in Tennessee," Rebecca said. "He served in the Army of Virginia, and moved north only under duress. Our mama," and here she nodded at Clemens, "was his younger sister. But Mama died in 'sixty-four. Uncle Edward had not heard word of this until after he arrived, but as we are his only remaining kin, he elected to stay in Iowa. I knew you were from Tennessee the moment I heard your voices."

"Blythe," Clemens said, in a tone of contradiction. "Blythe survived."

Rebecca nodded and agreed, "Yes, that's right, he did."

Only a small, feeble thread held together my sensibilities as they spoke of matters I cared nothing about. I shoved back my chair and paced to the window, saying, "I must go."

Where, I did not have the faintest idea; I only knew I could not continue to sit like a goddamn gamebird on a pond, unwary of the approaching huntsman.

"Sawyer," said Boyd, speaking for the first time since sitting. He had not touched his food. "We will find her. I swear I will not rest 'til she is found."

I looked gratefully at him, then passed a hand over my face. I could smell the stale scent of my fear, clinging to my clothing.

"I weren't gone no more'n ten minutes," Malcolm whispered. His fork clattered to the wooden floor but no one moved to retrieve it. "I ain't ever been so sorry, Sawyer. I didn't listen to Lorie an' now she's gone."

"It's not your fault," I said, holding his gaze. "It is not, Malcolm."

Clemens wiped his lips with the napkin and set it aside, requesting of Malcolm, "Young Mr. Carter, if you would relate the events again, just as you recall. I am unduly disturbed that a woman should simply disappear with no trace in a town as unremarkable as Iowa City. There is no reasonable explanation. Our instance of crime is quite low. Today's hanging marks the only evidence of it in months."

Malcolm said, "I only meant to peek at them ropes. I figured I'd run while Lorie was in the necessary an' come straight back. It was right crowded, an' I got jostled. I got me a look, an' then I spied you, Mr. Clemens, an' the other man, up on the top there…" His eyebrows drew inward in concentration. He recalled, "An' I seen that fella we was talkin' with when we first come to town, the scrawny-necked fella with the big mustache."

"Parmley," Rebecca said at once. "Lorie and I spoke of Parmley, as well. Trust him to advertise a hanging as though it was sport."

"Then what?" I asked, still standing, fidgeting as one awaiting his own execution.

"I saw the man carrying them hoods," Malcolm said, his gaze tilted upwards, as one drawing from memory. "An' then the prisoners was marched out, an' another fella made a picture. Startled me, it did. There was a loud swoosh, an' smoke from his picture contraption, an' the crowd sorta made a big breath, all at once. Them two fellas they was gonna hang was being led like cattle. I figured I been gone too long aw'ready, an' that Lorie-Lorie would be mad, so I run back for her. But then—she weren't there. I yelled and hollered for her, Sawyer, I swear on my life. I checked the necessary, an' I run into the hotel to ask after her, but no one seen her. An' then I run for you an' Boyd."

Boyd, Malcolm, and I went directly to the hotel where Lorie had last been, but as the hanging was still keeping everyone in Iowa City occupied, there was hardly a soul present to inquire. Immediately I'd called out to Lorie in my mind, certain she would respond. But there had been nothing. We flew from business to business, all along the main streets, but no one knew a thing. And now the sun was about to set on the day my wife had disappeared. Night was fast approaching and I had not a notion of where she was—or if she was safe.

Keep level, I reminded myself. *It won't do any good if you lose all control.*

Clemens asked, "I mean no disrespect, but is there any reason at all that your wife would choose to leave, of her own volition?"

I tried not to grit my teeth, thinking suddenly and unwelcomely of a man Boyd and I had known during the War, a soldier named Chalmers, from Alabama. The darkness had grown too severe for him to bear, the darkness of spirit, and he put his pistol to his temple by the light of a November dawn, and drew on the trigger.

Before I could respond, Boyd, having regained his sense of self-possession, said heatedly, "Of course there ain't no reason. Y'all wouldn't know, as you ain't well acquainted with us, but Sawyer an' Lorie's in possession of a love the likes of which most of us'll never have. They's been happier than I ever seen two folks, an' Lorie's missing because of some foul business of which we's unaware. I aim to find her an' I aim to do it fast. She's in danger an' we set here eatin' like nothing's wrong." He thrust his chin forward, eyes snapping with dark fire, and just as quickly he amended, "I apologize, ma'am, we appreciate your hospitality. But we ain't accomplishing nothing by settin' here. An' I know Sawyer agrees."

Boyd could always be counted upon. I said quietly, "I do."

Malcolm's eyes likewise glinted.

Rebecca drew her gaze from Boyd with seeming difficulty, appearing slightly startled by his impassioned outburst. She lifted her chin and said decisively, "Uncle Edward is able to mind the boys at home a while longer, I am certain. Let us make the rounds and assist Billings. We shall ask everyone we meet if they have word. Young Malcolm, if you'll accompany me?"

"Do you believe your wife is still within town limits?" asked Clemens.

Relying on nothing more than deep-seated instinct, I said quietly, "No."

REBECCA AND Malcolm ranged east, Clemens south, while Boyd and I took ourselves north, which proved to be a district comprised mainly of saloons. The activity on the streets increased as the sun sank; we skirted high-spirited men and trotting horses, buggies and carriages and wagons. The day's execution had drawn a crowd that seemed now to wish for nothing more than to seek refuge in drink.

There was a time when I'd been unable to resist the urge to seek solace in a bottle, though I had not let it overpower me since long before we left Tennessee. That wretched summer of 1865, returning home to ashes. To a family dead and buried, every last Davis but for me. Father, mother, grandparents, two brothers younger than I—all snuffed from existence as candle flames pinched between dispassionate fingers. Most days by the time dusk fell that long, cruel summer, I'd lost nearly all sense of who I was, though that suited me. If I allowed myself to dwell on what had been, upon my family that lay in a straight, evenly-spaced row, as seeds planted in a garden, dropped from a warm palm and covered over with earth, then I wanted nothing but death.

What had grown from their buried bodies, the seeds of them, were equally-placed headstones of rough gray rock, inches high and with slanted tops bearing their names, and the years of their births and deaths. I traced my fingers over each name every night that I could still see clearly enough, as part of a ritual of self-punishment. I'd been unable to save my brothers on the battlefield, I'd failed to return home in time to bid my parents farewell, and now my wife was missing—it seemed that ragged guilt intended to stalk me to my demise. Unwittingly I envisioned the crow—a creature whose presence I had not sensed so strongly in years. And yet now it hovered, wings widespread and talons extended, as though about to land.

Perhaps you've been allowed all the time you deserve with Lorie.

"Boyd," I whispered, in effort to slay the terrible thought.

He gripped my upper arm in an old gesture of comfort, responding instantly, "We'll find her."

"She's not here," I said. The helplessness brought me to a halt. A band cinched my chest and it was greater effort than I possessed to continue walking. The darkening town closed around me, seeming to revolve on a wobbly axis, like a child's toy. I sank to a crouch, the sights and sounds just as quickly receding. I felt stranded at the edge of a gaping chasm.

Boyd crouched at my side, preventing me from plunging into the nothingness as he had after many a battle, the two of us left reeling at what we'd been forced by circumstance to do—the guilty misery descending over our bodies, two green boys from the holler who had never killed more than wild game before becoming soldiers. Two boys who watched our beloved brothers, all four of them, slaughtered like animals before our eyes.

What I recalled most about that chaotic gray battlefield was the blank surprise upon Ethan's features as a round pierced him from behind, taking out the entire front of his throat in a burst of dark-red chunks. Not fear or pain on the face I had known my entire life, only absolute stun. His mouth opened and closed like that of a hooked fish before he plunged forward; I tried to stop his fall from where I knelt nearby, but I was already clutching my youngest brother, Jeremiah, whose blood flowed over my lap, obscenely warm. Jere stared with fading sight at the distant, weeping sky above the rocky field at Murfreesboro on that icy January morning. Sleet fell into Jere's cedar-green eyes and he did not blink.

"Jesus, *oh Jesus.*" I heard words being uttered, not quite realizing I spoke them. The horror of losing Lorie beat at me, allowing forth memories I did my damnedest to keep from ever surfacing.

"It's all right," Boyd said quietly, hovering over me and thereby shutting out the curious murmurs of attention we were attracting. "Sawyer, it's all right."

"She's not here," I repeated. "I don't know where she is."

"We'll find her," he said authoritatively. "Come, we's work to do. Come, Sawyer."

I allowed him to haul me to my feet, vulnerable as a goddamn kitten. To those looking on, Boyd commanded in the tone not a soul dared contradict, reminiscent of his father, "*Scat*, all of yous, before I make you wish you had!"

I resettled my hat and drew a deep breath, and together we continued on our way. Past saloon after saloon, where we parted batwing doors and inquired of those within, men mostly, though a woman or two graced the floor. No one knew a thing. I did not believe that anyone was intentionally misleading us—they truly had no idea. Most went straight back to their drinking, dredging forth no more than a momentary sympathy.

"It pains me fierce," Boyd said, as we walked to the final establishment, one at the very end of the street. "What coulda happened? I been wracking my brains. It don't make no sense."

"I know," I said roughly. I had regained a measure of calm. I would not think about the night hours passing without Lorie safe in my arms.

"Here, of all places, where we don't know a goddamn soul," Boyd continued, in his habit of thinking aloud. For all that he blustered and put forth a show of being brash, I knew Boyd to be a keen observer, a deep thinker. Little missed his attention. He mused, "If we ain't heard a word by morning's light, I aim to wire Charley Rawley. He's a fair-minded man, who knows these here parts. I believe he could help us."

I was so very grateful for Boyd's presence. He could never fully appreciate how much I depended on his levelheaded nature. I nodded agreement at his words. It was something, at least, a vague shadow of a plan. My gaze roved away from the bustling saloon and to the place where the street expired; beyond, the prairie stretched endlessly to the northern horizon, where we should have been just now, miles from Iowa City, encamped along the trail. It seemed such a simple desire—I well knew what a true gift had been bestowed upon me in my wife. Clasping Lorie's hand and making her my own, in all ways, was more than the most deeply moving moment of my life; it was a consecration. I felt born anew, allowed to experience contentment in ways I had not since my childhood, and joy as I had never known.

Boyd paused at this last set of doors, prepared to enter the bright, noisy space beyond. I told him, "I'll be just yonder," and nodded in the direction of the empty land to the north.

Boyd hesitated. At last he said, "I'll find you directly."

I walked swiftly into the darkness, no more than twenty steps from the street, before dropping to both knees in the tall, scratching grass. I studied the thinning moon and implored, "Lorie, answer me."

I strained, closing my eyes, stretching out to her with all the strength I possessed. I waited, but there was nothing, and grief stung the bridge of my nose.

"Tell me where you are," I whispered, tears falling chill upon my face, as though my innards had frozen. "Please, darlin', please answer. I feel like I am dying and I do not know where you are."

I ground my teeth, staring sightlessly at the heavens, seeing only my memories of her face, her precious face, the love in her beautiful eyes, which at times shown blue as chicory, at others the green of cedar boughs. I willed her to hear me.

"Lorie," I demanded, with quiet desperation.

Punishment was perhaps all I deserved. I reflected upon this, allowing myself no quarter, as I knelt there under a moon waning to new. I thought of Gus, good, kind Angus Warfield, who I had known from my birth. Rare were men as decent as Gus. And though it nearly killed me when he intended to marry Lorie, and claim his unborn child along with her, I forced myself to acknowledge that he would care for her with tender concern, love her to his final days, and would protect her with his life. And he had, to the very last.

I knew even without Lorie speaking the words that guilt over his death remained in her soul; I knew, as there was also the stinging backlash of guilt within me, for not being there when Gus was shot and Lorie was taken, and for the brutal harm that had come to her. And yet had Gus lived, Lorie would be his wife at this very moment. I would be a liar of the lowest rank, utterly dishonorable, if I did not recognize in the blackest part of my soul that if Gus had to die so that Lorie and I could be together, I would pay that price every time.

If I'm bound for hell, at least allow me a life with Lorie first. Dear God, you see into my heart, and know my sins, and what I have done to survive. Twice now I have not been present when she has disappeared from me, and I cannot bear it. If hell is where I shall spend eternity, I accept this. Please, before I die, restore my wife to me. Oh dear God, please...

And I was heartened beyond all relief to feel a sudden sense of her. Just the faintest flicker, but it was there.

She was there.

I rose swiftly and turned in a circle, struggling to retain the connection.

"Lorie!" I shouted. "*Lorie!*"

Though I could not discern a word from her, even an edge of a word, I knew without a doubt that she was no longer in Iowa City, instead miles distant from my current position.

But which direction?

"Sawyer!" called Boyd, standing on the edge of the street, where it met the grasses of the prairie. He yelled, "Get over here!" and I got, at a run.

"I felt her," I said, short of breath, and Boyd clapped my back, not questioning how I came to this certainty. "I felt her, just now."

I noticed for the first time that another person stood beyond Boyd, recognizing the smug weasel of a man with whom we'd discoursed briefly and unpleasantly upon arrival to this town. Parmley, who had been so eager to inform us that a former Confederate soldier was to be hung today, swayed forward just slightly, as though drunk. Lantern light fell in slanted rectangles on the street at his feet.

Piano music tinkled from the nearby saloon, "Beautiful Dreamer," a song I disliked, as it was so sorrowful. I tried not to interpret this as an ominous sign. A field doc in Georgia had been fond of bowing this particular tune, sitting outside his medic's tent after a day's work. As dusk descended he would play. I spent a week recovering from a musket ball to the leg, and had listened to the fiddle weep over this same melody—the darkening air concealed the pile alongside the doc's tent, resembling nothing as much as slop intended for pigs, that of severed limbs that no one had yet buried or burned—though nothing could lessen their smell on the sticky Georgia air—

Stop.

Boyd wasted no time explaining, "Parmley, here, got a word for you."

I was in this man Parmley's space a second later, perhaps unduly threatening, as he retreated a step and lifted both palms in instinctive preparation to defend against an assault. I restrained the urge to clamp my fists about him and shake forth answers. I demanded, "Tell me."

"I saw your wife at the hanging," he said, his tone less composed than it had been earlier today. Drink discernibly slurred his speech.

"If you are lying to me, you cannot imagine how sorry I will make you," I promised, and he gulped, I could see even in the partial darkness.

"I am not lying," he insisted. "This fellow," and he nodded at Boyd, flanking me to the left, "says your wife is missing from town."

"What happened? What did you see?"

Parmley hesitated; anvils weighted my heart. He finally said, "The crowd was thick as beeswax, but I saw your wife across the square. She was..." and he seemed to be searching for an appropriate word, settling upon, "Detained. Two men spoke to her, one quite close to her ear. They led her away."

"What men?" I raged, this time unable to stop from grabbing his upper arms, tugging him nearly off his feet.

"Christ almighty," Parmley uttered, struggling to free himself. He shoved at me, ineffectually, but Boyd's grunt forced me to release the smaller man, who at once brushed at the arms of his clothing, as though my touch had soiled him. He said stiffly, "I did not recognize them as locals. I admit I'd not given it another thought...until this moment."

Blood beat at my temples.

Boyd asked for me, "What'd they look like? What do you recall?"

Parmley released a tense breath and replied, "I'm doubtful I could pick either from a crowd. One was of a decent height, and wore a marshal's star. The other was a scrawny, disheveled fellow." He gathered himself and insisted pompously, "I'll not be manhandled. I've told you what I know, and I'll return to my evening."

Though his attitude earlier repulsed me, he had helped me perhaps incalculably now, and I said with all sincerity, "Thank you."

Parmley retreated to the saloon without another word, bumping into the hinged doors and nearly falling, but Boyd and I had not a moment to spare for him.

"Let us find Billings," Boyd said.

I T WAS FULLY dark and Lorie had been missing for more than eight hours. Desperation lanced its beak into my flesh but I held the worst of my dread at bay, instead concentrating on the two pieces of information I'd received in the last half hour—that Lorie was alive, and that she had been led away by two men. I could not dwell upon why she was unable to respond. If I did, I would lose control. Given the slightest opportunity, I would destroy any barrier in my path to reach her side.

"I do believe I despise the moon when it is waning," Boyd muttered, his chin lifted to glare in the direction of the sullen-looking orb, misshapen now as it was pared back to new. When I did not respond, as we skirted men and horses on our return from speaking to Parmley, Boyd wondered aloud for the third time, "A marshal? I know we ain't got a reason under the sun to trust Parmley, but I believe he told us true. He ain't got a thing to gain from lyin' to us. What could a marshal want with Lorie-girl?"

"Rawley," I said, intending to mention that contacting him was an idea with merit. Though our acquaintance had been thus far brief, Charley Rawley seemed a trustworthy man. He may possess knowledge that could help us—I longed to believe this, but my thoughts were at present choked with panicked notions, as deadfall in a logjam...images flowed in succession across my mind, almost without my intending. I recalled sitting at the Rawleys' fire the night of the full moon...singing in celebration of the Fourth, whiskey jug making the rounds, Lorie in my arms, Malcolm curled near us...

Think, Sawyer, I commanded. There was something I hadn't considered, just at the periphery of my thoughts. I felt this as tangibly as a damp towel draped over my forehead.

Think, goddammit.

A marshal would cover a greater territory than a local lawman, and would possess a longer-reaching jurisdiction than either Billings or Clemens, who were county-appointed sheriffs; surely Billings and Clemens, and Charley Rawley, would know of any marshals assigned to this area. Lamps were lit upon street corners, creating pockets of light amongst the night, fully gathered by now, its black cloak draped over the town as Boyd and I ventured south and east. We were scarce a block from Tilson's office; I could see lantern glowing against the canvas-covered window, though the hitching rail before it was empty; Whistler and Fortune, along with all of our horses and the wagon, were stabled just behind Tilson's.

Sudden as a spirit, Malcolm ran from across the street. The boy was alone, and out of breath, and my footsteps faltered; I allowed myself to believe that he was approaching so quickly because he bore good news. But I should have known otherwise.

"Sawyer," the boy gasped. "We gotta go. Quick, before Billings gets here."

"What in the name of Christ are you talkin' about?" Boyd asked, catching his little brother's upper arms; Boyd had walked two or three paces ahead, not realizing that I'd halted.

Malcolm twitched free of Boyd and galloped to my side, gripping my shirtfront to further impress upon me his sincerity. He choked out, desperation tinging his plea, "Sawyer, there's a marshal come for you! He's at the doc's office with Mrs. Rebecca *just now*...we got to *go*..."

A marshal—perhaps the same man who had taken Lorie, earlier today. Perhaps she was as near as Tilson's. It was at best a wild hope, but I hoped keenly nonetheless, unaware that I was speaking these thoughts aloud, in great, disjointed chunks. I meant to run that direction as quickly as I was capable, but Boyd caught my arm in his iron grip and insisted, "Hold up." His voice cut in twain my lack of sense as would the blow of a well-placed ax and he hastily drew the three of us to the side, out of sight between two buildings, and asked, low, "How'd you come to this information, boy?"

It was then that I realized something, and it served to insert a hook into my soul.

Wait. There was a marshal present at the fire that night, at the Rawleys' place.

I could see a rim of white around each of Malcolm's eyes, as they were wide with fear. I demanded, "Is it Yancy? Is the marshal who came for me Yancy?"

"No. His name is Quade," Malcolm said, still gripping my shirt. "We met him not a quarter-hour past, comin' to find Clemens. He said to Mrs. Rebecca would she be kind enough to put on the coffee for him, as he's ridden hard to get here." His voice took on a confessional tone as he said breathlessly, "Boyd, Mrs. Rebecca asked Quade what he was after in such an all-fired hurry, an' he says, 'A former Reb named Davis, all's I know. Killed two fellas near the Missouri border, not a month past,' he says."

"Jesus H. Christ," Boyd uttered.

This could not be, and yet it was.

I felt again the dead weight of my brothers in my arms, stumbling, lurching over rocks slick with rain and dark blood. With a single-minded sort of madness, I had not wanted their bodies to touch the battlefield upon which they'd been slain. Not their lolling heads or splayed hands, not even their boots. Utterly helpless, just as I had been that January day at Murfreesboro. Vulnerable as a young boy from the holler in the midst of ferocious fighting, possessing nothing but flesh with which to stop a bullet's killing flight.

I saw again the man named Sam Rainey, the man who hurt Lorie in every way he believed himself capable, who would have taken her life without a moment's pause, if just for the satisfaction of wiping from the Earth another enemy, a woman from the Rebel state of Tennessee. I found him thrashing on the ground in his camp that night, howling, though in that moment of terror I heard nothing more than the sound of Lorie, screaming for me, screaming my name. In the light of that dying fire I witnessed my shot take out Rainey, silencing him forever after.

I saw again, knew I would never fully wipe clean from my memory, the man called Dixon kneeling over Lorie, intending to strangle her—her legs beneath him had been struggling, her feet bare, so hideously vulnerable to him that I could not kill him swiftly enough—I only wished that I could have caused him to suffer before dispatching him straight to whatever lay beyond. As had occurred countless times during the War, I was moving too quickly to take a shot, and had instead swung my rifle's stock against his skull, effectively cutting short his attempt to strangle Lorie.

"What's this-all mean?" Malcolm whimpered, and I drew him against me and bent my face to his hatless hair, as I had no answer that would offer comfort. He began quietly crying, doubtless perceiving the lack of choices left to us now.

Boyd's mind moved at a clip, at the pace of a cantering horse. He understood, "One of them survived, that's what. Which?"

"They killed Gus. They woulda killed Lorie," Malcolm said, his voice high-pitched with weeping.

Jack. It had to be that sawed-off runt, the little piece of horseshit who came into our camp back on the trail in Missouri, long before riding with Rainey and Dixon, acting on the orders of the woman who owned the saloon where Lorie had been a prisoner. This woman, this Ginny Hossiter, paid Jack to follow us from St. Louis, and he had, with dutiful obedience, sneaking into Lorie's tent with the intent of stealing her away. I wanted to kill Jack that very first night, and should have trusted my instinct then.

And given the opportunity to kill him a second time, I had tried, and failed miserably. Never mind that it had been nightfall, and that I acted in a stupor of agonized panic; despite the fact that I fired a rifle into his belly, Jack was no doubt still alive, and there was reason to believe that Lorie was in his company this very night. Jack had certainly spoken to the law, and now a marshal was upon my trail, no doubt ready to apprehend me for a crime I would justify to my deathbed.

"It's Jack," I said, with certainty.

"I reckon you's right," Boyd said, already comprehending the truth of this. "He'd be the scrawny fella Parmley described. But what about the marshal, with Jack? That was hours past, an' this Quade just arrived…"

"Yancy," I whispered, and Boyd's dark eyes burned through the darkness. He nodded without a word and I felt a sudden and terrible shifting in my bones.

You'll be hung, I thought. *They have Lorie, and you'll be hung. You'll be dead and she'll be alone…*

I hissed through my teeth and set Malcolm gently aside; unable to remain still, I paced and then felt blood surge into my skull, pulsing heatedly there. I raged, "It will never let us free, goddammit, *it will never fucking let us free!*"

Boyd was on me in the next instant, clenching my shoulders in his grasp. He meant to shush my anger, and I threw off his grip.

"There is no redemption for us, *don't you see?*" I demanded, overwhelmed by hopeless rage; the world seemed to tilt and pitch. "There is no redemption for what we've seen, and what we've done..."

"*Sawyer!*" Boyd yelled, not about to be deterred by my outburst, gripping my shirtfront and shaking me. He was one of few men strong enough to manage this, and did so forcefully; I was reminded of Bainbridge Carter, who had countless times administered such disciplinary shakings to all of us boys. Boyd ordered, "Catch hold of yourself!"

Malcolm clung to my elbow, his pleading voice echoing in my ear, "Sawyer, we got to *go*. I'll fetch the horses."

"Boy, you return to Doc Tilson's an' say not a word that you's seen us," Boyd said, his breathing uneven. Because I had calmed to his satisfaction, Boyd released my shirt. Malcolm hesitated, but Boyd seemed to have formed a plan, as he said, "Go now, boy, I'll be there directly to fetch you."

Malcolm hugged me tightly around the waist, his cheek against my ribs; then he disappeared into the night.

"I'll fetch Whistler, you stay put here. I'll be no more'n a minute," Boyd said, low and emphatically, before departing.

Left alone, the sounds of evening revelry in a busy town reaching my ears from the near-distance, I let my back touch the wooden boards of one of the buildings that bordered this alley, sliding to a crouch and burying my face in both hands. Stalked like an animal, cornered here in this place. Lorie taken by Jack and Yancy—God knew what their intent with her, and I released a heaving breath, unable to prevent the sudden surge of bile from rising. I rolled to the side and vomited. I despised this helplessness, and the fury in the face of it. Jack once intended to return Lorie to Ginny Hossiter back in St. Louis, and I had to assume this was still his plan. He alone would not have authority to take Lorie from town in broad daylight, and though there was no rationale other than a suspicion, I was sure that we were correct in our assumption that the marshal accompanying Jack was indeed Thomas Yancy.

Detained, Parmley said.

"Why?" I whispered, not addressing anyone in particular, not expecting an answer. Hunkered there, I was inundated with a sudden memory of a summer from my youth; perhaps seven or eight I had been, and sore because Mama scolded me for hitting Ethan in the eye, and because I knew a greater punishment was coming. I could not recall the exact offense for which I'd struck my brother; only that it had seemed the proper course of action at the time. Ethan and I were the ones to cause trouble on any given day, far too similar in temperament, behaving often in the manner of cats in a burlap sack.

Jeremiah was the soft-hearted one, the last born; behind the pressure of both hands against my face, I saw my youngest brother as a little boy, ruddy and freckled, leaning his cheek against Mama's upper arm and resting there as she stroked his curls, with tender affection. Jere never gave Mama a moment's trouble, whereas Ethan and I felt the lash of the strap meted out by Daddy on a regular basis, always deserved; we'd run wild as foxes, along with Beau, Boyd, and Grafton, amidst all the sunny days of our youths. It seemed illogical, even insane, to believe that the six of us would one day ride out from the holler as volunteer soldiers, as cavalrymen for the newly-minted Confederacy. So prideful we had been, with no more than a smoke wisp of an inkling of the horrors we would shortly behold.

My father was as fair-minded a man as any I had ever known, and always calmly explained to us his justification for any disciplinary action. I recalled twitching with nervous anticipation in the barn, where we were routinely punished, usually fidgeting side-by-side with Eth, unable to process more than a few words of Daddy's earnest speeches, my eyes roving repeatedly to the strap. Strappings hurt for days on end; the first night, it was often impossible to sit for longer than a few minutes. But this particular instance, Daddy had not yet returned home from town, and the livery stable; I knew as soon as he did I would have to accept my punishment with no excuses. Lying there in our hayfield, which was a good two months from harvest and smelled as sweet as heaven, I imagined remaining hidden until the morning.

It had been a lovely evening; even flat upon my back in the hay, the view was familiar—the topmost branches of the oaks that grew strong and sturdy on the north side of the house visible above the stalks of grain surrounding me; the oak limbs curled and twisted in the fashion of an old man's fingers, thick with summer leaves; the scent of supper wafted from our home. The swath of early-evening sky above lit my face with a rosy tint, smooth as the soft breast feathers of a hen, and I reached up as though to pet it, bringing together my hands and shaping my fingers to form an oval, through which I peered at the lace made by the thin, fair-weather clouds drifting lazily along in whatever gentle breeze was stirring the air in that summer of 1850, or perhaps 'fifty-one.

And across that sky, into the frame I created of my hands, a crow winged past, a blot of ink against a pale-smooth page, the death specter forcing an acknowledgment of its presence upon me, long before I'd killed another man. Perhaps even then it had a claim upon my soul.

Lorie, I thought now, nearly two decades later, driving away the memory of the crow before it further mangled my control. I dug the heels of my hands against my eye sockets and begged my wife, *Forgive me for not protecting you as I should have. God knows I will never forgive myself. I am coming for you. I will not rest until I find you. I will find you and I will face my punishment. Even if it means I will hang and be sent forthwith to hell, I would kill them again. I would save you no matter what the price.*

"Davis!" A man's voice, unfamiliar to my ears, approaching my position from the right. Again he bellowed, "Sawyer Davis! I've reason to believe you're hereabouts!"

I rose swiftly, grasping the hilt of my .44 without a moment's thought; before I could draw, Malcolm darted at me from the direction of Tilson's, sudden as a pheasant rising from a roadside ditch. He reached me only seconds before a stranger appeared at the opening of the alley behind him, and Malcolm uttered one word. He cried, "Run!"

I could not judge the best course of action—there was no time, and I turned blindly, unwilling to flee and thus leave the boy alone. It was too late, and unwise, to draw my pistol now.

"Stop, or I *will* shoot!" commanded another voice, before I could move one way or the other, and a second stranger blocked the opposite end of the alley, from the direction of the adjacent street, advancing with a double-barrel shotgun trained upon my gut.

"*No,*" Malcolm moaned.

"Son, I'll ask you to approach me, slowly now," said the man to the right, beckoning to Malcolm. I felt crushed beneath the weight of water, powerless as a drowning man.

"Goddammit, this man acted in defense! His wife has been *stolen!*" I could hear Boyd's voice, raised in fury, from out on the street. "*You'll not take him,* I say!"

"Step back, sir! I said, *step back!*" These words were directed at Boyd.

"Take me," I ordered at once, tossing my pistol to the ground with a cold thump, putting Malcolm immediately behind me. I lifted both hands, hearing the boy restraining sobs. My voice was scarcely audible as I spoke to him, lying, "It'll be all right."

Both strangers converged upon me, each stopping just out of arm's reach with firearms at the ready. I kept my gaze steady upon the man to my left, the one with the double-barrel.

"Sawyer Davis, formerly of the Second Corps?" asked the man to my right, brisk and businesslike. Both were dressed for hard riding; the man who addressed me wore a marshal's star.

"Yes."

"Very good," he said, holstering his pistol, producing instead a clanking set of irons. With an air of calm efficiency, he said, "Name's Quade. If you'll extend your wrists, *thank* you."

"Get back!" demanded the man with the shotgun, swinging it towards the end of the alley, where Boyd, in a fury and appearing twice his usual size, approached with a determined stride. His pistol was holstered, but his intent could be perceived as nothing other than deadly.

I regained control of my voice and said sharply, "*Boyd!*"

"Mr. Carter!" shouted a woman, from the street. Seconds later Rebecca Krage darted into view; Marshal Quade jerked visibly at the sound of her voice. We all watched with some degree of stun as she flew to Boyd and caught his right arm, tugging with considerable strength. This action was enough of a surprise that her aim of halting him was successful. She gasped out, "Stop this! You're endangering both yourself and Mr. Davis!"

"Jesus Christ, this is why I hate towns," muttered the man with the double-barrel.

"Becky, get back!" Quade thundered. "What in God's name?"

"Leverett, these men are searching for a woman," Rebecca said breathlessly, refusing to heed the marshal's order, still clutching Boyd's elbow. Directly beside Boyd, the top of her head scarcely reached his collarbones, but again her attitude lent her height. Clearly she was acquainted with Marshal Quade, who was discernibly upset at her presence, but who was not surprised enough to forgo his duty; my wrists were now tightly shackled, connected by a length of narrow metal links.

Quade asked Rebecca, with no small amount of shock, "You *know* this man?"

Boyd jerked determinedly from Rebecca's grasp and advanced another few steps, speaking furiously, "My sister, *this man's wife*, was taken from this *shit-pile town* this very afternoon, an' we's reason to believe that she is with men who wish her harm."

"Has Billings been informed of this?" asked Quade.

"No, as we only just come to the conclusion ourselves," Boyd said. His gaze held mine, then shifted to Malcolm; he gestured briefly to the boy to come to him, and Malcolm did. Rebecca, not to be deterred, moved forward and curled one arm about Malcolm, squeezing him close to her side.

"Please, Lev, let them tell you what they have learned," Rebecca insisted.

"I'm afraid I can't do a thing but take this fellow Davis to the jailhouse. He's a wanted man, Becky, and I'll not speak another word on the subject." The marshal was lean, built on the spare, but he spoke with authority, and in a tone that discouraged any sort of protest.

Rebecca protested, with no small amount of heat, "You must listen to what they have to say. A woman is missing from this town!"

"Sawyer done nothin' wrong," Malcolm said, imploring Marshal Quade, his eyes wide and earnest. "Them men was gonna kill Lorie. They beat her bloody. You ain't got a right to take Sawyer!" He was working himself into a frenzy, as though about to jump forward and into danger, and Boyd caught him by the scruff.

"Jesus Christ," muttered Quade's accomplice, for the second time. He let the shotgun barrel drift south and only for a second did I entertain the thought of lunging and removing it from his grasp.

Quade said to Malcolm, "Son, I've a duty to uphold. When a man is accused of murder, action must be taken. If you'll excuse us." So saying, he looped the chain from the irons around one hand, with the ease of a many-times-repeated action, and ordered, "Potts, go find Clemens and tell him we've got our man." And to me, "Come along, Davis."

I had no choice but to follow.

THE JAILHOUSE was lit by two separate lanterns. Within, we were met by Billings, now hatless and with unkempt hair. I had a sudden, absurd picture of him continuously raking his fingers through it; the way it stood on end suggested such a thing. He had been smoking, and removed the cigar from his teeth to inquire, "What the devil?"

"Billings," acknowledged Marshal Quade. In the yellow light I took stock of the marshal, who was perhaps ten years my senior, with a face baked brown by the sun but for white squint lines in the outer corners of his eyes. I found myself daring to hope that it was a scrap of reasonability I observed in his gaze as he regarded me just as frankly. Quade looked back to the sheriff and said, "You've received a wire about this man as of this afternoon, I'd wager. You been to the telegraph office since midday?"

"I've had my hands full with the hanging," Billings said defensively, eyes narrowing. "This fellow's wife was lost in our town just this afternoon. What's this about? I swear I've not had a longer day since the goddamn Vicksburg Campaign."

Quade said, "He'll need a room for the night, at least."

Billings heaved a sigh and unlocked the cell to the left, into which Quade led me. The iron-slatted door clanged closed with a sense of finality, and I felt once-removed from my own body, a strange sensation that had befallen me many a time after battle. But there was no time to lose focus. Still in irons, I remained standing and said as steadily as I could manage, "I believe I know who has taken my wife."

Billings released a cloud of cigar smoke; Quade studied me with fists planted on hips. Neither seemed inclined to reply, so I continued, "He is from St. Louis. His name is Jack. I do not know a thing about him, other than he attempted to take Lorie on two separate occasions, the second of which he succeeded." I beat down the subsequent wad of vicious anger and said as calmly as I could manage, "This Jack killed a man we were travelling with, Angus Warfield, near the Missouri—Iowa border, not a month past. He and two other men took Lorie then, and would have killed her. They were acting on orders of a woman named Ginny Hossiter—"

Quade shifted his weight from one hip to the other and interrupted, "You said 'would' have killed her? What prevented this?"

There was no use concocting a story—I would face what decision I had made. I straightened to my full height and said, "I rode day and night to get to her. I came to their camp to find Lorie being strangled..." I gritted my teeth and forced myself to finish explaining, "I killed all three. I believed that I had killed Jack that very night."

"You're admitting to killing two men and the attempted murder of a third, in Missouri?" Quade asked.

"I am. I will face whatever charges I must, you have my word. But I beg of you to let me go after my wife this night."

"Where is she?" Billings demanded. "You said you did not know."

"I did not, earlier today."

"Jack Barrow claims you shot clean through his side and left him for dead. Two bodies were recovered in Missouri, one shot and with an eye punctured out, the other with a skull so smashed the poor bastard wasn't even recognizable. Barrow claims was you killed these men and stole their horses. And you've all but admitted this." Quade spoke with a measured tone, watching me as one might a beast, wary and yet with a hint of fascination, too.

"They would have *killed my wife*," I said; my voice emerged as though a boot was planted on my gullet. I gripped the iron slats, though I did not recall moving. The irons about my wrists clanked, the chain between not allowing for more than a foot of separation.

"What would Barrow want with her?" Quade wondered. "How come you to believe that she is with him now?"

"He intends to bring her back to St. Louis, for compensation," I said. "I was told just earlier, by a man named Parmley, that Lorie was led from the crowd gathered for the hanging by two men, one a marshal. I have reason to believe this marshal is a man named Thomas Yancy. We made his acquaintance July the fourth, at Charley Rawley's homestead."

"Yancy? I've communicated with him regarding you," Quade said. "He volunteered to come after you, as he was closer to your position. Though Potts and I made good time." To Billings, he explained in an undertone, "He's been ripe to see his girl here."

Billings snorted, but muttered, "You, too, I would imagine."

I heard only the confirmation of what I suspected—and I knew beyond a shadow of a doubt that Lorie was in the company of Yancy and Jack. At that moment I felt capable of wrenching free of the cell in which I was locked. Sticky-hot sweat, nearly as thick as blood, manifested over my body; my grip slipped against the metal. I said, "*Let me free.* I must go after her."

"The woman you named is a saloon owner in St. Louis, and she's raising considerable hell," Quade said. "Her brother was one of the men you admitted to killing, Davis. Damn woman is a pain in my side, I'll not lie. Siblings all over the place, apparently, as she claims *her sister* was stolen this past spring."

"No," I whispered, the bootheel against my windpipe increasing its pressure. "That is untrue. Lorie is not her kin."

"Well, goddamn," Quade said. He scrubbed his knuckles over his face.

"Let me out of here," I whispered.

"Now, that I cannot do," Quade said. "You're a wanted man. We'll get you before a judge as soon as—"

"There isn't *time!*"

Quade's spine straightened at my obvious temper, and he repeated evenly, "We'll get you before a judge, you have my word. Until then, you cool your heels."

A haze, reddish and bloody, descended over my vision. I whispered, "Get me Boyd Carter. *Now.*"

Boyd would ride after Lorie. Surely they had headed south—back towards St. Louis and the promise of whatever Ginny Hossiter promised in exchange for Lorie.

"You're in no position to be making requests of any kind, Davis," Billings said.

"Goddammit, *get him.*"

"He'll be along in the morning," Billings said, with little sympathy. He collected the kerosene lanterns, sending light bouncing wildly about the space.

"Yancy is a marshal, not a criminal. I cannot believe your wife is in his company," Quade said, adjusting his hat brim. As an afterthought, he added, "We'll speak again by morning's light, Davis, this I promise."

And I was left in darkness in the sheriff's office.

W E RODE FOR an hour before morning light, pink as the inner curve of a river clam's shell, painted the eastern sky.

I had awoken curled on my side with the scent of ashes and unwashed flesh strong in my nostrils, having dozed perhaps a half hour, at most. What little rest I claimed was plagued by a jumbled, nauseating sequence of nightmares, of men huddled in groups beneath a reddish sky, moaning in anguish and terror as they burned slowly, kindling in an inescapable fire of monstrous proportion. Just before waking, I had spied Sawyer in this crackling landscape, distant from me, his soldier's uniform in rags, his long hair gone, scalp blackened and bleeding. Somehow I could clearly perceive this, despite the space between us. He had been too damaged to move.

I returned to consciousness screaming and thrashing, startling Yancy, who was stamping out the embers from last night's fire. He said, "Jesus *Christ*."

Yancy seemed tense, working swiftly to untie my wrists and ankles so that I could manage to ride unassisted. Jack had already saddled our mounts, silently awaiting us. Before climbing atop the pony, I rested my cheek to the animal's warm hide, seeking refuge in the familiar scent, pretending that he was Whistler. I did not ask the pony's name, and would not, but in my mind I referred to him as Sable, borrowing the name of a horse from my childhood; my father had once possessed a lovely dark-bay gelding he called such, so deep a brown as to appear black.

"Mount," Yancy commanded, riding near, and I had little choice but to obey.

We rode south across the dark prairie, beneath a rioting of early-morning stars, the moon long sunk beyond the horizon. I leaned close to Sable's warmth, shivering with chill, and aching fear, unable to escape, from either Yancy and Jack or my thoughts; I was uncertain for a time which was the worse. I knew I must form a plan, come to some sort of conclusion as to my next course of action, but my head ached with exhaustion, and the futility of my circumstances. I must accept being their prisoner for now. There was no other choice and I attempted to override my fears and consider, as we kept a steady canter, what would be the course of action most logical.

I revisited Yancy's words from yesterday, taking care to recall each detail; he said that a second marshal, a man named Quade, would soon be in Iowa City to collect Sawyer; Jack said this marshal would not delay bringing Sawyer before a judge. Yancy seemed confident that Sawyer would be hung, but I found room to hope that this Quade, bearing no similar grudge against my husband, would perhaps prove more reasonable. If only I could send word to Sawyer, so he would not be caught so dreadfully unawares—but then he and Whistler would be in immediate pursuit and everything I'd done my best to prevent would be for naught.

I clenched my jaw, releasing my tight grip on the reins in order to rest a palm against Sable's square jaw, stroking with my fingertips. For all that I despised that which had occurred since yesterday afternoon, the pony provided me a measure of solace, and I redoubled my efforts to form a plan. We would go before a judge. Sawyer and I would testify against Jack; I may have worked as a prostitute, I may be without means at present, but I was not uneducated. I was intelligent and articulate; I had been raised by the most proper of ladies, my mother, and I understood the basic rights afforded a person—

And yet, as I beheld Yancy's form, riding just a few dozen hoofbeats ahead, my determination seemed as substantial as the sigh of the wind, intangible as the breath of it across the prairie grass, giving way as my hopes were slaughtered by doubt.

People will perceive you as nothing better than a whore, at best a former whore. This fact negates all others. You were fortunate beyond all imagining that Sawyer is able to see past it, that he is able to love you even so. Others will not so easily accept what you have been, and will question your credibility, your very word, as you are surely intelligent and educated enough to realize.

And then, as I had last night, I understood, *They are going to kill you. To assume otherwise is foolish, and you are not a fool. Yancy is hiding you away for that very reason. You present to them a liability.*

If only I could set eyes upon Sawyer. I felt as though I could withstand the next mile, the next moment, if only for that. I had not allowed myself to reach outward for his thoughts, had hardened my soul and kept at bay the images of him back in Iowa City—and the resultant silence was nearly more than I could bear. But enduring the seemingly unendurable was a thing I had long practiced. I clung more tightly to Sable's mane, letting memories of Sawyer overtake my mind. I would fight to my last sight of the Earth for him. I would do whatever it took to keep him safe. This I knew beyond words.

We rode on at an unrelieved pace, in a southeasterly direction, over the trail that I had so innocently believed I would never see again.

THE DAY grew long, a blue-sky day unmarred by any clouds, and there was no sense of where we might be in relation to the nearest town, or homestead; I recalled Fannie Rawley saying that Iowa City was a good sixty miles from their farm. Surely we'd ridden nearly that far, by now. When Yancy reined his gelding to a walk, Jack and I did the same, though I stayed well back from Yancy's position, watching cautiously for any hint as to what he was about. He drew his sidearm and fired, once, twice, into the still air. Beneath me, Sable jerked at the crack of each bullet's report; it took a considerable amount of my strength to steady him. Yancy paid us no mind, and Jack chuckled.

The two of them seemed to be waiting; I would not give Jack the satisfaction of asking for what. When a rider appeared as a speck on the horizon to the west, I thought perhaps my eyes were deceived, but his horse gained ground rapidly; less than a quarter mile later, Yancy heeled his gelding and galloped out to meet this stranger. Jack simultaneously flanked me to the right, keeping a good two horse lengths between us, but I could sense him there, hovering like an ill wish. Taut with tension, sweat prickling beneath my blouse, I kept my gaze fixed on Yancy and this approaching rider, ready to seize any opportunity afforded me, drawing Sable to a cautious halt.

"It's Zeb, yonder," Jack said, and my spine twitched; how could this have escaped me?

"The man who burned a dog," I whispered, and my skin seemed to shrink upon itself, until each bone near the surface threatened to slice through. They intended to leave me with this man.

"Come again?" Jack asked impatiently, maneuvering closer. The air was very still; I could hear the whirring buzz of locusts in the prickly grass that rippled to the horizon on every side, a landlocked sea all about us. When I did not respond, he prodded, "What'd you say, girl?"

I did not answer, recognizing danger as swiftly would any animal of prey. Yancy and this man Zeb were small in the distance, horses drawn abreast. Zeb appeared as nothing more than a vague outline against an indigo backdrop, but implied threat emanated from him. Though I could hear no words, Zeb's gestures indicated agitation, one arm waving about. His horse snorted and sidestepped. This was the man Fannie feared, that Yancy described as a rabid hound, who wished to burn former Confederate soldiers alive.

Emblazoned upon my mind were the images from my nightmare—and then I thought unwillingly of Sam Rainey, who first despised me solely because of my birthplace; perhaps this man Zeb would be satisfied with any former resident of the Southern states. Jack had suggested that very thing last night, near the fire; as though discerning my thought, Jack edged his horse closer to Sable.

Calculating far more rapidly than I would have imagined myself capable, I took stock of what was before my eyes, hearing only the sound of my increasing heartbeat.

Yancy and the man Zeb were a good hundred yards away.

The ground sloped gradually downwards in that direction.

Their mounts would be at a disadvantage, being forced to run uphill.

I was a strong rider.

Sable was young, and not yet winded, even after a long day of hard riding.

I thought, *You cannot hope to outrun them. And you'll accomplish nothing. They'll pursue and ride you to the ground. You will help no one.*

Surely they were exaggerating this man Zeb's intentions, in order to frighten you...

But Fannie believed him capable of terrible acts...

My body nearly split with the tension, the indecision, in my blood; I was dizzy, about to fall from horseback. I slid weakly from the saddle, abandoning the mad desire to turn Sable north and flee, and Jack made a sound of surprise. He barked, "What're you about, girl?"

Keeping hold of Sable's halter rope, I stumbled several steps before sinking to the ground, refusing to respond. I buried my face against my dirty skirt, however briefly, arms sheltering my head, and shuddered with the futility of my position; I felt, at that moment, I could not go on another step. Eyes closed, I was helpless as an insect wrapped in spider silk, awaiting nothing more than the tremors on the web which would indicate the approach of final surrender.

Jack brought his horse near my crouching body. He ordered with an angry growl, "Get up."

I ignored him; it was surely foolhardy, but I was not unduly afraid of Jack; at least, not Jack alone.

"Get up now, Lila," he said, and I lifted my gaze to fix upon him all of my hatred, hiding nothing.

He only sat back in the saddle, and chuckled, fingering the small antler hilt of his belt knife. His body blocked the sunlight from my gaze, effectively creating the disturbing illusion that he possessed no face, only a crisp black outline of a human head, erringly haloed by the setting sun. I realized I had a question for him, as I'd had one for Yancy, last night.

"Why did you claim to have killed them?" I whispered. The prickling prairie grass scratched at my arms; Sable's halter was warm in my sweating grasp.

"Come again?" Jack demanded, shifting position in the saddle; a rogue beam of sunlight pierced into my eyes and I blinked.

"In Missouri," I insisted. "Why did you claim them dead, when they were not?"

"Sam," he said succinctly. A wad of chewing tobacco wedged into his bottom lip slightly distorted his speech. "Sam knew it would hurt you to hear it, and he was right angry that they wasn't killed. He liked to bluster, but Sam was wary as a hen in his own way. Didn't relish ridin' up on two Rebs. Claimed he didn't think I was a strong enough shot. Claimed all Rebs was shooters. 'Those boys are shooters,' was his exact words. Dixon was the one stole the horses, little as he was, and silent of foot, while Sam and I waited a hundred paces away."

"You knew Sam for a murderer of women," I said, and Jack spit a plug of tobacco. I did not allow this action to discomfit me, and hissed, "You *know* he killed women for sport. He was crazy, damaged by the War. Sawyer saved me from him. Dixon would have killed me!"

Jack leaned forward, his grizzled face repulsive in its resurgence of anger. Spittle flew from his lips as he said, "Davis is the goddamn killer! You never saw what he did to Dixon, not by day's light. Left us all three for dead, stole our horses. And I aim to see him hang for what he done. Sam was my goddamn friend, whore, you'll not speak poorly of the dead."

I rolled to my knees and restrained the urge to clench hold of his elbow, drag him as best I could from horseback. His repeating rifle was no more than an arm's length from me, holstered in its saddle scabbard. I tugged my tell-tale gaze from the smooth wooden stock.

"Get on your horse," Jack ordered, easing straight and running a hand over the lower half of his face, visibly restraining his anger.

I knew it was not worth my breath to attempt to persuade Jack. I rose, as slowly and insolently as I could, suffering his aggravated gaze, only to spy Yancy and Zeb riding our way, closing quickly. My knees faltered; I held fast to Sable's reins and the pony stepped closer to me, nosing near my waist. His brown eyes were eager, as if interested in determining my mood, and I leaned against him for support.

Do not show weakness, I thought abruptly, edging away from the reassurance of the pony's warmth, gathering my courage as best I could, despite the stench of my fearful sweat. *Yancy told Jack he would not take orders. There is no reason to think that this man Zeb wishes you any harm.*

Oh, dear God...

I clamped hold of my skirt, awkwardly, attempting to bare as little flesh as possible in climbing atop Sable's back. Not a moment too soon; I felt slightly less vulnerable on horseback, watching warily as Yancy drew near, halting his gelding perpendicular to my position, at Sable's nose. Yancy's demeanor bore no hint of sympathy; he hardly appeared to acknowledge our acquaintance, instead studying me with a flat gaze. Just as quickly my eyes flew to the man called Zeb, a stranger to me, who without hesitation rode too near and aligned his big mount with Sable, to the left. I felt thusly caged, all of my saliva dissipating, causing my throat to bob and scrape, robbing me of any ability to swallow.

"She's right comely," Zeb said, and his voice was deep, his pattern of speech deliberate, just perceptibly slower than that to which I was accustomed. I could hear my frightened breath, my escalating heartbeat, as though I had wedged wads of cotton batting into both ears. Sable sensed my gathering agitation and nickered, instinctively sidestepping away from both man and horse.

Immediately Zeb reached and clamped Sable's bridle, effectively halting the pony's motion. I gasped before I could bite down upon this evidence of weakness, my gaze jerking between Zeb's face and his inordinately large hand. His clenching knuckles formed a hard white ridge of peaks.

Jack said, with distinct satisfaction at relaying the information, "This here whore belongs to that Reb soldier."

Zeb was an enormous, curly-bearded man of an age with Jack, heavyset, with face and forearms burned red-brown. A hat shaded him to the brows, beneath which his eyes gaped, like two holes burned into the side of a wall tent. By contrast, Yancy seemed almost kindly.

Zeb said, "I wanted that soldier."

"He'll hang before the week is out," Jack said. "And this whore best be in shape to ride when I come back for her. She's worth money to me."

"How do I know you'll pay up?" Zeb asked Jack. "I ain't keeping watch of her for nothing."

"It'll be a plumb month before I can ride back this way from Missouri," Jack said, on a sigh. "You can trust me to return with your share, goddammit."

"I can take my share in other ways," Zeb said slowly, as though stumbling upon this realization.

I could not muffle a horrified sound as Zeb next grabbed hold of my braid with his unforgiving fist, forcing my head as he willed it, angling my face sharply towards the sky. I closed my eyes and clenched my jaw, clinging to Sable with thighs and fingers, both. Beneath me, the pony responded with a whooshing of breath; my own nostrils likewise flared.

Hang on, I fancied that Sable was conveying to me, and drew strength, regaining partial control of my breath. *Hang on.*

I cried out, arms flailing as I was yanked from the saddle in the next moment. Zeb had dismounted, summarily carting me with; he moved swiftly for someone of such girth and bulk, flattening me against the side of his horse—the saddle skirt dug into my breasts, the stirrup strap my stomach. I breathed as shallowly as I was able, tears springing to my eyes at both the pain and shock. Zeb loomed behind, massive as a bear on its hind legs, insinuating his mouth near my left ear. He asked in that voice with its too-slow cadence, "Do Reb whores take it like any other?"

"Jesus *Christ*," Yancy's voice penetrated the buzzing that pushed outward from my temples. I heard high-pitched wheezing; I did not at first understand that this sound emanated from my lips. Yancy spoke as one addressing a misbehaving pupil, reprimanding, "Wait until she's back to your place."

"Won't take long," the man called Zeb muttered. Tears fell wetly over my nose as he reached from behind and gripped me between the legs, his other arm anchoring about my waist. I could not stop from heaving; bile rose and I gagged, and Zeb clamped his hand around the flesh between my legs, hurting me even worse. His voice was somehow as heavy as was he. He muttered, "You want your pretty face black and blue?"

My sobs emerged as near-soundless whimpers. Zeb plunged two fingers into my body, roughly, and with my skirt and underskirt in the way. I was pinned inescapably, unable to struggle free of his vile touch. Zeb grunted a little, bunching my skirts in preparation to lift them, and it was then I heard the unmistakable click of a hammer being cocked. The sound of a pistol made ready to fire caused tears to further blur my vision.

"There *isn't time* for this, I said. Let the whore alone for now," Yancy ordered, in a tone that suggested he was not so much concerned over what happened to me as he was the ticking of a clock, a time frame he was obligated to obey.

"Don't rough her up too terrible," Jack complained. "She's gotta be fit to ride."

Zeb grunted a second time but stepped away from me. I kept utterly still against his horse, my knees as yet too weak for movement, clinging to the pommel with slippery hands. A small bit of underskirt remained inserted inside my body—and how swiftly I had been reduced to existing as nothing more than a body, a vessel into which a man felt at liberty to plunge his dirty fingers, or his swollen cock, spew his sticky seed, regarded as less than fully human at best, as a creature without a soul at worst. It was a sensation every whore, whether the first night spreading her legs or the thousandth, understood. Even if unable to exactly articulate, she understood. Men plundered our bodies, blind to us in all other ways, desiring only to satisfy a corporeal need.

"Move," Yancy ordered caustically, and though I was not looking his way, I knew he directed this word at me. I smelled saddle leather and horseflesh. I heard Jack spit another plug of tobacco. Insubstantial as my knees were, at present, I mustered the wherewithal to follow the order, vision wavering as I released my grip and forced my feet to obey the order to move in Sable's direction. The pony whickered and my fear-blind eyes lifted from the ground, able to focus upon the animal's face, his nose stretching to meet me. I was minutely heartened, no more than three steps from collecting his reins when Zeb caught my elbow and jerked me close; a whimper hooked itself in the back of my throat, emerging as a pitiful rush of air.

"You ain't getting out of nothing, whore," he muttered, close to my ear. "My place ain't but a half mile from here."

He released me with a vicious shove. I stumbled over my hem and went to one knee, agony both physical and mental sharply delineating the world around me; Sable's hide loomed before my nose, each strand of hair appearing stark, and individual—the prairie grass crackled with cruel whispers, suddenly resembling slender sword blades, far too bright beneath the sinking sun. Nausea accompanied this sensation—that all objects were just slightly removed from their usual aspect, their typical color. I crawled forward and dragged myself upward by Sable's left stirrup. A blowfly droned as loudly as water over a falls, lighting on my wrist. Sable's long black tail twitched.

Yancy heeled his mount and resumed riding, angling due west now, without sparing a backward glance. Zeb reclaimed the saddle, a big Henry rifle tucked into its scabbard, and followed directly behind. Left with Jack, who was again acting, surely involuntarily, as my keeper, I found the capability to slip my foot into the stirrup, hauling myself atop the pony. I neither spoke nor glanced at Jack, who heaved a martyred sigh and rode closer to us, drawing his horse abreast on the right. As though exchanging confidences, he leaned nearer to me and muttered, "He'll burn Davis yet, you mark my words."

I clung to the pony with trembling legs, wrapping my fingers into his thick, coarse mane.

Zeb will kill you, I understood. I was weak with this realization; no pretending otherwise now. *He'll use you, he'll beat you, and then he'll kill you. There is nothing to stop him.*

I was deathly afraid of Zeb. Even Sam Rainey, who had borne hatred for me from the instant he learned of my Tennessee roots, had not inspired such rampant fear in my soul. I knew my position would decline swiftly, into one of abject horror, the moment that Yancy and Jack left me behind. This man Zeb would use me mercilessly, with no compunctions, angry at being denied his prize, that of a Rebel soldier.

"Ride," Jack commanded, aggravated and impatient.

I won't, I thought. *You'll have to kill me right here.*

I had no hope of fleeing from them; rather, I recognized that it was far better to die on the prairie, killed by a bullet, than to face whatever Zeb had in store for me at his homestead. I was doomed—somehow I had known this from the moment Yancy led me from Iowa City. But I was determined that I would choose my own death.

I must force Jack to shoot me.

Let it not be too painful. Give me the strength to die quickly, oh dear God.

Yancy and Zeb grew smaller as they rode west and into the distance; clearly they were confident in Jack's ability to haul me along. After all, I was just a whore, a harmless little whore robbed of all means she had in the world. The worst I could do, in Yancy's eyes, was be allowed to testify against Jack, and Yancy had taken care of my ability to do that; in his mind, the deal was closed, the transaction completed. Things would work out according to his plan—he was confident of this.

"Come along," Jack ordered, and my heart thudded, sick and swift, as I gripped the reins more tightly. Jack and his horse were perhaps the length of a body away from me. Any second he would close the distance between us and take hold of Sable's halter. My blood rose as I came to my decision, annihilating all other sound; the prairie around me seemed to recede into the distance, still appearing tinted by the wrong colors in the evening light, the haze of fear creating odd gaps in my perception. But the way north, back to Iowa City, was there before me. I eased Sable in that direction, carefully.

"There's a good boy," I whispered to the pony, clenching my knees, and then I heeled him as hard as I could.

Behind me, Jack shouted in furious alarm.

"*Gidd-up!*" I cried urgently into Sable's ear, and the pony rippled into a canter at once, his slim black legs eating up the prairie as I allowed him the leeway to fly.

Two shots were fired, one directly after the other, and I screamed, though the sound was lost in the dry hollow that had become my mouth. I bent as low as I could over Sable, waiting for the deadly penetration of bullets into my back. When I remained unstruck, I thought, *He was signaling Yancy.*

"Go!" I cried, breathless, heeling Sable ruthlessly. The pony galloped valiantly, the grasses a blur at the edges of my vision, the wind raking its fingers over me, stealing my breath; ahead, the mellow, sinking sunlight appeared to flicker, as though communicating to me the right direction to follow.

I còuld hear hooves in rapid pursuit. No matter how swift and sure my mount, he was small; his legs were not the length of the horses', and they would overtake us.

"*C'mon, boy,*" I whispered into his velvet ear. "Oh God, please…"

Another shot, lower-pitched and clearly that of a rifle, cracked the air behind us.

At least a good three hours of night crawled past, though I had no way to know for certain; outside the windows, the activity of the town began to die out, revelers stumbling back to wherever they intended to spend the night hours. My eyes had long since grown accustomed to the darkness as I paced like an animal in a cage, endlessly, too agitated to remain still. Fear gnawed at my innards. Neither Quade nor Billings returned, leaving me to believe they would not before sunrise.

How far south could Yancy and Jack manage to travel before morning's light? The thought of Lorie being forced into such hard riding, as they would desire to put as many miles between Iowa City and themselves as possible, bit into me. She was a strong rider, I knew this, but I had no way of knowing what they had done to her, how they had forced her to accompany them— had they struck her, bound her?

Oh Jesus...oh dear God...please let no harm come to her...

Lorie, hold on, love...

I crouched in the corner of the cell, thinking of a conversation between Boyd and me, back on the trail in Missouri. The irons on my wrists clanked as I shifted with restless agony. Boyd and I had been riding together that morning, a good half-mile ahead of the wagon, upon which Lorie was sitting, cradling Malcolm's head in her lap as he slept; Angus rode Admiral at their side. Only the night before, Jack had crept into our camp while we slept and attempted to steal Lorie away; I woke that night knowing she was in danger.

You should have killed Jack then, I thought, punishing myself. *You knew it that night.*

"Is Lorie all right?" I had demanded of Boyd that morning.

Boyd nodded. "She's right as the rain. Truly. Gus said we'll camp early tonight, let everyone get some rest." He paused a moment and admitted quietly, "I felt some a-that old hatred when I saw that Federal bastard. I thought I was getting to a place where it was behind me. An' yet I coulda killed him simply for them goddamn blue trousers."

I whispered, "I felt the same. Christ, how many times did we aim for that blue? Every pair of those fucking trousers could belong to the men who killed Jere, who killed Ethan. I don't expect to ever fully escape that hatred, Boyd, not ever."

"I know, old friend, I do. Graf, Beau...all of them. For what, now?"

But there was no answer to that question, no matter how often it was asked, and in endless incarnations.

"Do you think we'll go to hell for it?" Boyd had asked, hardly a whisper, and I heard the vulnerable speculation in his words; he truly wished for my honest opinion.

"I think..." I paused. I'd considered the notion so very many times, usually in a half-drunken stupor. There were months after arriving home to Suttonville during which I barely dared to sleep, for fear of nightmares. When the crow would appear, waiting for me, if my eyes sank shut. At last I whispered, "I don't believe we're damned, Boyd. I used to think so, but in my heart I believe...somehow it will be all right."

Boyd sighed; whether he was uncertain or unwilling to respond, I did not know until he whispered, "If we're damned for what we was ordered to do, for saving our own skins, then hell would be a right crowded place."

I held that morning, our words, in my mind here in the dark jailhouse in Iowa City. I spoke the truth when I'd said, however tentatively, that I did not believe we were bound for hell, but I thought otherwise now. Perhaps I had always known. Of course I was damned—I killed dozens of men in my time as a soldier. No matter that it was a necessity of battle, of conflict on such a scale. They were dead, taken from this world long before the span of a usual life. They'd all been the sons of someone, the brothers and husbands, the fathers...fighting as they were ordered, just as I had been. Dispatched from the face of the Earth by my pistol, my saber, at times even my hands. And now, years after my service as a soldier, I'd killed more men.

And I understood, *I would kill all of them again, with no regrets, to save you,*

Lorie. I accept my punishment. There is no worse hell than being kept from you, not knowing if you are safe. Please speak to me. Please, give me a word.

But there remained only silence.

I gritted my teeth—tears streaked my face, slipping along the grime and dirt upon my skin, burning the back of my nose. I scraped them away, heavy with despair. Though I had no reason to believe, no evidence to assume that he would hear me, I thought, *Boyd. I need you to find Lorie. I need you, my oldest friend. Please, hear me.*

Another hour slipped past, as I floated in a numb fog. I tried to establish a picture of Lorie in my mind, where she might be this night, and how far south from me. She had been wearing her blue broadcloth skirt, one of her lightweight blouses this afternoon—she hadn't her shawl, which was tucked carefully into our trunk, nor so much as a blanket with which to keep warm. I knew, I truly did, that my wife had survived numerous horrors to which I was not yet privy. I understood her desire to reveal information to me as she felt I could handle it; or, more sobering, as *she* was able to bear the revelation of such dark memories. I did what I was able, held and comforted her, telling her even without words that she could trust me with any memories. If truth be known, there were scores of brutal memories which I would soon discard as reveal, but I wished to keep no secrets from my wife.

I thought for a time about how there is more than one sort of prison—how the mind becomes a torture chamber of its own and the one, in the end, most difficult to escape. Lorie was strong, I knew this well; she had endured. That she was able to laugh, and find joy—to think that I brought her these things—was gift enough for one man's lifetime. But none of these truths worked to ease the throb of guilty pain, the knowledge that I'd been unable to prevent someone from causing her harm. And now she was without me, depending upon her own resources to survive. At last, exhausted, I lay flat on the cold dirt floor, against the hard-packed earth, and covered my face. Bead-bright eyes appeared in the darkness before me, eyes that never blinked, but only waited. The crow had been waiting for me for so long now.

Oh Jesus—

Stop.

When a small sound alerted my ears, I thought I must be hearing things. But then another metallic clink issued nearby and I sprang instinctively into

a crouch, calculating any potential defenses; not that many options were at
hand.

The irons. You have the irons.

The sound arranged itself into sense and I realized a key was turning the
lock of the outer door, ever so slowly. I tensed, curling the dangling chain immediately into a weapon. The moon had descended past the single window,
allowing no light to illuminate the figure that slipped into the jailhouse.

What in the hell?

My mind streaked through possibilities. Quade, returning? Perhaps he
had no other place to spend the night hours. Billings, checking in on the
prisoner? But Billings would not skulk into his own space. I retreated to the
far edge of the cell, back to the wall, squinting into the darkness.

When a woman hissed, "Do not make a sound!" I jerked in surprise. She
eased the door closed behind her, moving quickly to the cell. I discerned the
dim shape of her body, the pale blur of a face. The woman whispered, "Come
along, be quick about it! Not a sound!"

It was Rebecca Krage, fumbling with a set of keys, which clanked loudly
as she attempted to find the correct one. She cursed under her breath, and
I met her at the barred door, wordless with bewilderment. The lock made a
grating sound and the door swung inward.

"Come!" she insisted, and there was no time for questions. I followed her
to the entrance, where she hesitated and peered cautiously into the night.
Determining that we could make our escape without witness, she said quietly, "Follow me."

She was wrapped in a shawl and bare-headed, hardly more than a vague
outline before me as I obeyed her order without question. She led us around
the jailhouse and then behind the edge of the building, where welcome relief
descended over me.

"Old friend, there ain't time," Boyd said low, sensing my deep desire to
understand what was happening. He sat astride Fortune in the small scrap of
yard beyond, Whistler saddled and ready at their side. The backsides of buildings adjacent to the jailhouse loomed large; a hundred unseen eyes seemed
to peer down at us.

"The irons," Rebecca muttered, coming near and indicating my wrists
with a tilt of her chin. She worked as quickly as possible, her hands small
white moths. After several futile attempts, she whispered miserably, "I haven't

the key. I believed that Clint's would work, but they shan't. I am terribly sorry, Mr. Davis."

"I'll shoot apart that chain once we's free of town," Boyd whispered. "Don't fret, ma'am, you's give us more'n we could repay already."

"You have," I agreed, finding my voice. Rebecca had helped us beyond all measure, beyond comprehension, and there was no rationale for these actions. I caught her cold hands briefly in mine and squeezed, saying wholeheartedly, "I could never thank you enough."

She nodded, and her gaze moved immediately upwards, seeking Boyd. He tipped his hat and said softly, "You are an angel, ma'am."

I climbed atop Whistler, her warm back so familiar beneath me, adjusting my hips in the saddle and gathering the reins; there was no helping the cumbersome irons shackling my wrists, but I had learned to ride almost before I could walk, and they would not hinder me.

"I shall watch over young Malcolm. Be safe, the both of you," Rebecca whispered. She implored, "Please, Mr. Carter."

"You have my word," Boyd promised.

WE DID not let the horses canter until we cleared the bridge over the Iowa, and therefore the town limits. For hours we rode without speaking, quiet until dawn crested the eastern horizon; it was strange to feel the morning beams touching us from the left when we'd grown accustomed to riding north—the sun was supposed to rise on our right. The day appeared fair and fine, blue without a shred of a cloud. I threw all my senses forward, straining for a hint of Lorie, ahead of me on this trail. Southbound, I was certain, en route to St. Louis with Yancy and Jack.

"They's been riding since yesterday afternoon, we gotta figure," Boyd said when we walked the horses for a spell; everything within me rebelled against slowing our pace, but I loved Whistler and knew she needed the respite in order to keep moving. Boyd and I rode alongside one another, as we had countless times since our youth, he to the right, as usual. Our horses touched noses and nickered to one another; Fortune was sired by the same stud as Whistler, back in Cumberland County in our old lives. The sire had been of Piney Chapman's finest stock, a long-limbed stallion that passed on his build to both animals, though only Fortune retained his coloring; Whistler resembled her mother, Viola, a lovely quarter horse with a paint coat.

I nodded agreement of Boyd's words. We'd ridden hard and had not yet been allowed a chance to talk, Iowa City far behind. I asked only after Malcolm and Boyd explained that he had all but hog-tied the boy so he would stay put at Rebecca's until we returned for him. Once upon the trail, we'd dismounted long enough for me to stretch the length of chain taut against the ground, bracing well away, while Boyd took careful aim and fired. It took two tries, and my wrists were still cuffed as though with metal bracelets, but at least the irons were no longer linked together and inhibiting my movements.

Now, hours later as the sun crept into existence, I asked, "Why would she help us?"

"Mrs. Krage's a courageous woman," Boyd said in response. "I wouldn't have figured a Yankee gal would be so kind-hearted to a couple of former soldiers, I tell you true. I know she took a shine to Lorie, an' is awful worried for her. After the marshal took you last night she hurried me an' the boy to the doc's, said she could fetch her brother's keys once the town settled into quiet. I ain't got a reason under the sun to trust the woman, an' yet I do. Hell, the boy's with her, and she said she would take care of him. I asked her what of herself, would she be in a fix, an' she said not to worry about her. Malcolm was in a black temper to be left behind." And Boyd chuckled a little.

"We can never repay her enough," I said, my eyes fixed on the vast prairie, stretching endlessly, all the way back to Missouri. Urgency overtook me, gliding along my body and into Whistler, who snorted in response, her walk becoming a trot.

"What of when we overtake 'em?" Boyd asked, as Fortune kept pace.

Grimly I said, "I aim to shoot them dead. This time I won't miss. I curse my goddamn self for not checking that night, Boyd. If I'd have made sure, none of this would be happening. I don't aim to make the same mistake again."

"You can't hardly blame yourself," Boyd said. "Dammit, Sawyer. You done what you could, you saved your woman that night. We'll find her, I swear to you, but you can't shoot them fellas dead."

But I was resolute.

Boyd reached and grabbed the rein nearest him, jerking it sharply towards himself, stalling us. He said, "Beg pardon, Whistler-girl, but I gotta talk sense into him." He saw the warning in my eyes, but Boyd had known me longer than anyone left alive, and he was not intimidated by me. He released his grip but said in no uncertain terms, "You's already in a fix the likes of which we ain't been in since the War. Dammit, they'd hang you soon as look at you, back in town. Now, I'd bet good money ain't a soul would care about you shooting Jack stone-dead, but Yancy is federal marshal, an' there'd be nobody to save you if you kill him. I figure you's got a chance right now. We can explain what happened in Missouri, an' Lorie can tell her side, too. We's got a chance. But if you kill a marshal this day, that chance is gone like ice in the summer sun."

As much as my fingers twitched with the heat of bloodlust, I knew Boyd's words were accurate. I knew he was right. I rode for a spell without responding, stubbornly, the both of us cantering our mounts again, the wind from our passage rushing over our ears as daylight struck the left sides of our faces. I sensed his aggravation with me even as I mulled over his words; maybe there was a shred of hope—perhaps I would not be summarily executed upon my return to Iowa City, where Quade and Billings waited, no doubt in a stupor of rage; Quade might even pursue us. If I killed Yancy, I had to acknowledge that there would be no chance of my survival.

At last I said, "Then we must form a plan."

T HE SHOT, DELIVERED most certainly from the big Henry rifle, took Sable in his right flank; I felt the tremendous impact jar him. He shrieked in pain, sides heaving; his hoofbeats faltered precipitously. I moaned in agony—it had not occurred to me, in my foolish, pitiful attempt to goad Jack into killing me, that Sable may be an unwary victim.

He's a larger target, my floundering mind understood, even in the midst of panic. *Of course you would stop a fleeing rider by shooting his horse from beneath him.*

I could conceive of nothing more than continuing to run away from my pursuers—blindly I touched my heels to Sable's belly, praying beyond hope that the poor pony would continue his forward flight. But he had flagged considerably, losing ground.

"Stop!" I heard Jack bellow from behind me.

Sable veered sharply left, fleeing no more than a few dozen paces before skittering to a walk, then a complete halt, his front legs giving out as though weighted. I slid from his back, stumbling amid the prairie grass and falling to my knees at his face, tears blurring my vision. I held the pony's nose and cried, "*I'm so sorry, boy…*"

Sable's back legs buckled and he sank almost gracefully to the ground; just beyond him I could see Jack, closing fast. The others were not far behind. I sobbed, despising what my actions had caused; Sable snorted against my skirts. The legs on the left side of his body twitched. He had long eyelashes; his dark eyes held mine, as though he understood that he was dying. Blood, shiny against his dark coat, gushed in perfectly-timed spurts from the deep hole in his side, echoing his failing heartbeat. I wrapped myself around his narrow head as though to protect him, sobbing harshly. The evening light was a deep-orange in color, striking me in the face and hazing my sight. The endless prairie grass shifted, whispering and cackling, all around me; I could hear it even above my sobs, and the sounds of men shouting.

Jack dismounted and grabbed me around the waist, hauling me away from the dying pony. I fought him with every bit of my strength, beyond sense, thrashing against his wiry arms, bucking and kicking; my heels made stout contact with his legs, doing little more than angering him. I twisted, and clawed his face, tearing deep grooves into his cheeks. He yelped, flinging me away from him and planting a boot against my ribs, shoving me to the ground. From this vantage point stalks of prickly grass touched my nose, and beyond that, I observed as Yancy galloped near and drew his pistol, aiming between Sable's ears. He fired and the pony fell utterly still.

Jack slammed me flat to my back, my gaze directed suddenly towards the sweeping expanse of evening sky, a sight at once impeded as he bent over me, dark fury blooming upon his face. I writhed beneath him, tears seeping over my temples, unable to completely struggle free. Blood dripped from the wounds I had opened upon Jack's face and onto my nose.

"You ain't worth this," he growled, grasping my neck with one hand, digging a hard thumb into the soft hollow between my collarbones. I realized he was fumbling for his knife and bucked with renewed vigor, sounds that would have been screams emerging as pitiful gulps of air. Jack, not appreciably much bigger than me, jerked sideways and grunted, abandoning the knife and clenching me now with both hands. He slammed my skull to the ground, eyes gleaming. He breathed harshly, muttering, "Sam was...my friend..."

Later, I could not remember the exact sequence of events. Jack straddled my waist. With the bottom edge of my panicked vision, I realized his pistol was tucked into the cross-holster only inches from my left hand. I closed my fingers around the smooth wooden grip as easily as I would have a door knob; the piece slid free as if greased. My thumb slipped on the hammer, the slim protrusion of steel instantly slick with my terrified sweat; I felt rather than heard it click into place. Jack released his grip and reared backwards, intending to grab his pistol, but it was too late for him. I saw Jack's face as I squeezed the trigger, aiming just above the middle of his stomach; his eyes widened with surprise.

Jack made a horrible sound, like someone gargling salt water, and fell heavily over my legs, but I determinedly retained my grip on the .44, the singing aftershock of the bullet's report muffling everything but my heartbeat. I struggled frantically and cocked the hammer a second time; my hands were shaking so badly that the shot I fired at Zeb only succeeded in startling him, rather than punching a hole into his massive chest, as I had intended. He grunted in stun, otherwise undeterred by the near-graze of the bullet, plucking the pistol from my grip as effortlessly as one picking a berry from a bush and tucking it into his trousers. I kicked free of Jack's limp form, scrambling to all fours, and crawled madly through the grass, but Zeb caught my braid in his fist, twirling me around to face him.

Yancy was laughing, the kind of mirth born of shock, of someone stunned into a sort of hysteria. He was still mounted and his hat had fallen to the ground; his gelding and Zeb's were restless, high-stepping at the scent of so much blood, and Yancy sawed the reins to keep his animal in line. My ears rang and I could not determine any sense from the words Yancy was speaking to me; his jaws flapped meaninglessly. He realized I could not hear him and leaned forward to yell, "By God, you are a resourceful little whore! I'll be *goddamned!*"

I was positioned between two bodies, those of Sable and Jack—both of them were dead because of me. I killed Jack. I shot him with his own pistol. I squinted at his motionless form, trying to make sense of what I had done. He sprawled face-down, one arm curled beneath him, the other flung to the side. He still wore his hat, though it was tipped askew. A red hole the size of a fist had been opened between his shoulder blades. I choked on the surge of bile, and Zeb jumped back, cursing as vomit struck the tips of his boots. I rolled to one arm and heaved repeatedly, sick beyond measure. I fumbled at my skirt, wet with Jack's blood. Blood seemed to be everywhere.

"The Reb whore shot at me," Zeb said, in his slow voice. My hearing was slowly being restored, the ringing diminishing. He said, disbelievingly, "She kilt Jack dead."

Yancy dismounted and swept his hat from the ground, replacing it with an extra flourish, as would an Eastern dandy. Or a Southern gentlemen from days long gone. He came near, looming large before my eyes, and seemed to be actually seeing me for the first time. Studying my face, he said, "You *did* stab out Rainey's eye back in Missouri, didn't you? I didn't believe it until just now. We've sorely underestimated you."

I wiped my chin with my knuckles; my stomach heaved again and I bit down on the urge to continue vomiting, keeping one fist against my lips.

"Goddamn, this is a turn of events," Yancy said, still chuckling. "You've robbed me of my witness against Davis, but you've given me a gift in return. No reason to hide you away at Zeb's now. We'll deliver you back to Iowa City and I'll personally bring you before the circuit judge. They hang murdering women just as quickly in Iowa as in Missouri. Jesus, here I thought I'd be attending Davis's hanging in a few days, and instead I'll be at his side while his little whore wife has her neck stretched. I said it before, life is a *goddamn* funny thing."

No, I tried to say, but no sound emerged.

"She kilt Jack," Zeb said again.

"As we're well aware," Yancy responded, acerbically. Directing his words at Zeb, he said, "You're not hurt. Get Jack up and over the back of your horse. Christ, he's a goddamn mess. Point-blank. The bastard never took a shot in the entirety of the War, and now look at him. Dammit, we'll have to fetch his mount." The horse had bolted at the gunfire.

"We oughta kill this murdering whore," Zeb said, remaining still despite Yancy's orders, looking down at me. He appeared as large as a barn in the dying light of day. I was so numb I felt not so much as a stir at his words. He clarified, "We oughtn't to let her live after this, Yancy."

"No, she's in a heap of trouble. Killing her now would be a kindness. You and I will testify that we saw her shoot Jack Barrow."

Trouble. It was a word Mama would never have chosen from the thesaurus, as it was so simple, would not present enough of a challenge to her well-educated daughter. But I responded anyway, dutifully.

Trouble. Synonyms include: danger, misfortune, woe, dilemma, tribulation.

Zeb raised his pistol before I could think, let alone react. As one deaf and dumb, utterly mindless, I simply stared at its small, gunmetal-gray nose; the rush of movement to my left only made sense afterwards—Zeb fired, but not before Yancy rode near and kicked his shooting arm—the bullet that would have caught me squarely in the breastbone instead only tore a chunk from the muscle of my right arm.

The shot took me backwards; I do not recall making a sound. I thought, *This is how Sable felt, just now, when he was struck.*

Blood is hot, especially so when flowing from one's own body. With cautious fingers I explored the gash opened in my skin, hardly daring to look at it, picturing the gushing hole in my poor pony's hide. My entire right arm was momentarily rendered incapacitated; blood streaked wetly and obscenely between my fingers. I heard the sound of my breath, rapid and wheezing.

Yancy and Zeb shouted at one another, arms waving. Yancy's face was red, his eyes bulging with fury, but I had no time for them.

Think, Lorie…

I rolled to my left hip. Sweat decorated my eyelids, stung my eyes. I braved a look—I had to know what damage was done to me—my cupped hand shone as though with scarlet paint; I lifted it away, trembling and sickened, but determined to see. I heard small, sharp gasps. Sable lay only a few feet away from me and I scooted over to him and leaned my back against his hide. There positioned, I inspected the bullet's path over my flesh. A wound, however shallow, gaped in the muscle, raggedy-edged and weeping blood, but I did not believe there was a bullet lodged in my body.

Yancy leaned down to my level, his face less composed than it had been thus far. He commanded, "Let me see."

I stared at him as though his words were an incomprehensible jumble.

"Goddammit," he said, swiping at his mustache with a thumb. Behind him, Zeb mounted and loped away in the direction of Jack's errant horse. Yancy said, "You're not badly hurt. I'm sure it stings like the devil himself, but you'll make it back to Iowa City." There was not a dram of compassion in his tone; he might have been addressing a soldier of lesser rank and station. He produced the same handkerchief that had contained his dinner, tying it without fuss around my upper arm, tight enough that my fingers grew bloodless. He said, "You'll ride Jack's horse."

Zeb returned with the horse, stripped clean Jack's pockets, and summarily loaded the man's ragdoll body over the rump of his gelding; the big animal was unhappy with this burden and sidestepped nervously while Zeb secured Jack in place the same way in which he would have a deer carcass. Yancy, in an uncharacteristic display of manners, helped me mount Jack's horse; I sat woodenly, my right arm burning; I was fearful I would not be able to grip the reins on that side. With this in mind, I curled the reins around my left wrist and then gripped the bay's thick mane.

By the time we rode away from Sable's body it was dusk, the air silvering all around us, the last of the sunset awash with blood—reds and oranges streaking and spilling across the horizon. For a time, until I grew dizzy, I watched Sable recede as we rode north; when I looked back a second time, crows had begun circling, riding the air currents above my poor dead pony. One arched downward, a lithe black arrow, just as the sun blinked out of existence over the edge of the prairie.

WE RODE in silence. I did not know if Yancy intended to mock me somehow, allowing Zeb to take the lead and therefore forcing the sight of Jack's flopping limbs before my eyes; I concentrated instead on sitting the saddle. I was so cold, a trembling having overtaken my belly. To counteract this shaking I leaned forward, therefore closer to the warmth the animal provided. I tried to concentrate on what was happening, but it was as though I'd sunk into a jar containing honey; thus suspended, I watched everything from behind an amber-tinted haze. I felt slow, and thick, numbed by shock and exhaustion. At first I thought I was perhaps hallucinating, allowing a dream to take possession of me as I rode, when I realized that a horse and rider approached parallel to our position and against the darker eastern horizon, fast-moving.

Zeb and Yancy caught sight of this and reacted instantly, halting and facing their mounts that direction. Yancy reached and caught my horse's halter rope. A rifle was fired, north of us, once, then twice. I jerked as though stabbed with an iron poker fresh from the fire, and then was dealt a blow to the heart with the same instrument, swift and sure, the numbness evaporating as swiftly as it had settled.

"*Yancy!*"

This single demand was delivered in the deep voice I knew better than all others. My entire being surged to painful life as I heard Sawyer. A sharp joy pierced me before anything else, the knowledge that he was near and that I would be allowed the sight of him, overpowering the onrushing realization that this meant I could do nothing more to save him.

"I'm riding in!" Sawyer shouted.

"No!" I gasped, my feet inadvertently twitching, wishing to spur the horse forward.

"How in the goddamn hell..." Yancy growled, sounding truly confounded, his teeth clenched, a hissing sound emanating from between them. He looped the halter rope more firmly into his grip; he and Zeb lifted their sidearms, Zeb aiming at the rider to the east while Yancy directed his pistol towards the sound of Sawyer's voice.

And then there he was, cantering near on Whistler.

He had found me.

I stared at Sawyer riding towards me in the gloaming as one deprived of all that was pure and true, beautiful and whole, in the world. I was unable to gallop forward; instead I held him with my eyes. Tears swam across my vision and I let the strength of my thoughts flow freely to his mind, at last, *Forgive me. Forgive me for what's happened here.*

Zeb watched Sawyer and Whistler come near, though he kept the Henry aimed east, at the other rider; Boyd, atop Fortune, had positioned himself fifty yards out. Yancy abruptly changed his mind and held his .44 to my right temple. The barrel pressed coldly against my skin.

"You will *let her free!*" Sawyer commanded, his rifle trained upon Yancy. His face was as severe with fury as I had ever seen it, his gaze devouring me exactly as I longed to be consumed; he rode to within a dozen paces and immediate pain and terror raked him, I could plainly see this as he tried to make sense of what had been done to me. Jack's blood was all over my skirt, dried upon my face. Yancy cocked the hammer. Unable to advance closer, Sawyer demanded, "Set her free."

"I shot Jack," I said, finding my voice, hoarse though it was, holding fast to his gaze with mine. I explained, tripping over the syllables, "I tried to flee... but they sh...shot the pony from under me...and then Jack *grabbed me*..."

"You have been hurt," Sawyer said, and he was in anguish at this fact.

"I am all right," I said, with as much fortitude as I could muster.

"You have harmed her and I will kill you," Sawyer said to the men, and there was such menace in his tone that Zeb clutched the Henry a little tighter. I noticed the irons clamped around Sawyer's wrists, though the linked chain meant to band them together dangled free. Whistler made a small whooshing noise.

"You won't," Yancy said calmly. "I figure you'd not enjoy the sight of her clever brains decorating the grass."

Sawyer's jaw bulged.

"Your little whore wife shot a man to death, not an hour past," Yancy continued, with a tone of mocking gaiety. "A most extraordinary shot. Too bad you weren't here to see it, Davis. But you and I will be sure to stand together to watch her hang for it." He noticed the broken irons on Sawyer's wrists and observed, "You're a fugitive on more than one charge now, aren't you? You escaped Quade? I wouldn't have figured that possible. You blasted Rebs are full of surprises," and Yancy contorted his voice into an imitation of Sawyer's slight drawl, concluding, "*Ain't y'all?*"

Sawyer's self-possession was returning to him, incrementally. He did not remove his eyes from me as he said, "You will let Lorie go and you will take me in her place, and you will do this thing *now.*"

"I'll do no such," Yancy said.

Sawyer's eyes flickered briefly to the threat of Zeb's rifle made ready to shoot him, surely at the least provocation. He advanced Whistler another step and she nickered. My heart pulsed with agony. Sawyer's face appeared chiseled of stone with the hostility emanating from him, its angles sharp, his nostrils flaring. Sweat trickled over his temples, beneath his hat; he was near enough now that I could see the pulse beating furiously at the base of his throat.

His voice hardly more than a whisper, he ordered, "You will let Lorie free, and you will take me instead. Or you will be killed where you stand."

Zeb laughed at this, a scraping sound much like a rusty nail sliding free of an old board. He muttered, "He's bluffing. He won't chance it."

"He is most assuredly not bluffing," Yancy disagreed. He indicated by tilting his chin at the vast expanse of prairie stretching east. He recognized, "That other Reb bastard has a bead upon us, even as we speak."

Sawyer's gaze engulfed me, taking in each detail. He said, "I will not ask again."

"Then we get you, soldier, with no fight," Zeb demanded in his slow voice, and knocked his hat back a peg; even from the corner of my vision I could see the dark, twisted delight that this information afforded him.

"No, please, *no,*" I begged, unable to remain silent. "They will kill you. Yancy *knows* you, from the War. That night in the clearing, he was one of the men who tried to steal the horses and it was *his brother,* Sawyer –" I stared hard into his eyes, imparting these truths upon him. Sawyer's eyebrows drew together as he attempted to make sense of this revelation. I watched the new shock as it took him in the center, spreading rapidly outwards, though he remained otherwise motionless.

"*Be still.*" Yancy spoke around gritting teeth.

Sawyer's face remained impassive but I heard his thoughts, as clearly as though he whispered the words into my ear. And then I envisioned that, as he had intended, picturing his hands cupping my face with utmost tenderness as he thought, *Lorie, I want you to listen to me. Boyd is just east. He will take you safely to the Rawleys' with him. You must let them take me. I will be all right.*

No, I begged, shaking my head.

Lorie, he implored. I understood the intensity of his desire for things to happen as he had told me.

Whistler advanced another step.

Zeb whooped suddenly; all of us startled at the sound, even Yancy, who muttered, "Jesus *Christ.*"

"Take this goddamn Reb soldier and be done with it," Zeb said.

Yancy was in a rage, though he sat unmoving. With an air of unwitting defeat, he removed the pistol from its position of threat against my head. He said, "Then *you've* done this thing, Davis. You killed Jack Barrow before my eyes, shot him dead as a coffin nail. Two witnesses. You testify to this, and you hang. And your little whore wife can be a little whore widow."

Sawyer holstered his pistol and curtly nodded his acquiescence. I slid to the ground before Yancy could prevent it, running to Whistler's side. Sawyer dismounted and I was safe in his arms before I could blink—I cried out in pain, inadvertently, as he caught me close, cradling me, running his hands over me as gently as he was able in his intensity. I clutched his shirt, inhaling the scent of him in great gulping breaths.

"You've been shot," he said, attempting to determine the extent of the injury in the gathering darkness, murderously angry at this fact.

Before I could respond Sawyer's expression changed markedly and he moved fluidly, pushing me instantly behind him and away, taking the brunt of the strike; Zeb had dismounted and swung the Henry, clubbing Sawyer with its stock, taking him to his knees. Whistler reared at this action, making a sound very much like a scream.

Sawyer shifted rapidly to a crouch, shoulders curling inward, and lunged from the ground, catching Zeb in the gut, propelling the barn-sized man backwards. I scrambled to the side. Yancy cursed at them, unable to fire into the melee without risking shooting Zeb. And then Boyd suddenly charged into view on Fortune, gripping the reins between his teeth so that he could aim his repeater. The moment Fortune halted, Boyd spit free the reins, transferred the rifle to one hand, and drew his pistol with the other. He performed these tasks so rapidly I could have blinked and missed it.

There was a sudden grit of furious male voices, shouting over the top of one another.

"*I will kill the lot of you Federal bastards!*"

"You sonsabitchin' Rebs!"

"Goddammit, *stop*, I say!"

Sawyer twisted free of Zeb's grip, heaving with breath, and said, "Boyd!"

Boyd held his repeater braced against his ribs, aiming directly at Zeb's torso, his dark eyes burning with an unholy light I had never there beheld, Fortune neatly sidestepping as he tightened his knees; with his free hand, Boyd directed the long snout of his .44 between Yancy's eyes. Whistler was agitated, stomping her hooves. My panicked gaze jerked from Boyd to Sawyer, and in the next instant Sawyer moved with purpose, bringing me close, where I clung, seeking refuge, knowing we would be ripped apart at any second.

Against my hair, he whispered, "Go now with Boyd."

"No," I moaned, understanding the depth of what Sawyer was asking—to leave him here alone with Yancy and Zeb, who would haul him back to Iowa City and condemn him, thereby saving my life. I knew this, and Yancy may as well have produced a long-bladed knife and sliced open my body, nose to belly.

Sawyer said to Yancy, "You will take me in Lorie's place, or you will die right here. It is your choice." I felt these words rumble in his chest as he spoke.

Yancy nearly spat in his frustration. At last he muttered to Boyd, "Take that *goddamn whore* out of here."

"I will be all right," Sawyer whispered, cupping my jaws, and I beheld his eyes at close range, just inches from mine as he studied my face intently—as though he knew he would never see it again. I could not move; I already knew what he would do, which was as Yancy insisted. Sawyer would claim responsibility for killing Jack. I knew he would insist that he had done this thing, saving me as best he could.

He put his face to my hair and whispered, "Go now, with Boyd. You've been hurt and you need care."

"No," I begged. "Sawyer, *no…*"

"I must know that you're safe, Lorie," he insisted quietly. Behind us, there was a clanking of metal upon metal, and I felt that sound as if the irons were about to clamp around my heart.

"Lorie," Boyd commanded, not to be argued with. "Come along."

Panic created small explosions throughout my body. At the same instant, I recognized that I must be strong—Sawyer was risking everything for me, and I must find the strength to accept this; he would not allow me to act against what he wanted, not in this matter. He understood the toll extracted from my soul as I released my hold; I saw the same one, mirrored in his eyes. There was a bleeding welt upon his temple, a purpling bruise rapidly forming; what would they do to him, once alone?

Agony twisted hot fingers into my gut.

"This man will be unharmed when we meet again," Boyd said, his thoughts running a similar direction. His voice was thick with barely-contained fury, his drawl more pronounced than usual. "Which'll be exactly as quickly as I can meet up with Charley Rawley an' ride t'Iowa City, where you *will be* with Sawyer. He'll be *unharmed*, or I'll hunt down the two of yous like goddamn dogs an' make y'all wish you never lived to see the sun rise. There's plenty worse things than a quick death, an' I know where you lay yer head at night, *Yancy*, you bastard."

"You *son of a bitch*, don't you threaten me," Yancy hissed. "I'll gut you."

"You Rebs is meat for the hounds," Zeb growled at Boyd. He had maneuvered the Henry back into place, the barrel directed at Boyd's gut. Boyd's nostrils flared, dark eyes flashing with revulsion. The hatred between them was dense as a swamp.

Sawyer held my gaze steadily. Without words, he said, *I will be there, waiting for you.*

Yancy shouldered me aside and ordered, "Hold out your wrists, Davis."

Sawyer obliged, allowing Yancy to shackle him, this new set of irons upon his wrists above the old. Yancy moved with a brisk, businesslike attitude, but he tightened the shackles mercilessly.

"I will find you there," I told my husband, keeping my voice even with effort.

"Lorie, come," Boyd said succinctly, not removing his gaze from Zeb. Clearly he perceived Zeb as the greatest threat—and he was correct in that assumption. I wished the fearsome bear of a man struck dead—I wished the loathing in my gaze had the power to slash him down, never to rise again.

You're leaving Sawyer with him...

Oh God, no...

They'll hang him...

"Go now, sweetheart," Sawyer whispered. His left eye was beginning to swell closed. Tears burned the back of my nose.

I nodded with short, jerking motions.

Boyd drew Fortune near; I slipped my foot to the stirrup and climbed quickly behind him. I felt a measure of comfort that Whistler was here; I knew she would keep watch over Sawyer as best she could.

"Until then," Boyd said fiercely, directing these words at Yancy. To Sawyer he said, "Old friend, you count on me."

Sawyer nodded. He was shackled, his fair hair coming loose from where he had tied it at the back of his neck. The welt on his face gleamed with blood, raw-looking, and no one would tend to it—I choked on harsh sobs, gripping Boyd around the waist as he took Fortune at a careful backward walk, her rump warm and firm beneath me. Boyd kept his repeater and .44 both directed at them; likewise, he kept Fortune's nose aimed in their direction, walking us slowly away. I watched in agonized silence as Sawyer receded from me. Against all of my instincts, I was being taken from him.

When we'd retreated a good twenty yards in the gloaming light, Boyd muttered, "Hold tight," and holstered his weapons, turning Fortune with quick movements, heeling her flanks and galloping us away and into the gathering night, in the opposite direction that Sawyer would be led.

Once we'd ridden a fair distance southeast, away from them, Boyd reined Fortune to an abrupt halt. Overcome with pain, I wept wretchedly, and Boyd helped me down with great care, gathering me close in a hug, rocking us side to side, one palm against my braid. He smelled strongly, but familiar, and comforting. He heaved with an angry breath and said roughly, "I hated t'leave him there, too, Lorie-girl, but we ain't got no choice."

"*They'll hurt him,*" I moaned. "They will, Zeb is crazy and they'll hurt him, Boyd...*oh Jesus*...they'll hang him..."

Boyd took me by both shoulders and spoke quietly. He said, "I would kill both of them without a moment's hesitation, I want you to know that. Vermin, both a-them. But Sawyer's in enough trouble as it is, an' we can't risk no more. They ain't gonna hang him without a judge giving the order. What in God's name happened back there? Was that Jack, dead over the horse?"

"I shot Jack," I said, between ragged gulps of air. "I grabbed his pistol… and shot him. And then I shot at Zeb…and he shot at me."

"Jesus fucking Christ," Boyd said, cupping my elbow and examining the wound. "It bled a fair piece, but it's dryin' up, I can tell. Can you manage to sit Fortune for a spell?"

I nodded, but I was so cold, and shaking hard now, and Boyd made a sound of concern and gathered me back against his warmth. He kissed the top of my head and said firmly, "Little sis, you listen up. You done good." He spoke in my ear, making sure I heard his earnest words, "It ain't wrong to kill a bad man. It *ain't*, though I'm sorry you had to do such. Aw, sweetheart. We's gotta ride hard to the Rawleys' place. Charley Rawley will help us, I feel certain, an' they's heaps closer than town. Sawyer's entrusted you in my care, an' I aim to keep you safe. I love him like my brother, an' he loves you like he's never loved a soul on this earth. Come, we gotta ride. You hold fast to Fortune, you hear? I aim to be there by dawn, if we can help it."

CLOUDS ROLLED from the west as the night advanced, dense as a pudding, blotting out the stars. In the distance, lightning sizzled periodically, and we were due for a soaking within the hour. I sat in the saddle in front of Boyd, clutching Fortune's thick mane; Boyd's knuckles formed stubborn peaks as he gripped the reins; his forearms were sturdy as oak limbs about my waist. I asked after my sweet Malcolm first, aching to see the boy and tell him none of this was his fault, and then, though I was dirty, blood-smeared and sick with exhausted worry, I told Boyd everything I had learned since leaving Iowa City in Yancy and Jack's company.

"I'll be damned," he said slowly at last, his voice low and stunned. He asked for the second time, "You told Sawyer this?" At my emphatic nod, he continued, "Yancy knew us that night at the Rawleys' place. He knew us at the fire that night." Boyd seemed far removed, his voice emerging as if from a great distance, from the impassable reaches of the past. He whispered, "I told Gus that very night—I said we oughta ride after an' kill them other two thievin' bastards…Jesus *Christ*…"

"Boyd, I'm so scared," I moaned. "What if they –"

"They ain't gonna kill him," Boyd said, with such harsh certainty that I allowed myself to believe him. "Yancy wishes to, but he won't risk it. He knows I would find him an' open his gullet an' bleed him like a hog, marshal or no. They'll meet us in Iowa City. An' Mrs. Krage says that Marshal Quade is a man of reason."

I prayed that Boyd believed these words, and was not simply pacifying me. He, in turn, spoke of what had occurred in my absence, and of Rebecca Krage's incredible help.

"Malcolm is safe with her, I feel sure, or I would never have left him," Boyd said. "The boy's in a right fix, Lorie-girl, that I left him behind, an' that it's his fault that all a-this happened."

"No," I said at once. "No. Malcolm bought us time. If it wasn't for him, Sawyer would have been taken days ago. He may have been hung by now." Another round of sobbing smote me, as would fists; I was quite unable to gain control for longer than a few minutes at a time, and even then it was tenuous. I murmured, in misery, "*Sable...*" The little pony had done his best to save me, I knew this, and now rain would fall on his body, the crows would eat him, and no one would stop this from happening; Sable was dead because of me. And Sawyer intended to claim responsibility for Jack, the man I had killed, this same day.

Boyd sat wordless as I wept, stoic and solid. He only murmured, "Dammit," as rain began to strike the earth, growing ever steadier on the heels of a brisk wind. The sky to our right, due west, grew more menacing with each sizzle of lightning. The storm advanced rapidly and Boyd halted Fortune to dismount and root about in his saddle bag, extracting a wool cloak, which he handed up to me before reclaiming the saddle.

"Mrs. Krage sent this along for you," he explained, resettling his hat more firmly.

I clutched the cloak tightly together with my uninjured arm; there was an aching sore spot whenever I swallowed—both inside and out. I began to shake again, seeing Jack's grizzled face poised above mine each time I blinked. I could hardly articulate to myself what I felt—I was not the least sorry for killing Jack, for taking his life as he had been about to take mine—and yet, simultaneously, I could not escape the sight of his eyes widening as the pistol fired. He had been surprised. His death surprised him. I wanted only to see Sawyer, and instead Jack's dying face reappeared continuously behind my eyelids.

Sawyer, I begged, frantic with the need to hear his voice. *Forgive me. Oh dear God, forgive me.*

Lorie-love, he responded, miles away in the storm. *Don't fear.*

And the strength of him reached me; Sawyer's will eradicated all else and I was inundated with a picture of being held tightly to his body, as I had been every night until Yancy took me away.

Thus cradled, I allowed myself to sleep for a time.

Boyd and I were silent as the rain continued well past a low-slung gray dawn, hampering the speed of our travel, at times sheeting sideways with the wind. By the time we came upon the gate leading to the Rawleys' homestead, it felt as though we had been riding in the rain for more than two lifetimes. Boyd brought Fortune right into the dooryard and when Fannie Rawley appeared in the window, surely wondering what unexpected riders approached her house on this storming early morning, I began to sob again.

I T REQUIRED INSISTENT effort on my part to convince Boyd to allow me to accompany him to Iowa City.

"I will not be left behind," I told him, quietly, but in no uncertain terms. Never mind that at the moment of speaking those words I lay resting on the feather bed in Fannie and Charley's room, my wound cleaned and wrapped neatly in a new binding.

Shortly after our arrival, I perched upon a stool positioned near the squat, pot-bellied stove while Fannie thoroughly cleaned and dressed the wound where Zeb's bullet had grazed me; the Tennessee in Fannie's voice asserted itself more strongly the angrier she became, and angry she was as Boyd and I worked together to relate the events. I was crawling with the restless desire to return to Sawyer, to ride to Iowa City and see him safely delivered, and could hardly bear to remain still long enough for Fannie to administer care, all five of her boys crowding and shoving at one another to get a gander at my misfortune; they were unanimously disappointed that Malcolm was not with us.

"You got shot?" asked little Willie, who had been so industriously turning the crank on the ice cream maker the last time we'd been in one another's company. His dark eyes grew wide with wonder as he elbowed around the oldest brother, Grant. Willie marveled, "With a pistol?"

"'Course with a pistol, you dolt," said Miles, slapping at the back of Willie's hair. "What else you gonna get shot with?"

Grant asked incredulously, "What man would shoot a woman?"

"Does it hurt?" asked Silas. "I bet it smarts right fierce!"

"It's a bullet hole, 'course it hurts!" Miles said, now administering a punch to Silas's arm. "What's wrong with you?"

"Boys!" Fannie thundered. "Go play in the barn for a spell. Go on now, *get!*"

In the absence of the children, Boyd and I proceeded to relate to the Rawleys everything that had occurred since Yancy's arrival in Iowa City, as completely and concisely as possible. We left no piece of the tale unspoken—Boyd and I decided this before we reached their homestead; both of us believed the only choice left to us was to reveal everything, the charges against Sawyer in Missouri, his escape from Quade in Iowa City, his past encounter with Yancy, and finally, the fact that I was the one to fire a pistol into Jack's belly.

"That Thomas could allow such things to happen to a woman," Fannie said for the second time, softly resting her touch upon my bare arm. She provided for me a new set of clothing, underskirts and a thick shawl, for which I was grateful; I was still overcome by spells of chills and trembling. She railed, "I told you that Zeb Crawford was a fiend, Charles Rawley, *did I not?* Look at what he has done!" She composed herself slightly and muttered, "Why, we've been checking in on Fallon and Dredd these days, as Thomas has been away. If I'd known his errand, I would have stopped him, forthwith!"

Charley, sitting at the table with Boyd, sighed deeply and fixed upon me a troubled gaze, making a steeple of his fingers and resting them against his lips. He was a thoughtful man, one of quiet speculation, and I found myself daring to trust him; though it was far too late now, should Boyd and I change our minds. But our supply of those to trust was meager.

"If there are charges against your husband, as there seem to be, then Thomas is within his rights to apprehend him," Charley said somberly. "However, past events are affecting Thomas's proper judgment. I have known him for a fair-minded man, yet his actions these past days have proven otherwise." He sighed again, and said, "I knew something was amiss the night of the Fourth, when Thomas made such bold statements, but he spoke nothing of his past to me, of having known you and Sawyer from the days after the Surrender. That was a desperate time, for many. In truth, though I have known Thomas these past years, I cannot claim to know him well. And the War riddled each of us, in different ways. You know, of course," he said to Boyd, who nodded briefly.

"What are we able to do?" I asked Charley. "Sawyer will claim that he has killed Jack, and it is untrue. I must tell them the truth."

"You were defending yourself, as any judge would see," Fannie insisted.

Charley said, "Judge Hamm is on circuit, and due in Iowa City before the month is out. I would imagine he'll be in from Cedar Falls by next week, and he travels with a small contingent of lawyers. Sawyer could potentially be held until then, or he may be escorted to the nearest town with its own judiciary members, which I believe is Des Moines."

Boyd nodded at this information.

I spoke my worst fear, asking, "What if Sawyer confesses and Yancy hangs him without waiting for a judge?"

Charley said, "Thomas must wait for a judge's order, even with a wanted man," and the tension clenching me in its barbed fist eased, if only slightly.

"What of Marshal Quade?" asked Boyd. "He struck me as a reasonable sort. He ain't gonna be too pleased that Sawyer jumped his jailhouse an' fled, but we hadn't a choice. We had t'get to Lorie, an' we was almost too late. She's been beaten, an' *shot*, for Christ's sake," and Boyd's jaw tightened with anger. His eyes took on the look of a man you'd do best to hightail it away from, though he spoke in measured tones as he said, "I ain't ever been near so many fellas would hurt a woman as I've been in the North, I ain't gonna lie. Back home, we treated ladies proper, with gentleness, as *befitting* them."

Fannie's mouth softened at Boyd's words. She said quietly, "You are a Tennessee boy, born an' bred, of that I've no doubt. But not all men in these parts are the brutes you've described, son. I'm certain when you've had time to simmer down, you shall see that I'm right."

"Ma'am," Boyd said, tugging his forelock in place of tipping his hat brim. He said, on a sigh, "You's right, a-course. I'm addled with exhaustion, that's what."

"I would that the two of you eat, and rest, before you ride out," Fannie said, helping me to fit my arm back into the sleeve of the borrowed blouse. She gathered up my ragged braid and asked, "May I brush your hair, dear girl?"

Within the little room she shared with her husband, Fannie eased the door closed and placed me on the edge of their feather tick. The numbness was settling over me again and she sensed this, wordless as she unbraided my dirty hair, spreading it gently over my shoulders; after collecting an ivory brush from her night table, she worked the bristles over my scalp. I shivered and tears slid wetly down my face. Fannie said nothing, only continued her quiet work; long minutes passed, and it was me who spoke first.

I whispered, "I'm not Boyd and Malcolm's sister."

The motion of the brush momentarily ceased, replaced by Fannie's warm hand, which smoothed a gentle path over my hair. She whispered, "I thought not."

"May I tell you something?" I could hardly send the question past the pain in my chest.

"Of course you may," she whispered.

FANNIE WAS reluctant to see us go—especially since she wanted me to remain at the homestead, and subsequently out of harm's way. She insisted we could ride the wagon to Iowa City when I was feeling up to this act. But I knew, despite everything, that she understood my determination.

As we hugged farewell, she said, "If it was Charley there in your husband's place, I would not sit home idle, either."

I wore a pair of Grant's trousers, cinched tightly with a length of rope; more womanly clothing was tied in a bundle to the back of the horse they lent me to ride northwest, a solid, coffee-colored mare; I would harden my heart and not think of little Sable. It was an hour before dawn, misting rain, but Charley insisted that we could reach Iowa City by nightfall if we pressed hard; he could not accompany us so quickly but promised to ride to Iowa City within a day or two. By evening, it would have been more than twenty-four hours since I'd seen Sawyer.

The sky was utterly starless, moonless, heavy as a layer of quilts on a wintertime bed. I stared up at the lusterless, unrelieved black, clouds thickly spread. I struggled to envision Sawyer, to form a picture in my mind—and then I saw him sprawled upon the burning battlefield from my nightmare and drew a harsh breath before I could banish the hateful image.

"What is it, Lorie-girl?" Boyd asked, bringing Fortune near. His voice was a low murmur, laced with concern. "Are you hurting?"

"I'm not hurting," I said, which was a lie; the bullet wound stung as though dipped in undiluted lye. But I was not about to confess to this. I explained, "I'm fearful." In the dimness Boyd appeared as a near-shapeless blur, but his voice was familiar as ever. Comforting and steady, as though he truly was my brother. I wished he was. I admitted, "I'm so fearful."

Boyd said, "I am, too, I don't aim to lie to you. I'm half-worried that big fella will be lying in wait for us, somewhere up the trail."

I shuddered violently at the thought.

Boyd said, "At least there ain't much for trees on the route. I figure he can't hide out as well as he'd wish."

After we had ridden in silence for quite some time, I said softly, "I told Fannie the truth about me. She knows what I was."

"What you was, an' what you still is, is a woman to be proud of," Boyd said, in what I considered his Bainbridge Carter tone, that of a man not to be altered from a particular mindset. He concluded, quietly and insistently, "A woman who knows her mind an' who does what's right, that's what. Ain't nothing else you's ever been, Lorie-girl."

My throat cinched shut, not allowing speech, but I reached and squeezed his forearm, tightly, thanking him for such heartfelt words; he patted me, once, twice. And thus fortified, we rode on.

THE HOMESTEAD of Rebecca Krage and her sons, her brother, Clint Clemens, and her uncle, Edward Tilson, came into view on the northwestern horizon just at sunset, as we emerged from the southeast, dirty and saddle-sore, having ridden without let-up through intermittent rain since leaving the Rawleys' dooryard. A burning blaze of scarlet light crisply cast the house, the barn, and the wide corral in black relief, etching them upon the backsides of my eyelids when I blinked. The horses, perhaps sensing rest, increased their pace, until we were near enough to discern figures in the yard, drawn as though in ink against the rim of red sky—a woman and three boys, one of whom recognized us, and came at a run.

Almost before we'd cleared the yard I dismounted, so eager to hold Malcolm close; my knees, weakened from the day's long and difficult riding, buckled as soon as my boots touched ground. Malcolm issued a sound of alarm and caught me by both elbows as I sank, and then burrowed against me; we were almost of a height, though he felt slender and tensile in my embrace. I hugged him for all I was worth, still clutching the mare's halter rope, never minding my aching arm. The clucking sounds of others speaking around us ran over my ears as would flowing water, conveying just as little sense as the burble of a creek.

"Lorie-Lorie, I'm so sorry," the boy choked out, sobbing unashamedly.

I cradled him to me, rocking side to side. I murmured into his shaggy hair,

"It's not your fault. None of this is your fault." When my words of comfort did not prove enough, I cupped his cheek and implored his dear face, "You saved Sawyer that day. You bought him time. Yancy would have taken him that very afternoon, if not for you sneaking away."

Tears continued to roll over his dirty, freckled cheeks. He whispered, "I ain't never gonna disobey you again, I swear."

Boyd crushed us into a hug, burying his nose against his brother's hair. He murmured, "Boy. You behave?"

Malcolm nodded vigorously as we drew apart. I sensed the curiosity of our observers; Rebecca approached on Malcolm's bootheels, however tentatively. In the sunset's crimson glow she resembled Deirdre more than ever; I blinked, thrown backwards across time and space, to the balcony at Ginny's that Deirdre and I favored after a night's work, sitting alongside one another for a moment's respite before taking to our beds as the sun rose. Rebecca's hair was neatly pinned, her blouse a utilitarian blue and buttoned to her chin, her lovely, delicate face rife with momentary relief—but her eyes were lit by the sinking sun, and the concern brimming within their depths frightened me to my very bones.

She needed to tell me something, I could unmistakably see.

"You've been delivered," she said, and even the sound of her voice reminded me of my old friend, my sweet Deirdre. "We have been so worried, Lorie, I must tell you," and she drew me into her gentle arms; the scent of wood smoke clung to her hair, and whatever she had been baking prior to our arrival.

"Thank you," I whispered, embracing her tightly. "We are indebted."

"I wish to help you," she said, easing back and lightly grasping my forearms, to better emphasize her words. She studied me minutely before continuing, "I felt the first day we spoke that you and I were meant to be friends."

I whispered truthfully, "I felt the same."

Rebecca's eyes flashed upwards, to Boyd, standing near my left side, and as he was positioned just slightly behind me I could not ascertain any particular emotion from his face; there was, however, plenty of such upon Rebecca's as she appeared to drink in the sight of him. I saw her throat bob as she swallowed but her voice was steady as she said, "And I have watched over young Malcolm, Mr. Carter, as you requested. He has been most helpful."

"Ma'am," Boyd replied, and his voice was low and soft in polite acknowledgment of her words.

Rebecca looked again to me and said briskly, "Clint informed us only hours ago that your husband was taken to the jailhouse by Marshal Yancy, earlier this afternoon. I know you shall be most eager to see him."

Malcolm said, "I saw Sawyer, Lorie-Lorie, Mrs. Rebecca brought me into town, an' we talked with him for a spell."

"Mr. Davis was struck in the side of the face," Rebecca said. "Uncle Edward was able to examine him, and he shall accompany you, momentarily." Her eyes roved along my arm, followed by her gentle fingertips, and she noted with alarm, "You've been harmed. What has been done to you?"

"I am well," I insisted. "I must get to Sawyer."

Boyd must have perceived Rebecca's need to convey information to us, as he asked her, "What did Sawyer tell you?"

Rebecca said to Malcolm, "Be a dear and fetch Lorie's shawl," and the boy nodded at once, and jogged to do her bidding. In his absence Rebecca's hand stilled upon my arm, her fingers curling about my elbow as she said, quietly and forthrightly, "Mr. Davis has confessed to killing three men. Yancy wired Judge Hamm, who is at present in Cedar Falls, claiming he witnessed Mr. Davis shoot the man called Jack Barrow. Hamm gave consent, and they've plans to hang him by the day after tomorrow. I did not tell young Malcolm, as Mr. Davis requested."

Her words hurt me worse than a knife laying open my flesh; I brought one fist to my lips, pressing hard enough to displace my own teeth.

"They ain't hanging him," Boyd said, with bristling anger. "They ain't about to, not while I draw breath."

The fear I'd held at bay crouched and sprang, gripping my heart to sustain itself; my lips grew numb, and cold. I whispered, "I must go to him. *At once.*"

"Uncle Edward shall accompany you," Rebecca said, nodding across the yard to a man near the open door of the house, a tall man a good three score in age, who had braced his right arm against the frame of the door above him. Rebecca's boys tugged at his shirt, chattering at him; he kept issuing speculative gazes in our direction but did not venture forward, as though politely allowing Rebecca a moment with us before requesting an introduction. It wasn't so much the sight of this fellow, who was surely Edward Tilson, as the cadence of his speech as he spoke to his great-nephews that chimed like a bell within my mind—here was a voice of home, a particular drawl, a slight over-elongation of vowels—the sound of a man from Tennessee.

"Let us go," I said, and took the saddle, heedless of any words spoken to me, heeling the mare's flanks, resuming a northward course towards the wide bridge I knew was no more than a few miles away. Fortune overtook the mare before I reached the river, but Boyd had no words of anger or reprimand; he was as intent as I to see Sawyer. As Fortune came abreast, he said only, "Tilson's not a shout behind."

We were forced to slow our pace once within the town limits, and sudden disorientation hazed my vision; I realized I did not know exactly where to go.

"Boyd..." I said desperately, and he took the lead, keeping Fortune at a brisk trot as he navigated along the dusty streets; once within range of the jailhouse, I heeled the mare again, cantering ahead and dismounting clumsily, jamming a splinter into my finger in my haste to wind the lead rope about the hitching rail.

Sawyer was near and I cared for nothing else but reaching him.

I burst into the small building, not pausing to explain myself to the young man who rose with a startled exclamation, dropping his quill pen to the floor. Sawyer bounded to his feet and met me at the slatted iron bars which served to separate our bodies. I clutched him as closely as I was able; his hands curled possessively around me, the shackles removed from his wrists, both of us speaking over the top of one another.

"Lorie...*you're here*..."

"Sawyer, oh Sawyer..."

"I've been so frightened, darlin'..."

"Are you hurt, *did they hurt you*..."

There was a small, metallic clinking near my right elbow; I had failed to notice the approach of the man with whom we shared this small room. He was in the process of unlocking the cell door and said quietly, "Mr. Davis, I shall grant you a moment's privacy with your wife."

Sawyer made a sound of deep gratitude. I released him only long enough to fly through the barred door, now open for me, and Sawyer caught me into his arms. I felt the shudder that trembled over him as we held one another, and I kissed his jaw, his ear; our lips were flush as we clung, breathing each other's scent, reveling in the gift of being allowed to touch, unimpeded. His hair was loose, dirty and tangled, and the welt on his temple was discolored and raw. I drew back, urgent to look fully upon his face. He was here in my arms just now, but Rebecca had said...

She had said...

"Lorie, I've been so frightened," Sawyer said, bringing his forehead to mine. He kissed my nose, my eyes and mouth and chin, in a fever of intensity. He whispered, "You disappeared..."

I couldn't speak past the gathering sobs; tears stung my eyes, which were blinded by the sight of him, unable to look upon him enough to satisfy my hunger. I shook my head, telling him without words that I was not physically harmed, but of course he saw the agony on my face and understood, "Mrs. Krage told you."

A jagged sob wrenched free. I was furious at myself for weeping this way, when I wished to speak coherently. The jailhouse door opened a second time, emitting Boyd, who crossed the space in three strides.

"I told you I'd get her to you," Boyd said, and his voice was gruff. With hardly more than a whisper, he said, "Jesus Christ...Sawyer..."

Keeping me at his side, Sawyer stepped closer and gripped Boyd's outstretched hand. My husband whispered to his oldest friend, "I'm counting on you."

Boyd's eyes were rife with desperate agony, but he said, "We's gonna get you before a judge."

"No," Sawyer said, and his tone brooked no argument. Outside, horses and riders approached; we would be inundated by others in no time. Sawyer said firmly, "I confessed and it will go no further. *No further.*"

"They are plannin' to hang you," Boyd said, over-enunciating each word. "I ain't about to let that happen, you understand."

Sawyer said with all of the considerable force of his willpower, "You will. And you will take care of Lorie after I am gone, and see that—"

"*Sawyer,*" I interrupted, regaining a loose hold on my self-possession, allowing anger to burn away a little of the fear. I said firmly, "*No.* I am going to tell them everything. We will get you before a judge, no matter what it takes."

"You will *not,*" Sawyer said, fiercely, almost growling his words, but I would not be strayed from my course—I would not allow him to die without a fighting chance.

"I *will,*" I insisted. "You *will not* be hung for something that I did."

"Lorie," and he had never addressed me with such formidable severity. He said, "I struck a deal with Yancy, and it will go *no further* than this. He will *hang you* if not me. Do you hear me?"

"I do not accept this," I said, and his hawk eyes blazed into mine. Sawyer had never been so angry at me but I would weather this fury, which masked his terror that Yancy would act upon the threat and attempt to convict me instead; I was determined to explain to Marshal Quade what had actually happened. Charley Rawley believed that Quade would hear me out, that the defense of one's self was just cause for taking another's life. And more importantly, that Sawyer was not to blame.

Clemens, along with Edward Tilson, to whom I'd not yet been properly introduced, crowded into the jailhouse, both talking, and in this hubbub Sawyer held me closer, leaning to my ear and whispering, "I beg you, do not say a thing. Lorie. *I beg you.*"

I whispered, "I must."

"If they take you from me again, *I am as good as dead,*" he said, jaw clenched, low and furious. "You think I would let you die for me?"

"What of me? Would I allow the same?" I yelled at him, in a hissing whisper.

Clemens came near and instructed, "Mrs. Davis, I must lock the door."

I would not release my grip on Sawyer; his hold was equally as stubborn as our eyes clashed.

Lorie, he warned.

Forgive me, I said.

"Mrs. Davis?" invited Clemens, his tone that of hesitance; I recalled Rebecca saying she believed he would be better suited as a schoolmaster.

"Lorie," Sawyer said again, but I was resolute. Clemens relocked the iron door behind me.

There was no discernible tremble in my voice as I said, "I must speak to Marshal Quade."

"*Lorie!*" and all eyes in the room were drawn to Sawyer at what they perceived as his inexplicable fury; only Boyd understood, and he watched silently, his posture tense. Gripping the iron slats as though to rip them free of their bolts, my husband thundered, "*You will do no such thing!*"

I darted outside, sweating and nauseous, but unwilling to face his rage at present; I would do what I could to save him, or I would die trying. I was in no way attempting at melodrama—the stakes were as simple as that. Boyd followed me and there was a cacophony of raised voices inside the jailhouse, but the door clunked closed behind Boyd, and I could not distinguish words.

"Lorie-girl," Boyd said. "*Damnation*."

Clemens popped outside next and said, "Marshal Quade boards with us, and is at present situated in Uncle Edward's office."

"Thank you," I said to the slim young deputy, Rebecca's brother, who resembled her but had inherited none of her plain-spoken attitude, nor confidence.

"If you'll accompany me," Clemens said, politely indicating.

"Where is my husband's horse?" I asked. Through the thick walls I could still hear the sound of Sawyer in a rage. I closed my eyes until the dizzy rush threatening to pull me under subsided, and asked as calmly as I was able, "Where is Whistler?"

"His mare has been taken to the livery, just two blocks east," Clemens said, as he led the way, Boyd and I bringing up the rear. Evening decorated the town with glints of lamplight, windows aglow as lanterns were lit. Though the town was quieter than the last time I had walked its streets, it was still a bustling place, horses and wagons and foot traffic heavy along the walkways.

"May I claim her after we've spoken with Marshal Quade?" I asked.

"Damn right," Boyd said.

"Of course," Clemens echoed, coughing a little as though to excuse Boyd's less dignified response. He noted of a rangy gelding at the hitching post, "Quade's horse is here."

We reached Tilson's office and Clemens held the door; within, a lantern was centered upon a crocheted doily atop an otherwise rough wooden table. The marshal sat at this table sipping from a tin cup, which drifted southward to the table at our entrance.

"Good evening, Leverett," began Clemens, but the man he addressed neatly interrupted by holding up a single index finger.

"Well, if it isn't the escape artist," Quade said, speaking drily to Boyd, but before Boyd could respond Quade's shrewd gaze moved to me and he asked, "Who have we here, Clint?"

Clemens said courteously, "This is Mrs. Lorissa Davis, whose husband is at present in custody. Mrs. Davis, may I present Marshal Leverett Quade."

"My pleasure," the marshal said.

Again Clemens acted as a gentleman, drawing out a chair and indicating that I sit. I did so, directly opposite Marshal Quade, while Boyd spun another chair around and straddled it, keeping his focus steady upon the marshal as well. Clemens remained standing, clearly uncomfortable; he shuffled and then removed his hat, holding it to his chest.

"I should clap you in irons," Quade said to Boyd, however conversationally, and reclaimed his drink; from the scent, the tin contained whiskey, neat. I prayed he was sober enough for serious conversation; I couldn't bear to acknowledge that Quade was our only hope of delaying the hanging. He was perhaps middle-thirties, long-faced and wiry, and while his dark blue eyes were stern and observant, I believed I detected reason, perhaps even a sense of humor, in their depths.

"You'd do well to listen to my sister," Boyd replied, unperturbed at Quade's words. "She's a few things to tell you this night."

I leaned across the table to implore the marshal. "My husband was brought here under the custody of Thomas Yancy and a man called Zeb."

"Zebadiah Crawford, yes," Quade confirmed. "I've not seen hide nor hair of either since they deposited Davis back at the jailhouse."

"They are still here," I said, with dark certainty. "They will have claimed that my husband confessed to killing three men, two in Missouri, and the other just a day past, south of here."

"Davis claimed such, himself," Quade said. "Scarce have I come across a wanted man so forthcoming. Never mind that he evaded me, though exactly *how*, he will not admit. I've a good idea," and he narrowed his eyes at Boyd, but continued, "Though that's the least of my concerns at present. Davis tied up the matter for Yancy and me, neat as a pin. I almost hate to hang a man so easy to work with." So saying, he drained the last of his booze and lightly reset the cup upon the table.

"*I* shot Jack," I said, feverish with need to convey the truth to him. I felt capable of emitting flames from my eyes. "My husband did not kill him."

"And Lorie *was* shot, for her trouble," Boyd said, indicating my injury.

Quade's eyebrows drew tighter and he ordered, "Explain."

I did, as concisely and accurately as I was able, clasping my hands as so not to wring them as I spoke. I was still clad in Grant Rawley's trousers.

"You left with Yancy to ensure that your husband be given more time? To do what? To flee?" Quade demanded when I paused for breath.

"Yancy does not seek justice in this instance. He seeks revenge," I said, doing my best to temper the desperation in my voice. "He knows my husband from the War, from the days following the Surrender. Please, you must understand. Yancy took me from Iowa City so that it would hurt Sawyer, and because I could speak for my husband, and contradict Jack's story. Yancy planned to leave me with Zeb Crawford until after Sawyer had been hung."

"You are indeed alleging that Thomas Yancy, a federal marshal, *kidnapped* you?" Quade demanded.

"Not exactly," I countered. "I accompanied him because I thought it was the only option." I longed to clench Quade by the shirtfront and shake the truth into him. "Yancy wished to hang Sawyer that very day, as the gallows were already prepared. He implied that he would shoot my husband if I did not accompany them."

"Jesus *Christ*," Quade muttered. "And how then did Jack Barrow come to die?"

"He pinned me to the ground..." I whispered, but found myself struggling to recount the moments between Jack gripping me and his subsequent death—my voice faltered, maddeningly, as I strove to recall exactly, and both Clemens and Boyd, with almost comic unison, each put a fortifying hand upon my back. I blinked and saw nothing but the bulging surprise in Jack's eyes as a hole was opened in his gut. I had done this thing to another person, had created a bloody tunnel of his midsection.

And I would do so again, with no hesitation.

The outer door opened before I could continue speaking.

"Quade, you sanctimonious son of a bitch, if you are treating a lady with any less than she deserves, under *my roof*, I'll wring your scrawny, good-for-nothing Yankee gullet," was the first thing I heard. This outrageous statement was delivered in a deep voice, no less commanding for its oddly hoarse quality.

For a split second, before he could contain it, the faintest hint of a smile tugged at Boyd's lips. We turned as one to confront the man who filled the entire space before the door, with his stature, stance, and demeanor, all three. It was Edward Tilson, Rebecca and Clemens' uncle, and I could see from where Rebecca gleaned her sense of self. The man before us stood with fists planted upon hips, glaring down at Quade from beneath the brim of a bone-colored duster. Doffing this, his outward expression changed markedly as he caught my gaze, and he bowed to me, bringing hat to chest.

"Mrs. Davis, I am Edward Tilson," he said in that rasping voice, resettling his hat.

I heard Mama, low and soft, whispering at me to curtsy, but as I was seated and the room narrow, and crowded with bodies, I made no attempt. Instead I took his proffered hand and said respectfully, "Mr. Tilson," and then withstood his unapologetic perusal of my face.

In the lantern's flicker Tilson's skin resembled well-aged leather, baked a deep brown and etched with a latticework of wrinkles; two deep grooves formed crevices alongside his mouth. His hair was iron-gray and fell past his shoulders, his features strong and clean-shaven, dominated by a long nose; his eyes were a smoky shade of blue and held more than their share of sorrow, which I could sense if not yet understand, and perhaps a trace of humor, in addition. He held my fingers gently in his grasp and at last murmured, "You's a woman of some spirit, I'd wager."

I recognized this as a compliment of the highest order and felt something akin to a smile touch my eyes, an acknowledgment of his sincere words.

Boyd said, "Damn right she is. Sir, we's been attempting here to explain to Marshal Quade why Sawyer ain't gonna hang." Boyd's jaw clenched and he concluded, "Not while I am alive."

"Where's that goddamn bottle, Clint?" Quade demanded, tipping his chair on its back legs, with an air of good-humored defeat; Clemens, glad to be given a task, hurried into the adjoining room. Quade said, with no little amount of sardonic stringency, "Mrs. Davis was in the midst of her story when *you* so rudely interrupted her, Edward. 'Sanctimonious,' my white Yankee ass. I doubt you know the meaning of the goddamn word."

"'Sanctimonious,'" repeated Tilson. "Synonymous with *self-righteous, holier-than-thou, pompous, censorious.*" Tilson stopped his nephew en route back to the table, swept the whiskey from Clemens, neatly uncorked the bottle with a deft swipe of his thumb, and drew a healthy swig. He winked at me before asking Quade, "Need I go on?"

"Goddammit, pass that here," Quade muttered, and Tilson did so, while I sat in silence, unable to stop from staring at this imposing elderly man who spoke with the inflection of home, and who recited synonyms as neatly as though reading from a thesaurus.

Tilson turned his observant gaze next to Boyd, framing his question as a demand, "So you's Boyd Carter? Pleased to make your acquaintance, son."

"Sir," Boyd said, shaking Tilson's hand.

Tilson's eyes were nearly lost in a webbing of wrinkles as he smiled, though the animation faded from his face as he said, with all seriousness, "I aim to help you, Mr. Carter, if I am able. My niece is adamant that I do so, an' I admit I'm a mite curious about the four of you. Young Malcolm has proven most true-hearted. It's been long since I've seen the likes of the boy's love for you, Mr. Carter, an' you, Mrs. Davis, as well as your husband. I left Mr. Davis in a fine fury, back yonder. He's sore worried about what you are saying in here, Mrs. Davis."

No small amount of astonishment in his tone, Quade asked, "*Becky* is adamant that you help these people?"

I found my voice and said desperately, "Mr. Tilson, my husband is not guilty of killing Jack Barrow, though he confessed it."

Tilson seated himself opposite Quade, on my left, leaning over his elbows on the tabletop to commandeer the whiskey. He said, "I treated the goose egg on your husband's head, just earlier this day. He's a decent fella, of sound stock, I'd stake my life, an' his love for you is plainer than a beetle in the butter dish. Tell me why he would claim to have killed three men, if it ain't true."

Four men watched me with gazes unwavering in the candlelight. Not so very long, and yet more than a hundred lifetimes ago, I would have been forced to adopt a certain posture in this same situation, to tilt my chin at a particular angle and smile just so, to thrust forward my cleavage and walk with a gentle sway in my hips, each and every gesture calculated to increase a man's arousal. I would have led each of them, by turns, to that dreadful brass bed in my room at Ginny's and allowed use of my body, pretending to enjoy the rutting grunts of a man reduced to the satisfaction of his bodily urges. It was all I could do to restrain the violence of a shudder—but here, in this place, I sensed nothing other than their collective desire to listen to what I had to say.

"Sawyer did kill Sam Rainey, and Dixon, which he has confessed, but only to save me. And it wasn't Sawyer who killed Jack. It was me. I shot him," I said quietly, though my heart bumped loudly enough to overshadow my statements. I had sweat so much in the past days and nights that it seemed as though no fluid could remain within me; even so, moisture gathered at my hairline.

"Well, that makes sense of a few things," Tilson said, while Clemens vis-

ibly paled at my words, as he had several times during my explanation prior
to his uncle's arrival. Tilson regarded me with admiration, I was not mistaking the glint of this in his eyes. He murmured, "I figured you for a woman
that gets things done."

"The fact remains, Jack Barrow is dead, as are two of his companions, in
Missouri," Quade said. "We aren't in the Territories, Edward. We're in peace-
time, might I remind you, and this isn't In'jun country, goddammit. A man
isn't allowed to take another's life without consequences."

"Sawyer don't just take men's lives, as you's implying," Boyd growled. "He
was saving Lorie's *life*. As she has explained."

"How do I know this isn't a fabrication? *I* was not present at said events,"
Quade said evenly, and an unexpected snippet of my first conversation with
Rebecca flittered across my memory—

But now the marshal is courting Mama, her son Cort had said, and I recognized, belatedly, that of course Cort was referring to Marshal Quade. I
found myself regarding the man anew—surely anyone with whom Rebecca
would associate in such a fashion possessed a good heart, however concealed
at present.

"Because I ain't no liar," Boyd said, and his jaw clenched. It seemed to
me that there was perhaps a touch more challenge in Boyd's dark eyes than
warranted, as he studied Quade with an unwavering gaze. Boyd maintained,
"Lorie an' Sawyer can tell you the same tale. She would have been killed. *Both*
times."

"How fortunate that the only other person present is now dead," Quade
said. I did not perceive a challenge in those words as much as I did the rationality of a seasoned lawman. I sensed that he was edging towards being
persuaded by what we had to say, but would not swallow a story without
further proof.

"Sawyer is claiming to have killed Jack to save me. He said he struck a
deal with Yancy," I explained, and the man's name was bitter as rust upon my
tongue. I lifted my chin and said, "I will hang before I allow that to happen.
You must allow him before a judge. Please do not let Yancy hang my husband. *I beg of you.*"

Quade appeared consternated; he did not know exactly what to make of
me, as if yet uncertain regarding my sincerity. He laced his fingers and fit
together his thumbnails, precisely, and I was reminded of the way men at

Ginny's poker tables displayed such 'tells.' Of course, I did not know Quade well enough to read any of his.

"Don't be cross with Mrs. Davis just because you ain't never had a woman love you that-a-way, Leverett," Tilson said, and I could hear the grin in his impertinent tone. He caught my eye and guessed, "You're wondering about my rasp. I'd a run-in with a group of Yanks in 'sixty-four, thought to hang me. I was halfway to hell before they realized their mistake. Violates the rules of wartime to hang a physician. Left me with a goddamn necklace of a scar. Ain't been much of a singer since, neither."

"You served, is that so?" Boyd asked.

"Fifty-Ninth Mounted, Cooke's Regiment," Tilson said immediately. "You're Second Corps, yourself, is that right? I believe the boy Malcolm said as much."

"That I was," Boyd said. "From 'sixty-two."

"Last thing I want to do is interrupt a regimental reunion," Quade interjected, a statement laced with exasperation. "But do please explain why you had been taken in the first place, Mrs. Davis, in Missouri. Why in God's name would Virginia Hossiter claim that you are her sister, stolen from your home in St. Louis? I am admittedly confused."

I felt the grit of my teeth grinding together. I had to close my eyes before gaining enough composure to say, "That woman is no kin of mine. I was forced into her employ in the autumn of 'sixty-five. I lived as a prisoner within those walls and she wishes me returned. I…" Here I gulped, but Boyd curled one hand around both of mine, gently stilling their nervous fluttering. I gripped him tightly and was able to finish, "I earned a great deal of money for her."

"What sort of employ?" Quade stipulated.

I lifted my chin and directed my gaze at the place where the wall met the ceiling; the lamplight was broken into pieces here at this long juncture. I observed a small spider dangling above us, its legs working frantically at the skein suspending it. At last I whispered, too exhausted to feel shame, "I worked as a whore for her."

Quade's demeanor did not alter. He said only, "I see."

Clemens was still standing, and had removed his spectacles, using the edge of his shirt to clean the glass lenses. Peering somewhat nearsightedly as us, he said in his studious way, "The circuit judge, Hamm, is due within a week. We've cause to wait for him, I firmly believe. Mr. Davis shall remain in custody until that time, if that suits you, Leverett."

Quade slapped the butts of both palms against the edge of the table and said dismissively, "I figure you're right. I'll speak with Yancy in the daylight hours, but he won't be pleased. I feel the need of another bottle of bourbon, if that suits the lot of you Southern gents." He tipped his hat at me and acknowledged politely, "Mrs. Davis." Rising, he concluded, "I'll be yonder, at the Forked Hoof."

And he took his unceremonious leave.

"Lorie, you's ready to collapse," Boyd said in the silence that followed.

"Your wagon, an' horses, are in my barn," Tilson said, and his tone had changed, growing somehow gentler. He said, "If you'll accompany me home, I believe Becky baked bread this day. I'd be honored to have your company."

"Please, let me see Sawyer first," I whispered.

Clemens said tentatively, "I'll allow a few minutes, no more, or Billings will be angered. He is furious enough that Mr. Davis escaped the jailhouse once already."

"Your sister is a woman that gets things done, too," Tilson commented wryly.

TILSON AGREED to collect Whistler from the livery stable, while Boyd, Clemens, and I rode to the jailhouse, which was dark and empty of anyone but Sawyer at this hour. Clemens unlocked the heavy outer door and said, "I shall knock to collect you," before pulling it closed behind me, remaining outside with Boyd.

"Lorie," Sawyer said. He rose at once, from where he sat on the narrow cot in the cell.

Though I longed to fly to him I approached with caution, studying his eyes in the dimness of the small room, and said quietly, "You're to be allowed to go before the circuit judge. And Tilson is collecting Whistler."

Sawyer exhaled slowly, as though unable at first to comprehend my words. His anger was still evident as he whispered, "I did not want you to tell them."

"I know," and my words were little more than a breath. I stopped only a few paces away from the cell.

"Do you know what your death would do to me?" Sawyer asked, and his tone was dangerous, his voice far more harsh than usual. When I did not immediately respond, he insisted, "*Do you?*"

My temper flared in the manner of the sun clearing a cloud bank on a day steeped in humidity, sudden and broiling. I said, with considerable heat, "Of course I do! I believed you dead in Missouri, Sawyer, and I will not go through that again!"

"*I will not allow you—*" he yelled, but I interrupted him, shouting, "I will do what *I have to do!*" Breathless anger cuffed me; I was shocked by how disposed I was to yell at him.

"You will not risk yourself!" he raged, advancing to the iron slats, gripping them tightly.

"How *dare* you tell me what to do!" Hot tears inundated my vision, boiling over onto my cheeks.

"I will when you do not listen to reason!"

"Sawyer…" and the anger leaked away with my tears. There was no satisfactory outcome to our argument; neither of us was willing to concede to the other, not regarding this matter. The stakes were too high.

He said, low and insistent, "Come here."

We clung between the damnable irons, arranged in a lattice pattern, crisscrossing both vertically and horizontally, as they did over the window. Sawyer commandeered my face and kissed me, possessing my mouth. The taste of him, the strength and sensuality of him, so near and yet I could not fully embrace him—I moaned and pressed as close as I could.

"Lorie," he breathed, kissing my eyes, my chin, jaws and neck; he went to his knees and I brought my breasts to his face, working swiftly to unbutton the top of my blouse, fumbling in my haste, at last parting it and allowing him access to my bare flesh, where he pressed his face, overcome. The iron was cold and unforgiving against my skin, but he was all heat, and so very welcome.

"Sawyer," I gasped. "I love you. You do not comprehend *how much I love you.*"

"Lorissa Davis," he said, harsh and intense, bracketing my waist, his chin between my breasts as he knelt while I stood. His hawk eyes burned in the darkness. He said, "*They will never take you from me again.*"

"Tell them the truth, Sawyer," I begged, tears rolling over my face, dripping upon my bare collarbones. "Tell the judge the truth. We stand a chance—I believe we stand a chance." A sob escaped before I could contain it, and his fingers tightened their protective grip.

He rested his cheek against my heartbeat and glided both hands possessively around my waist.

He said hoarsely, "Forgive my temper, Lorie, there is no rationality within me when I think of you being harmed. I lose all control I possess. I pray that we stand a chance, but you will not hang for me. No matter what happens, you will not hang for me."

"Did they hurt you?" I whispered, smoothing my fingers repeatedly over the curve of his skull.

"They are only able to hurt me through you," Sawyer said, and he was raw with emotion. He drew back so that he could see my eyes, and my heart jolted all over again.

"What did Yancy say to you that night?" I asked.

"We spoke very little on the ride north. He said nothing of what had occurred that night, in the clearing." Even more determinedly, Sawyer asked, "Who shot at you?"

"Zeb," I whispered, and a trembling moved upwards from my legs; Sawyer felt this. I explained miserably, "I shot at him, but I aimed wrong, and he shot back. Yancy told me that Zeb wishes to burn Rebel soldiers alive, because a group of them burned his sons, in the War. Oh God, Sawyer...he scares me so..."

"What else did he do to you?" Sawyer asked roughly. "He claimed all manner of despicable acts as we rode north. I would not allow myself to believe him, and even Yancy reprimanded him to be silent."

"He would have used me until I was nearly dead, and I believe he would have killed me," I whispered. "That was why I fled..." I gulped, before continuing, "I thought that if Jack shot me right then, it would be better than going with Zeb to his home..."

"They were taking you there?" Sawyer asked.

"Yes," I whispered. "He was supposed to keep me away until after you'd been..." I choked out, "After you'd been hung..."

Sawyer bent lower and brought his face to my belly, cupping me around the backs of my hips. He kissed me there, so gently, before rising to his full height. He said, "I am so sorry I did not stop them from taking you. I am so sorry."

"They shot Sable from beneath me…" I wept.

"Sable?" he questioned softly, stroking damp hair from my temples. He worked with gentle efficiency, buttoning my blouse, cradling my breasts with aching tenderness.

"The pony they gave me to ride," I whispered, sheltered against him.

A knocking on the door, and startled, I bit the inside of my cheek.

"Mrs. Davis? You must come along," Clemens said, but Boyd shouldered around him and stalked to my side.

"They's gonna let you before a judge," Boyd said, with quiet confidence. "We told them the truth. An' I aim to see this through. They ain't gonna hang you."

There was the slightest easing of distress within Sawyer; I felt it minutely, my cheek tucked to his heartbeat, as his to mine just earlier. I closed my eyes so that I might pretend I was not about to be separated from Sawyer.

"Thank you, for everything," Sawyer said, wholeheartedly; I could feel the pace of his blood. "I know you'll watch over Lorie, while I cannot."

"Mrs. Davis! Mr. Carter!" Clemens was agitated, poking his head around the jailhouse door, and Boyd chuckled, though quietly.

"That one's tetchy as a schoolmarm," Boyd muttered. "We'll return in the daylight, old friend. An' you know I'll keep her safe, with my life."

"Sawyer," I whispered.

He knew, and held me closer still. He whispered, "Darlin', I will see you in the morning. And I will think of you every second until then."

Boyd clasped Sawyer's outstretched hand, holding fast for a last second, and then we left with Clemens.

W HISTLER WAS WAITING in the corral at Tilson's homestead. I climbed the split-rail fence, reaching for her, and she trotted over to me at once, seeking a pat or two, whooshing a loud breath against my side. I hugged her face, lavishing her with affection, my tears soaking into her hide. Even in the advancing darkness I recognized the understanding in her kind eyes, the sense of knowing she exuded. I kissed the white snip at the end of her nose and whispered, "I love you so. You kept him safe, didn't you? I won't let him die, I promise you."

Whistler nickered; I knew she believed me. I leaned against her, this horse that had been born on my tenth birthday, though I would not know this fact until many years later. She had come into the world under Sawyer's observant eye in his daddy's livery stable when he was only sixteen, during the sweet, unaffected contentment of the years prior to War, and he raised her from that moment. She carried him through the hell of a conflict which dragged on longer than anyone could have foreseen, eventually to me, all the way from Tennessee across the wide Missouri prairies, and at last to the night of our handfasting.

My heart ached with fortitude, and purpose, and I said again, "*I promise you.*"

Malcolm ran from indoors and monkeyed beside me, curling around Whistler from the opposite side and laying his cheek against her, which she patiently allowed, shifting her back hooves in the way she had. Malcolm said, "Tilson told us the news."

I whispered, "Oh, Malcolm. It will be all right." I spoke these words to reassure him and to simultaneously comfort myself. Malcolm hopped from the fence and wrapped his arms around my waist, burying his face against my ribs. I stepped gently down and embraced him fully, petting his hair, kissing his cheek; he held my braid the way he'd cradled the stems of the flowers he and Sawyer picked for me to carry at our handfasting—with utmost care, and tenderness.

"Ain't nothing feels right without you an' Sawyer," Malcolm murmured, clinging as a barnacle to a ship's hull. "Lorie-Lorie, don't go away again, please never go away again."

I inhaled familiar scents—that of ripe, sunbaked earth at our feet, clover growing tall and fragrant somewhere near, manure from the corral, dinner wafting on the faintest stir in the air from the direction of the warmly-lit house, where Rebecca, Clemens, Tilson, and Rebecca's boys could be heard, talking over the top of one another in the pleasant, half-exasperated way of families. The sky was a rich indigo and pinpricked by stars; I caught sight of the old crescent, a perfect, creamy cup to cradle the new moon—Deirdre would have said that meant a fair day on the morrow.

The new moon in the embrace of the old, she'd whisper.

Tonight I did not hate the waning sliver of a moon with such a violent fervor.

Malcolm's breath, soft on my cheek, was tinged with lemon.

I whispered, "Had you lemon candy earlier?"

A small sound issued from him, a muffled laugh, which tickled me. He drew away and grinned, saying, "Yep. An' guess what? I near forgot to tell you!"

"What's that, sweetheart?"

"It's my birthday," the boy said. "I'm thirteen years this day. Mrs. Rebecca has a calendar, an' so I know for certain. Boyd can't boss me no more. She done made me a special dinner."

"What's that I hear?" asked Boyd, coming across the yard. He was trailed by one of Rebecca's boys and slowed to accommodate the little one's pace. As they walked, Cort tugged on Boyd's shirt, jabbering at him; Boyd ruffled the boy's hair and said something that made Cort giggle.

"I ain't gotta listen to you no mores!" Malcolm proclaimed joyfully, then yelped and squirreled away as Boyd attempted to curl him into a headlock.

"Dinner's ready!" Cort said, bouncing near my elbow, and I smiled at him; like most youngsters, he remained in perpetual motion. He resembled his mother a great deal; Rebecca's beautiful hazel eyes peered quite plainly from his face. Cort announced, "Mama made a cake!"

"We got more'n one reason to celebrate this night, ain't we?" Boyd said, before successfully harnessing Malcolm about the neck. To his little brother, he invited, "You's free to quit obeying me when you can escape a solid hold."

"Lemme go!" Malcolm yelped, landing rabbit punches against Boyd's ribs, to no effect. Cort giggled and dodged them, then shrieked with laughter as Boyd shifted fluidly, releasing Malcolm and slinging Cort over his back, carrying him towards the house, upside-down.

"The sound of boys playing in the yard does my old heart good," Tilson rumbled, coming outside as well. Silhouetted against the lantern light in the door, he appeared statuesque, tall and imposing—he could almost have been Sawyer, or a man related to my husband, perhaps a father or uncle. And his voice, with its echo of Cumberland County, of home. I found myself willing, however rashly, to trust this stranger, just as I'd been compelled to trust Rebecca.

Tilson leaned back at the waist and commented, "My, but it's a fine night, ain't it?" He ambled across the dooryard and presented his arm to me, asking next, "May I escort a lady to dinner?"

I obligingly took his elbow and saw his teeth flash in a grin. He said, "It's a pleasure, Mrs. Davis."

"Thank you kindly," I said.

"We'll take a leisurely pace," he decided. "As the evening is so fine."

"It is," I agreed, almost shyly, and Tilson patted my hand companionably.

We ambled behind the others on the way to the house, and Tilson said quietly, "Once I had me four fine boys an' a baby girl."

Somehow his gruff voice lent the words an additional quality of wistfulness; I found myself looking up at him as he continued speaking.

"I loved them more'n I can rightly explain. A part of me always wondered if it weren't downright foolish to love anyone that much, but I was a fool for them little ones. They bust up my heart with loving them, an' their mama, my Adeline. She gave me five blessed children. We lost our little Ina Rose when she wasn't but one, an' I thought I couldn't grieve harder'n I did back then."

He paused to draw a sigh, as I studied his imposing profile, wordless as he offered to me these confidences. He continued softly, "But my boys grew tall an' strong. My youngest, my Bridger, weren't but seventeen when the shots was fired at Sumter that cursed spring. All of them, Blythe, Amon, Justus an' Bridger, were a-fired to join the Cause. Couldn't stop 'em, an' I respected their spirit, I did. I joined up to keep my boys safe. An' not a one but Blythe survived that godforsaken conflict, Mrs. Davis, an' their daddy a goddamn physician. My eldest son ain't fit to live with, since. I ain't seen him in near three years, the last of my boys."

Ahead of us, Boyd, Malcolm, and Cort had entered the house; I could hear Rebecca scolding all of them for bumping the table with their wild roughhousing. Tilson and I stopped walking at the same moment. A pair of brown bats fluttered in the sky directly above.

"Where is your son now?" I whispered.

"The Territories south of Kansas, last I heard," Tilson said. He lifted his chin and appeared to be studying the heavens. He said, "I ain't got so much as a reason to believe that Blythe is still living, but I swear on my soul that I'd sense it if he left this Earth before me, I truly do, Mrs. Davis." He admitted, "The way you spoke for your man this eve reminded me something fierce of my wife, my Adeline. She loved me in such a way, an' God knows I didn't always deserve it. Had someone tried to hang me back when she was living, they'd a-been forced to get past her first." And he chuckled, the sound colored with winsome nostalgia.

For no other reason than simple instinct, I rested my cheek upon his arm, however briefly, and without guile, and then, as a gentleman to a formal dinner, Tilson led the way inside.

"Lorie," Rebecca said, coming at once to me. "I am ever so grateful at the news."

"Thank you," I said, realizing she still believed that I was kin to Boyd and Malcolm, and had not been informed of my revelation before the others, at Tilson's office. Impulsively, I leaned and kissed her cheek and though her eyebrows lifted in surprise, a sweet smile overtook her features.

"Come, dear Lorie, we've cake in honor of young Malcolm," Rebecca said, directing me to the chair that Clemens had politely withdrawn.

Rebecca had indeed baked a cake, rich with walnuts and cinnamon, frosted with thick cream; it waited in a tin pan on the sideboard, tempting as the flicker of clear creek water to sweating skin. We crowded about the small wooden table positioned beneath the central ceiling beam, everyone's elbows in each other's way, talking of what had occurred this evening, abridging details as necessary for the little boys. Rebecca was in agreement that Judge Hamm would hear us out when he arrived in Iowa City.

"Leverett Quade is no one's fool, but not an unreasonable man, as I am certain you have realized," Rebecca said, seeming not to remain still for more than a breath, her capable hands buttering bread and passing serving dishes, nudging aside her son's roving fingers when he attempted to steal a swipe of the frosting. I watched Rebecca as discreetly as I was able as she spoke of the marshal, attempting to determine a deeper sense of her feelings for the man. She had quickly parried the subject of Quade's courtship the day of our first meeting, though perhaps that was the result of simple embarrassment at her son's forthright words.

"Yancy is the one needs convincing, foremost," Boyd said. "What do you know of this man, Tilson?"

Boyd sat at the foot of the table, Tilson the head; Clemens was to his uncle's right, while I was to his left. Rebecca sat beside me, Malcolm directly across, feeding bits of food to his gray kitten, the little boys competing for his attention. The knot in my stomach had eased with the relief of knowing we were not utterly helpless, and I found that I was able to eat.

"Not a great deal," Tilson answered in response to Boyd's question, clapping a second helping of boiled potatoes to his plate. "Yancy's on circuit here, every few months. I ain't had a run-in with him, nor that big fella Zeb Crawford, but I aim to have a word with them tomorrow. You're planning the same, ain't you, Carter?"

"That I am," said Boyd. "I got words, real specific-like, for the both of them."

Clemens said, "As have I. I was most troubled by your accounts this evening, Mrs. Davis."

"Where are they now?" I asked, attempting to restrain the urge to cast my eyes about the room and into the darkness outside. Merely the thought of Zeb caused fearful sweat to form along my spine.

"Yancy is within city limits, I am certain," Clemens said. "I imagine him the type to prefer the comforts of the hotel, while Zeb, from what I am able to deduce, may very well be bedded down in an empty stall in the livery. Or perhaps he has left town. I am uncertain of his whereabouts."

"Do you believe Sawyer is safe in the jailhouse?" I asked, suddenly considering the possibility that he was not. "What if—"

"It is a secure building," Clemens assured me. "And either Billings or I am within reasonable distance each night. Billings is presently on duty, but I plan to sleep at the office, as is my habit during weekdays, and I promise I shall check in on Mr. Davis before I retire."

"In town limits, a man's less likely to take action," Tilson said. "I ain't saying it's impossible, but a man's perspective is different in a town. He considers his actions more closely when there's the possibility of being observed, and caught. Your good man is safe, I do believe, Mrs. Davis."

I looked to Boyd, who nodded and then assured me, "I would sit out front of it, if I thought otherwise, Lorie-girl."

Clemens addressed Rebecca next, saying, "I invited Leverett to dinner, but he asked me to relay to you that he would call tomorrow evening, if that suits you."

Rebecca's movement stalled for the first time since we'd all been seated. Instead of replying, she only nodded.

"Will he bring flowers, like last time?" Cort asked his mother. Before she could respond, he informed us, "He brings flowers for Mama near every time he comes," and I found myself struggling to imagine the incongruous picture of stern-faced, businesslike Quade astride his horse and bearing a bouquet.

"Hold your tongue, boy," Tilson scolded, though he softened the words by winking at his great-nephew.

I had only by chance been looking Boyd's way at the start of this exchange, and though I could not interpret his thoughts as I could Sawyer's, I was quite adept at reading his face. The emotion present there was not one which I could have exactly articulated; I saw his gaze flicker briefly but intently to Rebecca, whose chair was angled in such a way that she would have had to turn her head to look directly at him. And then, quite suddenly, she did— though only for a heartbeat, before turning her gaze to me.

"I apologize. Here we talk of trivial things, when your exhaustion must be extreme," Rebecca said; I wondered if I was perhaps reading too much into the slight scald on her cheeks.

"We are indebted to you," I told her. "Please do not apologize, not for a thing."

"We ain't had such good company as yours in a long while," Tilson said, with an unmistakable glint in his eyes; I wondered if he'd intended to subtly jab at Marshal Quade with this statement.

"Boy, you oughtn't to have that critter at the table," Boyd said cantankerously, abruptly directing his focus upon Malcolm, who was quietly feeding scraps to the gray kitten, cuddled on his lap.

"Aw," Malcolm wheedled. "He likes being at my side," but he gamely returned the animal to the wooden crate near the woodstove; immediately it stood on its back legs to peek over the edge.

"You haven't named him yet," Cort reminded Malcolm, and the three boys took up what was certainly a previous conversation, discussing a variety of options.

Boyd sat with his forearms surrounding his plate; I knew he was every bit as fatigued as I, shadows dark beneath his eyes, but Rebecca's table was a proper place, and I caught his gaze with a small motion, frowning unobtrusively; he took my meaning and eased back, politely removing his elbows from the table. Boyd's dark hair was flattened from his hat, his shirt dirty, though he'd washed his arms to the elbow, outside at the pump. He was a good-looking man, solid as an ox and with strong features, black brows above expressive eyes in which the given mood was rarely a mystery. Unable to prevent drawing upon past experience, I considered how the girls in any whorehouse would fight each other for his attention—he and Sawyer, both, and very nearly had, the first night I'd met the two of them.

Though Rebecca sat to his right and within arm's reach, she seemed to be now avoiding looking his way, but he addressed her, saying courteously, "Ma'am, I apologize for my lack of manners. There ain't no excuse. My dear mama would have plenty to say about me appearing in such a state at a proper dinner table."

"On my birthday, too!" Malcolm said, before Rebecca could reply, his brown eyes twinkling, and I was heartened to hear his usual good-humored tone. "Mama wouldn't let you hear the end of it. You look like you ain't combed your hair in days, Boyd!"

"You have ridden far, and hard, this day, Mr. Carter," Rebecca said, politely ignoring the giggles that emerged from her boys at Malcolm's teasing. "Please, do not apologize. You are my guest. *Our* guest," she corrected hastily, and she was flustered, I was not imagining this. Boyd's face remained solemn; I sensed that she caused him unexpected agitation, and he did not know exactly what to make of this.

Boyd said, "Well, I appreciate your hospitality all the same. Makin' a cake for the boy was downright sweet of you."

Rebecca's cheeks were broiling now; I peeked at her from the corner of my left eye, mildly astonished, observing the way she deliberately buried her face behind a sip of water. Boyd continued eating as though he had no notion of her slight discomposure, and perhaps he did not—but then his gaze was drawn again, resting upon her for the space of a breath, before he continued eating.

"Oh, I surely am thankful," Malcolm said. "I ain't had me a birthday cake in *ages*. Not since Mama was alive. I'm most grateful, Mrs. Rebecca."

She smiled warmly at him and said, "And you are most welcome. I have grown quite fond of your company, dear Malcolm. The boys have as well, haven't you, boys?"

"Young Malcolm knows how to entertain the ladies, same as myself," said Tilson, using his fork and knife with a proper air, as of a well-bred gentleman. His hair was parted unevenly, ragged at the ends and tucked behind his ears. I found myself wondering if Tilson had noticed the undercurrent flowing between Boyd and Rebecca; of course it would be unseemly of me to ask him, even if I could catch him for a moment alone. He caught me studying him and offered an affable wink, then regarded his great-nephews, one on either side of Malcolm, advising, "Pay attention, young fellas."

"Maybe we can have a fire this night, Uncle Edward?" asked Cort.

"I suspect we could," Tilson said. "After all, it ain't every Friday that a boy celebrates the day of his birth."

Tilson built a fire in the stone-ringed pit in the side yard, and we sat long into the evening; I collected Sawyer's jacket from the wagon, wrapping into its ample warmth, which blessedly retained the scent of him. Snuggling into it, I thought his name. And moments later he acknowledged softly, *Lorie*.

Rebecca served cake on small tin plates; Malcolm was allowed two pieces, topped with thick, sugar-laced whipped cream. After eating his dessert, and despite now being a boy of thirteen years, Malcolm hooked an elbow over my lap and there lay his head, and I stroked his soft hair.

"Boyd, might you play a spell?" I asked, and he obliged.

For the span of an hour, while Boyd made the fiddle sing, bowing out melodies sweet and haunting, I felt removed from time, suspended between moments; perhaps simple physical exhaustion was at fault, as Boyd and I had

traveled dozens of miles on horseback this day. And still the level of emotional strain we had withstood was incomparable to the physical, far more
taxing. I leaned against a split log meant for a seat, propping my elbow, and
the firelight shimmered as my eyelids grew heavier. My fingers sank into
Malcolm's hair, and I let myself drift to sleep.

It seemed only seconds later that I woke to the scent of tobacco and the
absence of music; the fire had burned to embers, though still radiated heat. I
was curled in Sawyer's jacket and leaning against the split log, while Malcolm
snored. My lap prickled with needles and pins from the weight of him, my
left arm sore from its position against the raw wood, but I felt oddly rested, as
though my body claimed at least a part of what it required. Tilson and Boyd
spoke in low, hushed tones; Clemens was no longer present at the fire, surely
having ridden for town, and Rebecca's boys had settled with their heads upon
her skirt, also asleep. Boyd's fiddle case rested near his right thigh, and he and
Tilson were both smoking.

"We've all a need to leave behind the darkness," Tilson said in a quiet
murmur, drawing on a pipe. "I keep the dear memories tucked close, but I
ain't got use for the others. Drives a man mad, after a time."

"I wish it was that easy," Boyd said in response, low and soft.

"You's a young man," Tilson said, his eyes in the fire. "You'll outlive the
worst of them memories, even if it don't seem that way, at present."

"I still can't hardly figure that many men dead in one fell swoop," Boyd
said, in his fashion of thinking aloud. "An' the horses. All them broken bodies, lying there under the sun an' rotting away. Like as I would to believe that
they'll leave me at peace, I feel them sights'll be with me 'til I leave this earth."

Rebecca was silently studying him, her body angled just slightly in my
direction, while Boyd and Tilson sat opposite, beside one another.

"Ma'am, I apologize," Boyd said, interrupting himself, his dark eyes lighting upon Rebecca and holding fast. He said, "It's the late hour, I s'pose, that's
loosening my tongue. I ain't fond of the idea of you bein' forced to think of
such terrible things."

Rebecca only shook her head, gently dismissing his concerns. Her eyes
were steady on Boyd's; no more than a few feet separated them and yet it
somehow seemed an impassable distance. Boyd swallowed as their gaze remained intertwined and unbroken; something far more complex than any
words passed between them. And then a log snapped with an explosion of

little sparks, and broke the stillness. Rebecca blinked and looked discreetly away from him.

"Maybe it ain't even right to forget, much as we want to," Boyd murmured, and passed a hand over his face as if swiping at unwelcome memories. He explained, "If we forget, I start to feel as though my kin died for nothing. My brothers, my cousins, my folks, all gone. Once I coulda spoke of the Cause, justified it to my last breath. An' now, I can't remember a goddamn thing about the *why* of it. My kin died for no reason a'tall but to satisfy the needs of those in power, them that would let others die in their place. Once there was more Carters in the holler than you could count in a day, an' now there ain't but the boy an' me left to bear our name."

"We like to blame the devil for the evil in the world," Tilson said, and sighed, exhaling smoke. Tilson possessed what Deirdre would have called a solid 'poker face,' in that his expression was carefully neutral, and therefore difficult to read. He elaborated, "It's easier that way, see? The way I see it, the true evil ain't the work of any old devil. It comes from the capacity of one man to hate another man. A man he ain't ever met, ain't ever spoke to, but that he's made to hate right to his very guts. A man he'd just as soon shoot as look at. The speed with which a man can be galled into taking sides, an' overlooking all else, that's evil."

"I do not disagree," Boyd said.

"I cared not for causes, or politics. I begged Elijah not to go," Rebecca said, with quiet bitterness, and I looked her way at these unexpected words. She was to my left, wrapped in a shawl and with her palms resting upon her boys; her gaze was deep in the embers, snagged there, though it was clear she was not seeing the pile of glowing coals. The fire danced over her fine features. I knew well the blade of loss. It had cut into all of us—robbing us of fathers, brothers, husbands, sons; inescapable, it struck without mercy and sliced indiscriminately, caring not for any of our foolish hopes. The War had made widows and orphans of an entire generation; I heard this sentiment expressed many times while employed at Ginny's.

"Now, honey," Tilson began, drawing the pipe from between his lips.

"Elijah never crossed me a day in our marriage, and yet he would not be persuaded in this matter. I pleaded with him to stay home. I wanted my *husband,* not a soldier. I may not have been to battle, but memories plague me,"

Rebecca said. "There are days I wish I had none. They could hurt me no more if I held both hands in the fire."

Compassion lifted Tilson's brows and yet there was an edge of caution about his demeanor, as if he knew from experience that his words could yield anger. He said quietly, "Elijah believed he was doing his part for his country."

Rebecca's chin jerked to the side, as if she wished to hide tears, but her voice emerged steadily as she whispered, "What of his part for his family? What of that?"

"He believed he was serving his family the only way he could," Tilson murmured, pausing to relight his pipe, shifting his focus and thereby allowing her a moment in which to compose herself.

Boyd sat wordlessly, a tobacco roll caught between his teeth, and his eyes remained fixed upon Rebecca as she stirred with restless energy. I tried to gauge his current thoughts, and was unable. He was as stone-faced as I had ever seen him.

"I *begged* him not to go," Rebecca repeated, imploring Tilson, as though it had been his duty to prevent her husband from taking up arms and marching to fight. Her eyes shone wet with tear-shine. She choked, "He was killed before he ever saw Nathaniel. I haven't even my husband's body, nor so much as a grave to visit. I have *nothing left* but memories and promises unfulfilled."

"You have two fine sons," Tilson reminded her.

Rebecca closed her eyes and bent her head; the pale smoothness of the back of her neck resembled the delicate stalk of a flower in the faint light. Her nostrils flared as she released a breath and used her knuckles to scrape away her tears, but when she lifted her face, she had regained control. "You are right, of course, Uncle Edward." She looked to me and whispered, "Forgive me for behaving this way, and before company. I am overcome."

I was just far enough from her that I could not reach and offer a comforting touch; I wanted to gather her close. Not simply so that I could pretend she was Deirdre, at long last acknowledging the fervency with which I'd begged absolution for her death since the night it happened, but because I truly cared for Rebecca. I understood her words, and the intensity behind them, as well as anyone could.

I said, "There is not one thing to forgive."

Rebecca managed a ghost of a smile before whispering, "Thank you, Lorie. Uncle Edward, shall you help me with the boys?"

"Of course I will, honey," said Tilson, but Boyd rose first, stepping around the fire and to her side, gathering Cort into his arms with capable strength.

"Show me where this little fella belongs," he said to Rebecca.

Malcolm stirred and sat up as Boyd followed Rebecca to the house, each of them toting a sleeping boy. Malcolm rubbed both eyes and then bent his arms about his knees, catching one wrist in the opposite hand; I had to smile at his posture, as Sawyer always positioned himself in the same fashion at the fire.

"If it ain't the birthday boy," Tilson said, winking at Malcolm.

"I don't feel older," Malcolm said. "I feel like I oughta *feel* older."

"What is today's date?" I asked. "I just realized I have no idea."

"The seventeenth of July," Tilson said obligingly.

"We very nearly share a birthday," I told Malcolm, pleased at this revelation. "Mine was only yesterday, though it has passed without my noticing."

"Lorie-Lorie!" Malcolm reprimanded. "You shoulda had another piece of cake," and his dark eyes shone in the ember glow. He said, "We's nearly twins, then."

"Nearly," I agreed, scooting closer so that I could rest my cheek upon him. I held close Sawyer's jacket and Malcolm wrapped one wiry arm around me, letting me snuggle to him this time, as Boyd rejoined us, ruffling Malcolm's hair as he sat.

"Many happy returns, boy," he murmured to his little brother.

"That was kind of you to help Becky," Tilson commented.

"Ain't nothin'," Boyd insisted politely. "We's all tuckered."

"Today is Becky and Elijah's wedding anniversary," Tilson explained, low and soft, and Boyd's hands fell still; he had been in the process of relighting his smoke. Tilson continued, "I weren't present for their wedding, but Becky's mama, my dear little sister, wrote of the account an' mailed it to us back home."

A beat of quietude surrounded us as we absorbed this knowledge.

"How long was they wed?" Boyd asked at last, and there was a husky quality to his voice that was not entirely from the smoke.

"Well, they were joined in 'fifty-eight, an' Elijah was killed in action the summer of 'sixty-three," Tilson said. "So, a good five years. I cannot claim to have known Elijah, but my niece loved him dearly. Becky was carrying Nathaniel, you see, when his daddy was killed."

Boyd flinched, just slightly; I felt a similar lashing of pain at this information.

Tilson said, "Don't let on that I've said a thing, if you would. Becky can't hardly speak Elijah's name without shedding tears for him, an' so I don't mention the man if I can help it."

Boyd whispered hoarsely, "Killed in which engagement that summer?"

Tilson knew exactly what Boyd indirectly asked, and replied, "Ain't one that you boys was in, I can say with near certainty. Elijah died outside Vicksburg, in June of that year."

Boyd's shoulders eased; he changed subjects abruptly, saying, "Lorie-girl, I made ready a pile of quilts for you in the wagon. An' I set up our tent, boy."

"I ain't tired," Malcolm said, yawning wide enough to nearly crack his skull.

"A quarter hour and you will be sound asleep," I teased. "Thank you, Boyd."

"Ain't nothin'," he said again, and I longed to ask him what was on his mind—a penny for his thoughts, as Mama would have said.

"Lorie-Lorie, let's have a bet," Malcolm encouraged, with enthusiasm. Sitting straighter, he elaborated, "I'll bet you a penny I'll still be awake in a quarter-hour."

Boyd snorted and said, "You ain't got a penny to speak of."

"A gambler's life is no easy path," Tilson said, grinning at Malcolm. "You's a bit young to be considering it."

"I ain't gonna be a gambler," Malcolm assured us. "Soon as I'm able, I'll homestead an' build me a cabin in them woods Uncle Jacob is so fond of writing about."

"I know life in Minnesota ain't gonna be what we's used to," Boyd said, exhaling smoke from both nostrils. Resting his forearms on his bent knees, he murmured, "I scarce go a full day when home don't cross my mind. But I aim to take my chances in the wilds north of here. I swore to myself that I would get us there."

"What's wrong?" I asked Boyd, sensing the uneasiness in him whether he intended it or not; I thought not, as his brows drew inward.

Boyd looked between the three of us, Tilson and Malcolm and me, his face somber and his eyes unreadable. At last he admitted, "It's being in the North, in enemy territory. I know it ain't the same as when we was fighting, but all a-these Yankees about. I feel they would see us harmed for being Southern. Tell us to go straight to hell."

"But the fighting's all done," Malcolm said quietly. "It's over."

"Some things ain't ever truly over, boy," Boyd said, in an equally hushed voice. "There's an open wound in our country yet, bubbling over an' refusing to heal. I don't know when it'll heal over. An' the scar will always be there, I feel it in my bones, boy."

I shivered at his words, which resonated with undeniable truth.

Tilson said, "There's truth to that. We ain't to see its end, not in my lifetime. Perhaps in yours, boy." He sighed, exhaling a thin cloud of smoke, and concluded kindly, "But you get used to being in Yankee country. Took me a fair amount, an' the winters are fearsome cold for a Tennessee boy, but there ain't no life back home. Not for us, not these days. You'll find your way, all of yous. Your good man, too, Mrs. Davis."

And I prayed that he was right.

I washed my hands and face as quickly as I was able, at the pump to the rear of the house, beneath which grew a thick patch of daisies; their soft white petals brushed against the material of my borrowed trousers. I shuddered at the icy water that snaked down my blouse while I scrubbed at my skin; my closed eyes felt like boiled eggs against my fingertips, and this observation caused another shudder to clutch at me. It was dark and cold, but I could hear Boyd and Malcolm murmuring to each other as they settled into their tent, just as they usually did on the trail, and this familiarity allowed for a sense of relief, however small. I smiled a little as I used the edge of my sleeve to dry my face, and then observed Rebecca coming across the darkened yard and towards me.

"I came to offer you my bed," she said. "I shall bunk in with my boys in the loft."

"Heavens, no," I replied. "I have a bed in the wagon."

"But it is so cold out here, for a July night," she protested, bundled into a shawl, her hair a long braid. Her feet were bare, and the ground was wet with dew. I imagined her hem was similarly damp. She looked almost like a little girl in the dimness. She whispered, "I am sorry for my behavior at the fire. Please do not think me discourteous."

"Of course I do not think such," I said, gently scolding, thinking of that which Tilson had related at the fire, of this night being the anniversary of Rebecca's marriage to Elijah. I clutched her arm and said, "I wish that I had words of comfort. But I know there are not any, not when your husband was taken from you."

"Come indoors, let me fetch you another quilt, at least," Rebecca said, and led the way. The house was warm, and lit dimly by the fire in the potbelly of the woodstove; a chorus of snores met our ears, from the loft above. Outside, Tilson remained at the fire, stirring the embers with a long stick, meditatively smoking his pipe.

"Your uncle told us some about your husband," I admitted as Rebecca handed me a quilt from the trunk against the north wall. I found myself wanting to talk with her, hopeful that she would be willing.

"Please, sit a moment, let us speak," she whispered, as though sensing my thoughts. "That is, if you are not too exhausted…my manners are inexcusable…"

I sat at the dinner table, folding the quilt over my arms, and Rebecca seated herself just opposite. The quiet darkness of the room inspired confidences, and I said, "You remind me a great deal of a girl I used to know. I felt it from the first moment I saw you."

"Malcolm said as much," Rebecca acknowledged. "Dear Lorie. When Clint told me that day that you were missing, I was sick with worry. Far beyond that which is logical, as we had only just met, but it struck me soundly. I knew that I was to help you. I know it still."

"You risked yourself, Sawyer told me," I whispered. "I cannot thank you enough."

"I did only that which I believed I should," she said, her voice low and soft. "Your husband was ready to tear apart this town to find you. Clint is quite terrified of him, and of your brother, though he shan't admit it. And I must tell you, your brother's words…Mr. Carter's, that is…moved me greatly. You see, Clint asked your husband was it possible that you had left Iowa City of your own accord, and before anyone could speak your brother responded with an impassioned answer the likes of which I have never heard. It was beautifully spoken, so very sincere. He understands the depth of love between you and your husband, Lorie, and more than that, he was unashamed in his opinions." She whispered again, "It moved me greatly."

"He and Sawyer have been friends all their lives," I whispered. The tone with which she spoke of Boyd told me far more than any thousand words. I acknowledged softly, "Boyd is a good man."

"I shall admit, the thought of harm befalling him, or any of you, troubles me greatly. When he and Mr. Davis rode after you, I was fearful that I may never see him again…I can scarcely fathom the strength of this sentiment, even now…I was fearful I would never see *any* of you again, and I find that unbearable, as irrational as that may be…"

"It is not irrational," I said. "It is not, Rebecca."

"What of your family? Your mother, your father? What of your other siblings?"

I hesitated less than a second; after all, her brother and uncle knew the truth about my past. I asked, "May I tell you something?"

"Of course you may," Rebecca said.

A log in the stove snapped, momentarily intensifying the reddish glow in the small room. Snores provided a background cadence both reassuring and oddly peaceful. I studied what I could see of Rebecca's eyes, and whispered, "Boyd and Malcolm are not my brothers. And yet, I could not love them more. They are more brothers to me than were Jesse and Dalton, God rest their souls."

"I do not understand…"

"I used to work in St. Louis for a woman named Ginny Hossiter. I had worked for her since I was fifteen years old. Sawyer and Boyd, and Malcolm, were traveling from Tennessee, had been on the trail since April, and they were accompanied then by a man named Angus Warfield. Angus knew my father, Rebecca, and he…he took me from Ginny's place. That very night, he brought me with them…" I stuttered to a halt, unwittingly yanked amongst nightmarish memories. Not those of Angus taking me from Ginny's; he had rescued me as surely as I still drew breath, but of the night he had been killed for his trouble.

Rebecca whispered, "You will think me dense as a stump, but I still do not understand…"

"I worked for her as a whore," I said, without rancor or challenge. It was the simple truth, after all. "Since I was fifteen I worked as a whore."

There was a beat of silence; Rebecca's gaze remained unwavering.

"Oh, Lorie," she whispered, and then reached across the table to grasp my hands; hers were small and delicate, but warm as they surrounded mine, which were chilled from the pump. Rebecca said, "Oh, my dear. But you are so very young…"

"When you spoke earlier of memories…you see, I understand better than you could have known. I know what it means to lie awake, plagued by the past." I threaded my fingers into hers and held tightly; she was the second woman in whom I had confided, Fannie Rawley being the first, and neither had been horrified, or summarily repulsed. I sensed only sympathy, and compassion.

She whispered, "What of this Angus? Where is he now?"

And so I told her.

IN THE MORNING I was anxious as a flea-bitten horse to ride into town and set eyes upon Sawyer.

"But we done hauled water for you," Malcolm complained, when I voiced this desire. "Just so's you could take a bath. Why in tarnation you gotta wash *again*, Lorie-Lorie?"

His query was delivered in such a manner to suggest true curiosity rather than overt exasperation, and I caught him by the elbow and kissed his cheek. I explained, "Because my scalp is itching."

Malcolm said, "You's got longer fingernails than me. Just scratch it, an' you'll be right as *rain*."

Rebecca had prepared a breakfast of fried eggs and onions, and delicious corn grits; there was strong coffee, accompanied by fine white sugar in a porcelain bowl painted with daisies, and a jar of sticky-sweet blackberry preserves. Just these small luxuries were worth the cramped eating space, all of us again crowded at the table; I had grown so accustomed to taking meals out-of-doors, in the wide-openness provided by the endless prairies. After breakfast, I stole into the small bedroom at the back of the house, narrow and hardly large enough for the brass-framed bed pushed beneath the solitary window. Studying its neatly-made surface under the scattering of a fair morning's light, I knew this was the same bed Rebecca had shared with Elijah.

Last night she had spoken of him, in copious detail. From her descriptions, I pieced together a solid picture of a good-natured man to whom she was wed at age eighteen.

"His eyes were blue as cornflowers, just like Nathaniel's. Elijah never met his youngest son, and yet it is Nathaniel who most resembles him," Rebecca had said. "Elijah never failed to speak dearly to me. He was the kindest soul alive, Lorie. I cannot tell you how greatly I long for the sound of his voice. If I could hear it once more before I die, I should be content. When I read the letters he wrote to me, I imagine his voice speaking the words."

Elijah had fought with a battalion for the state of Iowa, from 'sixty-two until his death; his only remaining relative, an older brother, had died prior to that, in March of the same year.

"Uncle Edward never begrudged us for being Yankees," Rebecca had explained. "Clint and I were raised in Illinois and Iowa, both—our papa was from Illinois—though I do believe a part of Mama's heart always remained back home, in Tennessee. She and Papa met there, after all, when Papa was on a business trip with his own father, in the summer of 'thirty-nine. She and Papa fell in love and courted there, and later he brought Mama, Clint, and me to this very homestead, where Mama remained until she died."

In the relative privacy of Rebecca's bedroom, I stripped to the skin, noting the blood that had congealed and scabbed over my wound, and proceeded to scrub scalp and body, hunkering in the tin washtub that Malcolm and the boys had dutifully filled with water from the pump; I had hoped it would warm a little during breakfast, but it was still shocking to my skin. At least it was wet, and cleansed away the dust and grime. Rebecca and I talked the night away, and this morning found me still so very tired; I indulged in a moment's rest, even propped uncomfortably as I was in the washtub with its rim no more than two feet in diameter. The hard edge dug into my back, but I had positioned it near the sunlight spilling into the room, and closed my eyes to appreciate the warmth.

Zeb was here, last night, I realized, the thought utterly unbidden, and my stomach lurched; my eyes opened at once, and roved the small room.

No. You are mistaken.

He was here, my mind insisted, despite my best efforts to disbelieve. *He looked upon you as you lay sleeping in the wagon.*

Water sloshed as I sat straight and twisted all of my hair to the side, scanning the small window; covered as it was in oiled canvas, I could not directly view the yard, but the glow of a cloudless sky was translucently visible, and nothing more. Not the hulking figure that terrorized my thoughts if I let down my guard. I did not understand how I came to an understanding of

Zeb's presence with such certainty—I had not woken in the early morning hours to spy him, I had heard nothing out of the ordinary.

You sensed him as you walked to bed, remember?

I recalled hurrying through the darkness to the quilts waiting in the back of the wagon. The wagon itself was parked between the house and the barn, nearer still to the wall tent in which Boyd and Malcolm slept last night; I had not felt unsafe. *And yet...*

A shiver overtook me as I climbed within the canvas-covered space. I gave no thought to this, other than that it signified I was cold, which I had been. But what if Zeb truly had risked creeping near in the night hours, hiding out of sight and watching Tilson's homestead, angered that he had been denied his prize, hoping to enact additional harm upon us? Zeb knew that Boyd and I were here, and he bore each of us no little hatred. He would as soon kill Boyd as look at him; he had tried to kill me, and Yancy had been forced to stop him.

You are allowing your imagination to get the better of your judgment, I reprimanded myself, hurrying from the tub and wrapping into a length of toweling, unwilling to sit motionless any longer, determined to set aside these fears. I combed my hair with Mama's brush, one of the only items of hers retained from my old life, braiding and pinning up its length. I dressed in my own clothing, with reluctance, acknowledging that I much preferred the ease of trousers to layers of skirts—how I had once longed to be a boy, understanding even as a child that they were allowed far more privileges than was I, as a girl. Mama had been predictably horrified.

"You are my daughter, and a *lady*," she had said, on many an occasion. "And a lady allows the men in her life the privilege of taking care of her, at all times."

I mean no disrespect, Mama, but I must disagree. And I believe you would understand, I truly do.

"Lorie! You ready?" Malcolm called, in his usual impatient fashion. "Boyd says we gotta post a letter to Jacob."

Tilson left for town an hour past, while Boyd settled at the table to compose a word to his uncle; Jacob and Hannah expected us before autumn, and now we were well behind our original schedule.

We will get to Minnesota, and to their home. We will reach this place, I swear it, I vowed, thinking of what Boyd had said last night at the fire, opening the door to see him and Malcolm seated at the table, Boyd bent over his letter to Jacob, quill pen scratching along. Malcolm, from what I had already ascertained through the closed door, was in the process of begging for an evening dinner of pan-fried chicken.

"It's been such a piece since I had me some," Malcolm said, in the appealing, persuasive tone I knew well. He sighed, "Oh, what I wouldn't give."

"I would have to wring a few pullets' necks, and I had not intended such this day. It is not pleasant work," Rebecca said, her hip near Boyd's shoulder as she stood drying the cake pan with an embroidered towel; Malcolm sat just across the table from his brother, the gray kitten upon his lap, and he leaned forward to ply Rebecca with his considerable charm, sensing the slightest give in her protests.

"*Please*, pretty please?" Malcolm wheedled, teasing the kitten with his fingertip. "I got me a real hankerin', now that we's talked of it. It's me an' Boyd's most *favoritest*..."

This statement gave Rebecca just the slightest pause; in her scholarly fashion, every word precise, she murmured, "I am uncertain if I have enough cornmeal..."

Boyd looked up from his writing. Rebecca, positioned as she was, could not see his face; he sent Malcolm the briefest flicker of a wink and then sighed, lamenting with apparent nonchalance, "Leave off, boy. Besides, it just ain't a dish done *right*, outside the South."

The towel in Rebecca's hand fell still and Boyd surely felt the sudden charge in the air behind him, similar to the instant before bolt lightning pierced a cloud to strike the earth; his dark eyes were merry and he bit back a smile even as Rebecca asked, with considerable snap, "*Mr.* Carter, did I not hear from your mouth this *very* morning what fine grits I had prepared for breakfast?"

He said demurely, "You did, indeed."

Gesturing with the pan, Rebecca demanded, "Are not grits a dish commonly prepared in the Southern states of this country?"

"They are, at that." A dimple appeared in Boyd's right cheek, though he kept his eyes downcast.

Rebecca continued, with asperity, "Or perhaps you were offering an empty compliment."

At this, Boyd immediately hooked an elbow over the chair back, turning so that he could see her face. All teasing gone from his voice, he said, "I was most certainly not."

The faintest suggestion of a smile nudged her softly-bowed lips as their eyes held, and caressed; there was no mistaking this. In a sweeter tone, Rebecca said, "My mama herself taught me to fry pullets, and she was born and bred in Tennessee. See if I haven't learned a thing or two." She turned to settle the pan on its shelf, concluding breezily, "That is, *if* I decide to fry any."

Not minutes later, Malcolm and I turned to wave farewell to Cort and Nathaniel, who had agreed to mind the kitten in our absence; both boys hung on the corral fence to watch us rumble away in the wagon while Boyd rode Fortune, just to our right.

"You two best thank her profusely," I said, elbowing Malcolm and then leaning to address Boyd, who rode immediately closer. I elaborated, "After that trick."

"What trick, Lorie-girl?" Boyd asked innocently, though his eyes danced beneath the brim of his hat.

"You know very well," I said, the ribbons anchoring my hat fluttering in the light breeze. "Even if that chicken isn't better than you have ever tasted, you will tell Rebecca it is."

Boyd said, "She weren't fooled a moment. She saw right through me." He added, half-wickedly, "An' I got me a notion it'll be the *best* thing I ever tasted."

Billings was at the jailhouse this morning, sour-faced and unwilling to leave the room so that I might speak alone with Sawyer.

"Must I be plagued until you are gone from here?" Billings grumbled, his back to us as he reseated himself at the writing desk. He muttered, "Goddamn marshals everywhere, and wives..."

"Well, just the one wife," Sawyer whispered, for my benefit alone. A hint of his good humor had been restored to him—perhaps it was the bright sun outside, the sense of purpose and promise of hope, and perhaps it was erroneous, even foolish, to allow such feelings, but I was abundantly grateful nonetheless.

He asked quietly, "Did you sleep well, darlin'? Holy Jesus, I miss you..."

I held fast to him, my fingers curled around the material of his shirt, absorbing the feel of him, storing up for when we would be apart. I demanded, "Are you warm at night? I worry so much...I miss you, too..."

"All I need to keep warm are my thoughts of you," he murmured.

"Boyd tricked Rebecca into making fried chicken," I said.

Sawyer grinned, and the sight of it upon his face came close to caving in my heart, same as always. He asked, "How did he manage that? She seems a woman not easily fooled."

I was about to respond when Billings sighed, and said acerbically, "I'll thank you to state your business and take your leave, Mrs. Davis."

"Keep near Boyd," Sawyer said, growing serious again, his eyes intense as he took my face in his strong, lithe hands, stroking my lips with his thumbs. "Please, darlin', keep near him. Yancy is not to be trusted, and he's in a black fury that I am to see the judge. I can't see him acting on his own, but Zeb may, in his place. And with Yancy's consent."

"Yancy is a federal marshal," Billings said, overhearing this last remark. "He is a law-abiding citizen."

Sawyer kept his eyes upon mine, ignoring Billings and his blustering.

Keep near Boyd, he said again.

And I nodded my understanding.

It was Saturday, the eighteenth of July, and we should have been bound for Minnesota. Instead, I sat on a chair in Tilson's office, while Malcolm stacked and restacked a deck of cards that Tilson lent him, an untouched cup of water at his elbow.

"It's healing up right nice," Tilson murmured. He donned a pair of silver-rimmed spectacles to examine my arm. His hands were large, but simultaneously light and careful, his fingertips gentle over my skin. "I don't see signs of infection."

"Fannie Rawley cleansed it with garlic, and lye soap," I said, as Tilson eased the blouse back over my shoulder, and I refastened the two buttons I had undone in order to bare the wound.

"Just as I would have done," Tilson said.

Though I had promised to stay near Boyd, he was insistent that I remain here while he sought out Quade, and Yancy, ideally both at once. Yancy had been to the jailhouse in the early morning hours, as Billings informed me, and though there appeared to be no sign in town of Zeb Crawford, I knew better. He was lingering here, somewhere. Tilson promised to keep an eye on both Malcolm and me, and allowed Malcolm to peek into the satchel containing what medical supplies he possessed, answering the boy's subsequent numerous questions. It was otherwise quiet in his office, occupied by nothing more than our bodies and specks of rainbow-tinted dust, visible in the bars of golden sun leaking through the canvas-covered window.

And so we passed the long hours of the summer day, eating cold biscuits and bacon for lunch; later, near mid-afternoon, a man came seeking Tilson, explaining that his wife had been in labor since dawn, and was requesting the doc.

"How is she faring, Billy?" Tilson asked, up and gathering supplies, which he tucked into his satchel.

"She's paining, doc, I hated to leave her," Billy responded. He was young, revealing a bearded, sunburned face when he doffed his hat at Malcolm and me. "She's asking after her mama, and her mama's been gone some five years."

"You return to Letty, we'll be on your heels," Tilson said, and Billy did not need to be told twice.

"This is the woman you mentioned earlier?" I asked, tying the ribbons of my hat beneath my chin.

"She is, at that. I expect I'll haul you two along," Tilson said. "Letty will be glad of a woman, Mrs. Davis, an' perhaps you'll assist me, if you've a mind to. Malcolm, bring them cards, son. You'll be setting and waiting a fair piece, I fear, as this is her first babe."

We left a note for Boyd and then climbed atop Tilson's flatbed wagon, into which he tucked his satchel and his rifle, riding over the prairie and to a neighboring farm, several miles west of town and along the river, a small homestead bordered by pines and with a pen full of pigs. Despite the heat of the day smoke curled from the chimney, as the lone window in the structure was covered with canvas rather than glass, and it would have been dark as evening without the fire. The man who had come to request Tilson's presence met us at the door.

"Billy, leave it propped open, if you would," Tilson said to him. "I can't see a blessed thing otherwise. And the afternoon is a lovely one."

Malcolm and I hovered behind Tilson with the uncertainty of strangers; the wedge of daylight allowed into the space by the open door fell upon a slice of dirt floor and the right leg of a low-slung bed, upon which a woman knelt, her bare feet cast in light, the rest of her body in shadow; her pale feet,

slim and narrow and lit by the sun, appeared oddly vulnerable, and I wished
to protect them, perhaps cover them with a blanket. Smoke from the hearth
fire fled out the door, at once freshening the air.

"It's a fine day to welcome a child, ain't it, Letty?" Tilson calmly inquired
of the woman, despite her obvious distress. He continued, already moving to
her side, "This here is Mrs. Davis, an' she'll assist me. How would that be?"

"That'd be…right fine," the woman managed to say, in a breathless moan.
Her voice was scarcely audible.

"Lorie, come around the side here," Tilson said, retaining a tranquil confidence that transferred to me; I obeyed, rolling back my sleeves, no longer
steeped in hesitancy. It was the first time Tilson had referred to me by my
given name; I felt oddly pleased by this informality.

"What can I do?" Malcolm asked earnestly.

"Bless you, boy, but I'd rather you wait out near the crik. Have Billy show
you where them trout is biting," Tilson said. "Keep him busy, won't you, son?"

And Malcolm nodded his understanding.

I joined Tilson at the bedside, my eyes having adjusted to the dimness,
and did my best to offer the woman a smile, even as I realized that she was
much more girl than woman, hardly appearing old enough to issue forth a
child of her own. Her hair lay in a lank braid; her belly was distended un-
imaginably beyond its usual girth. A pale face round as a gourd lifted to peer
at mine before pain doubled her forward. She wore a drooping dress designed
to accommodate her girth, rucked now about her hips. The bedding beneath
her knees was damp and soiled. She moaned again and remained hunched
over her midsection.

"Letty, lay back an' let me see how far along," Tilson said, and his very
demeanor established and maintained a sense of steady calm. He invited,
"Hold to Lorie."

Together we lowered her and then I took her chilled hands, letting her
grip as she would, and despite the fragility of her fingers, she grasped with
considerable force. Tilson gently raised her skirts, and I was struck by a memory of the night Sawyer found me in Sam Rainey's camp, the way Sawyer had
lifted my dirty garments using similar motions, with absolute tenderness and
yet an urgency of need to determine the extent of the damage. Letty's knees
splayed wide and her hips lifted from the bedding as she emitted a hissing
groan, nearly grinding my bones as she clutched.

I tried to read Tilson's face as his big, capable hands roved her belly; he appeared to be peering into the middle distance as he explored the flesh between her thighs in his careful assessment. I was fairly certain that I detected a hint of concern about him, though outwardly he gave little sign, and it was merely a guess upon my part. But then his eyes met mine, and I knew I was not wrong.

He looked back to Letty and said quietly, "Honey, you're right far along, but the babe ain't positioned properly just yet. I'd like for you to get to all fours."

She nodded roughly, and again we assisted her motions. She breathed heavily as Tilson gripped her hips, easing her into position. He spoke in low murmurs, soothing her. To me, he said, "I can't quite tell if I felt a foot or an elbow, but sure not the little one's head."

"It...hurts..." she groaned, gasping between breaths, and I put both hands immediately to her back, patting and soothing as well as I could.

"Pull in a deep breath," Tilson said. "There's a good one, now another..."

From this new angle he reached to cup her belly, his eyes fixed on a single point upon the wall but truly seeing inward, to the child contained within her, a writhing mass of life demanding entry into the world. Letty's position brought to my mind a laboring horse, perhaps uncharitably, but it was the only picture I had upon which to draw; I had witnessed many birthings in Daddy's stable. Letty's heaving ribs and hanging head were akin to what I had seen as a little girl—I almost expected forelegs to emerge from between her parted thighs.

"He's near sideways," Tilson muttered, gritting his teeth a little, as though in sympathy. He said, "Feel here," and commandeered my hands, guiding them to the child within her; he was correct in his statement, and a sudden splash of apprehension caught me in the face. He asked, low, "Have you seen a child born?"

"No," I said. "Only horses."

"It's much the same," Tilson acknowledged. "Though just now, we's got a piece of work." He said to Letty, "Honey, we have to turn the babe. He's pointing the wrong way."

"Help him..." she begged, rearing upwards as much as she was able, imploring Tilson. "Please...help him..."

"We will, but it'll hurt, an' you must be strong. Stay like this, darlin', as that will ease the pain a little."

Letty sagged forward, chin to chest, braced upon the bedding and watching her belly upside-down. Her dress had sunk and I carefully eased it up past her hips, determined not to shy away from the task at hand; if Letty could bear the pain, I could certainly find the courage to remain near, and assist as well as I could.

"In my satchel, Lorie, there's strips of linen. Fetch those, set them near, an' stoke that fire, get the kettle boiling. Just there," and Tilson nodded, while I hurried to do his bidding, glad to be given a task, busying myself. While I worked, Tilson spoke softly to Letty, rubbing her side. Glancing their way, I beheld dark blood seeping from between her legs, creating small rivulets. At the sight I fell completely still, inadvertently clenching my teeth, involuntarily remembering.

Blood, with its unmistakable scent.

Blood that spilled forth with no regard for the life it was stealing.

Letty hissed and her back suddenly arched, and I understood that I could not let the darkness of my memories overwhelm me, not now. I gathered the linens and hurried to the bedside. Letty's lower body was bared and her knees spread wide, her genitals appearing purple and swollen. I said firmly, "Tell me what to do."

"Set those here, then hold her shoulders, try to keep her still," Tilson said, and I followed his orders at once. Letty seemed not to hear his words, locked in her own private chamber of pain, but Tilson addressed her, explaining, "Hold as still as you can, darlin', but don't be afraid to yell out."

Without further ado, he gripped her stomach as one would a large, ripe watermelon, and then he bore down, forcibly attempting to maneuver the child into place.

Letty screamed, harshly, her muscles rigid under my grip. I was baring my teeth and did not realize, shocked and horrified at the noises torn from her, even as I silently begged Tilson to succeed in his endeavor, or to stop.

"She's bleeding so much," I choked out, unable to remain silent.

"He's shifted," Tilson said, with an air of purpose, setting free Letty's mid-section and putting his hands upon her lower back. He ordered, "You must push, Letty, he's shifted."

"I...can't..." she moaned.

Blood flowed faster, escalating at the pace of her breath. Though I was doing little but observing, sweat greased my skin and my breathing matched hers; I was fearful she would die, here before our eyes.

"You can," Tilson encouraged. "You must."

Letty tried to nod, and she strained hard, sagging and then pushing again, to no avail. She was sobbing now, in between great gulps of air. She gasped, "I...can't..."

"Make a dart of your fingertips, Lorie, and I'll show you what to do," Tilson said, not to be contradicted. "Quickly now," and he demonstrated with his own.

I understood even before his explanation.

"She's narrow across the pelvis, an' we must get the babe free," Tilson said. "It's just what your daddy would do to help birth a foal, you'll recall. I'll press an' you pull, darlin', it's the only way."

I braced myself at Letty's hips, given over to necessity now, no space in my mind for thoughts, or for any lingering squeamishness. I hesitated only a fraction, my own innards seeming to seize in response, and then slid my fingers into her body. Tight heat, and wetness. Blood to my wrist. I felt the need to apologize profusely, to beg forgiveness of Letty for this repugnant intrusion. But then, in the depths of her, I felt the child, sturdy and firm, and there.

"I feel him!" I heard myself yelp.

"Good, now guide him," Tilson said, and it was as though we were tussling with a wild animal, taming a creature between us, as he massaged and kneaded while I did my best to tug.

Letty wailed repeatedly, the sound shredding the air.

"C'mon now," Tilson urged. "Letty, you must push. Push!"

Her entire frame heaved and subsequently expelled my hand. Before my eyes, equal parts alarmed and amazed, the skin between her legs parted further, bulging unfathomably; an oval of wet black hair appeared.

"I see him!" I cried.

"Once more," Tilson insisted. "Letty, once more." She gasped and strained again; Tilson said, "There he comes!"

And there it was, indeed, a perfectly round human head emerging from her womb, an entirely new person entering the world.

"Be ready, Lorie!" Tilson said, and just that quickly I curved my palms and received into them a purple-blue creature, madly wriggling. Tilson took a linen cloth and wiped fluid from the baby's eyes and nose, while I wept, whether in relief, shock, or pure exhilaration, I was not entirely sure.

"It's a girl," I babbled, using my shoulder to swipe at my tears.

A thin, crimped length kept them connected; my eyes followed this cord between mother and child, and then I nearly dropped the infant, so stunned was I by what I saw.

"Dear Lord, it's twins," Tilson said, noticing this at the same moment. "Letty, you've another babe in you."

The poor girl seemed beyond sense, ready to collapse, but she delivered the second child, this one a boy, into Tilson's waiting hands.

"You done good, little mother," Tilson congratulated her, beaming and joyful. "Here's two fine youngsters you've brought into the world." And then he leaned and bestowed a kiss upon my forehead, his eyes crinkling as he grinned at me, as proud as any daddy. He said, "You done good, too, honey."

A T DINNER THAT evening, Malcolm related events with enthusiasm. "Lorie-Lorie near saved that gal's life," he said. "Ain't that right?"

"Darn right," Tilson agreed, and I flushed with pleasure. He had complimented me without end, all the way back to Iowa City while I leaned against Malcolm on the wagon, physically depleted but brimming with the pride of a task well done.

"It was such a joy to see her with them, afterwards," I said. "During, I was terribly frightened, I'll admit."

"I would never have known. You carried yourself right nobly, an' it's a fine hand you have," Tilson said. "Small an' strong, just what was required. There's some say a man ain't got a place at the birthing bed, an' I think you proved them folks right this day."

"Mama used to say that," Boyd said, well into his third piece of chicken, fried to a perfect golden crisp. His lips were shiny and his eyes downright devilish as he explained, "Mama would say that a man more'n did his part nine months *before* the birthin'."

Rebecca flushed hotly, hiding a smile by hooking an index finger over her mouth, while everyone else laughed uproariously.

"You mean like we done talked about, back on the trail?" Malcolm asked eagerly. "That is, when a man—"

I kicked his ankle at once. Malcolm knitted his brows in my direction, but obediently discontinued this line of questions.

"Son, it seems someone has taken your education to heart," Tilson teased the boy. "But your brother's got the time frame about right." And he winked at Boyd.

"It was good to feel so useful," I said, in all sincerity.

"Useful you was, indeed," Tilson said, this time with a wink in my direction. "Indispensable, darlin', an' I thank you."

Another swell of pride, and capability, bloomed over my soul. I had insisted upon stopping at the jailhouse before returning to the homestead. Clemens, on duty at that hour, was dear and kind enough to unlock the cell, before ambling outside to speak with Malcolm and his uncle. Sawyer led me to the narrow cot where he slept and there settled us. I tucked myself against him and traced my fingers over the healing wound on his temple. He appeared drawn, the skin beneath his eyes darkened with strain.

"Let me look at you," he whispered. "Let me touch you."

"You haven't been fed properly," I worried, gently stroking my thumbs along his cheekbones. "Oh, Sawyer…"

"I am well," he assured me, touching his forehead to mine, telling me so with eyes and unceasing touch, both. "I promise you. Compared to where I slept as a soldier, this is downright luxurious. Tell me how you spent your day, *mo mhuirnín milis.*"

"I birthed two babies," I said, clinging tightly to him. The pleasure of him in my arms was so forceful, so immediate, that I felt dizzy with it, as though it was a gift I perhaps did not deserve. One that would be taken from me, forthwith, and I clung all the more tightly.

"Two?" he repeated. "From the same mama?"

I nodded. And then my words came gushing, "It was terrible and beautiful, both at once. I cannot explain better than that. I feared she would die—she sounded as though she might, Sawyer, it was frightful—and there was so much blood. But Tilson needed my help. The girl, Letty was her name, needed my help, and there was no other choice. I helped pull the child from her body. I felt it, *inside* of her. It was a girl, a little girl, and I helped her come into the world. And only seconds later, another head appeared. Her brother. Twins!" Sawyer's gaze was steady, bathing me with the warmth of his admiration, the sweetness of his attention; tears brimmed in my eyes as I continued to the dearest part, "And you know what? Letty named her daughter Mabel Lorissa, after her mama, and after *me.*"

Sawyer grinned, cupping my elbows, gliding his palms up my arms to take my face between them. He whispered, "You are the most amazing woman I've ever had the privilege of knowing."

I smiled even as tears splashed over my face. I said, "Tilson said I could learn to midwife."

"For certain you could. Tilson seems a decent fellow," Sawyer said. "He has been twice to speak with me."

"He was proud of me," I whispered. "And being there, with all of the blood…at first I could think of nothing but Deirdre…of when she lost the child in the hallway at Ginny's." I closed my eyes before continuing. "But then, I set that aside. I knew I had to help, that this time I was *able* to help, when before I could not. With Deirdre, there was nothing I could have done." It seemed to me as though I had only just stumbled upon acknowledgment of this. I said, gaining momentum, "Perhaps it is foolish, but I feel redeemed somehow, Sawyer."

"It is not foolish," he said. "I would that you feel delivered from all that plagues you. Lorie, look at me," and I did, opening my eyes to the intensity of his. "My wife, you are not at fault. Not for your friend, or Gus, or for me. These things were beyond your control, darlin', and I *would* that you know this. You torture yourself, and I will not have it."

I wanted so badly to believe what he said—that I was not to blame for the deaths of good people, people I had cared deeply for. God knew I blamed myself—and surely whatever judge I may face after death would blame me. If not entirely for those I had loved, then certainly for causing Jack's death.

Oh God…

There was a knock at the door, and seconds later Tilson entered, doffing his hat and saying, "Good evening, Mr. Davis. Your wife has delivered two children this day." He approached the cell door, still gaping open, and curled one hand about an iron slat, regarding us with a half-smile.

"As I have just learned," Sawyer said, and his voice grew slightly deeper with emotion as he said, "I thank you for watching out for Lorie, while I cannot."

"It is my honor," Tilson said. "I've grown right fond of her company, I'll admit. I believe you would make a sound apprentice."

"Thank you," I whispered. I knew it was futile to consider asking if I could be allowed to remain here, at the jailhouse with Sawyer. Billings would be quite apoplectic, and Clemens had already more than bent the rules for us.

"Sawyer!" And Malcolm darted inside, scurrying past Tilson and throwing his arms around Sawyer. "If Mrs. Rebecca fried up chicken, like I been pray-ing for all day, then I aim to bring you a piece tomorrow."

Sawyer laughed, low and soft, and freed one arm to hug the boy. He said, "I would be *most* grateful, kid."

"We must go," Tilson said, his tone recognizing my reluctance to do so.

Sawyer nodded, crushing both Malcolm and me all the more tightly. I kissed his jaw, stroking his loose hair with both hands.

Into my ear Sawyer whispered, "Whenever you go, it's as though a new piece of me is torn away."

"It's the same for me," I said, hurting so badly I did not believe I had the wherewithal to leave him here. "We'll return in the daylight."

"I'm counting the hours," he said.

Tilson crossed the meager space and placed a hand upon Sawyer's shoul-der. He said gruffly, "You are a fortunate man, Mr. Davis. I hope you know this."

Only because I could read Sawyer's thoughts so well did I fully understand what crossed his mind just then; standing as he was, Tilson's face was shad-owed, his imposing form outlined with light from behind. The way Tilson spoke, his unconsciously paternal gesture, tore at my husband's memory. As plain as though he'd spoken aloud, I sensed Sawyer long for his father, James Davis, gone these many years.

Sawyer said quietly, "That I do know, sir."

And there was no choice but to leave him alone in the jailhouse.

"Mama was here to help me, both times," Rebecca was saying, drawing me from thoughts of my husband and back to the dinner table. "She was calm as a summer day, you shall recall that about her, Uncle Edward."

"It sounded right awful," Malcolm said. "The screaming, that is. What was you doing to her?"

"Well, it's a painful business all around, son," Tilson said. "An' in this case, the child, both of them, was positioned wrong. We was fortunate this time. It ain't always so."

"Boy, you's watched horses give birth," Boyd added. His elbows were on the table again, forearms surrounding his plate, as though to guard against anyone intending to separate him from Rebecca's delectable cooking. He concluded, "It's much the same process."

Malcolm's mouth twisted into a knot, his brows beetling, as he surely pictured just such a thing.

"Twins," I said again, still marveling at what I had witnessed. "When the second child appeared, I thought perhaps I was having a vision."

"It ain't always easy to tell there's two," Tilson said. "I've been surprised by a second babe once or twice before. I've even heard tell of three at once, but I've never seen such in my lifetime."

"A woman ain't got but two breasts," Malcolm said, with real wonder, as though the rest of us had no notion of this anatomical truth. "How could she feed three babes at once?"

"Oh, dear *Lord*," Boyd muttered, amidst more hilarity, Tilson tipping back in his chair with wholehearted merriment; little Nathaniel clapped one hand over his mouth in the manner of someone who knows he is in for trouble, blue eyes shining with delight in the mischief. Boyd said, "Mama would skin me alive to hear the way you talk, boy. I ain't taught you *nothin'*."

"Perhaps I oughtn't to allow you a piece of plum cake," Rebecca said, her eyes lighting upon Malcolm with an air of affectionate teasing.

"Plum cake?" Boyd repeated. "Fried chicken *and* plum cake? Woman, you *are* an angel."

"Aw, please, Mrs. Rebecca?" Malcolm begged, not seeming to notice how Boyd's words had affected her. He promised, "I swear I won't mention breasts no more."

Tilson said somberly, "You might kick yourself later in life for swearing such a thing, young Malcolm."

Later I helped Rebecca with the dinner dishes, drying as she washed. The door was propped open to the fine summer evening, and we listened to Malcolm and Boyd playing with the little boys, while Tilson settled into a low-slung canvas chair and smoked his pipe.

"It is so fine to have a woman here, with whom to converse," Rebecca said. "I cannot tell you how much, Lorie. I would beg you to remain here, for always."

"I wish we could have met under better circumstances, but I am so glad to know you," I said, scraping at a stray strand of hair with my thumb, damp from the dishwater. "You are kindness itself, and a true kindred spirit."

"Uncle Edward is most adamant that he will convince you to settle near here," she said, with a subtle air of hope. "He has confessed as such to me this very day. He has taken a keen liking to all of you. Malcolm reminds him greatly of his own boys. I never met my cousins, and of course now it is too late, unless Blythe ever ventures north. I wish he would, for Uncle Edward's sake. There has been not a word from the man in nearly three years. How the world has changed since the War."

"I believe Boyd could be convinced if not for Jacob and Hannah. They are expecting us. We'll be long overdue by the time we arrive."

"I understand," Rebecca said. Her eyes flickered outside, only briefly, but I knew she sought Boyd. She acknowledged quietly, "He is set on his course."

For the first time, I thought, *Perhaps we could settle near this place.* But I left the words unspoken, for now.

"Boyd spoke with Yancy this morning," I said instead, my eyes also roving to the dooryard. "Yancy is fearsomely angry at this turn of events. It is only Marshal Quade preventing him from moving forward with his plan to hang Sawyer. And of Zeb, no one has heard a word."

Rebecca knew my terror of this man, as I had told her everything that occurred while in his and Yancy's company. She said, "Perhaps he has given up and returned to his homestead."

I whispered, "I wish I could believe so."

Rebecca said, "Leverett will keep his word. He is a stubborn man, and an honorable one."

I was more than a little curious to know more, but would not relent to my impulse to beg her for additional information; as much as we had spoken in the past two days, she had confessed nothing of her feelings for, or relationship with, Marshal Leverett Quade.

"Lorie! Mrs. Rebecca! Come along!" Malcolm called from outside, waving both arms at us. He ran to the open door and caught the edges of the frame, on either side. He enthused, "There's fireflies!"

Rebecca and I joined them, each of us wrapping into our shawls. I leaned over the top rung of the corral and Whistler came to me; I entwined her mane around my fingers and found room to delight in the sight before my eyes. The prairie surrounding the homestead teemed with the golden-green sparks of lightning bugs, flickering and signaling to one another, seeming thousands strong.

"July is their month," Rebecca said, lifting Nathaniel into her arms. He snuggled his cheek upon her and popped a thumb into his mouth. She sighed, "What a marvelous sight."

Malcolm and Cort darted like moths across the ditch to the far side of the road, attempting to catch one of the tiny creatures, and Rebecca walked slowly in their direction, murmuring to her youngest.

Tilson called from his chair, "Rain before morning, that's what they's telling us."

Boyd joined me at the corral, hooking his arms over the topmost beam. He said softly, "Whistler-girl," and scratched her jaw. "You's wondering after Sawyer, ain't you, girl?" He scratched beneath her jaws and said, "I wrote Jacob that we been delayed, but I pray we'll be on the trail before he gets word back."

"I can scarce think that far," I whispered. "I can't think beyond Sawyer being free of that miserable jail."

"He will be," Boyd said, low and steady. "We gotta trust in that, Lorie-girl." When I remained silent, he leaned a hair closer and intentionally lowered his eyebrows, imparting the seriousness of his words. He said, "You's been stronger than I coulda guessed, through all a-this. I want you to know that."

"It doesn't seem that way, to me," I said at last, stroking the soft spot beneath Whistler's forelock. She nickered and nudged with her nose, encouraging me to continue such ministrations upon her face. I admitted, "I feel a right wreck, most days."

"No, you's nothing of the kind," Boyd said. He tilted back at the waist and studied the sky for a few breaths. Still looking that direction, he said softly, "I was thinking this evening of a girl I knew from back home, named Livy. Had there been no War, had we stayed in Suttonville, I woulda married her."

He had spoken of many girls from his past, but never with such a somber demeanor. Though I was fearful he might say she had died, I asked quietly, "Where is she now?"

"I looked for her when we got home that spring, in 'sixty-five. Her daddy raised corn an' flax a few miles from the Bledsoe holler, an' in my foolish pride, I thought she mighta waited for me. She hadn't, as I shoulda well known. She'd married Charles Main when he come home, near six months before. Already expecting a young'un by the time my sorry self showed up at her door."

"Had you been promised?" I asked. I thought of the customs of my old life, the tendency of the older generation to arrange early matches, to cast their speculative gazes to neighboring sons and daughters as potential mates for their own children.

Boyd met my eyes with a half-rueful grin. He said, "Me an' Livy shared a few kisses, I'll not deny, long before I ever dreamed of bein' a soldier. She was one of the few girls in the holler not sweet on Ethan Davis in them days. He knew the ladies all adored him, an' he was right shameless."

"Sawyer has told me a few stories about Ethan," I said, smiling a little. It seemed as if there had been trouble to scare up anywhere near, then Ethan Davis sought it out.

"It seems like a dream of another time," Boyd said, on a sigh. "I swear, sometimes I think I only just imagined them days in the holler, runnin' wild with Sawyer an' the twins, an' my brothers. We was carefree as the wind."

"Sawyer speaks much the same of those times," I said. "We were all so blessed in our upbringings. I wish I would have fully understood that, at the time, but we never know what we have, not as children, do we?"

"That's so," Boyd agreed. "Though I can't reckon a time when I weren't thankful, deep inside. Lord knows we never had much, scarce two coins to rub together at any one time, but Daddy an' Mama made our house a home. Never wanted for love in them days. Shucks, I aimed to raise me a passel of my own boys in the same holler. Live near my brothers, an' the Davis boys. Surely that weren't too much to ask for. But life had other plans for us."

"It did," I whispered.

"An' the path we's on now, however painful, is the right one, I believe this," Boyd said. "I aim to get us all north, like I promised. I am fixin' to see the sun rise in Minnesota before next month is out." But just now his eyes were fixed on Rebecca.

My heart gave a sudden, hopeful thump, but before I could speak, Boyd said, "Partly for Gus's sake, too. He longed to begin afresh. I'd like to get there for him," and tears came to my eyes, even though I knew Boyd had not intended that.

"Boyd…" my voice faltered, and he looked at me, eyebrows lifted in question. I whispered, "I am sorry…for Gus…"

Understanding descended over his features and he said adamantly, "I didn't mean to hurt you by sayin' that, Lorie. Gus loved you, an' he woulda done right by you. I knew him my whole life, an' if giving his life was what it took to save the woman he cared for, he woulda paid that price. It ain't your fault."

I rested my forehead against Whistler.

"C'mere," Boyd said gruffly, and enfolded me into a brotherly headlock. He gently knuckled my scalp, as I'd watched him knuckle Malcolm's a hundred times. Against my hair, he whispered, "It's all right, Lorie-girl."

"Mama, it's the marshal!" Cort suddenly heralded, and I felt the tense shifting in Boyd's frame as he drew back; together, we turned in the direction Cort was indicating, to see a rider approaching at an elegant trot through the lovely purple dusk.

"Evening, folks," Quade acknowledged all of us with poised politeness. He walked his mount into the dooryard with the ease of someone familiar with the space, tipping his hat brim. Tilson rose from his chair to greet him, and Quade said, "Evening, Edward."

I looked at once to Rebecca, who had let Nathaniel carefully back to the ground. She stood silently, her son gripping her skirt, watching as Quade spoke briefly with her uncle.

"Lookit, Marshal, I caught a firefly!" Cort said, running near with his hands clasped. Quade took a moment to exclaim over the boy's find, while Rebecca drew closer her shawl and slowly followed in her eldest son's footsteps.

"Good evening, Becky," Quade said, removing his hat as she drew near. His voice held clear fondness for her; he seemed unable to get enough of the sight of her face and reached immediately to appropriate her hand, kissing the back of it, however politely. I regarded Quade anew; he was not as old as I had first taken him to be, dressed this evening a hair finer than he had yet been, and appearing far more approachable—a noticeably handsome man come to pay a call, rather than a strictly law-minded marshal. He said, "I apologize I haven't been yet to visit. Perhaps you would accompany me for a walk, as the evening is so fair?"

Beside me, Boyd stood still as a salt pillar.

Rebecca nodded assent, and Tilson said, "We'll just have to enjoy ourselves without your company for a spell, honey."

Boyd muttered, barely audibly, "I believe I'll retire."

And without another word, he disappeared within his and Malcolm's tent.

I T RAINED IN the deep of night, a soft cadence which at first incorporated into my dream. I lay within a pile of quilts, half untucked in the chill of the darkened air, and the gentle pattering of droplets upon the wagon cover transformed into the beat of drums in the distance, advancing ever closer. I shifted restlessly, half-asleep, and saw against the canvas of my mind a dim gray battlefield, upon which a ragged line of soldiers appeared. Before I could retreat, I was inundated by them. Hunched and broken they were, some marching without boots, their faces robbed of all purpose but one.

Sawyer! I screamed, the ground cold and hard-packed beneath my bare feet, riddled with ruts and loose rocks. I scrambled, stumbling to gain a solid foothold, searching the faces of those passing near me with mounting desperation. *Where are you? Answer me!*

Do you know Sawyer Davis? I begged the soldiers, one after the other, but they did not answer, scarcely heeded my presence, as though, here in this place, I did not truly exist. Horses brushed near my skirts as they followed in the same direction, some with blood dried stiff on their hides, others with injured limbs, hobbling as painfully as their masters.

Please, I sobbed, trying unsuccessfully to grasp at tattered coat sleeves. *Please, where is he? You are his Company, this I know!*

A boy sat on a split stone, a few yards away, a heavy battle drum poised on his lap. He watched with solemn eyes as I crawled towards him, on all fours now, as Letty had been upon the birthing bed. Blood, cold and wet, seeped around my hands and then my wrists, but I believed the boy possessed answers. I had nearly reached him when a crow the size of which I had never beheld, blacker than the absence of all light, landed atop his slender shoulder. The boy sagged under its weight.

*Oh, Jesus…*I gasped, falling utterly still.

We are dead, ma'am, the boy said, politely and slowly, as though speaking to someone who required exaggerated explanation of a simple fact. His flesh was mushroom-colored, slick with the misting rain. He did not acknowledge the crow, though it sank its talons to gain a firmer hold in order to adjust its enormous wings. Its beak was poised near the boy's ear.

Where is Sawyer? I whispered, dragging forth my resolve. I demanded, *Answer me.*

They's bound for heaven, Lorie-Lorie, the boy murmured in a different voice, my sweet Malcolm's voice, and my heart shriveled. He concluded, *But it's a right tough march to get there.*

Teeth bared and grinding together in my horror, I gasped, *This is not real. I do not believe you are real.*

Witness, the crow whispered.

Blue-white lightning bit into the sky; I felt its electric pulse deep within. Rain increased its frantic tempo, and thunder sounded loudly enough to crack apart the atmosphere. I turned away from boy and crow to spy the land-scape choked now with soldiers, lurching and stumbling, some trampled in the crush of bodies and falling over one another, until their ranks resembled stacked wood. Heads thrown back, chests gashed open and ribs displayed, like gutted animals in a butcher's window, fingers limp and dangling; there a boot yet connected to a torn pant leg, though the soldier within the uniform had rotted away.

I can't hardly figure that many men dead in one fell swoop, I heard Boyd say, somewhere beyond my sight.

A growling came from between my teeth and I thrashed at the crow, wishing fervently to destroy it, but it remained maddeningly unperturbed, impervious to my gesticulating arms, only cocking its skull and angling a small black eye to peer behind itself. Again on all fours, I scrabbled around the rock and another sizzle of lightning perfectly illuminated for me the scene just beyond.

Screaming split my skull, thunder tore the skin from my bones.

Someone shook me, forcefully.

"Lorie!"

Even when my eyes opened and I comprehended that it had been a night-mare of hellish proportions, I could not stop screaming. Boyd and Malcolm had nearly climbed over the top of one another to reach me in the wagon, having been sleeping only paces away in their wall tent, both of them now crouching in the cramped space beside me, and damp with rain. Thunder exploded as would a discharged bullet, causing the ground to tremble and tins to rattle, gaining strength as the storm increased in fury.

"Lorie, what's wrong?" Boyd demanded in the pause between bursts of ear-walloping sound. Lightning flared, briefly creating the illusion of daylight. "What is it?"

I could not catch hold of my wits enough to answer, and he shook me, demanding, "Lorie!" Thunder detonated just ahead of another sizzle of lightning, and new wariness jerked Boyd straight. "That was a rifle," he said, trepidation weighting his voice.

Malcolm, clutching my other arm, suddenly issued a noise somewhere between a hiss and a strangled cry, his gaze fixed behind me. I turned in time to observe as a flash of brilliance momentarily backlit the hulking figure of a man on horseback and toting a long-barreled firearm, the noise of his sneaking passage muffled by the rain. Just outside the wagon he was, advancing, no more than steps away.

Boyd shoved both of us to the wooden floorboards, so swiftly and with such force that my lungs emptied of all air. He aligned his body over his brother and me, breathing hard, and thunder shattered just as a round was fired into the side of the wagon. It was such a double blast of reverberation that only buzzing nonsense could be heard in the aftermath. Pinned under Boyd's weight and effectively deafened, I made little sense of the next events.

Wood had splintered.

Boyd's elbow jabbed into my side.

Rain grazed us from the hole now opened in the canvas.

I tried to turn my face to see what was happening—

Another volley of chaos, thunder or rifle report, I could not discern.

Boyd jerked sideways and the bones of his forearm dug harder into my face.

Boyd, I tried to say, hideously worried, hearing shouting from outside. And then suddenly he was up and moving fast.

Lightning highlighted the huge man and the length of his rifle, but he was angled differently now, away from the wagon.

Malcolm scrambled after his brother, even as Boyd absolutely leaped to the ground and hollered, "Stay *put!*"

A horse galloped away; I could hear its hoofbeats.

I rolled to my knees and through the oval opening at the back of the wagon could see Tilson with his rifle braced to his shoulder, firing repeatedly. Malcolm disobeyed his brother's command and followed directly after, into the drenching rain; I was on his heels, and only one thing crossed my mind.

"Sawyer!" I screamed, cupping my temples and thinking his name, begging for his attention. I was certain that it had been Zeb wielding the rifle—and, having met resistance here at Tilson's, there was nothing to stop him from riding into Iowa City and shooting his way into the jailhouse.

Perhaps he already had, and with all my energy, I called silently to Sawyer.

Fortune raced past, Boyd bent low; the mare cleared the yard at a gallop, and horse and rider were nearly instantly blotted from sight by the storm.

Lorie, oh God, what is it? What's wrong? Sawyer's frantic voice filled my mind, and my knees went weak with relief, momentary though it was.

Zeb was here, I told him, closing my eyes, sending the thoughts as hard as I was able. *Boyd is following him, but he may be coming for you, oh Sawyer...*

Are you harmed? he demanded.

No, but I am so scared...

And in a dark corner of my mind, the crow landed smoothly, dragging sideways the slender frame of the dead drummer boy.

Malcolm caught my arm and cried, "Where's Boyd going?"

"To Sawyer," I said, with certainty, leaning close to the boy's ear so that my words were audible above the rain. Thunder echoed over the land, shuddering the ground, which was cold and soggy beneath my bare feet.

"You two! Come along!" Tilson yelled, gesturing at us. "C'mon!"

"Where is Boyd?" Rebecca asked frantically, grasping at my arm as we hurried inside. She was clad in her nightclothes, her long dark hair loose, the worry in her eyes leaping forth and into mine.

"He's riding to Sawyer," I said, as Tilson shut the door and moved at once to flank the window. "We've endangered you," I said, in anguish. "I am so sorry..."

Rebecca took me into her embrace, and Malcolm wrapped his arms about the both of us, shivering in his wet clothes.

"That fella Zeb, I do believe, was firing on the wagon, in this very yard," Tilson said, shaking water from his hair, keeping firm hold of his repeater. "Damnation, I thought it was thunder woke me. By the time I gathered my senses an' fired on the big son of a bitch, he could have killed the lot of you. Some solider I am, Jesus *Christ*."

"Uncle Edward," Rebecca admonished. Her face was pale as a dogwood blossom, though she kept purposefully preoccupied, shushing her boys, sending them back up to the loft with murmured reassurances, before stoking the fire in the woodstove.

"Are you hurt, either of you?" Tilson demanded, his eyes roving over us in search of any injuries. "What of Carter?"

"I don't know," I said, miserable at this lack of knowledge. Boyd had moved so quickly, mounting Fortune and riding out, that I had not noticed one way or the other if he was wounded.

"I fear Boyd was hit. He jerked so strange-like," Malcolm whispered painfully, unconsciously echoing my trepidation. Rebecca, a kettle poised in her hand, flinched at these words as though struck; she closed her eyes and I could see the struggle within her to continue the task. I tugged Malcolm to a chair and settled him.

"I believe he is all right," I said with as much fortitude as I could muster, sitting next to Malcolm so that I could see his face. Tears decorated his long lashes and his lips trembled. I elaborated, "He would not have been able to rise so quickly, nor ride Fortune, if he was badly injured."

"That is true," Rebecca whispered, drawing a deep breath; she crossed the room to a trunk positioned near the loft ladder and withdrew two quilts, draping one over Malcolm.

"Boyd is all right," I whispered to her, as she placed the second quilt over my shoulders, and our eyes held fast; Rebecca was in torment, I could plainly see, but she nodded acknowledgment.

The night dragged itself into early morning. Tilson at last abandoned his position near the window and joined us at the table; Rebecca, better able to manage her concern when moving, prepared coffee and boiled oats. I stayed near Malcolm at the table, all four of us uncharacteristically quiet as the storm rolled westward, its fury gradually decreasing. More than an hour ticked past before hoofbeats approached in the slackening rain, and Malcolm bolted outside into the first faint stirrings of silver daylight, leaving the door gaping.

Rebecca flew to the open door.

"Thank God," Tilson said, as we all saw Boyd ride into view.

I ran in Malcolm's footsteps; Boyd dismounted and led Fortune to the corral, and he called to me, "I been at the jailhouse. I couldn't get inside at first, but Sawyer is all right, I spoke to him through the window. Clemens arrived an' I told him what happened, then hightailed it back here."

"It was Zeb, wasn't it?" I asked breathlessly.

Boyd nodded brusquely. He was soaked to the skin, his thick dark hair so wet it fell nearly to his shoulders. He growled, "He's a goddamn dead man, the moment I see him again."

"What did Sawyer say?" I begged.

Malcolm had been assessing his brother's appearance, and his voice trembled an octave higher than usual as he observed, "You's bleeding."

"Let me see," I demanded, catching at Boyd's arm.

Boyd craned to look and said, "Shit, I figured as much. Bastard didn't get a bullet into me, try as he might. But I believe I got a few splinters."

Once inside, Boyd remained a frenzy of livid motion, nearly unable to sit still long enough to let Tilson examine the wounds that bits of the wagon, made into weapons by the force of a bullet's impact, had opened in his skin. Rebecca said not a word, but her relief was palpable; she was nearly unable to tear her gaze from him. Rain and blood streaked Boyd's shirt, and his eyes blazed with dark fury.

"Get that fire roaring, if you would," Tilson directed Malcolm, and then to Boyd, "Son, let's get you settled so's I can look you over."

"He is a goddamn *dead man*," Boyd muttered for the third time, as Tilson dragged a chair nearer to the woodstove.

Tilson said calmly, "I aim to help you go after this Crawford fella, but first I must clean out these wounds, or you'll be in a sore fix. You gonna take off that shirt, so's I can look?"

With impatient jerks, Boyd did so, and I winced to see the multiple gashes upon his muscles; though none appeared deep, I could see wooden splinters jammed into his flesh.

"Here, you shall catch a chill," Rebecca said, her voice low and soft. Without ceremony, she handed him a quilt, which Boyd accepted with the slightest relaxing of the stern set to his jaw. He studied her face as he murmured, "Thank you, ma'am."

"Let me take a look," Tilson told Boyd, having donned his spectacles. To his niece, he added, "Becky, be ready with that witch hazel."

He and Rebecca proceeded to work with quiet efficiency, Tilson removing each bit of wood with a small needle-nosed pincher, setting these upon an enamel plate at the table as they came clean. As he freed each, Rebecca was waiting with a damp cloth to gently wipe away the blood, before dabbing a mixture of the antiseptic solution into each wound. Malcolm sat near and watched the entire process unblinkingly, while I attempted to make myself useful by serving Cort and Nathaniel their breakfast.

Near the end of their ministrations, Boyd grew chilled; he was still clad in his damp trousers, and despite the quilt draped over his lap, he could not suppress a shiver. Tilson finished his work and removed his spectacles, and was busy gathering the supplies; Malcolm, satisfied that his brother was safely delivered from his injuries, ran outside to the necessary. Cort held the kitten, and he and Nathaniel were feeding it bits of oatmeal. Rebecca stood alone near Boyd; she had tied her dark hair into a braid, but had not pinned it up as usual. The bottle of witch hazel was still clutched in her right hand, and I watched as she, with a small, swift motion, placed her left upon his back, near the nape of his neck; her fingers curled inward, caressing the damp curls the rain had formed in his hair.

Boyd's chin turned sharply towards her, his nose at a level with her breasts, as she stood while he sat. A heartbeat, no more, their eyes held; I could not see Rebecca's face. Even witnessing from the space of a room away, I sensed the strength of her passionate desire to continue touching him, a feeling which shocked her; I understood the single caress was as boldly out of character for her as would be appearing without clothing in town. And she withdrew her hand as quickly as she had placed it on his bare skin; her hem brushed the tops of his boots as she turned rapidly away.

Tilson, rummaging in his satchel, groused at Boyd, "I would ask that you rest a spell, young man, but I believe it's a futile effort."

Boyd dragged his concentrated gaze from Rebecca, who had busied herself helping Tilson to tidy away the supplies; he was taken aback, I could clearly see, but he wadded up his damp shirt and said only, "You believe right."

I HAD not seen Yancy since that night on the prairie. He was dressed in fresh clothing and had since been trimmed, perhaps by a barber; his face was clean-shaven but for his mustache. Simply observing him from afar, little would one guess the dreadful things of which he was capable; he appeared a person of upstanding virtues, his marshal's star winking in the light of the lantern upon Tilson's table, a necessity on such a gloomy-skied day.

"Might it be possible for us to converse without the presence of this woman?" Yancy said as Boyd, Tilson, and I entered Tilson's office. He spoke the word *woman* in the exact tone with which he had spoken *whore*, and I discerned no difference in his meaning.

Quade, back in full marshal form, was already present, furious but professional enough to contain it, enraged that Tilson's property had been invaded in such a fashion, thereby indirectly endangering Rebecca. We had converged upon Tilson's office; Billings told Clemens that he would thank us to discuss this matter elsewhere than the jailhouse, as he had his hands full with a pair of disorderly drunkards from the night before, and Clemens had dutifully relayed the message. Billings refused to let me see Sawyer this morning, but I knew my husband was safe at present, and contented myself with that.

"You shut your goddamn mouth," Boyd growled, in response to Yancy. "Your man attacked us last night."

Yancy interrupted with a supercilious tone, scoffing, "That is an absurd declaration."

Tilson stood with his jaw thrust forward. He interjected sharply, "Then it weren't Zeb Crawford shootin' his rifle near my home this past night? Shootin' to kill my guests? Coming into *my* dooryard?"

"Crawford left town two days ago," Yancy snapped, his gaze cutting to include me in his words. "He is hardly in my employ, and I will not be lowered by such suggestions. There are plenty of respectable folks in this town concerned about a pair of dangerous former Rebs in their midst. It could have been any one of them. Ask around, see if I am mistaken."

"I have heard a fair amount of grumblings to that effect," Quade affirmed, leaning back in his chair and heaving a small sigh. "But that in no way excuses such an assault."

"An' who put such notions into their fool heads?" Boyd raged.

"Dangerous to whom, exactly?" Tilson asked, his face thunderous in its anger. "For Christ's sake, one of these 'Rebs' is in custody, as we speak."

"'Fool heads?'" Yancy repeated. "Hear that, Quade?"

Tilson did not remove his gaze from Yancy, and asked levelly, "Where is Zeb Crawford now? He ain't left town, which I know *you* know well. I have a question or two for him."

Regaining a firmer hold of his temper, Yancy said, "I was informed by Judge Hamm that I was able to hang my prisoner, *a wanted man*, and now I have been informed that I am forced to wait, rendering me incapable of leaving this town and returning to my sons. Zeb and I parted ways after I delivered Davis to the jailhouse."

"Ain't that handy, him leaving town," Boyd said, low and dangerously, and Yancy could not quite contain the hatred in his eyes as he regarded Boyd.

"I'll thank you to leave off this line of inquiry," Yancy said tightly.

"Or what?" Boyd asked, his upper lip curling.

I had remained silent, intimidated by the angry male energy in the small space, but I lifted my chin and said, "We saw his face. There is no question that he intended to kill us last night."

"You've spoken to him, then?" Yancy asked, all but baring his teeth at me. "He has confirmed this?"

"We *saw* him," I said, as evenly as I could. It took considerable effort to keep my eyes upon Yancy's; the vicious anger rolling from him was nearly tangible, heated and dense. Boyd's solid presence at my side lent me strength.

Quade said angrily, "Goddammit. I won't have Becky and the boys in harm's way. I won't hear of it. This is madness."

Boyd's shoulders squared anew; he looked hard at Quade, fists clenched, desiring to challenge Quade's right to concern for Rebecca. But wisely, he held his tongue.

"It was Crawford," Tilson confirmed. "Get him in here an' I'll identify him. Unless my word as a *Reb* is too suspect."

"Christ almighty, don't you be adopting that attitude, too," Quade said. "Last thing I want is a rehash of old recriminations. War is over, boys."

"Zeb's place is near a full day south, close to my own," Yancy said. "He'll have long since returned there."

"Then you best get packing," Tilson said mildly.

"Are you out of your mind?" Yancy asked. "Have Billings search the town. Send his deputy on a goose hunt. I will ride south, and return to my home, when Davis is properly hung, God willing no later than midweek, and not before."

I could not contain my flinching at these cruel words.

The door swung suddenly open and a man peered around it, saying, "Doc, Campbells' oldest boy had his foot stomped by that new mare. They need you at the stable, pronto."

"I'll be right along, Clyde," Tilson said.

"You tell Zeb we's waitin' on him," Boyd said, exaggerating his drawl just slightly, as though to taunt Yancy.

"I don't plan to speak with him in the near future," Yancy said, an arrogant set to his features. He resettled his hat with an air of lofty dismissal.

Boyd only said, with quiet menace, "You tell him."

"Lorie, you best join me," Tilson said, once the office had emptied of all but Boyd and me. "You were fine help yesterday, an' I don't aim to leave you here alone."

I nodded, weak with exhaustion but desirous of something to occupy the hours of the day, other than spending them drowning in worry.

"I'll get back there," Boyd said. "The horses need attention, an' I'll mend the canvases, best I can manage." Zeb had discharged one of his rounds into the tent in which Boyd and Malcolm slept last night—if they had not been in the wagon with me, at that moment, one of them likely would have been killed. Boyd murmured, "An' I don't much care for the thought of them alone too long, neither."

"Becky is a right fine shot with the Springfield," Tilson said, with a half-smile that emphasized the wrinkles aligning his eyes, referring to the rifle he had left with Rebecca and Malcolm. "But I'm sure she'd appreciate your concern."

"I mean every word. We can't thank you enough," Boyd said, gruff and emotional. He elaborated, "Stabling our horses, feeding us, an' now we's put you in danger. There ain't no way we can repay you."

"Just having your company has been payment enough," Tilson said. "I told Becky I'd do my damnedest to convince y'all to stay near this area."

Boyd searched Tilson's eyes and found only sincerity. He said again, "Thank you."

I was at last able to see Sawyer late that afternoon, after spending the otherwise quiet, rainy Sunday with Tilson; he and I hastened to the livery stable, where the oldest son's foot was badly bruised and sore, but not broken. In the noon hour, I accompanied him to the homestead of Billy and Letty Dawes, where Letty was resting, nursing her new son and daughter, all of them faring well after their difficult entry into the world.

Sawyer was distressed, hollow-eyed with fatigue and worry. Clemens did not allow the door to be unlocked this time, as the second cell was still occupied by the men retained for disorderly conduct; both of them watched me with ill-disguised interest. Clad as I was in my trousers, for riding, they were keen-eyed, but I ignored them as well as I could.

"There's been no sign of him since last night. Yancy claims Zeb left town," I told Sawyer, speaking low.

He said painfully, "I cannot keep you safe. I am going mad in this place, shut away while you are in danger."

"Zeb could have come here last night, and you are unarmed," I said, agonized.

"Zeb's intent is to go after you, as Yancy fears what you might say to the judge, Lorie, and I am ill with worry over it. My fury alone seems enough to kill him," Sawyer said. "Should he appear before me, I could destroy him with a look, I swear on my soul."

"Yancy is fostering talk," I whispered.

Sawyer touched my neck, gently caressing the hollow at the base of my skull with his thumb. He said, "Boyd told me as much. But I don't believe for a moment that anyone other than Zeb would take such action. Stay near Boyd, and Tilson. Promise me."

"I pray this will soon be behind us," I whispered, attempting to lighten my tone, unwilling to leave for the night on such a low note. Unbidden, Yancy's words pierced me—*when Davis is properly hung, God willing no later than midweek.*

Midweek was two days from now.

Sick with desperation, I reached to hold my husband's face; he was unshaven to a degree that I had not yet witnessed as his wife, his stubble many shades darker than his flaxen hair, a color far more similar to his eyelashes. His beautiful hawk eyes held mine, and he told me, *I pray it, too.*

Tilson leaned around the door and said, "I apologize for stealing Lorie away just now. But we best hightail it for home."

Sawyer nodded acknowledgment, and then kissed my lips with chaste sweetness, mindful of our rapt audience. He whispered, "Let me know when you get there. Kiss Whistler for me."

I will, I promised.

"'Til the morning, then," Tilson said, retaining a cheerful air. He advised the men in the adjacent cell, "You boys best get your jaws up off the floor."

"Ma'am, I got *terrible* trouble sleeping. Might be a kiss would help me, too," said one of the men, speaking with a jokingly hopeful tone; both were standing as close as they were able, with their forearms braced between the iron slats and wrists dangling. I issued a small, unexpected huff of laughter, and even Sawyer was mildly amused as he carefully released his hold on my waist, catching my hands and kissing my knuckles before fully letting go.

Although I should have bucked up and offered to help Rebecca with dinner, as another guest had arrived in the form of Charley Rawley, his horse in the barn and his presence very much welcomed, my temples ached with a dull, heavy pain by the time we had arrived back at the homestead. Instead of venturing indoors, I strayed to the corral and fetched Whistler, using the fence to climb astride her back, with no saddle in place. She allowed this and together we left the yard, with little purpose other than my inability to remain stationary, angling away from the house and towards the west, where the dirt of the yard gave way to taller grasses and uneven ground.

"C'mon, girl," I whispered to the mare, thinking of the first time I had ridden her, far back along the prairie in Missouri, the afternoon Sawyer and I sat together beside the river in the shade of an enormous willow and spoken of our childhoods. He had attempted to cheer me by offering the use of his beloved mare, and I had willingly and enthusiastically accepted. A rush of affection, and love, for both man and horse swept over me. I leaned forward and hugged Whistler, feeling the rough-textured hair of her rusty-red mane, and she nickered and whooshed a loud breath through her velvet nostrils, in response. I kissed her mane and whispered, "That is from Sawyer."

My body, hot and rigid with emotional energy, slowly calmed as Whistler carried me along; I was mindful of our vulnerability, not venturing beyond the copse of oaks on the western edge of the property, keeping the homestead in sight. Whistler was singularly the most well behaved animal I had ever known; few horses would remain so responsive without benefit of bridle and bit, but Whistler was more human than any horse I'd ever encountered. Her ears quirked in my direction and I told her, "I know you miss him, too." And then I heard myself whisper, "A little pony called Sable died."

The sun had not completely vanished beneath the horizon, about half-sunk in a rich, cloudless copper spill of light, bathing my face with the last of its radiance. Tears rolled from my jaw, and I used my knuckles to smudge them away, to no avail; more followed in their wake. I halted Whistler with a tightening of my knees, and she stopped obediently. I sat just behind the gentle swell of her withers, her red-and-cream calico hide warm and firm beneath me, so solidly reassuring. She smelled of horse, a scent in which I had sought and found comfort since I was a little girl, safe in my daddy's stable.

"He was a good pony," I told Whistler, and though my words were true, I spoke them now with the sole purpose of punishing myself. "I fancied him coming north with us, did you know that? Even as scared as I was with those men, I imagined that Sable would be your friend, and Aces', and everyone's. He was little, and so sweet, and he ran so hard for me…and then he was sh…" I gulped, before explaining in a whisper, "Shot from beneath me."

Whistler sidestepped delicately; I began to cry, dismounting so that I might move to her face and embrace it. No matter how dear I held Sawyer's opinions, and Boyd's and Malcolm's, there was no denying that good people and innocent creatures like Sable had died because of me. *For* me, and I grappled with the depths of my guilt, holding fast to the solid comfort Whistler offered. She nuzzled my chest as the sun sank and twilight came leaping on silent feet; mosquitoes whined near my ears as the darkness advanced. I wept until I turned quickly from Whistler and vomited, unable to stop the flow of dreadful thoughts.

What if the circuit judge, when he arrived, was compelled to believe Yancy? I searched my memory for any reference, passing or intentional, that I had ever gleaned regarding the law. Mama had done her best to educate me in matters both consequential and practical, but I could not recall much in the way of pertinent legal matters. A circuit judge had the power to convict and execute; could his decision be overturned, or appealed, or was it final? Ought we to pursue obtaining a lawyer?

I do not know, I thought, misery fisting around my stomach.

And, worse yet, I was not wholly certain Sawyer would allow me to tell the truth, that I had been the one to pull the trigger on Jack; if Sawyer determined that the best course of action was to claim all responsibility, regardless of the outcome of this, then he would, and I would be powerless to stop him. Sawyer would never let anything happen to me that he could prevent, this I knew absolutely, and I could feel the strength of his guilt over the fact that I had left Iowa City with Yancy and Jack biting deeply into him.

I would have struggled to articulate what I was feeling, but I understood at some level that I wished we had the chance to face Yancy and Zeb on a playing field outside the law—on the prairie, far from any judicial proceedings, courtrooms and the suited men therein. Before a judge, lies could be told and subsequently heeded; on the prairie, under the sun, victory could be won by means other than parrying words, or depending on the whim of a stranger.

That is barbaric. That is not civilization.

But is it any less barbaric, or civilized, to allow the lies of one man to condemn another?

This is a Yankee court. Their bias towards you, as Southerners, will color the outcome, this you know.

The War is over, and law is blind.

It should be, but it never is—you are surely astute enough to realize. Law is an abstract concept, and in theory is blind, but men, who are paid to uphold it, are surely not.

I bent forward and braced over my knees, struggling for a solid breath, but there was nothing left in my guts to expel. I knew not what this week, with the arrival of the judge, may bring—I could not hope to predict any potential resolution. There was only one certainty in my mind, and it allowed for me a shred of comfort.

No matter what, I would not go on without Sawyer. I intended no histrionics, nor did I intend exaggeration by making this claim. It simply *was*. Our paths had been intertwined before what we knew in this life—in other places, other centuries, inextricably braided together, a connection never fully severed, by death or passing time. I understood, however, we were not allowed to find one another in each subsequent life. Here, in the latter half of the nineteenth century, we had been given the gift of one another, born within ten years of the other and bestowed with the consent—whether heavenly or otherwise—to meet.

And I refused to allow death to part us so rapidly, not in this life.

"Come, girl," I murmured to our horse, kissing her face before leading her back towards the homestead with one hand curved beneath her jaw; I was unable to mount without the benefit of the corral fence, and had no halter with which to lead her, but she followed dutifully, towards the lantern light spilling out into the evening.

Charley joined us around the fire this night; he had a room at the hotel, but lingered with us for a time before continuing into Iowa City. I leaned against Malcolm, Rebecca on my other side, and Charley accompanied Boyd, playing his harmonica while Boyd fiddled. Waltzes and reels, songs of our lost homeland, rendered so masterfully that tears glistened in Rebecca's eyes time and again; I was only privy to this because we sat so near, and reached to briefly curl my hand around hers, thinking of the way she had touched Boyd this morning. He was bowing with eyes closed, as was his usual fashion, overtaken in the music.

But between songs, he sought Rebecca's gaze.

Above, the moon had vanished from the heavens, allowing stars free reign across an echoing black canvas, stretched taut, pinned to Earth just beyond the edges of our vision. Enmeshed in worry, exhausted, I intermittently experienced the odd feeling that I sat alongside myself, connected by only the thinnest of threads to reality. Tilson's pipe smoke filled my nostrils. The men had positioned their rifles within reach. Malcolm rested his head on me, and the fiddle dusted our hair with shivering notes.

Sawyer is all right, I told myself, time and again. *It is all right.*

Of course Sawyer, alone in the dark jailhouse, could sense my restive thoughts, try as I might to prevent him further distress; but he felt the unpolished edge of fear that cut into my heart, and sought at once to reassure me.

I am here, darlin', I am safe, he thought, and I relented, allowing him welcome access, closing my eyes to better allow the picture he, too, was envisioning, that of him aligning our bodies so that I was protected, enfolded in his love. He parted my lips with his, claiming full possession of my mouth, his fingers lacing together low on my back; here, at the fire, I wrapped carefully into my own arms, letting Sawyer flood my mind with other pictures, his golden hair loose and his eyes fierce with passion, my body rigid with the aching need to join with his—to feel him held deeply inside, letting me believe for those consecrated moments in time that we could never be forced apart.

On and on the music played. My physical presence remained here at the fire, while my soul flew with wild joy to Sawyer's, together becoming one entity under the new moon on this July night, in the year of 1868.

THE MENFOLK sat up long past the time that Rebecca, Malcolm, the little boys and I retired. Malcolm tucked in with Cort and Nathaniel in the loft, while Rebecca insisted that I share her bed, and we lay together in the dimness, hearing the comforting rise and fall of the men speaking together at the fire. The scent of tobacco drifted inside, ghost-like.

Rebecca and I whispered our good-nights, and enough time had passed that I believed her to be asleep; I lay inches away beneath the quilt, exhausted and yet alert, my heart taking up periodic bouts of thunderous beating, which frightened me, though it had happened time and again when I lived at Ginny's—my anxieties taking on physical form, manifesting as a rapid heart. I tried to draw a steadying breath and it was then that I became aware that Rebecca was weeping. She made not a sound, hardly a movement to indicate, but I knew.

Without a word, only because it felt as natural as reaching for a sister, I slid my left arm over her waist and cuddled closer. It was the fashion in which Deirdre had always held me, offering comfort with her touch, her murmured assurances, until I calmed. Rebecca heaved a painful breath and caught close my hand, curling both of hers around it; I could feel her trembling.

"What is it?" I whispered, letting the warmth of her comfort me, in return.

"Lor…" her breath hitched and broke apart my name. She drew a breath and managed, "I am so…sorry…to wake you."

"I wasn't sleeping," I whispered.

"I feel so…selfish," she gasped out.

"You are anything but selfish," I reprimanded in a whisper.

"I *am* selfish, crying for myself," Rebecca explained at last, in a hushed and broken voice.

"What do you mean?" I whispered, though I knew.

"I loved Elijah so," she whispered, half-moaning the words, as another sob shuddered over her. She bent her head before continuing, "I am a widow, a mother, and I have less than no right to feel possessive of any of you. I know your journey is only just beginning, and that mine is stationary, here in this place. But I shall not deny, the full extent of my loneliness has struck me so forcefully since all of you arrived…"

Squeezing tighter her hands, I whispered, "You have every right to your feelings. I hate to think of you being lonely."

She sighed, releasing a soft breath, and whispered, "I have felt a closeness with you since the day we met. Around all of you, I almost dare to feel like a young girl again." The sound of Boyd's laugh, low and fleeting though it was, reached our ears where we lay curled together. So softly I could barely discern her words, she said, "I was so frightened this morning." She shivered, violently, before whispering, "I love hearing him play his fiddle. He is very talented, and so…*engulfed* in the music. It is a joy to simply watch him." She paused and I could almost feel the increase in her pulse. She whispered fervently, "But please, speak not of such things to anyone. Please. I shall never mention them again. I have behaved very foolishly."

"That is not so," I insisted, rolling to one elbow. In the dimness, Rebecca's face was a pale blur, her hair a dark spill over the pillow. At Ginny's, Deirdre had been the only person with whom I had spoken freely; I wished for a similar honesty to exist among Rebecca and myself, and whispered, "There is something between you and Boyd, and I know you realize this. You have not behaved foolishly."

Her words hinging on a sob, she contradicted, "But I have. Leverett intends to marry me, eventually, and I care for Leverett, I truly do. He is a good man, earnest, and willing to accept the charge of my boys, along with me." She did not sigh, but I heard the desolation hiding in her words, regardless. She whispered, "I must accept this, and besides, I could never leave this place. I could not venture north and bring my children into unknown country."

Tears prickled my eyes, blurring the outline of her. I whispered, "I care for you. I do not want to leave you behind."

Rebecca whispered, "I care for you, as well, and I shall do whatever I am able to support you, when you go before the judge. I'll demand that Leverett do the same. I believe we have a fighting chance against this marshal, this Yancy."

"I pray it," I whispered, closing my eyes. "Oh God, Rebecca, I pray it."

"I shall see you in the morning," she whispered. "Please do rest, dear, your eyes were red with weeping when you returned from your ride. Rest. We are safe indoors."

I nodded my acquiescence, whispering to reassure her, "I intend to sleep until morning."

But it was not to be on this night.

THE ROAD beneath my bare feet was familiar, though I had never stood shoeless upon its surface; in fact, rarely had I ever set more than my eyes on it—and then usually from the second-floor balcony where I had spent years of my life, walking each evening as the sun died and bright stars were pinned with eager fingers to the darkening heaven. In my whore's costumes I had paraded that balcony in a nightly attempt to attract more customers, and therefore more gold, to Ginny Hossiter's establishment. Music tinkled from between the batwing doors I had once known well, the ones leading into the prison of her whorehouse. People were milling about the boardwalks, talking and paying little mind to me; when two men carrying a large, ornately-bordered mirror between them passed near, I caught a glimpse of my reflection.

My eyes had been made unfamiliar, enlarged and outlined with the thick black smudge of a kohl stick, my lips redder than warm blood, cheeks decorated with perfectly-round spots of fuchsia rouge. My hair hung loose and my breasts were lifted outrageously high by the pinching of a black satin corset, my waist likewise cinched and ludicrously diminutive, as if I was nothing more than a caricature of a prostitute, drawn in ink by the mocking hand of an Eastern cartoonist peddling pulp novels. Twin straps of black dangled down my thighs, but there were no stockings attached to these garters, and I was in fact naked from navel downward, with no additional garments to cover my lower regions.

Before I could react bodily to the heated shame at this recognition, rough hands clutched my waist from behind, thrusting me to my knees upon the dirt of the road. The mirror was positioned directly in front of me now, the evening sky appearing in its smooth glass surface at a cockeyed angle, stars flaring into view and then away. The man behind me was faceless and savage, brutally penetrating my flesh—and try as I may, I could not look away from the vicious scene. My body twisted and writhed to escape his assault; I heard the raw screams issued, but another part of me, my spirit perhaps, remained oddly still and silent, observing from a brief distance.

A woman whispered in my ear, and somehow I could hear her words despite my cries and desperate pleas, the animal grunting of my attacker.

They used your body, Lorie, but not you.

You must understand this difference.

They used you, but they cannot destroy you, do you understand?

The stars twirled and pitched in the reflected surface of the mirror, as a child's rotating toy, distorting my awareness. I was both within and without my physical form. The woman whispering so urgently to me possessed eyes of a very vivid blue.

Do you understand?

I understand, I whispered at last.

You must go on.

You must, no matter what, Lorie.

You must.

A horror beyond even the violence of the rape seeped coldly into me. I did not comprehend just exactly what she meant, but I knew suddenly that I could not agree. I would not agree.

No, I said. *No. Leave me. Leave me!*

The crow glided into view, large and gorgeously black, supple and lissome as a catamount, a predator that had never known a day's hunger. It landed elegantly atop the golden gilt of the mirror's frame, and suddenly there was nothing besides it—and me. The landscape receded and faded to gray featurelessness, but in the mirror, red light suddenly leaped and grew, monstrous and demonic, consuming everything in its path.

I ran to the water pump in the side yard at Ginny's, where I had once spent the days of my monthly bleeding hanging laundry, and cranked fiercely upon the handle, filling a heavy bucket, stumbling over the ash-covered ground in my haste to douse the fire. I threw the water upon the flames with all of my strength, but the liquid struck nothing more than the flat surface of the mirror, scattering in droplets, utterly ineffective.

The fire burned higher.

I WAS NOT simply seeking to reassure Lorie when I said that there were plenty worse places I had slept, as a soldier. Many a night during the War had I spent the long hours of darkness entrenched in dampness, or outright mud, hollow with fear and loss, hunger and fatigue, wrapped in nothing more than my army-issued coat; after time, that had grown threadbare and pitiful. We were lucky to come across occasional Companies with whom we could trade—though it was anyone's guess which was the better trade, that for food, or warmer garments. By War's end, I felt less human than an old dog, flea-bitten and ragged, chiseled away to bones, each rib prominent. A skinny bag of innards held together by little more than the dream of returning to Cumberland County, and the family I believed there, waiting for me.

And yet tonight, lying here on the lumpy, unwashed cot upon which many another prisoner had rested his sorry self, I truly felt as though no place could be worse; now that I had found Lorie, nothing hurt as desperately as our physical separation. A part of what kept me sane during my time as a soldier had been my dream of finding her—the woman meant for me, and to whom I would equally belong, a belief to which I clung with stubborn determination since one early morning in the summer of my twelfth year, when I returned to the haunted cave in the Bledsoe holler to retrieve my lost boot. Upon arriving at the mouth of the cave in the silvering light of dawn, I found my boot, which the night previous had been wedged between two rocks, now unstuck and waiting patiently as a pup for its master.

This had been strange enough, sending a chill along my young spine—I was not nearly as brave as I pretended to be, in front of Boyd and our brothers—but I had reached for it gamely enough, the thoughts of fey creatures from Mama's stories in the forefront of my mind. As my fingers closed around the familiar old leather, a voice deep within the cave had told me two words. *The angel,* I heard. And from that moment forth there had arisen in my soul the need to find her, my angel, the woman meant for me.

Boyd and Ethan laughed themselves sick when I informed them of this truth, later that same morning.

"You's crazy as a jaybird," Boyd had said. "Ain't no voices in caves, 'less you's hearing things that other folks ain't."

"I'll tell you who's an angel, is that Helen Sue Gottlender," had been my brother's contribution, once his laughter died away. He continued, with an air of reverence, "You think her legs are as fair an' freckled as her arms? I aim to find out."

And Ethan had, by his and her sixteenth summer.

I turned to my other side, alone after the two men in the adjacent cell had been released earlier in the evening. There was no moon this night, and the jailhouse was dark as a tomb, but my thoughts were elsewhere, far away back home, and I allowed the memories of my old life momentary sway in my thoughts, a faint amusement tugging at me as I remembered my brother and his never-ending accounts; he had inherited Mama's gift for storytelling.

As eldest, I felt it should have been me earning the right to tell such tales of girls and the softness of their limbs, and yet Ethan had been the bold one in those days, always knowing just the right words to draw forth giggles and blushes in the local girls. I had been jealous and Jeremiah simply in awe, as he was far too painfully shy to be within a country mile of any girl not related to us, unless forced, as he was at school. The three of us shared a room, Eth and Jere a bed, and many a night had we crowded near Ethan as he related his exploits in hushed, excited whispers.

"I tell you, her daddy would skin me alive," I heard Ethan say, and if I closed my eyes I could plainly see his face in the moon-spill entering into our bedroom that long ago summer night. He insisted, "I tell you, we was kissing, an' she weren't wearing a thing beneath all them layers of skirts, an' her legs sorta opened up, an' she sorta *lifted* up, as if she *wanted* me to keep going." He paused purposely at this critical juncture in the story, grinning impishly. Ethan dearly relished being able to hold our rapt attention.

Jere, effectively bated, whispered breathlessly, "Then what?"

I had scoffed, restacking both hands beneath my head and directing my gaze at the wooden beams of the ceiling. I muttered irritably, "She did *not*."

Undaunted, Ethan said, "Shows how much you know, Sawyer. She did. An' then, sweet Jesus, I felt *right between* her legs. It was so soft, an' wet…an' she made a sweet little sound that I swear I want to hear every night for the rest of my livin' life…"

Jere interrupted to dutifully inform, "Reverend Wheeler would say it's a sin, Eth."

Ethan snorted a laugh and replied confidently, "It ain't no sin, *deartháir beag*. Nothing so precious could be sinful. If it is, curse me straight to the devil!"

Now, many years after the fact, I held close my brothers in my mind— Ethan and Jeremiah, the three of us inseparable, right to the horrific end. As I had so many times since returning from War, I thought, *Forgive me for not taking better care of you. I know we were grown men when we left home, but I was eldest. I intended to keep you safe, mo dheartháireacha daor, and I did not. Forgive me.*

Boyd had known Ethan and Jere nearly as well as I, and loved them as I had loved Beau and Grafton Carter as my own kin. Malcolm was too little to share the same depth of memories, only seven years when we left the holler in November of 1862. Of course, our plan was to drive out the Yankee invaders and return home victorious, no later than the eve of the New Year. The worst kind of foolishness, and blind pride, and it had killed everyone but Boyd and me, and little Malcolm. I understood I could hardly assign myself blame for the fevers that had taken a third of Suttonville the final winter of the War, a population weakened considerably by loss and starvation, a toll exacted upon those we were fighting for, left behind with little word, and even less food.

Rumors reached our ears after returning home, that Bainbridge Carter had been killed by a bullet to the gut, rather than illness. Tales of the crimes of retreating Federal troops were often grossly exaggerated, but I had seen with my own eyes of what desperate men were capable, on both sides of the fight; in any event, Boyd had not heeded these rumors, but I knew they troubled him still. The vision of his father defending their home to the last—making a stand against enemy soldiers and being cut down for his efforts—was at once valiant and terrible. Bainbridge and Clairee had been buried by the time we returned, near the headstones erected for their lost sons in the family's plot near their home; my own folks were likewise already beneath the ground, our homes burned out and looted. Our paths forever and indisputably altered.

And yet, as I had told Lorie that night at the Rawleys', had we not been to War, had they survived, I would likely never have ventured from Cumberland County, and home, and I would not have found her—and that price was the only one too great to pay. I had survived the loss of everything I once held dear, but I would not survive the loss of this woman, my wife.

And then I prayed, sending my thoughts upwards into the night.

Let us live out our natural lives together. Please, let Lorie live to be an old woman, with me at her side. Let us watch one another age, our hair gone gray and our faces lined. Please. It cannot be unfathomable to ask of this.

I would not consider all of the unheeded prayers of my past, the abject begging in the midst of one filthy, bloody battlefield after another. The whisperings I had made as I lay in the Suttonville cemetery that terrible summer of 'sixty-five, when I had wished for nothing but my own death, if for no other reason than to end the ceaseless torture of a functioning memory.

Please. Do not let me die in a hangman's noose. Not now. Not when I have so much to live for. If I must die, I will feign bravery, for Lorie's sake, but please do not let it come to that, oh sweet Jesus, please.

It was surely beyond midnight. I was restless with dormant energy, exhausted but unable to sleep, the threat of Zeb and Yancy never far from my mind. I had been rabid with fury at the news of Zeb firing on our wagon, our tent, during the hours of last night, possessed anew with the need to kill both men with my bare hands. What sadistic satisfaction I would find in wrapping my fingers about their throats and crushing away their worthless lives. Zeb, who had taken it upon himself during the ride back into Iowa City to tell me just what vile things he had done and would do to Lorie, when given the slightest opportunity. Zeb's halting voice and odd manner of speech reminded me of a man I had known in the War, who had been kicked brutally in the head by a horse, but had survived.

Zeb, who was surely hiding somewhere near, coward-like, awaiting his next chance to strike.

Yancy, by contrast, remained quiet and aloof on the ride north, and related to me none of what he told Lorie when she was his prisoner. I might have been a complete stranger to him for as little as he spoke, the wound on my temple leaking blood; at least I had been granted the assurance that Lorie was safe with Boyd. And Whistler remained with me. My horse, whose gait was near as familiar to me as my own, who had survived the duration of the War. My horse, who I would not allow to be stolen that dreadful night in April of 'sixty-five. In the saving of my horse, I had taken the life of a Federal—one of too many to count, at that point in my life—but the very act of marching home in the wake of formal surrender, defeated and hollowed-out, should have suggested that the killing was over.

I am not attempting to manufacture excuses, I am not, I thought, uncertain exactly to whom I directed these words; perhaps nothing more than my own conscience. *He fired upon my face, and I would have been dead these past years, killed right there in that clearing if not for a misfire. I would have let him ride free, but he engaged further—he drew the saber first.*

Yancy's brother chose his own death.

I did not intend to kill him, not until he attacked and I had no choice.

Did the hereafter take such things into account? I thought of Reverend Wheeler, the clergyman of my youth, whose sermons I had only ever listened to with half an ear, always on the lookout to catch my brothers' gazes and exchange some joke. Boyd, Beau, and Grafton were likewise always near, and privy to our irreverent conduct, more than willing to contribute; many a strappings had we earned after misbehavior during Sunday service. The reverend was a fairly tolerant man, at least in my memory, with docile brown eyes that Ethan once commented reminded him of a milking cow.

Would you have told me I could be forgiven? I wondered of the reverend, who, were he still living, would undoubtedly find it difficult to envision the boy he once knew should I appear before him now, changed as I was, both inwardly and outwardly. Young Sawyer Davis, eldest son of a kind-natured liveryman, would never have dreamed of the ferocity that would one day be enacted in battle, and endured; even in boyish speculation, and visions of imagined heroism, I had never considered there might come a time when I would be forced to kill another man.

But I am not sorry for killing Yancy's brother. I am only sorry for the terrible things that have come of it, since.

My thoughts continued, heedless of my need for at least an hour's sleep.

I am not sorry, nor do I believe it is wrong to kill a man who intends you harm, who would as soon kill you. I would do so again. I would do so to save the life of those I love, without a moment's hesitation.

I would help Lorie come to understand this; I refused to allow her to be plagued by the guilt of taking Jack's life, of being forced to bear witness to his violent death. That she had been under such circumstances again, defending herself against assault beyond imagining, was unbearable to me—as though life continually mocked my attempts to protect those I loved, and even as I lay there in flat-black darkness, I swore I felt the shadow of the crow.

You could not save Ethan, or Jeremiah.

Lorie could have been killed.

Even now she is unsafe and you are able to do exactly nothing.

"No," I whispered, struggling beyond these thoughts, instead picturing Lorie as I had envisioned her earlier in the night. When our thoughts had intertwined in the way I had come to cherish and depend upon, the connection that bound her heart with mine, stronger than all else previously known to me. I closed my eyes and reached for her, and then, in the deeper dimness behind my eyelids, I suddenly beheld the red and unmistakable menace of growing flames.

I sat up in a rush.

The window glass was not quite enough to muffle the faint sounds of passage just outside the jailhouse—had I been asleep, had it been raining, I would not have heard it at all. Instinct drove me to crouch into the corner of the cell, seeking refuge, throwing my awareness outward; there was no reason for a soul to be here at this hour, and it was not Boyd, or Tilson, carefully turning a key in the lock.

Yancy?

Would he dare to act on his own?

He would not.

He would send Zeb to act for him.

My thoughts raced, as a hog fleeing a butcher.

You have no defenses.

You are unarmed, a perfect target.

The door opened just enough to emit a hulking figure, an enormous, smudged outline darker even than the blackness of the small room. He entered and closed the door, just as quietly. My heart was shredding itself to bits with beating, blood flowing hot and fast, preparing me to fight. I had no weapon. I hadn't even the chain of the irons, which I might have used to choke him, and it would be a battle for my life. I understood clearly that one of us would die this night, and it would not be me.

"Come along," he murmured into the thick stillness, as though his presence had been anticipated. His voice emerged slowly, but he spoke with confidence—he would not be contradicted.

I did not respond, though there was no hope of remaining hidden for long; he knew I was here.

Zeb advanced and began working the key upon the lock of the barred door to the cell. Like a prey animal, I hunkered in the corner with sweat gliding into my eyes, and observed. He would not be carrying his Henry—it was undesirable in this sort of close-quarters situation. Instead he would have a pistol, and sure enough, there was the shape of the shorter barrel, trained in my direction. The door swung inward and he took one step closer.

"Step to, Johnny," he said.

Leap.

The thought had not fully formed before I followed it, lunging at him with a roar, seeking to grip the nose of the piece and disable his ability to place a bullet. He sidestepped faster than someone of his girth should have been able, striking with his free hand, and the downward blow of his fist caught the edge of my jaw. The shock of it sang through my entire frame, but I was focused with deadly purpose and my aim proved true, closing around the barrel and redirecting its threat. He grunted and thrust all of his weight forward upon me, taking us to the dirt floor of the cell.

I heard furious breathing, mine and his, as we grappled. He struck my face repeatedly, rendering me nearly stupefied, though I felt little pain. My world had narrowed to a slim corridor of resolve—that of keeping control of his primary weapon. The pistol was pinned uselessly beneath my torso and Zeb wrapped his left hand about my face, his thumb groping obscenely towards my eye, as though seeking entry into the socket. I grunted with the effort of battling him, shifting as best I could to knee his exposed side with all of my strength, and he wheezed, releasing his grip on my skull and turning in attempt to contain my lower half.

"Son of a...*bitch*," he uttered, as I continued my assault, intending to bust apart his ribs as I would have kindling. He lurched to the side in an attempt to trap my legs, not releasing his hold on the pistol. It discharged, whether by his action or mine, I did not know, and I felt the audible *whoosh* of the bullet as it sailed past my ear, lodging in the far wall with a thud. A red haze descended over my vision, my ears muffled as though with cotton batting, as they had been so often in battle. I was accustomed to this feeling, and let it envelop me, wrestling for control of the upper hand.

Zeb was formidable, and I could sense he was the stronger of us. He bore down upon me, striking with a hard-knuckled fist, bent on my subjugation. I felt and tasted blood, coppery and slick, and was forced to relinquish one hand from its feverish grip on the barrel, catching at Zeb's wrist in an upward swing. A growling issued from him, primal and inhuman, and before I could hope to dodge, blood and sweat trickling into my eyes, he butted his forehead viciously against mine. With this blow I reeled inescapably backwards, white-hot stars colliding across my vision.

I had a vague sense of movement, and then the pistol was discharged again. A poker, fresh from the fire, jabbed into my left arm. No more than half-conscious, I suddenly observed my daddy, his frame cast in a vermilion halo by the blaze of his forge, as I had seen it a thousand times in my youth, his familiar mustached face with no trace of a shadow upon it as he worked the bellows and stoked the fire, heating an iron bar to a yellow-white glow so that it was malleable for shaping into a proper horseshoe. Sparks flew from the cinders therein and Daddy used his tongs to lift forth the metal, an inanimate object brought to life in the flames, which issued a painful, groaning hiss.

I rolled to my uninjured side but could not escape Zeb. He holstered his piece and then bent, grunting with effort, and hooked his shoulder beneath my armpit, hauling me up as the burning agony bit deeper, and I groaned again. He hefted me, impossible a task as it may seem, and stumbled forward, out into the darkness of the street. No one had been roused by the gunfire. Or perhaps no one was choosing to investigate. Two horses waited, and he let me drop over the unsaddled of the two, face down and draping; before my consciousness fled, Zeb had efficiently cinched together my wrists and ankles beneath the horse's belly. Breathing hard, he mounted his own and summarily led us from town.

I FELL FROM the bed before I was fully awake, inadvertently dragging half the quilt behind me, propelled by the urgency of the nightmare. Blindly, I crawled across the space that separated me from the door. I heard panicked gasps and realized I was the one issuing them. I floundered, hunkering upon all fours on the wooden floorboards, disoriented, cloaked still in unreality— only seconds ago I had been half-naked on the street in St. Louis. I swore I could smell the acrid scent of a blazing fire, one intending to consume all in its ravenous path. Soot seemed to be in my nostrils.

"Rebecca!" I begged, startling her awake.

She sat at once, and whispered urgently, "What is it, Lorie? Are you hurt?"

I stumbled to my feet, heart thrashing with tremendous and powerful fear. Its presence overrode all else in my body but did not yet have a direct object. I only knew that something was terribly wrong.

What is it, what is it...

The window, I realized.

Though it was deep into a moonless night, a sort of glow backlit the oiled canvas covering, tinting it the shade of whiskey in a clear bottle. I blinked, absorbing this sight, and it was then that an unmistakable Rebel yell rolled across the night. At the incongruity of the sound in this time and place, my spine went rigid, each individual hair upon my nape standing straight. There was a brief, tense pause, and then another, simultaneously piercing and mocking. The person issuing the yell was no more than a quarter mile away.

"What in the *goddamn hell?*"

I heard Boyd utter this, and the thundering of his footsteps. I hesitated not a second, running barefoot through the small living space made dim and red by the banked fire in the woodstove; Boyd leaped the last three rungs of the loft ladder to reach the floor. Tilson was already up, strapping on his gun belt, hurrying into his boots.

"You Rebel *sons-a-bitches!*" came a low-pitched howl, Zeb's voice, profanely joyous at uttering these words. It continued, "Come out, come out... *wherever you are!*"

"Stay away from the window!" Tilson commanded sharply, moving to the closed door, rifle in hand and directed at the ceiling beams.

"Boy! You stay put!" Boyd ordered Malcolm, an arm outstretched to prevent disobedience of this issuance, as it was clear the boy intended to follow his brother and Tilson. Boyd grabbed his repeating rifle from where he had propped it near the door, moving to Tilson's side.

"*Boyd,*" Malcolm protested, his eyes intense, and in the fire's glow he looked less like a boy than I had yet witnessed, as though his adult self was unexpectedly granted this moment to peer briefly outward.

"Do not go out there," Rebecca pleaded, looking desperately between Boyd and her uncle. Cort and Nathaniel cuddled close, peering from the loft like possums in a tree.

"Where you grayback boys hidin'? Y'all ain't cowards, are yous?" Zeb yelled from outside, affecting a taunting and rancorous drawl.

"He is a *dead man,*" Boyd muttered, with unqualified resolve. "He will not see the sunrise, I swear this."

"He *wants* for you to come out there, do not you see?" Rebecca said, and I saw the tears in her eyes despite the dimness of the room.

Using her given name for the first time, Boyd ordered adamantly, "Rebecca, take them an' stay away from the door, an' the windows, no matter what." He called up to Cort and Nathaniel, "Boys, I need for you to come down here, an' stay by your mama," and they clambered down the ladder as he bade, without question, moving to Rebecca's open arms.

"Boyd," she implored, desperately, when it seemed apparent he could not heed her words, that he would surely be forced to venture outside.

"Bastard's around back," Tilson said, clearly calculating options. "Best I can figure he's positioned in the stand of oaks, yonder. Damnation. We must figure it's Zeb and Yancy, both. Goddamn. Do they think we're about to come running out?"

"You want me to ride for the marshal?" Malcolm asked. "I can make me a run for the corral."

No sooner had he uttered these words when Zeb bellowed, "He's a right pretty sight! You ain't gonna come see?"

And hearing that question, I knew.

"What the hell?" Boyd growled, advancing to the window, though it faced the front yard and offered no explanation for Zeb's words. "What's he about?"

I evaded Boyd and opened the door, racing into the night before the thought fully formed, even as Boyd roared at me to stop. But I was compelled by a force outside of myself as I flew around the edge of the house.

And then I saw.

Never before in my life had time so hideously folded over upon itself. The only way my mind could comprehend what it beheld was to deny all truth, to disbelieve all senses, and therefore continue existing. A scream rang in my skull. I heeded nothing in my path as I ran—far too slowly, as though mired in viscous mud—ran and ran, but I could not get there in time. As if I already knew it was too late.

Rifle in hand, Boyd pursued and overtook me, and though I did not hear the shot, I saw its impact strike him down. I loved Boyd as deeply as any blood kin, but I could not stop for him, not now, mindless and deranged but for one purpose. I fell, skittering to my knees, gasping and sobbing, raking at the flames as if I had any hope of dousing them with no water source. Burning chunks of wood tumbled to my skirt and I felt nothing. All of the pain, wrenching and destroying me, was internal, centered in my heart.

A crude, low-lying wooden pyre had been constructed beyond the house, far enough that the man building it could go unnoticed in the dark, but with every intention of letting those in the house see the blaze, once lit. It was very near the spot I had hugged Whistler, just earlier this evening. The pyre was burning now, and Sawyer had been draped atop, on his back; I could see the perfectly-formed arch of his pale throat in the scarlet glow—his hands were blackened. The ends of his hair were afire. In that moment, I was certain he was dead.

But I climbed that blaze.

It began to collapse beneath me, spreading over a greater surface area, and I lunged, getting my arms around his waist and using the combined force of my heft and momentum to deliver us from the fire. Sawyer was weighted as lead, but I rolled with him, finding the strength to maneuver us out of direct flame and to bare ground; the motion kicked up showering bursts of sparks from the pyre. In the midst of this hell I worked feverishly, beating out the last of the flames upon him. Still I could hear nothing; my sight had narrowed to a slim tunnel of frantic need, sharply focused, my fingertips seeking evidence of life.

There was a pulse pressing back against my fingertips, and sobs of relief splashed through the cavern of agony within me; sounds rushed back to beat at my ears—that of my labored breathing, furious shouting, rapid gunfire—and the taunting crackle of the fire no more than an arm's length from my left elbow. Wetness poured from my eyes and nose as I grasped Sawyer's face, bending close, the glow of the fire upon which he had been placed to die now offering light so that I could attempt to assess the damage to him. His clothing was in blackened tatters but had perhaps provided meager protection. My hands shook violently as I parted the ragged material of his shirt, in order to better see his wounded flesh.

And then Zeb was there.

He emerged from the darkness of the trees, scant yards away, and into the glow of the fire like a creature from the underworld, toting his Henry rifle. Crouched animal-like on the ground, and lit from beneath as Zeb was by the fire he had kindled into existence, the angle from which I viewed him created holes of his eye sockets. He seemed in that moment to possess no eyes, but instead deep black chasms, without end, mimicking nothing so much as his ancient hatred, an abyss across which there was no hope of rationale, or reason. His beard glinted ruby. His chest was massive as a steamboat's hull. He appeared to smile as I spread myself over Sawyer.

No, I begged as he directed a cocked pistol at my right ear, though no sound emerged from between my lips. Before he could discharge a bullet, something caught his attention and he moved surprisingly quickly, as he had on the prairie, stepping to the side and bringing the Henry rifle into play, the smooth stock braced against his stomach.

"I'll kill her," Zeb said, a statement no less true for its stilted delivery; he seemed to be breathing harder than normal.

"And then I will kill you," Tilson said in return, almost conversationally. I did not dare to turn my head to see, but Tilson sounded close. Perhaps just on the opposite side of the collapsed pyre.

"You goddamn Rebs," Zeb said. He advanced one pace closer and put the pistol to the top of my scalp, pressing hard with the cold and unyielding barrel. He kept the rifle on Tilson, and said slowly, "Goddamn you to hell. You burned my boys. Nothing left of them but black bones when I found them."

"I didn't kill your sons, an' neither did this man," Tilson said harshly. "No one here had a goddamn thing to do with that."

"Burned them alive," Zeb continued, as though Tilson had not spoken. "When I sleep, I hear them, screaming for me."

"Who is with you?" Tilson demanded. "Where is Yancy?"

Zeb said, "He washed his hands of it. Said the judge might believe the whore after last night. He gave me the key to the jail and said to finish it, this night."

"You take that pistol away from Lorie," Tilson said, menace edging aside his composure, even if he did not intend for that.

"She kilt Jack," Zeb said. "Shot him dead."

I didn't dare to move a thing but my eyes, feeling Sawyer beneath me. His shirt was wet with blood. Twenty running paces away, where the long grass met the dirt of the yard, I saw Boyd stagger upright, stumble two steps, and then fall to his knees.

"Take that pistol away, an' I ain't gonna tell you again," Tilson said.

"No," said Zeb.

"You's as good as dead," Tilson warned.

"I been dead since the War," Zeb said, in the tone of one conversing with a dimwit.

"Holster that piece, you *fucking Federal bastard!*" Boyd shouted hoarsely, reeling to his feet again, aiming his .44. He stood half-hunched, the barrel weaving in his grip.

"No," Zeb said, with an air of finality. A stick snapped in the pyre, sending a plume of red sparks.

And suddenly Malcolm was there, approaching quietly from behind, a repeater carried gracefully in the crook of his arms. In the fire's glow, and to my terror-dazed eyes, Malcolm appeared eldritch and otherworldly, his features cast in scarlet. He stopped ten paces away and said with admirable calm, "I got a bead dead center on your back, Mr. Crawford."

Zeb's attention was momentarily distracted at the sound of this new voice;

the pistol shifted slightly from its position of threat against my head, and that was all it took.

Tilson bellowed, "Lorie, get down!" and then he and Boyd fired repeatedly into Zeb.

The big man jerked, arms twitching, and dropped his heavy rifle with a thud. I had flattened myself to the ground at Tilson's order; the cracking report of gunfire seared the air above me.

"There's Yancy!" I heard Malcolm shout, his voice high-pitched with alarm.

Three things happened then, one directly after the other, and though I was in the very midst and witnessed each as it occurred, later I would recall the moment as something viewed through thick smoke, with its opaque haze, its capacity to blind and choke. The moment when the path of my life was forever after altered.

You must go on, the blue-eyed woman had told me.

Zeb went heavily to his knees, bleeding from multiple gaping wounds; his eyes were painted a flat, mortal red. Malcolm executed a swift half-turn and raised the rifle with the fluid movements of a dancer, bringing it to his shoulder and taking aim, firing into someone riding away at a full gallop. And Zeb, dying, blood gushing over his bottom lip, hoisted the pistol he still clutched in his fist and committed the final act of his life by firing it into Sawyer's face.

TILSON AND MALCOLM converged within a heartbeat, Tilson shouting at me to get back, but I would not release my hold on Sawyer. I did not hear Tilson order Malcolm to grab me and fought the boy with all of my strength, out of my mind, thrown far and viciously beyond all reason. Malcolm gasped, struggling to restrain my attempts to break free his hold; Tilson knelt quickly and his free hand went to the juncture of Sawyer's collarbones. Almost instantly, he was on his feet again.

"Lorie!" Tilson put his face near mine, clamping hold of my chin so that he could issue his words and know that I heard them. "You listen here! You calm down! I need you, an' Sawyer needs you!"

These words penetrated the churning madness, and I found the strength to stop screaming. Malcolm, consequently, relaxed his gripping arms. Weeping, lurching, I flew back to Sawyer's side and dropped to my knees as a rock into a lake, gone forever as it settled on the bottom, no farther to fall.

"*Please please please...*" I wheezed and gasped this single word.

"Boy! Get over here, help me lift him!" Tilson said, brusque and efficient. "I'll collect his torso, you two his legs, come along now! Get him inside!"

Between the three of us, we lifted Sawyer's inert form and carried him with slow, careful progress. I could not stop gasping, choking on each breath, as I studied his face—his precious face, black with blood and soot; blood pooled in his eye socket. I could not begin to determine the destruction the bullet had wreaked. Behind us, Zeb lay dead near the pyre he had built. Ahead of us, in the long grass roughly halfway back to the house, Boyd was bent forward but still standing.

"Boyd!" Malcolm bleated his brother's name.

Boyd managed a step, immediately stumbled, righted himself, and then came to us at a halting run. His face in the firelight bore a sickly pallor; his voice emerged as a grating whisper as he asked, "Is he dead? *Oh, Jesus...*"

"He ain't dead," Tilson said. "An' he won't be, if I have anything to say about it. Son, you's been cut up there."

"Boyd," I begged.

"Knocked me straight down," Boyd said, dogging us. Blood seeped from his lower right side.

"You's hurt," Malcolm said, and he was weeping, nearly silently, tears washing over his face.

"Becky!" Tilson bellowed, but Rebecca was already running to us.

"I dressed the bed and put on a kettle," Rebecca said breathlessly, her tone steady despite the obvious terror in her eyes. Her shocked gaze held Sawyer and roved urgently over Boyd, taking into account his every last detail, but she submerged everything other than necessity and hurried to hold the door for us.

"Get him onto the bed," Tilson said, unable to cease issuing orders, and we did so. "Becky, get the extra lanterns going. Lorie, get him undressed as quick as you's able. We must see the extent of the damage. I know you been burned, honey, but it's gotta wait."

I nodded understanding; my own wounds were the last thing I was thinking about. I could not have explained how grateful I was for Tilson's presence, unflappable and knowledgeable; I felt that if anyone could save my husband, it was he.

"Son," Tilson said to Malcolm, removing Sawyer's boots even as he spoke. "Did you hit him? That was Yancy, riding swift away?"

"It was," Malcolm said quietly, his tearful eyes transfixed on Sawyer's face in a combination of shock and grief. He blinked and then said, "I hope I got him, but I couldn't tell. He was hidin' in them pines to the south."

Rebecca appeared with two additional lanterns, and Tilson shoved aside the crocheted doily and ivory hairbrush set positioned neatly atop the bureau, nodding for the lights to be placed there.

"Linens," he told his niece. "And my satchel."

Boyd joined me at the bedside and together we worked to remove what was left of Sawyer's clothing; I could not catch my breath but my hands were steady, focused only upon doing whatever it took to save him. The sight of the damage sent arrow points of throbbing agony through my center. Bearing witness to how wretchedly, and purposely, he had been hurt served to constrict my heart into a self-preserving knot surely no larger than a pebble. Each moment stretched longer than time itself.

Sprawled limply atop the bed, Sawyer was nearly unrecognizable, as though painted with red and black. He had been severely beaten. His hair had burned away nearly to scalp. The familiar muscled flesh I had touched so many times was streaked with drying blood—a bullet had entered his left shoulder, as the acorn-sized hole there attested. His lips were parted and he breathed, however faintly—and this fact alone kept me from tumbling over the cliff's edge. Zeb's final shot had taken him in the left side of the face—there was a ragged trench over his eye—and so much blood.

"Son," Tilson said, addressing Malcolm. He had rolled back his sleeves and hooked his spectacles behind his ears. "I must ask of you a task. I must ask you to ride into town to fetch Clint an' Rawley. They'll be at the hotel yet. Billings, as well. Quade, if you can find him. Rouse Billings from dead sleep if need be, the bastard. You tell them we've been attacked."

Malcolm nodded at once, passing Rebecca as she reentered the room bearing a kettle and linens, using one to clutch the heated handle. She set these on the nightstand, dragging it closer to her uncle. I heard the outer door close behind Malcolm, as he left on the errand.

"Lorie, I must treat him, an' I'll need help. Can I count on you to do what I ask, without hysterics? Otherwise you must leave this room," Tilson said, not unkindly; he simply needed to know the answer. His big, capable hands were already upon Sawyer and moving with deliberate delicacy, just as they had traced over Letty's flesh only days ago; the lines between Tilson's brows suddenly deepened, and this outward sign of concern stabbed anew at my heart.

I nodded in response to his question, quite unable to speak.

"Good. Boyd, let's get him over. I fear there's still lead inside," Tilson said. "Gentle now."

"His eye..." Boyd said, and there was grit in his tone, the hesitance to pose a question for fear of its answer.

"We'll clean it out, but there ain't lead lodged there," Tilson responded. "I fear the eye is lost, but it ain't the greatest danger just now." The two of them carefully maneuvered Sawyer, exposing a bulging lump near the top of his shoulder blade, that which provided clear evidence of a bullet's presence. Tilson muttered, "*Dammit.*"

"I've the penknife, witch hazel, and whiskey," Rebecca said, coming near. She had donned a full-length apron over her nightclothes, her hair twisted back from her delicate face. She placed these items beside the lanterns and proceeded to pour steaming water from the kettle into a shallow basin.

"Lorie, turn your head," Tilson said. As he spoke, he uncorked the whiskey, collected a linen and wet a part of it using the whiskey bottle, releasing the strong fumes of grain alcohol. His gaze was sympathetic, but unwavering in its resolve. Boyd watched me, with seeming caution, as though he already knew I would disobey Tilson's request.

I lifted my chin only a fraction, and whispered, "Please. Let me help."

Tilson's mouth compressed into a stern line, but he only nodded briefly, acknowledging my words, and then said, "We can't delay. Boyd, Becky, you two bolster him, keep that shoulder exposed for me. I don't want him prone, not with that eye. Lorie, take that cloth and see if you can't cleanse some of that soot from his legs. Use water and vinegar, both, darlin'." I realized Tilson was attempting to position and busy me away from direct view, but he had allowed me to remain here, and so I did not protest.

With characteristic calm, Tilson dabbed clean the area surrounding the bullet's bulge. I gathered my wits and moved to the foot of the bed, gently taking Sawyer's right ankle into my hand and applying the damp cloth.

I am here, I told my husband, clamping fiercely upon the urge to give way to abject weeping, willing my thoughts into his mind. *We will save you, I swear to you. We will save you.*

Boyd and Rebecca held Sawyer in place, angling his torso so that Tilson could work. Tilson sat upon a chair, and with marked, exact effort, opened an incision small and neat, just beneath the lump of lead. A thick line of blood immediately welled. Tilson set aside the penknife, then squeezed precisely with his thumbs; I was reminded of Sawyer working over the abscess on Juniper's hoof. The bullet popped forth like a bloody pit emerging from an overripe cherry. It fell to the bed and Tilson, sounding cautiously satisfied, muttered, "There," and stoppered the flow of blood with the whiskey-drenched linen.

"Helps combat the seepage an' infection," he explained. "Learned the trick in the War."

"He's hurt so terrible," Boyd said roughly.

"We'll clean an' poultice him, patch up this cut, an' then we'll see to that eye," Tilson said. He looked abruptly at me, his blue-gray gaze searching my face, and his voice softened. He said, "Darlin', you's the bravest woman I ever knew. This man of yours owes you his life."

"Help him," I begged in a whisper.

"I aim to, you rest assured of that," Tilson said, and a ghost of a smile touched his lips.

HOURS LATER, Boyd, Malcolm, and I sat together, three hardback chairs drawn close. Tilson had climbed to the loft and joined his great-nephews, intending to rest as best he could before dawn, no more than an hour away; he had worked tirelessly over Sawyer, with Rebecca's competent help, Boyd and I assisting as we were able, before turning his attention to Boyd, and to me, assessing and treating each of us, all without a word of complaint.

I had not felt the pain of my wounds in the extremity of my distress, had hardly determined the extent of them, but now, left in the quiet dimness of one lantern with my husband, and the man and boy I loved as brothers, the multiple burns throbbed with a stinging ache. My feet had borne the worst of it, lacerated with multiple burns, and I sat now with my bare toes curled under against the floor, leaning sideways against Boyd's comforting solidness to my right, exhaustion having sapped all remaining strength.

"You hurting?" Boyd whispered.

I admitted, "Yes. Are you?"

A bullet tore a sizeable chunk of flesh from his lower right side, just above his hip; Tilson called it a goddamn lucky shot, as it could have easily been lodged in the bone. Rebecca had been the one to place the poultice, her head near Boyd's waist as he stood while she sat, quietly tying the bandage about him, her fingers competent and tender upon his flesh, not lifting her gaze higher than her work. Boyd, holding up his shirt, dared to let his eyes linger upon her; I was the only one to notice, seated as I was at the end of the bed while Tilson carefully smudged a thick salve over the burns on my soles, before binding them.

Boyd whispered to me, "I'm hurting some, but I'll heal. Carters is fast healers, always has been."

"Thank you," I whispered. "Both of you. You saved him. You killed that…
that…" Hatred broke the word in two, twisted apart my voice. I managed,
"That *bastard*."

"You was the one climbed into the fire," Malcolm said, low and yet with
wonder in his words. "My heart near quit beating, I was so scared."

"Tilson was right, you's brave as a warrior, Lorie-girl," Boyd said, and
kissed my cheek. "Sawyer loves you with all his heart, an' I know you love him
as much. But then, I knew that from the first."

"I do, and I love the both of you, too," I whispered. "I can't imagine my life
without all of you."

Malcolm, to my left, rested his cheek on my upper arm.

"We's family, no matter that we ain't blood kin," Boyd agreed. "An' I don't
aim to lose one of us, not now." He whispered, "You hear that, old friend?"

For a time, we sat wordlessly; Boyd held both of us close, Malcolm snuggled against my side, one of his slender arms resting upon my lap. I let their
collective security sink into my soul, so very grateful for them. But no amount
of comfort, or wishing, could banish the memory of Sawyer's blood, so much
spilled this night; I was unable to stop thinking of it, and my helplessness
in the face of his suffering was torturous, so potent was the pain of the unknown.

Tilson had treated Sawyer to the best of his ability, of this I had no doubt,
and now we were forced to wait. To watch for signs of infection and to wait—
and I despised this with a rabid ferocity. Long ago I had waited for Daddy
to return home, and for Dalton and Jesse with him; I had waited for Mama
to recover, to find the strength to resume her role as my mother, my only
remaining security. I had waited for eventual death at Ginny's—and at the
cruel hands of Sam Rainey. And now I was forced again to wait, and my fury
had burned itself into an ember-field of bitter exhaustion, no less powerful.

After a long spell of silence, Malcolm whispered, "I wish my shot woulda
killed Yancy. I tried, Boyd, I done tried to kill him."

Boyd said firmly, "Malcolm, you done good, an' I couldn't be no prouder
than Daddy would be this night. You saved Lorie by coming from behind,
an' thinking to stay hidden. Zeb wanted us in the open, so's we would be easy
targets."

"But Yancy's still alive out there," Malcolm said, and I reached a hand to
him; he understood without words and collected it within the warmth of his.

"He was watching everything from the pines, makin' sure we was all killed. When we wasn't, he run like the coward he is."

"Charley lit out to find him," Boyd said. "Yancy ain't gonna get away for long."

Charley Rawley had departed an hour before, southbound and determined to find Thomas Yancy; Clemens had arrived with Quade, and the two of them were still quietly conversing near the woodstove in the other room; Rebecca, allowing herself not a moment's respite, had made coffee and now sat with her brother and Quade. Billings had come from town, and had since likewise left, riding north rather than south, leading a second horse, with Zeb's body dangling over its back.

"But he will get away," Malcolm insisted, using his thumbs and forefingers to feel each part of my hand, almost unconsciously, as if intending to assemble it into an entirely new configuration. He explained, "Yancy's the law. Ain't no lawman gonna believe us over him. Yancy'll say that Mr. Crawford did this on his own. An' Quade, who mighta believed us, wasn't here to see what really happened. You heard Mr. Crawford call us 'Rebs.' That's all we is to the Yankees—Southern Rebs who ain't fit to live."

"Once I thought I'd never utter these words, but not all Yankees hold that opinion, boy," Boyd murmured, though I could sense from his tone that he was rather taken aback at Malcolm's adult perusal of the situation.

"But they do," Malcolm said, with keen insistence. His pupils reflected the glimmer of the single candle in the space, burnt low and guttering. "They's all got kin that was kilt by Reb bullets. Even Mrs. Rebecca, who been sweeter'n honey to us, lost her husband to a Southerner. We ain't but the enemy."

"Rebecca doesn't see us that way," I whispered. "She truly does not. And she loves Tilson, who saved Confederate lives for the duration of the War."

"But Tilson is her kin," Malcolm protested.

"She has helped us more'n we could ever repay," Boyd whispered, and I wanted to look at him, to gauge from his expression what he was feeling, but I could not call forth the strength required to lift my head. His tone was reflective, and subtly tinged with wistfulness. Boyd had helped Rebecca administer a dose of laudanum to Sawyer an hour earlier, but she had not spoken to him other than to direct his movements in keeping Sawyer's head steady so that she could manipulate the spoonful down his throat.

When Quade arrived, he had taken Rebecca into his arms and held her.

"Thank God for her, and Tilson, both," I whispered, and bent nearer the bed so that I could press my lips to Sawyer; so little of his face was exposed, bound and wrapped as it was, but I kissed his jaw, gently. He was alive, and every breath I took begged him to continue living—I had not yet allowed myself to contemplate that his left eye was gone. At present, I refused to concentrate on anything other than ensuring his continued survival.

Boyd placed one hand on Sawyer, lightly and with great reverence. He whispered, "Old friend, we's been through too much together for you to leave us now."

"Dawn's coming," Malcolm murmured.

Dawn offered a false sense of fair weather, the land outside the front door appearing lovely and benevolent beneath a placid sky; within a quarter hour, however, the sun would lift into the massing clouds, all of its tranquility subsequently eradicated, and would display for us instead a day devoid of color, a sky flat-white, humid air heavy as stale breath. I had not slept, could not think of sleeping, but I had countless reasons to be thankful.

Sawyer was still breathing.

He had survived the night.

Rebecca was frying eggs, talking quietly to her boys. I found it difficult to walk—my feet felt as if they had been scrubbed free of all skin. I sat and rested my forearms on the edge of the bed, my cheek upon them, and was drifting in a state of partial stupor when Sawyer's left arm jerked violently and he groaned. I sprang to immediate attention. Tilson had covered both of Sawyer's eyes with a single strip of linen in order to hold the poultice in place. Surely by now the laudanum was wearing away, and Sawyer would require another round or the pain would be too intense.

"I'm here," I said, my eyes roving frantically over his face, searching for further signs of consciousness. I touched him with great care, leaning as close as I dared without jostling the bed, and said firmly, "Sawyer, you're safe. I'm here, and you're safe at Tilson's."

He groaned, low and harsh.

Rebecca appeared swiftly in the room, bearing a spoon and the small, brown-glass bottle, in addition to a tin cup of water. She asked, "Is he waking?"

"He's hurting," I said, retaining calm with all of my effort. His limbs had begun to shake, despite the quilts atop him. His jaw clenched and he issued forth another grating moan. I began to cry, begging, "Hurry."

"Lift his head, just as we did last night," Rebecca instructed. "There, now."

I assisted her as she plied the liquid painkiller, gently fitting the spoon between Sawyer's teeth; he appeared to swallow, and Rebecca administered a sip of water. As careful and experienced as her touch, most of it dribbled and wet his chin, as it had last night; it took us four attempts for Rebecca to be satisfied with the amount he took.

She said, "I've a beef bone simmering. By noon I shall have a hearty stock." Studying my face, Rebecca whispered, "Dear Lorie, I would be pleased if you would rest. Lie on his far side and sleep for a few hours." She implored, "Please."

I nodded; Rebecca eased shut the door behind her.

I climbed gingerly over the foot of the bed, settling near the window and lying upon my side, facing Sawyer, though I left a careful distance between our bodies. Blurring waves of dizziness lapped across my mind, as small waves to a creek bank, and I made a pillow of one arm and there rested my head, as the room brightened, albeit dimly, with day. I told him, "I will be right here."

But for the slightest rising and lowering of his chest, Sawyer was so frighteningly still, resting now upon his back; any position was undesirable at present, considering the burns upon his flesh and the small, neat stitches Tilson had sewn into his shoulder, but Tilson deemed it best for Sawyer to lie thusly. His face was angled my direction, the linen covering his eyes dampened by blood on the left side, but not an alarming amount. I studied what I could see of his face, his face that I loved more than all else in this world, and would never cease to love.

You must go on, the blue-eyed woman seemed to whisper, somewhere at the edges of the room.

Not without Sawyer, I contradicted, fiercely. *Not without him. I will not wait countless additional lifetimes to find his soul again. I will not.*

It is a sin to consider taking your own life, my mother murmured in my ear.

Half-dreaming, I whispered in response, *I am a sinner many times over, Mama, and I have finally reached a point that I acknowledge this with no shame. And what of you? You left me behind. I know that I cannot seek to blame you for contracting the typhus, for being ill, but you left me long before that. After news of Daddy, you had already retreated into your mind. I was alone from that moment forth. I never understood my anger, the resentment I bore you, until now. It is unfair, this I understand, and I will always love you, but you did wrong by me. So please, never speak to me of sinning, not ever again.*

For a time I drifted along in a languid torpor, allowing one foot to touch the side of Sawyer's leg beneath the quilts, unable to bear having no physical contact with him. In my mind, I sailed freely a few dozen feet over the land, expeditiously retracing my footsteps many hundreds upon hundreds of miles south and east, spying endless acres of grasses, vast as an ocean, rippling with the wind. Light as a scrap of down, I flew farther, observing the red dirt roads of central Tennessee, the ditches ripe and bursting with flowers in this month of July.

I saw Lake Royal, glimmering blue-green under the summer sunshine. I saw my brothers playing beneath that same sun, their curly auburn hair glinting like a promise that would remain forever unfulfilled. I realized I had become almost completely without substance, somehow understanding I was nothing more than a piece of my mother's fair hair, a strand unintentionally set free from the lock she had given to Daddy before he left home. He had bound it with a length of green satin ribbon and Mama and I had each kissed it, before he tucked it for safekeeping into the breast of his uniform. I had sometimes wondered, in the depths of my darkness when I still lived at Ginny's, what had become of that lock. In the most macabre of my thoughts, I envisioned it impervious to the rot that overtook flesh; perhaps it fluttered free of Daddy's uniform before his body was buried, and was even now blowing along in the wind somewhere in Virginia.

For luck, Mama had told him.

A crow soared with effortless elegance, wingtips so near I could feel the rush of air created by its soundless passage. For a time we flew together, our eyes directed to the ground below, where the land had taken on the unmistakable appearance of flesh, ragged and wounded, the waterways its arteries, bright red with flowing blood.

A long time in healing, the crow whispered. *Long after your death, the land will still be recovering from such a conflict.*

I saw people then, thousands of them, perhaps even millions, busy as ants as they moved over the damaged landscape.

And in their souls, longer still, the crow told me, with no menace. Its words were simple, unavoidable truth. *They will live. Some will even prosper. In time, they will forget what has been done here. But their souls will still bear the injury.*

Go, I raged. My voice was hollow and fragile, as though the words had passed across a wide plain in order to be heard. *Go from me. Never return to me again. I despise you.*

It does not matter. Oblivion is where I exist, it whispered.

I grew weighted then, abruptly cut free from my airy freedom. I screamed after the huge, black-feathered bird as I plunged to earth, but on it flew without looking back, flapping once its sleek ebony wings before disappearing into the distance of the wide blue sky that arched over Tennessee.

REBECCA SPOKE heatedly, just out in the yard.

My eyelids were stuck shut, as though my tears had solidified and become sticky, tangling together my eyelashes. The house smelled of beef broth. I rose to one elbow, rubbing furiously at my eye sockets, looking at once to Sawyer. The quality of the light had changed in the small bedroom, the sun having advanced over the roof of the house, creating pockets of shadow. Sawyer appeared unchanged. An unsettling sense of disorientation, of plummeting endlessly, hovered near, and though I was uncomfortably warm beneath the quilt, I shivered.

I heard the second voice then, which seemed vaguely familiar, and I strained to listen.

"Shall not...if I have..." I could only discern every few words.

"Only require...few moments..."

The journalist, I realized. The man named Parmley was in the dooryard with Rebecca.

I eased from under the covers, sweat slick on my skin, but I intended to help Rebecca shoo the objectionable man away. It was then that I realized heat was emanating from Sawyer; just as swiftly, my stomach grew cold. I rested my palm against his cheek, and knew.

Fever.

I stumbled outside, heedless of both my aching feet and my ragged appearance. Cort and Nathaniel were hanging on the fence, watching silently as Rebecca stood with fists planted on hips, facing Parmley as he sat horseback. I observed that Fortune and Aces were absent from the corral, as was Kingfisher, Tilson's solid chestnut gelding. Without preamble, my voice scratching over the words, I told Rebecca, "He's fevered."

Rebecca nodded at once. To Parmley, she snapped, "Ride for town, fetch my uncle, and be quick about it!"

Parmley's insincerely sycophantic interest was immediately directed at me. He gushed, "Mrs. Davis, you have been delivered from your ordeal. Sheriff Billings has informed me of your misfortune. If you'd allow me to ask a few questions…"

He dismounted and seemed about to follow on our heels, and Rebecca rounded on him, ordering, "Go, now! I shall not ask you again. I require my uncle, forthwith!"

Parmley lifted both hands, clutching his mare's halter in the right. He said cajolingly, "Rebecca, you know I mean no harm. I only wish to…"

"I swear on my life, Horace, I shall wring your neck," Rebecca interrupted, speaking through her teeth, and Parmley instinctively retreated a step.

Cort muffled a giggle.

"Very well," Parmley conceded, remounting his mare. As he rode from the yard, he called, "Good day. Perhaps when Mr. Davis is well, you'll allow me a moment of your time!"

"Come, Lorie, do not be troubled by that fool," Rebecca said. She called to her boys, "Finish sweeping out the stalls, and you may have another tart each."

"I woke just now," I said. "And Sawyer is feverish. Oh, Rebecca…"

She rested the backs of her fingertips lightly against his temple, her features taking on an expression that echoed Tilson's. She whispered, "Indeed." Then her eyes flashed to mine and she said, "A fever is not always a sign of trouble. It means he is healing, and his body is fighting an infection. At times, it is best to let it run its course."

I tried to draw a full breath past my trembling lips. I whispered, "But he is so very hot…"

"Let us see what Uncle Edward says," Rebecca said, and gathered me into a hug. Against my hair she whispered, "I wish I could do more to put you at ease. You have been very brave, Lorie."

Tilson arrived within the next half hour, along with Malcolm and Boyd. Boyd, despite Tilson's exasperated orders to stay put, had ridden into town to speak with Billings, to see what had been done regarding Zeb's role in last

night's events; I could only imagine the resultant firecrackers. I listened with
one ear as the three of them cantered into the yard.

"Boyd Carter!" Rebecca said, and her tone was nearly the same with which
she had addressed Parmley; she was in an obvious temper. The conversation
between the men came abruptly to a halt, and Rebecca snapped, "You are
bleeding, sir, and should not be horseback!"

There was a beat of silence, and then Tilson whistled, low, as though to
indicate danger. He asked his niece, "How is Sawyer?"

"He's fevered, as I told that imbecile Horace to relate to you," Rebecca
steamed, and I envisioned the storm blazing in her eyes.

Tilson said, "Parmley received the sharp side of your tongue this day, as
well, it seems."

"It ain't but a little blood. I ain't hurting," Boyd said, coming indoors; he
called, "How is he, Lorie?"

Malcolm had walked around the house to use the pump; I could hear him
just out the bedroom window, wise enough to avoid Rebecca in her current
state. I reflected that she had slept as little as any of us, but I had not heard so
much as an utterance of complaint from her.

"Sit here, and let me see for myself," she ordered Boyd, before I managed
to respond to him.

Tilson appeared around the partly-open bedroom door. He set aside his
hat and came near, laying a hand upon my shoulder.

"You was dozing when I left," he said. "I'm glad of it. You needed the rest."

Tilson moved closer to the bed, inspecting Sawyer with practiced and
tender thoroughness, asking of me questions concerning his intake of water,
and beef broth. He said, "He is warm, but I ain't ready to panic. Let us change
out these bindings, and reapply the poultices. I wish I could tell you there
was a way other than waiting, but there ain't." Tilson sighed, recognizing my
despair. He said quietly, "I mean to restore your good man to you. Do you
trust me?"

My throat was dry, but I whispered, "I do."

RAIN FELL IN the night hours, spattering the canvas over the window. When thunder issued forth a crescendo of spine-jolting bursts, I cowered instinctively, imagining I heard in it the crack of multiple firearms. Beside me, Sawyer jerked and groaned.

"He's shaking again," I moaned, horrified by how swiftly these tremors overtook his body. "Malcolm…"

But he had already disappeared to fetch Boyd.

Hastily I gathered up the layer of quilts near the foot of the bed; these, I alternately removed from his scalding body or, as now, attempted to tuck closer about his shuddering limbs. Boyd came, toting a lantern, and helped me prevent Sawyer from thrashing too violently, as he and Tilson had been intermittently for the past three hours. Boyd kept a steady flow of reassurance, speaking in low, measured tones, the way a man would to a spooked horse. I prayed that Sawyer was able to understand that we were here, and near him, that we were caring for him. He had not yet demonstrated any signs of lucidity, and when his voice suddenly emerged, harsh and hoarse, nearly a growl, my heart convulsed.

"Get…*back*…"

"Sawyer!" I said, with unintentional sharpness, consumed by the need to hear him speak again. "We're here. It's me, it's Lorie."

"*Get back*…" he ground out, his teeth clenched.

Bracing his forearms over Sawyer's chest, on either side, Boyd said firmly, "Sawyer! It's us, we's right here with you. You's safe now, old friend."

"*Son of a bitch...I will kill you...*" Sawyer tried to lift his head; his hands became fists, and he jolted against Boyd's careful hold.

"Boyd..." I implored, as new fear throttled me.

"He's in a fever dream," Boyd said, and his breath came fast with the exertion of keeping Sawyer from inadvertently hurting himself. He insisted, "He ain't talking to us."

Tilson entered behind Malcolm, bearing the laudanum, and it took him and Boyd both to administer the dose. I clung to Malcolm, who petted my hair with slow, gentle strokes. Within another minute, Sawyer calmed enough to fall still; Tilson had swapped out the poultice over his lost eye no more than a few hours ago, with my assistance. I refused to be afraid or squeamish to look upon the damage; I only feared what would be the reaction when he came to full consciousness.

"Try an' get some rest, please, Lorie," Boyd whispered, once calm, if not peace, had been restored to the room. His face was lit by the single lantern, positioned to his right, highlighting his strong features and casting odd, dancing shadows over the left portion of his countenance. His brows were knitted.

To alleviate his nearly-palpable concern, I whispered, "I will."

"Sawyer wouldn't like the way you's mistreating yourself," Boyd murmured, clearly understanding that I was pacifying him. "You ain't eating, or sleeping. You know this."

"I do," I whispered in acknowledgment.

"Rest," Boyd repeated.

Tilson corked the laudanum and settled it at the bedside. He asked, "You hurting, honey?"

I was hurting, desperately so, though far less than was Sawyer; I despised that I could do so very little to alleviate any of it, forced to wait and see what the next hour would bring.

"Lorie?" Boyd pressed, and his shoulders rose and lowered with an indrawn breath. I knew he had slept nearly as little as had I, was approaching the end of his considerable emotional strength, and so I drew forth enough resolve to whisper, "I am not hurting, not that way. I will try to rest, I promise you."

"Good," he muttered, low.

The lack of knowing drove iron nails beneath my skin, carved out great patches of my sanity, trenches as ragged as hastily-dug graves. I rested my fingertips upon Sawyer's chest, allowing myself to feel the rise and fall of his breathing. As long as he breathed, he continued living.

Tilson said, "I'll be near."

Rebecca entered the bedroom as Tilson retired to his bed near the wood-stove, bearing a second lantern and a tin cup in her hands. She moved word-lessly, clad in her nightclothes and shawl, her long, dark hair in a thick braid. Boyd stepped aside to allow her nearer to me; the air between the two of them was rife with crackling tension, which seemed to increase each passing hour.

"I've tea for you, Lorie," she whispered, and staved off my apology, whispering, "The thunder woke me, do not concern yourself."

Dutifully, unable to refuse her, I took the cup. In the glow of the candles, Rebecca regarded me with as much solemnity as Boyd. He stood less than an arm's length from her, just slightly behind her right shoulder, and I saw how his dark eyes lighted intently upon her. Rebecca could not have been more aware of his quiet presence had he stood shouting and making a scene, but she kept her gaze directed at me, and as I managed a second sip, she mur-mured, "That's good."

"Thank you," I whispered in response. The tea was warm and laced with mint, soothing upon my dry tongue. "Thank you so much."

"He is unchanged?" she whispered, reaching gracefully to set the lantern upon the bureau top. She rested her hand to Sawyer's face, briefly, and with utmost gentleness.

His voice more gruff than usual, even in a murmur, Boyd said, "He came to for a moment there."

"Perhaps by morning he shall be fully awake," Rebecca whispered, perch-ing gently at the edge of the feather tick laid over the very bed within which she had spent her wedding night, where she had delivered each of her sons, and where she had unknowingly spent the last hours allowed to her in Eli-jah's company, only months before his formal discharge would have occurred. And now my husband battled for his life upon the same narrow mattress.

"I pray it," I whispered. Sawyer's face, so familiar and beloved to me, was now altered, and I was admittedly terrified for him to become aware of this unwitting change; I cared only that he survived. I assisted Tilson both times he changed the poultice over the wound; he insisted it would heal measurably, even within a month. The bullet had burst through the slim bone on the outer edge of the socket and therefore had not lodged within Sawyer, but there was no hope of saving his eye. Had the shot been placed even another hair's breadth to the left, he would have been killed instantly.

And even knowing it had not, I had to clench my teeth against the wretched pain of that thought.

"How are your feet?" Rebecca asked, and almost unconsciously, I slipped them under the hem of my nightdress. They were still bound with two strips of linen, and I did not wish to admit to my own pain, not now.

"They are not hurting worse," I said, and this was not a lie.

Rebecca turned her attention to Boyd, who stood still and silent, only a pace or two away; he watched her steadily, as though unable to help himself, and I saw how their eyes held fast, fancying that I could very nearly discern the increase in the pulse of blood throughout Rebecca's body. Boyd swallowed, though he did not move otherwise. Quietly, she asked him, "Would you like me to change that dressing before morning?"

I knew the injury pained him, but he would not admit it to Rebecca, who had soundly scolded him yesterday.

"There ain't no need," Boyd whispered, his gaze tangled into hers. His hair fell in a tumbled mess over his forehead, his shirt undone two past the top button; we had all long travelled beyond any strict adherence to propriety, even Rebecca, sitting here in her nightclothes, which only a husband, as decorum dictated, should ever be allowed to see. The lantern light flickered over Boyd's strong, striking features, the stubborn set to his mouth, his dark eyes and the solid lines of his jaws and chin, thick with black stubble long due for a shaving.

"It is no trouble," Rebecca whispered. She sat with hands tightly clasped, as though to forcibly prevent herself from reaching for him.

"I am well," he assured her. His tone soft, he whispered, "I promise, I am well. Don't fret."

She nodded, rising abruptly and collecting from me the cup. She whispered, "Call for me, if you need, and there is a fresh cloth on the basin. Sleep well, Lorie." She did not offer any such pleasantry to Boyd. He watched her leave the room, tugging close her shawl.

"It brings her comfort to ascertain for herself that you are not hurting," I told him, speaking just above a whisper, and Boyd's eyes flashed at once to me; he was plainly consternated. I elaborated, "You're being difficult."

At my words, the faintest hint of a smile tugged sideways his mouth. He whispered, "My mama's words, many a time, Lorie-girl."

"Rebecca worries for you," I whispered, nagging at him. "She…" I gulped back the admission that she cared deeply for him, but Boyd was nobody's fool; surely he realized. Instead, I concluded, "She cares for all of us. I find myself wishing she was my sister."

"Well, it's a waste of time t'wish for things we can't have," he whispered, his pupils burning with the reflection of the lantern's flame. His posture changed and he briefly closed his eyes, then murmured contritely, "Don't mind me. I aim to fetch a few hours' sleep, an' wake in a better temper. C'mere," and he reached to catch me in a hug. I held fast, squeezing him tightly, and kissed his cheek.

"G'night," he whispered, and left me alone with Sawyer.

In Boyd's absence, I gently drew the quilt back to Sawyer's shoulders, studying his face.

"It is too quiet without your voice," I whispered. The linen tied over his eyes was a pale white slash in the gray dimness of the room. The laudanum had slightly altered his scent, and I prayed the need of the drug would soon be past. Recognizing the pain he suffered, being subsequently deprived of him, was torturous, unbearable to me, and yet I would bear it; so long as he lived, I would bear the torture.

"Boyd played for you earlier this night," I murmured. "The same waltz that he'd played on the prairie for us, the night we were handfast." Tears spilled to my cheeks, there was no helping this, as I continued, "No church ceremony could have been half so lovely, so *real*. To be there with you, as the sun set and the moon rose. I felt as we spoke that even the Earth itself heard our words, and acknowledged them. I know some might find that foolish, but you understand. You *know*, as you always do, what is in my heart." I bent to kiss him, my lips wet with tears; I carefully brushed away the resultant moisture left behind upon his fevered skin. I whispered miserably, "You are so heated, love."

I collected the folded linen Rebecca had placed over the edge of the basin, now half-empty. I dipped the cloth, wringing the excess; the drops plummeting back into the water seemed absurdly loud in the quietness of the room, the orange lantern light skipping wildly over the disturbance in the liquid. Sawyer lay naked, the burns upon his body treated with salve, and carefully bound. In addition, his left side was wrapped in linen, protecting the injury left behind by the bullet Zeb had fired into his shoulder; eight precise stitches now held closed the exit wound. Tilson had instructed the binding over Sawyer's eyes remain dry, and so I placed the coolness of the damp linen across his collarbones instead, mimicking Rebecca's actions. Sawyer shuddered at the touch of the damp cloth, and my hands jerked in surprised response, instantly removing it.

"Is it too cold? Oh, Sawyer...I am so sorry..."

A rope snared my heart and I nearly dropped the damp linen as he groaned one word—my name.

"I'm here, I am here with you," I told him, desperate for him to realize this truth. For all he knew, he was still trapped in the jail in Iowa City—I had not allowed myself to speculate how he had suffered that night—even before being draped atop a burning pyre; Zeb had come for him while he was still locked within the cell in the sheriff's office, and the battle to submit Sawyer to his will had surely been horrific; Sawyer's body bore marked evidence of this.

"Lorie," he moaned, and I held his burning face between my palms; he flinched, his hands fisting. He sounded frightened, as though perhaps in the clutches of a dream, he could not find me, or did not realize that I was safe. His hoarse voice burst forth, calling for me. And then he choked, roughly and in terror, "*I can't see...*"

I was unable to prevent him from ripping the binding away from his eyes. His right eye was a mere slit, glossy with fever; the poultice over the left was in danger of falling away, and Sawyer struggled to sit. And then suddenly Tilson was beside me, curling his big hands about Sawyer's upper arms and easing him back to the bedding, speaking in the quiet and comforting way of a longtime physician. His gray hair swung against the sides of his jaws as he held my husband carefully prone and called, "*Becky!*"

Sawyer was agitated, his eye rolling backward in the socket, alarmingly, his jaw clenching as though in fury, bucking against Tilson's grip. He issued a low growling sound and fought Tilson's hold, but the doctor was of a size with my husband, as few men were, and did not allow Sawyer to thrash free.

He said firmly, "Son, you're all right. Listen to me, you are safe." In a different tone, Tilson shouted, "Quick now! It weren't enough."

Rebecca came at a run, and Tilson held Sawyer while his niece administered another spoon of laudanum. Once Sawyer had sunk again into full unconsciousness, Tilson carefully resettled the poultice and tied the linen about his eyes. Tilson was breathing slightly heavier than normal; when he turned, his eyebrows were stern with worry. Studying my face, he said, "He'll rest for a spell now." Seeing that I was not consoled, he added, "Sawyer knows you love him. He has something to live for, an' that's more than a good start, Lorie."

I intended to rejoin Sawyer on the bed, but I stepped wrong with my bound and aching feet, faltering. Without a word, Tilson swept me into his arms, as he would have a wayward child. Despite my protests he carried me forthwith into the adjoining living space, to the rope bed situated near the woodstove, upon which Rebecca already had a kettle boiling, cooking oats for breakfast. Atop the ropes was spread a bear skin, a tattered quilt, and a single pillow, and Tilson deposited me here with great care, drawing the quilt over me. He said in a voice not to be contradicted, "You will take a dose and you will sleep."

I knew he would not be denied, and I was near the end of my ability to continue functioning; my eyelids were already sinking. The pillow smelled rather strongly of Tilson himself, who typically bedded here during the night hours, but when he held a spoonful of laudanum gently to my lips, I accepted with no protests. The thick syrup of it was sweet on my tongue, and left an unpleasant aftertaste, but a silken black shawl encased my mind nearly at once, and however unwillingly, I gave over to unconsciousness.

WHEN NEXT I woke, the room was still swathed in darkness, broken only by the red glimmer of a low-burning fire in the woodstove; woozy from the drug still holding sway in my blood, I saw in its glow a pair of malevolent eyes, and sat with a gasp, tumbling from the rope bed and to the floorboards. The resultant thunk drew forth the sound of swiftly-moving feet, and Boyd crouched near me, cupping my shoulders in a gentle hold. Malcolm bent just behind his brother, and in the fire's scarlet tint I blinked at them; their resemblance, already strong, was further increased by the depth of concern present on their faces. The ember-light carved out odd patterns upon their features and I blinked once more, attempting to focus, prompting Malcolm to explain in a hushed voice, "Lorie-Lorie, it's just us. Boyd an' me." He added helpfully, "It's night again."

"You been asleep for near sixteen hours," Boyd murmured. "We's sitting with Sawyer just now, me an' the boy."

I reached and clutched at Boyd's forearms, to steady myself. I begged, "Let me see him."

"He ain't come to yet," Boyd said softly, lifting me to my feet and subsequently tucking me to his side; he knew it hurt me to walk. "We changed out the bedding today, while you was sleeping. Tilson wished to spare you that, an' I agree."

I held to Boyd and allowed him to assist me to the bedroom; there, he helped me atop the bed, where I climbed to the far side, nearer the wall, and minutely assessed Sawyer's face. The haze in my mind was slowly shredding apart, as clouds before a rising wind.

I whispered, "Thank you."

"It was right good you slept so long, you needed the shut-eye," Boyd said. He and Malcolm took up their positions on chairs settled near the bedside. Malcolm dragged his seat closer and leaned both elbows on the edge of the feather tick.

"Has he spoken today? Has he dreamed?" I asked.

"He's been dreaming a fair amount," Boyd said, placing a gentle hand on Sawyer. "He's been calling for you, Lorie-girl, but he ain't woke yet."

"Early this morning, he said..." I bit back the onrushing fear and whispered, "He said that he *couldn't see*...oh, Boyd..."

Malcolm whispered, "He's still got one good eye. We gotta remember that."

"The drug is addling his mind. I wish he'd break into a good sweat, and be done with it," Boyd said. "Tilson said that would be the best sign just now, would show us that the fever didn't have a hold on him no more."

"Where is Tilson?" I asked. The house seemed empty of all but the four of us.

Malcolm explained, "Him an' Mrs. Rebecca lit out to attend a woman whose birth pains came on too early, a few hours back. Me an' Boyd's been watching the boys." Malcolm added, "They's got Stormy up in the loft with them."

"You finally named the kitten," I guessed.

"You hungry, Lorie-girl?" Boyd asked, and I nodded.

The three of us sat in silence as I sipped beef broth. My stomach seemed shriveled, and I was unable to consume more than meager portions, but I heeded Boyd's words—Sawyer would be angered that I was not taking better care of myself.

"What did Billings have to say when you were in town?" I asked, after a time.

Boyd shifted on the chair, his jaw squaring. His gaze was directed at the ceiling beams as he said, "They had Crawford in a pine box at the undertaker's. He had no kin, an' Billings said there ain't a thing to be done 'til the judge arrives from Cedar Falls. It was all I could not to fire a few more rounds into that bastard's coffin, propped as it was against the side of the building. More'n one person was standing near to gawk at it, an' talk is a-flying in town."

"What of Yancy?" I whispered, hardly able to speak the man's name.

"He can't hide forever," Boyd said.

"I wish I woulda kilt him," Malcolm muttered intensely, his dark eyes fixed on a single point upon the quilt.

"No—that would be too great a burden for you to endure," I whispered at once, reaching to clasp my fingers about his hand.

"It ain't no more than what you bear," Malcolm insisted, and his face was wreathed in stubborn sincerity. He whispered, "I aim to protect the folks I love, an' I love you, an' Sawyer, with all my heart. If I woulda aimed truer, Yancy wouldn't be a threat to us, no more."

"Malcolm," I said, tenderness and concern knotting about my heart. Though perhaps I should have chastised in that moment, or offered one of many insipid excuses why he should reconsider this position, I only whispered, "Still, I am glad you did not."

"You's possessed of a fine, brave soul, but you's still just a boy," Boyd said firmly. "An' young'uns ain't oughta think on such things."

Malcolm would not be placated. He insisted, "I ain't a young'un. An' I don't believe it's wrong to kill a bad man. Or one that would send another man in his place to do the bad work for him."

"Yancy is a coward to his core," I said, troubled by the passion of Malcolm's statements. "And I agree wholeheartedly with Boyd, that you are fine and brave, both, sweetheart. But when all is said and done, it would have been a terrible burden for a boy of twelve to carry with him."

"I'm *thirteen!*" Malcolm corrected, his words tinged with indignant moodiness. "I ain't twelve no more."

"Don't you sass Lorie," Boyd said sharply, and Malcolm jolted to his feet, scraping back the chair.

"I'll be in the barn," the boy muttered, and disappeared without another word.

"He's tired," I whispered, as the outer door closed behind Malcolm with a soft thud. "That he must consider such ideas is what troubles me most. But his opinion is valid."

"It's my damn fault," Boyd allowed, plunging both hands through his black hair. "I done told him that very thing. It *ain't* wrong to kill someone who'd wish you harm, an' no one could persuade me otherwise. But at his age, I never thought on such things. Shit, I could hardly think past the next meal, or which girl's braids I might tug at Sunday service. Times have changed since the War, that's God's truth." Boyd smiled, unexpectedly, his teeth flashing white in the gloom. He said, with teasing emphasis, "When I was *thirteen*, that is."

"What did Sawyer look like, at that age?" I whispered. "I can imagine, but I do so love when you tell stories about those days."

Boyd said amiably, "Sawyer grew fast as an ox-eye weed one summer. I can't recall which summer exactly, as they sorta blur together a bit for me now, but Sawyer went from small an' skinny to the height of a spring sapling, all of a sudden-like, but still just as skinny. I swore you coulda counted each of his ribs. He ate like a horse, couldn't eat enough to fill up, but he didn't gain no weight for a year or two."

I smiled at this picture.

Boyd went on, "Sawyer's hair weren't so long then, though it was of enough length to tie back. He's always been a bit vain about his hair, I ain't gonna lie. I believe it started the autumn he heard tell that the girls in our school liked it, when we was maybe eleven or so. I teased him that if any girls approached him from behind, they'd confuse him for one of them. The fights we'd get into. *Shit*. We was black an' blue half the time, just from beating on each other."

After a time, I whispered, "I am so grateful that he has you. That you share his memories, as would a brother. He depends upon you a great deal, you know this."

Boyd covered his face with both hands, his elbows braced against the bed. He was silent long enough that I grew tense with concern; at last he said, "I grieve for the loss of his eye, Lorie-girl. I'm fearful of his reaction." And then he whispered, "If I'd aimed truer into that bastard Crawford, he woulda been dead when he hit the ground. Oh *Jesus*…"

"You did everything you could," I whispered. "You cannot blame yourself."

"So fast. It happened so goddamn fast," Boyd said, lifting his face. My heart folded inward to see the evidence of tears on his cheeks. His upper lip curled in self-punishing anger as he all but growled his words, "He coulda killed Sawyer, coulda taken him from us forever. There's so few people in this world that I call my own, that I love, an' so fast life sees fit to rob me of them." He heaved a half-choked sigh, and I reached, curling my hand around his. He squeezed my fingers and said, "I know you understand, I do. I apologize."

"Do not," I whispered. "Please, Boyd, do not apologize."

"I can't hardly dare to care for a living soul, Lorie, not when I fear the loss so terrible. I cherish the thought of my own young'uns…but what if I lost one of them? What if I can't keep watch all the time?"

I whispered, "No one is able, not all the time. Loving someone is never completely without pain, even the dearest love that exists. We are all vulnerable to it, Boyd." He studied my eyes, and I heard myself ask, "You think it is any easier for Rebecca?"

Everything about him changed in an instant, growing defensive and rigid; his jaw tightened. He sat back in the chair, folding his arms. He whispered hoarsely, "She's a *Yankee widow*, for the love of all that's holy."

"She is far more than that." I dared to say, "You know she cares for you. It is plain upon her face every time she looks at you."

Boyd closed his eyes; I was left with the feeling that I had slapped him. He whispered painfully, "Ain't nothing can come of it. She's a promised woman. An' we's headed north."

"She and Quade are not yet engaged," I contradicted. "Boyd, if you care for her, you must tell her. You cannot ride away from her."

He held my gaze steadily; I knew he was thinking, as was I, of the terrible night Sawyer had understood there was no other choice but to ride ahead, to leave me behind in Angus's care.

"I do care for Rebecca," he whispered, nearly inaudibly, and my heart gave a small, glad thump at his admission; how tenderly he spoke her name, how sweet it sounded in his deep, soft drawl. He repeated, "But ain't nothing can come of it. She is every breath a lady. I am nowhere nears good enough for her. An' I aim to make it north, late or no. I aim to do what I set out to do."

"You are—" But my words were cut short as Sawyer issued a low groan. His arms twitched and his head rolled to one side, angling towards us.

"Sawyer," I begged, touching him, but he had already sunk back under; his arm was inert, hot as a kettle on the fire. I kept my fingers upon him.

Boyd said, "When you was fevered, on the prairie back in Missouri, he was feral, Lorie-girl. Wouldn't let a soul near you but for him when you was caught in fever dreams. None of us could get him to sleep, an' hardly would he eat, he was so a-feared for your life."

I bent my head to my folded arms, there on the bedside.

After a long spell of silence, Boyd whispered, "It's worth the pain, or we would never love, would we?"

"We would not," I murmured in agreement.

B Y MID-MORNING'S CLOUDY light, I trimmed and washed what remained of Sawyer's hair; the thick flaxen length of it had burned away,
and what was left to adorn his scalp was no longer than the top joints of
my fingers. Tilson had helped me to shave away Sawyer's heavy beard, only
yesterday afternoon.

I whispered to my husband, "Now I can see your ears."

Malcolm helped me, tenderly cradling Sawyer's head upon the pillow so
that I could administer a linen cloth, damp with warm water and apple-cider
vinegar, cleansing his skin. Malcolm, whether consciously or not, kept a soft,
steady flow of words, effectively holding at bay my tears.

"When I was little, I remember always begging Sawyer to lift me on his
shoulders. I felt I was on top of the whole world, up there."

"He has told me of that," I whispered, tenderly applying the cloth, mindful of the binding over Sawyer's eyes. The scent of vinegar was strong in my
nose.

Malcolm continued, "He let me ride Whistler when I was only little, I
recall settin' on her back an' clutching her mane, while Sawyer led her about
the dooryard. I've always knew he loved me, Lorie-Lorie." The boy's eyes glistened with tears, though he did not let them fall as he whispered, "I thought
there weren't nothing worse than when Mama an' Daddy died, an' Mrs. Elmira took me in to live with her. There hadn't been no word from Boyd in
months. I didn't know if he'd survived. I had all but give up hope before he an'
Sawyer come for me that spring."

Rebecca entered the room to hear Malcolm's last few words, bringing a
new basin of water, which she set carefully upon the nightstand.

Malcolm whispered earnestly, "I won't never forget the sight of them two, ridin' up the lane to Mrs. Elmira's. I thought I was maybe having me a vision, that I'd wished so hard an' so long for Boyd to come for me that I was just imagining it. I ran outside an' it was raining a little, but I didn't care, I was just so happy to see them. I slipped on the mud an' Boyd near fell off of Fortune to collect me up in his arms."

"Your brother loves you very much," Rebecca said, stroking Malcolm's hair. I looked up at her and beheld the wistful aching, carefully guarded, present in her eyes.

Boyd, I understood. *She loves him, and she will not admit it.*

Malcolm whispered, "An' then him an' Sawyer hugged me between them, an' I felt so safe, Lorie-Lorie. I felt like nothin' could hurt me again, not when they was near."

The rapid beat of hooves approaching deterred my intended reply, and Tilson said from the outer door, "Clint's riding in!"

Clemens' voice was slightly breathless, though his words reached us with no trouble. He called, "Uncle Edward, the judge has arrived, not an hour past."

Rebecca's eyes flew to mine.

"Then we must go to him," I whispered.

"Hamm has not ridden markedly far this day, though he is often insufferable concerning his 'delicate' personage, and does not hear the caseload until properly rested," Clemens said upon entering the house, between long swallows from the dipper. He was sweating and appeared slightly flustered, the first I had seen him so. He politely used the cloth Rebecca handed him to blot his mouth, and said, "He shall hear us after his noon meal, he has promised."

Tilson said, "There's no word yet from Rawley, but we'll have to do without him, for now."

Clemens looked to me and asked, "Mrs. Davis, are you feeling up to riding into town this afternoon?"

I whispered, "Damn right I am."

"IT'S A fine woman can appreciate a good horse," Tilson said, spying me hugging Whistler beneath the oppressive, pewter-gray afternoon sky. I had laced into my boots and stood now in a tremendous amount of pain, but bear it I would; Rebecca lent me a dress of finely-woven ecru lawn and helped me to pin up my hair, in deference to the judge's sensibilities. I looked as proper as a woman who had worked for three years as a prostitute could possibly hope. Tilson offered his elbow; I believed I startled him when I surrendered to instinct and tucked close, hugging him, unable to resist the sudden need for paternal affection.

"Thank you," I whispered, and he briefly rested his cheek against my hair. I admitted, "I am so scared. I despise that our fate rests so completely in someone else's hand."

"Ain't that the way of it, for all of us?" he asked, gently. "Whether you believe in a higher order, or no, our fate ain't in our own palms, much as we might wish it." He patted my back and said, "We'll see this through. No matter what happens, we'll see this through."

I rode alongside Tilson on the buckboard, my hat brim flapping as the wheels struck ruts. He sat with carriage erect, as would a soldier, handling the reins with calm competence, and from the corner of my vision I could nearly pretend that he was Sawyer, as an older and far more grizzled version of himself. Rebecca and Malcolm had remained behind, and Malcolm promised to stay near Sawyer's side until I returned. I prayed doubly hard as we headed for town that when I saw them again, I would bear good news. Boyd and Clemens rode just ahead of the wagon, both with hats pulled low, as the sky had begun to spit.

It was raining steadily by the time we reached the church where Judge Hamm held court, as the town itself had no formal judicial buildings. The church was adjacent to the green where the gallows had been erected, and I was stunned to discover there was a crowd seeking entry to the main room from the cramped vestibule, filling the narrow anteroom with their damp, restless bodies. Horses were tethered by the dozens to the hitching posts. Residents of town were clearly eager to observe this afternoon's session before Judge Hamm and his traveling lawyers; Yancy, despite his continued absence, had been successful in rousing suspicion amongst the population of Iowa City, whose murmuring and grumbles reached my ears as we arrived and made our difficult way inside, through rain and crowd. I spied Parmley, the objectionable journalist, who snaked briskly between several others to reach my side.

"Mrs. Davis," he blustered, catching at my elbow. "I have sought an audience with you for days now."

Tilson shouldered Parmley none too gently aside, all without a word. Though a man of few admirable qualities, I had to acknowledge Parmley's stubbornness, as he remained undeterred, following directly behind, still attempting to catch my ear. I ignored Parmley, however rudely, and focused upon the sight of Marshal Quade at the double doors leading into the church itself, speaking calmly but in no uncertain terms refusing entrance to those seeking a seat.

"Mrs. Davis, Edward, good afternoon," the marshal greeted as Tilson and I stepped near, tipping his hat brim. In the murky light of the vestibule, a small room with scant and narrow windows, I allowed myself a moment to study Leverett Quade's face, seeking to view him as Rebecca would—her potential future husband. Rebecca claimed to care for him; he clearly cared for her. Quade did not seem to notice my brief scrutiny, and at close range I beheld a not-unpleasant face, lean and sunburned, upon which the evidence of no little amount of hard living was present, this tempered by a sense of calm and competency. His words and actions proved him a decent man; it was only because I cared so deeply for Rebecca that I found Quade lacking.

Besides, he was not Boyd. And for all his resistance, whether he would openly admit to such or not, I knew Boyd felt just as strongly for Rebecca as she did for him.

Other than those seeking to petition the judge, no one was allowed to enter the main room of the church—except for Parmley, toting a single-sided broadsheet and a small leaded pencil. He seated himself in the pew just behind Tilson, Boyd, Clemens and me, leaning on his forearms as though he believed proximity would somehow ingratiate him to us. Quade closed the double doors amidst protests and stood firmly planted before them, clutching one wrist in the opposite hand, feet widespread, awaiting the appearance of the judge. The altar at front had been replaced by a small wooden table holding an ink pot and a stack of documents, surrounded by four cane chairs. I found my gaze roving to the stained glass adornments set into the oblong windows to either side; the light filtering through was tinted with warm golds and bloody reds; a wooden cross bound at its juncture with a length of white satin ribbon had been hung upon the front wall.

I had not been within the walls of a church since the dismal spring of

1865, praying with the ardor of the condemned for my mother's return to health; this prayer, like so many, had gone unanswered, and perhaps it was this memory that served to cleave through my defenses just now. My mind thumbed desperately through its many images of Sawyer, and settled upon the sight of him tying back his golden hair to make ready for the day; so often now had I undone that very same bit of twine in order to comb my fingers through its flaxen length, at day's end. Here I sat prepared to do battle for my husband's life, even as he simultaneously battled for it on a separate front—miles from me, trapped behind the walls of a fever—and I reached to clench Boyd's hand, for strength.

Boyd twined our fingers and nudged my shoulder with his. He muttered, "Shore up, Lorie-girl, you's gone white as a catfish belly."

"There's Hamm," Clemens leaned around Tilson to murmur.

The judge, entering from the right, was a slope-shouldered man in dark clothing; the elbows of his suit coat were dusty. His mouth was dominated by a bristling gray mustache, which he fastidiously worried with his lower lip even as he walked; round spectacles rode low on his nose. He was of an age with Tilson. I tried, with no success, to determine if his face was one ever wreathed in gaiety, or even pleasantry; he appeared, at present, frighteningly dour. A quiet descended over everyone as the judge nodded to those of us assembled and seated himself without ceremony at the table. Three additional men sat to his sides, drawing close their chairs.

The judge said, "I am ready."

The lawyer to the judge's right, stage left from my perspective in the pew, lifted a document and cleared his throat with an officious air, one befitting proceedings set to begin without further delay. Reading from the paper, he intoned, "Sawyer James Davis, formerly Private Davis of the Rebel Army of Tennessee, is charged with the murders of Samuel Rainey, Gerald Dixon, and Jack Barrow, all formerly of Missouri."

I gulped at this meticulous recitation.

The judge looked our way as Tilson shifted in his seat. I remained still as a threatened rabbit, and the rabbit I had shot on the plains sprang obscenely to my mind, blood-smeared and lifeless. By nightfall I would recall very little of what was spoken; the afternoon remains in my memory as a series of disjointed chunks.

The lawyer addressed the small crowd before him, asking solicitously, "Is Sawyer Davis present today?"

"Due to his severely injured state, he is not," Tilson said, with as much stern clarity as his hoarse voice allowed. "But several of us, including his wife, are here to speak for him."

"YOU WORKED as a prostitute in St. Louis from 1865 until this past spring?"

"I did."

"Virginia Hossiter was your employer?"

"She was."

Parmley, listening raptly, scribbled notes with his pencil. Sitting as I was upon a chair positioned near the front table, I heard every scratch of that writing utensil, as though Parmley scribed the words into my flesh.

"You believe yourself somehow redeemed from this unfortunate circumstance?"

"I do, sir."

"You are now lawfully wed to Sawyer Davis?"

"I am."

"And you claim to have been the one to shoot Jack Barrow dead, rather than your husband?"

"Yes."

"Was Barrow a customer of yours? Did he owe you money?"

"No, neither of these things. He intended to strangle me."

Later, the flow of questions became a bottomless sea in which I would have floundered if not for the strength of my conviction. I sweat straight through Rebecca's beautiful lawn dress, but I answered each without lowering either chin or eyes. I looked steadily at the judge, whose gaze was dispassionate rather than censuring, and I was not ashamed.

"Rainey and Dixon, by all accounts, were brutally killed. What justification have you for such vicious behavior?"

"Samuel Rainey was a customer of yours?"

"Dixon was unknown to you?"

"Why would Virginia Hossiter claim you are her kin?"

"Zebadiah Crawford attempted to burn your husband alive?"

"You allege that Zebadiah Crawford acted upon the orders of Marshal Thomas Yancy?"

"Marshal Yancy is no longer present in Iowa City?"

"When did you last lay eyes upon Marshal Yancy?"

"He is considered a missing person until we receive word from him."

This last statement, delivered by one of the lawyers, prompted Tilson's immediate response; he said crisply, "When Yancy next sees my face, he'll wish he was a goddamn missing person."

"Edward, for the love of God," muttered Quade, still positioned at the back of the church.

Boyd, who had offered heated commentary several times thus far, said curtly, "Yancy wished us dead from the moment our paths crossed on July the fourth. He knows Sawyer an' me, from the days directly after the Surrender. I will explain."

The judge, sounding as if he wished he could heave a deep sigh in addition to the words, invited, "Come forward and state your next piece, young man."

REBECCA OPENED the door as the wagon rumbled up the lane, lantern in hand. The evening was well advanced due to the efforts of an expanding storm which had blotted out most of the appreciable remaining daylight. In the rising wind, the ends of her shawl flapped. Malcolm ducked around her and into the falling rain to take Fortune's reins, as Boyd had galloped the mare ahead. I heard Boyd deliver the news, informing them, "They ain't gonna hang him," and Malcolm bent his forehead to Fortune, nearly wilting with relief.

Without ceremony, without guile, Boyd went immediately to Rebecca and drew her into his arms. I believed he intended to keep the embrace brief, and proper to a fault, but was summarily unable; I saw how he crushed her close, as though never to let go, and bent his face to the side of her neck. Rebecca dropped the lantern to the wet ground, where it teetered precipitously before remaining upright, in order to wrap both arms around him. She cupped the back of his head, her fingers in his hair. His hat fell and remained disregarded.

"I figured," Tilson murmured, watching the two of them as he drew the wagon to a halt near the corral. He had procured for me a lap blanket, under which I huddled, nearly as limp with exhausted relief as Malcolm appeared.

He went on, "I may be an old codger these days, but I see the way my niece glows like a firefly when Carter is around, from near the first night she met him. Just the mention of his name is enough to set her to shining."

"Boyd cares for her, as well," I whispered.

"But I fear no good will come of it," Tilson said. "She will only be hurt all the more when he leaves, if either of them admit to it," and I understood that he was right.

Boyd collected the lantern and held the door for Rebecca, letting her enter the house ahead of him. Before I could reply, Malcolm gathered himself and hurried to us, leading Fortune, to help unhitch the team. Malcolm's hair was curlier than ever in the damp and he came directly to my side of the wagon, reaching to pat my leg.

"He ain't come to," Malcolm said. "I stayed near him, Lorie-Lorie, I promise."

Tilson hopped to the ground and lifted me down. I was chilled and my burned feet hurt so terribly I did not think I could walk the few yards required to gain entry into the house.

"I can't..." I started to say, but Tilson understood.

"I know," he said gently. "I know, honey. You saved your good man a second time today, the least I can do is carry you inside."

Sawyer Davis?

At first it was just a breath in my mind, hardly more than a whispered echo. I squinted as beams of sunlight angled low and into my right eye, blessedly eradicating the dark heat through which I had been aimlessly drifting, that had until this moment been rendering me blind. There was a scent in the air that I knew well, deepest memory stirred as I inhaled. When I blinked, the mellow beauty of a Tennessee evening spread placidly before me; immediately I blinked again, attempting to clear the lingering darkness from the left side of my head.

But it would not dissipate.

And then, closer than before, a jovial voice I knew well, and Bainbridge Carter demanded, *Sawyer, is that you? Where you been, boy? We ain't seen you in these parts in a month of Sundays!*

Bainbridge approached from behind, and I wanted so badly to turn and greet him, but I was rendered immobile, watching the sun as its upper curve gilded the crest of the holler I knew better than any landscape, rimming the Earth with crimson fire. I beheld familiar sights—*the Carters' house is just beyond that stand of blue ash, yonder. See, there's that lone blackgum growing tall in their midst*—and was inundated by familiar scents—*Bainbridge must be roasting a hog over a hickory fire*—which should have served to comfort my heart...

But instead it thrust faster, in alarm; my field of view appeared vertically bisected, as though an impenetrable black curtain had been draped over half of my head. My hands jerked upwards, but I was suddenly fearful to place my fingertips upon my own face.

Lorie, I thought, wild now with fear. I could not exactly recall the last time I had seen her, or where she was at this moment, and I shouted for her, stumbling forward, my voice echoing over the valley in which I had been born and raised.

I can't see—I can't see her—

Oh Jesus, what's wrong—something is wrong—what's happened –

"It's gone, Sawyer," my brother Ethan said, low and solemn, and then, inexplicably, there he was, standing on my right side, the sun bathing his familiar face. His throat was smooth, unmarked, bearing no trace of the gaping bullet wound which had killed him that cold and terrible January day. He was dressed as though to attend a church social, his red-gold hair shaggy on his neck; he did not appear to have aged past the day he died, when I carried him from the battlefield at Murfreesboro. When I turned my head, the dark curtain followed, obliterating that which was not directly in front of my right eye.

"Ethan," I whispered, so stunned by the sight of him restored to life that it overrode my fears. "Is it truly you?"

"It's me, brother," he said, and there was tenderness in his voice. He curled a hand over my right shoulder; immediately I placed mine atop his, to keep him near.

"What is this place? Where are we, Eth?"

Ethan's face took on an appearance I remembered well from our school days, the sort he wore when attempting to puzzle through a complicated mathematics figure. He finally said, "It's what is…beyond."

I demanded, "Have you been here in this place since the War? Eth, what's wrong with me…"

"Your eye is gone," Ethan said, with deep empathy. "I know the shock of it, Sawyer, I do. When I first got here I could not breathe, nor speak. I was in terror. But Jere found me right quick. Sawyer, I must tell you—"

"Sawyer!" called another voice, joyful and moving closer, and my youngest brother caught me around the waist, clinging tightly.

"*Jeremiah*," I whispered, choking on a sob, crushing his warm body closer. When last I saw him, he had been stiff and colorless, wrapped in a pieced calico quilt for burying.

"Sawyer, we wasn't expecting you yet. What's happened?" Jere asked, drawing back and minutely examining my face; he looked mildly appalled by what he saw. That he was *able* to see, that he was not lying buried in the Suttonville cemetery as he was the last I knew, served to rob me of speech. I could not muster words past the jamming of emotion in my chest, and Jere recognized, "You's confused. I was when I first arrived. But Granddaddy found me before too long, and Ethan was right on my bootheels. And you'll heal up." A smile seemed about to split my brother's face and he hugged me again, tucking close. He whispered contentedly, "Now we's all here," and over my brother's shoulder I squinted into the last of the light, and saw my mother and father.

Daddy and Mama came our way across the holler in the sunset, the light glinting scarlet in Mama's hair. Together, as they had always been in life, Daddy's arm wrapped protectively about Mama's waist.

"Daddy, look! Mama, it's Sawyer!" Jere called to them, and my mother pressed both hands to her mouth, staring, before lifting her hem so that she could run.

I went to both knees as swiftly as if sliced across the back of them, a supplicant, and my father was there to take my head against his stomach, holding fast, his big hand curving protectively about my skull, as it had when I was a child needing comfort.

"My boy," Daddy said, and his voice was just as I remembered, rife with happiness, and deep relief. He said, "You are home."

My mother's soft touch joined my father's, smoothing the hair from my brow, kissing my face, murmuring her concern over my appearance, and I wept, shamelessly, heaving sobs that wrenched my chest. In the near-distance, perhaps from the Carters' front porch, I could hear the sound of a fiddle player picking out the merry notes of "Buffalo Gals." Wrens chirped and called; I heard a mourning dove's soft warble.

Mama rejoiced, "My Sawyer, *mo mhac is sine,* you are finally home."

I was home.

Since leaving it at the age of nineteen, I had wanted nothing more than to return.

I had to tell them something, had to force it past the knot in my throat, and I whispered brokenly, "I am sorry, I am so sorry I couldn't keep you safe. I have never forgiven myself, in all this time. I never will."

"Sawyer," Jere said, in gentle reprimand. I could feel my family, all of them near to me at long last, their scents as familiar as my own. Somehow, I was here with them. It seemed as though I could stay.

"It wasn't your fault. It was never your fault," Ethan whispered. "Jesus, Sawyer, how could you blame yourself?"

"*Forgive me*," I begged.

Daddy's hand bracketed the right side of my face and he looked upon me with concern knitting his brows, his fair hair shot through with silver. He said, "You were never to blame, son."

"It was our time, brother," Ethan said.

"I knew it, I *knew* I seen Sawyer," Bainbridge said, with delight in his gruff voice, and I eased away from my family's embrace to behold all of them—Bainbridge and Clairee, Beaumont and Grafton, and my grandparents, Sawyer and Alice Davis. My heart clenched as they converged upon us, talking and exclaiming over me, all at once. They appeared hale and whole, vigorous and lighted from within, as though they had never suffered a day's hunger, sickness, or pain.

The darkness on the left side of my vision began to recede.

"All of you," I whispered. "Oh God, all of you, here…"

"Sawyer Davis, you handsome thing," Clairee said, and the teasing lilt in her tone was exactly as I recalled. She said, "How glad we are to see you, darlin'."

In the gentle brogue of her homeland, Mama said tenderly, "Come, let me clean your face, *mo buachaill milis*." She exulted, "Alice, look, it is our Sawyer, home at last," and tears streamed over my grandmother's cheeks as she kissed my face repeatedly.

"Sawyer, my boy," said Granddaddy, and he grinned. "You have grown well. Your grandmother always said you would be as tall as me, someday."

"You must be hungry as a bear in snowmelt," Beaumont laughed, lightly knuckling my scalp. Beau had been born scarcely nine months earlier than Boyd, and looked just like him. He shook his head, dark eyes lit by a sheen of happiness, and said, "Sakes alive, Sawyer, it's damn good to see you. I can't tell you."

"Boyd an' little Malcolm ain't with you?" Grafton asked, beset by evident disappointment. Before I could answer, he figured in his characteristically slow way, "I s'pose not yet. I s'pose I lost track of the time, just like I always done."

"Dinner's waiting just yonder, love," Granny said. "Your mama baked a cornbread this afternoon," and at her words, I could smell it, rich and delectable. Granny smoothed my hair and lamented, "Oh, if I had known you were coming this evening I would have rolled out a crust and made you a rhubarb pie, sweetling. Oh, *Sawyer*."

Bainbridge winked at me and rumbled, "An' I've a bottle of my best, just a-waitin' for you, boy."

Jere urged, "C'mon home with us."

Grafton said approvingly, "You's lookin' better already."

And indeed, he had hardly made this observation before my sight fully cleared. I blinked, imbibing the seemingly impossible—this place, this dear and familiar holler, which had been my home longer than any other on the earth.

"Sawyer?" a man called from a short distance, approaching around the blue ash grove. "Is that you?"

I recognized this voice—it was one known to me much more recently than any others' present. I struggled to recall how many months it had been since last hearing him speak, but before I could figure, Angus Warfield strode into view. He wore his hat, doffing it politely at the ladies as he approached, though he did not remove his startled gaze from me. Upon one arm he carried a child, a somber little boy with brown curls. Once the two of them were close enough, I saw that the boy's eyes were a deep gray—exactly like Angus's.

"Gus," I whispered. Not long ago, in a stupor of agonized unknowing, I found him lying near the ashes of a cookfire with his sightless gaze directed at the dawning pewter sky, a bullet hole splitting his breastbone. Lorie had been missing from their camp and in my panic to find her I had no time to bury Gus, a man I'd known my entire life, whose calm and quiet wisdom was a large part of what saved my soul after the War; I had wrapped this man's body in a quilt and rode madly away, across the endless prairie in search of Lorie.

I said painfully, "*Angus…*"

Still upon my knees, I reached a hand for him, which he took and held firmly. His chest was blessedly intact, and his eyes were deep and comforting, as they had never failed to be in life. He alone appeared perplexed at my presence and he asked intently, "Surely you are not here to stay?"

"Grace, don't you look well?" Mama said over her shoulder, reaching a welcoming arm. "My eldest son is home. You remember Sawyer."

A woman came near and smiled warmly at me. Her honey-brown hair hung loose, rippling over her shoulders, and her resemblance to Lorie, while not exact, was marked enough that I made a sound, part disbelief, part agony. A seizure of need for my wife obliterated any fleeting notion I had harbored of remaining in this place.

Grace said demurely, "Evenin', Sawyer."

"She was waiting for me," Angus explained softly, and brought her to his side, where she tucked close to him. He said with wonder, "My Grace was waiting for me, all this time. But Sawyer—why are *you* here? This cannot be right. What has happened?"

I caught Gus's forearm in my grip, begging, "Where is Lorie? Where is my wife? How do I get back?"

The sun was setting quickly now, pulling the warmth of the day with it. An indigo mist lifted from the land around us, melting into the greens of the holler, and I saw Lorie's eyes in the blending of those two colors.

I demanded again, "How do I get back?"

As I asked, the darkness encroached swiftly over my left side.

Gus knelt and brought the child on his arm to a level with me. The boy, though small, studied my face with the solemnity of someone much older. Gus whispered, "Tell her that I will never fail to care for him."

Love, and girding pain, simultaneously cinched my heart. I knew I was looking upon Lorie's son, who had been lost on the Missouri prairie, whose grave marker I had constructed. I rested my fingertips softly against the boy's round cheek, and saw my wife in his face. I whispered, "Of course I will tell her."

The air in the holler grew ever darker, but I could discern each of their faces in the faint afterglow of the vanishing sun, those I loved more than all others, save one. They had fallen silent at my exchange with Angus, watching wordlessly.

I sought my mother's eyes with my one-sided vision and whispered, "I cannot stay here."

Mama caressed my face. There was sorrow present upon hers as she regarded my mangled appearance, but she said at last, "I understand. *Téigh go dtí di, mo mhac. Bí láidir as a cuid, do i gcónaí.*"

"I will, I promise," I said, and she smiled, hearing the fervor in my voice.

"Your Lorissa loves you so," Mama whispered, and her expression was soft with fondness. "She is waiting for you. She will help you, my son."

Ethan's green eyes glinted in their old teasing way, and he cupped my shoulder, whispering in my ear, "*Tá mé in éad de do oíche, deartháir.* You've a fine, sweet woman."

"You go an' kiss my boys for me," Clairee said, and the soft floral scent of her enveloped me as she bent near, bestowing a kiss on my forehead. "You tell my sweet baby that I'd never forget his dear face. That I will recognize him no matter how old he is when he comes to me again."

"You tell Boyd an' Malcolm I am goddamn proud of 'em," Bainbridge said, with his stern affection.

"Your path ain't an easy one, my boy." Granddaddy's palm rested briefly upon my back. He said, "But you are my grandson, a Davis. You are stronger than you realize."

I felt time running out; there was no chance to question my grandfather's words; I said only, "I love you all."

"We never doubted that," Jere said. "Aw, Sawyer."

"They's waiting on you," Ethan told me. "You tell Boyd I still have it in me to whup him!"

"Go to her, son," Daddy said.

I turned and everything within me surged violently towards my wife, who had appeared between us and the far horizon. She was sitting with her head bent over her arms, and my soul constricted at this evidence of her pain—the connection that bound us pulsed and throbbed, itself alive.

"Good-bye, brother," Jere said, growing fainter at every passing second.

"We'll see you again someday, never you fear," Ethan whispered.

It was full dark then and I was left suddenly alone. Even with my limited, lopsided view, I observed in stun as the heavens above were at once gloriously ablaze with stars, riotous with every color I had ever witnessed and many I had not, and could not have named. Ruby and emerald, fiery oranges and yellows, searing azure, blinding in their intensity...

Lorie! I cried out, as my need for her seemed to wrench my physical body inside-out. I spun through wildly-swirling colors, sweating profusely, in motion and yet completely still, inexplicably, drawn by the force of my angel, my woman, waiting for me in the world somewhere beyond.

WHEN I WOKE to darkness, blinking wildly to regain a shred of sight, I knew that something had altered. I swallowed drily, the sound thunderous in my head, and then lurched abruptly upright, arms flailing, bumping Sawyer as he lay beside me.

"Oh!" I cried, as I inadvertently struck his shoulder. I huddled protectively over his form and found his face with my palms, cupping tenderly. Unexpectedly, my fingers slipped along his skin and I gasped, "You're sweating."

"Water," he whispered, so faintly I could scarcely discern, but I leaped as though prodded, using my heels to drag myself over the foot of the bed; my knees gave out as I touched the floor and a hoarse sound of alarm rose from Sawyer's throat as I promptly crumpled. He rasped, "*Lorie...*"

I crawled around to the basin, as it seemed faster than attempting to walk on my stinging feet. I eased upwards so that I could kneel and dipped a cup from the basin, filled with fresh water as of an hour ago, and then I stood, however painfully, and brought the cup to Sawyer's lips. It was not until his hand touched my wrist that sobs struck at me like clenched fists.

"Saw..." A gasp sliced in two my attempt at his name. A simultaneous swell of relief rendered me nearly without breath. I cupped his shorn head and helped him to drink; the sound of his swallows was as music to my ears. He held fast to my wrist and when he could take no more water, I set aside the cup and all but crawled atop him, mindful of his healing body. I whispered intently, "You are safe. I am here, and you are safe."

"Lorie," he whispered. No lantern burned in the bedroom this night, leaving us cloaked in dim grays; without hesitation, he reached and slipped the binding from his eyes.

I held his face, putting my lips to his forehead. He had been restored to me and I was dizzy with the respite of this knowledge. My hair swung around us as it did when we made love and I could feel his breath against my collarbones. I had to explain to him, though I struggled desperately for words. At last I whispered brokenly, "Your eye…"

I thought he said, "Ethan told me."

Certain my weight was hurting him in some way, I shifted immediately, but he curled an arm over my waist and kept me near.

"Stay close to me," he whispered, understanding why I had moved. "I need to feel you. You are not hurting me, darlin'."

His words, the sweet endearment, stroked over my skin and served to crack the dam restraining uncontrollable tears. I wept, bending my face to his neck, and he held me. I spoke in wild bursts, choked by fitful sobs, and Sawyer held me and stroked my hair. He was wet with sweat, and now my tears, but I could not catch hold of myself.

"You were burning…*you were burning on that pyre*…I thought you were dead…oh Jesus, *he shot at you*…I was so scared, *I was so scared…oh Sawyer…*"

"Lorie," he soothed, his mouth near my ear. I despised that I was unable to gather a handle on this outpouring of emotion. I had to tell him what had happened, coherently. He had not asked about his eye, and was instead offering me comfort. He murmured, "Lorie-love."

For a time we held fast in the darkness, until the rapid beating of my heart calmed—until we had at least partially sated ourselves upon the feel of one another. I lifted my head. My sight had adjusted to the darkness and Sawyer lay beneath me, studying my face. The pale blot of the poultice remained in place over his missing left eye. The lack of hair upon his scalp threw the shapes of his beautiful cheek and jaw bones into sharp relief; the curve of his mouth was slightly darker than the rest of his face.

"I have missed you so much," I whispered, my lips trembling, and tears continued to roll from my chin, splashing upon him.

"I had the strangest dream, just now," he whispered roughly.

"Tell me," I said, kissing his lips with utmost care, caressing his face.

Before he could respond, Malcolm whooped, "Sawyer's awake, you-all!" and bounded into the bedroom, knocking over the basin in his haste to reach the bedside. I squeaked as tepid liquid flooded the floor, catching my hem in passing, but I could not trouble myself to worry over spilled water. The basin clattered with a panging thud and anyone not aroused to wakefulness by the boy's hollering was certainly now alert. I heard Boyd slam through the front door from outside, where he had resumed sleeping in his tent, leaving the loft for Rebecca and the boys; seconds later he crowded beside Malcolm at the bedside. Boyd fell to his knees, bent his cheek to Sawyer's outstretched hand, and wept unashamedly.

"I'LL BREAK his neck," I heard Boyd say, coming in from outside the next afternoon.

"Whose unfortunate neck are you referencing?" Rebecca asked. She had been stirring cake batter, but now ceased the motion.

"That weasel, Parmley," Boyd said, and I heard him slap something upon the table.

Sawyer sat propped against the headboard, sipping beef broth from a tin cup. He appeared pale and drawn, the bones of his face more sharply defined than ever, as he had lost weight. He was shirtless, dressed in fresh bindings and with a new poultice, tied to accommodate his remaining eye; I had scarcely let him out of my sight since this early morning. He remained terribly woozy and slept intermittently through the day, requiring doses of laudanum to alleviate the intensity of the pain. But he was alive, the fever broken, and he would recover.

To Boyd, he called, "Why's that?" and Boyd stormed into the room brandishing a single-sided broadsheet; I recognized the town's circular.

"This," Boyd said through his teeth. "Damn, I oughtn't to upset you two, but I figure you's gonna see it sooner or later. Damn varmint."

The headline was an inch tall, emblazoned in riotous capital letters for all to read: FORMER WHORE SAVES REBEL SOLDIER'S LIFE. In smaller typeface the subheading promised a lurid tale to follow, *Once a Lady of the Night, Lorissa Davis, now reformed, repentant, and lawfully wedded, proves in a tearful display that a woman's heart is stronger than a man's will.* The byline read, *Horace W. Parmley.*

"Oh," I whispered weakly, rendered otherwise speechless.

Rebecca followed Boyd into the room and stood now at the foot of the bed, the bowl containing batter held against her stomach as she regarded my expression with a certain amount of circumspection. She said, "I dislike defending the man, but I do believe Horace presumes he is complimenting you."

"But aiming for his own gain, at the same time," Boyd said. "Story like this will cause a stir. Set folks in town to pure gossip. Damn the man."

"I do not disagree," Rebecca allowed. "All the same, he is misguided enough to believe his words are charitable. You shall notice his use of 'lawfully wedded.'" She sighed and resumed stirring, saying, "The man deserves no less than a sound thrashing, regardless."

Sawyer said, "If I felt even half myself, I would ride into town and deal with him." He sought my gaze. "But he is right on one count, Lorie-love. I never knew a stronger heart than yours."

Healing bruises discolored his face; healing burns welted his back, elbows, and legs. He had been ravaged physically and—as I related events to him as he was able to listen throughout the day—emotionally as well. He asked for the entire story and was predictably horrified that I had put myself in danger in so very many ways. That I had been forced to bare my soul before the judge and those listening, that I had climbed a burning pyre to save him and sustained injuries, that I'd witnessed the shot to his face, scraped Sawyer's heart nearly raw. Of that dreadful night, he could recall nothing beyond Zeb coming for him in the jailhouse.

And of Thomas Yancy, federal marshal, there was yet no word. Charley returned our way only this morning to pass along the lack of news; Yancy's sons were residing with the Rawleys for the time being.

I took from Boyd the broadsheet and folded it neatly in half, hiding from sight the audacious black ink. I said evenly, "Let people think what they will. I cannot change what I was, and I am no longer ashamed. Nor will I ever be, again. Besides," and I scooted closer to Sawyer on the bed. He took my hand into his and curled tight my fingers. I said, "There is little in this world that could trouble me today."

Boyd's chest rose and fell with a heavy sigh. He muttered, "You's right, Lorie-girl. I ain't oughta entertain fantasies of ridin' to town an' cranking the man through his own printing press."

Unable to resist teasing him, Rebecca said, "Your descriptions are most detailed. Perhaps a tendency towards poetry lies in you, Mr. Carter?" The deep and finely-wrought current of awareness that flowed between Rebecca and Boyd was one development I had not yet related to Sawyer—but then I realized that he, ever perceptive, was studying Boyd with an air of speculation.

"I got me a given name," Boyd complained, still surly on the surface, but then his dimple flashed, quick as he could have winked. Since shunning propriety and hugging her close in the dooryard, I had not observed Boyd make any additional moves to touch Rebecca, but I ascertained clearly that he *wanted* to touch her—and repeatedly. His eyes were nearly as hot as a coal bed beneath the pretended irritation.

But he had told me himself he meant to ride away when the time came.

"Perhaps you might ask politely for things that you want. And perhaps I ought to finish this cake and let Lorie alone with her husband," Rebecca said decorously, all but fluttering her lashes at Boyd. So saying, she nodded to us and returned to the other room.

Boyd's heated gaze followed directly after her.

Sawyer paused with the tin cup partway to his mouth and asked me silently, *Is this truly what it appears?*

And I nodded, just faintly, in response.

"TELL ME what you're thinking," I requested in a whisper, much later that night. Though I knew, I wanted for him to speak it—to set free what troubled him.

"I do not truly believe this, but I meant to ask. You are not...that is..." Sawyer faltered over the words and I pressed closer to him, as close as I dared. I lay along his right side on the bed, my skin completely bare in the glow of a single lantern, night pouring through the window covering and spilling darkly upon the floorboards. The quilt was bunched near our hips.

"Tell me," I insisted again, quietly.

"You are not repulsed by how I look...by how I *will* look, when I am healed, are you?" he finally asked.

"Sawyer," I reprimanded, mildly shocked despite everything. I rolled to one elbow in order to better regard his face. "Of course I am not." He kept his gaze stubbornly focused towards the wall beyond the foot of the bed, but I took his chin in my fingertips and made him look upon me, deliberately studying him. It twisted into me as would an auger bit that one of his beautiful hawk eyes was destroyed, that he was from now forth rendered half-blind.

I hoped, vengefully, that Zeb Crawford burned in some everlasting hell for what he had done to the man I loved. But Sawyer was alive and, God willing, I would never be asked to endure separation from him again.

I knew, however, that my reply must be delivered with care; Sawyer did not wish for, or deserve, a mollifying response. The beauty of his remaining eye was mine to behold in the candle's flame, the iris a gorgeous amalgamation of warm gold and cedar-green, ringed by a darker circle and fringed with enviable thick black lashes.

At last I said softly, "I mean to look upon both of your eyes again, when our first child is born."

Sawyer's throat bobbed with emotion. Gently I bent my thigh over his hips, pressing the juncture of my legs against him; his right hand curved firmly around my backside, drawing me even closer. From his throat rose the soft, husky sound I cherished, the one that was mine alone to treasure, which he uttered when we made love.

"I will provide for us, this I swear to you, Lorie. I will never fail to take care of you, or our children, even wounded as I am just now," he vowed.

"These things I know, with all of my heart," I said tenderly, peppering his jaw with little kisses.

"We will reach Minnesota. I intend to relinquish nothing that we have sought, and spoken of," he whispered. "Delayed, but not given up."

"This I know," I repeated, resting my palm over his heartbeat. "I do, love."

Sawyer drew a breath and carefully shifted so that his body was better aligned with mine, holding me from behind, caressing with both thumbs the hollows created by my hipbones. The patch tied over his missing eye lent his handsome face an unexpected aura of slight menace, like that of perhaps a brigand, or masked outlaw, and I recognized the inopportune nature of my powerful desire for him; our hunger for one another clashed with the restraint we must practice for a time.

His voice a husky murmur, he whispered, "Had I a thousand words and poetic skills in abundance, I could never describe your exquisiteness. Look at you. I could never be thankful enough that you are mine, Lorie." The orange fire of the lantern lit exactly half his bruised face as he softly kissed my mouth. "I want your skin against mine, every night of our lives. And every morning, and many times in between morning and night," and I smiled at this heartfelt description.

"We will accomplish very few tasks if we are so often naked," I replied, kissing his bottom lip, taking it into my mouth and lightly suckling.

He groaned a little, shivering at my teasing, and disagreed, "No, it is the very best sort of task we will accomplish, that way. I formally request that you wear not a stitch, at all times, you beautiful, naked woman. Holy Jesus, you are beautiful..."

"You make me blush," I whispered, kissing his top lip this time.

"I love watching such blushes overtake your skin," he said, following the flushing heat with his kisses, down my neck and to my breasts. He pressed his lips between them and inhaled as he was sweetly inclined to do, and I sensed the feeling overtake him just before he whispered intently, "Lorie. I would know that you forgive me."

"Sawyer," I scolded, encircling his head and holding him captive to hear my words; his shortened hair brushed softly against the sensitive skin of my inner arms, gleaming golden in the lantern. I said, "Never think that I do not forgive you. You came for me. I know that you will always come for me. You do not require forgiveness."

"I was not there when you were taken, not with Gus, and not this time. You risked your life. You were *hurt*, Lorie. Again you were hurt, and I could do nothing to stop it."

"No worse than you," I said, and my vision swam with tears, thinking about what he had spoken of earlier this day in relating to me the incredible dream bestowed upon him at the mercy of the fever's breaking point. "Remember what your grandfather said. You are stronger than you know. They forgave you for all the faults which you unduly blamed upon yourself. Now *you* must forgive yourself. Oh Sawyer, do not carry the burden of that any longer." He did not answer, and I implored, "Please, love, for me."

He finally nodded, pressing his mouth to my bare shoulder, where the wound from Zeb's bullet would forever scar my flesh. Both of us would bear markings of the man's hatred, but I vowed these scars would be bodily, nothing more. Our souls, mercifully, remained intact. Together, and therefore whole.

He lifted his head and I saw the shine of unshed tears in his eye. He whispered, "It is such an odd sensation to feel tears on only one side. It will take me a long while to grow accustomed to this change. How my head ached all day, just where my eye used to be. I can't rightly believe it's gone for good."

"Tilson said the headaches may be from the laudanum withdrawal, more than anything," I reminded him, smoothing my hands over his short hair, letting it bunch between my fingers. And then I confessed, "I tried closing my left eye this morning as I walked outside to the necessary. To get a feeling for it."

A faint smile tugged at his mouth as he said, "Malcolm told me."

"Malcolm tied a bandana about his eyes and roamed the yard after dinner, then bumped into the corral fence, and Rebecca said he would be black and blue before long, and made him take it off before her boys started begging for bandanas, too."

"I wondered what she was scolding him about." His expression grew thoughtful and he mused, "Boyd cares for Mrs. Krage and if I don't mistake it, she cares for him. Of course you have noticed this, my woman. You are a keen observer."

I nodded. "Even Tilson has noticed."

"What says he on the matter?"

"Tilson recognizes that Boyd will go north, and that Rebecca will not," I said. "Now that we are able to continue onward."

"I will speak with Boyd," Sawyer promised. "If he cares for her, he cannot ride away without her."

"That is just what I said," I whispered. "Oh, Sawyer..."

He drew me to his chest, where I tucked carefully close, attempting to fully acknowledge that we were safe. No marshal would come for him, not any longer; the judge had declared Sawyer absolved.

But Yancy is still out there...

"We have a long journey yet ahead," Sawyer murmured. "I pray that I am up to it."

"I will help you. I will be at your side," I whispered, nearly trembling with gratitude at this truth. Sawyer clutched my hips and I slid my hands again into his hair. "I will be a patient wife, I promise."

"I only expect your patience when I deserve it," he said tenderly, kissing my eyes, one after the other, and then my chin, which lifted at once, instinctively seeking his kiss upon my mouth. His lips a mere breath from mine, he cupped one hand between my legs and whispered, "You have been *most* patient with me, wife. But just now there are other matters I wish to discuss. Such as how you are also silken-soft. Oh holy God, Lorie, you feel good..."

"I know it is unseemly to ask, just now," I said, breathless with tears, and shivering joy, as he caressed inside me with slow and rhythmic strokes. I was still half in disbelief that he was awake, and coherent. I clarified, "But I would like very much for you to kiss me...here...*and here*..." and I indicated by tracing my fingertips between my breasts, flushing a little. How brazen I had become.

A genuine grin overtook his face.

"Nothing would make me happier. Come here to me, darlin'," he murmured, stroking in earnest as I moaned, and lowered his mouth.

"I DREAMED that there were stones over your eyes," I admitted later when we lay in darkness, the lantern extinguished for the night, bracing against the memory of the nightmare—the same night that Zeb had fired his rifle into the wagon, and Boyd and Malcolm's tent. I shuddered. "A crow showed me your body, and spoke to me."

After a moment of silence, in which I could sense his thoughts flowing backward through time, Sawyer murmured, "That was my old nightmare. I dreamed so often of the crow during the War. After many a battle it came to me as I lay sleeping, thinking to rob me of any peace I had salvaged in the aftermath. Many times I dreamed of stones covering my eyes, blocking my sight. You must have sensed it."

"I believe it is gone now, the shadow past," I whispered truthfully.

Sawyer did not at first respond; at last he murmured, "I do not believe it can ever fully be gone, but perhaps it will not darken our path again. I pray we have given it enough."

But even as I nodded agreement, I found myself wondering what monstrous toll—exacted throughout time in the fires of war and death, greed and savage destruction—would ever be enough to satisfy such a creature.

S ON, YOU WON'T be fit for travel for a time an' you must accept this," I heard Tilson tell my husband. Tilson was endlessly patient, and spoke with abundant practicality, but even through the closed door I could sense that this information was not what Sawyer wanted to hear, or heed. Boyd was also in the room with them, having recently returned from Iowa City bearing a new letter from Jacob.

"We cannot delay any longer than the end of August. July is gone as it is," Sawyer said, and his deep voice was respectful, yet rife with the desire for Tilson to understand.

"We got a month of travel ahead of us, at the least," Boyd seconded. "How soon will Sawyer be able to make the journey?"

Tilson must have sighed, as there was a pause before he said, "If it were up to me, an' I know it ain't since I am not your daddy, Sawyer, I would insist that you an' Lorie remain here through the winter. Consider it, son. You will reach the Northland just as autumn is heavy underway. You are already off schedule, an' haven't the proper food stores, or shelter, nor will you have time to build these things before the snow flies. You's in a weakened condition at present. The population that far north is sparse, at best. Hundreds of miles between any help, or neighboring folks. What if you fetch sick?"

Sawyer did not respond and I imagined him gazing at the window with a stubborn set to his jaw. He despised being subjected to these truths, I knew; he wanted to provide for us without question.

Tilson persisted, "Spend the winter recovering. Apply for land. Carter, you can apply for him, by proxy, there ain't nothing preventing that. You an' the boy get settled, an' Sawyer, you can gain back your strength, learn to manage with your limited sight. Once spring rolls around, you continue the journey, and have the entire summer to build a home." There was a pause, and then, "Dammit, I saw with my own eyes how Lorie suffered to see you hurt. I will never forget the sight of her screaming over your body. I been to War an' I ain't ever seen the likes of her eyes when she thought you was killed."

"That is a good point, old friend," Boyd said with a sense of quiet defeat, momentarily conceded though it was.

I rested my forehead to the door from the opposite side, reaching to Sawyer with my mind; he was in agony at this picture of my pain.

"I don't tell you this to hurt you," Tilson continued, in a tone less harsh. "I tell you because that is how very adamant I am that you do not venture north until you are able. It is what your own daddy would advise. Do you understand?"

"I do," Sawyer whispered roughly.

I knuckled my eyes, moving quietly away from my eavesdropping and wandering slowly outside, mindful of my sore feet, where Malcolm hung on the corral fence scratching Juniper's forehead; the old horse's hoof gave no sign of the wound he had suffered on the outskirts of Iowa City. I joined Malcolm on the fence, stroking a finger under Stormy's downy chin. The kitten had grown markedly since first we met, but still fancied his position on Malcolm's shoulder. Stormy offered a companionable rumble as I petted him.

"Heya," Malcolm greeted.

Rebecca had taken the buckboard into town, along with her boys, to bring supper to Clemens, who was boarding at the office for the time being. The yard was visited by a sense of abandonment in their absence. Malcolm read my face and guessed, "Sawyer don't like what Tilson's sayin'."

"Tilson believes that you and Boyd ought to ride on, and that Sawyer and I should winter here, in Iowa," I said. "And you are right, Sawyer dislikes being told what he is unable to do."

"Ride ahead? You mean, without you?" Woe and outright dismay crossed paths over Malcolm's features.

"I do not much like the thought, either," I said, pressing against the bridge of my nose to ward away sudden tears. "I thought to be settled by the winter months. But I have counted my blessings every moment since Sawyer woke, and if remaining behind is necessary for him to be fully well, then I accept it as a minor consequence." Eyes closed, I considered living here for the duration of the winter, and grew lost in thought. Whistler ambled over and nuzzled my chest, and I absently curled an arm about her neck. It meant we could remain in Rebecca's company for a time, and Tilson's, which certainly gladdened my heart. And the Rawleys were relatively near...

"But I can't be apart from you, like I done told you," Malcolm said miserably, and my eyes flew open. His lips trembled.

"Oh, sweetheart," I said, heart flinching, and reached an arm for him. He tucked immediately against my side, smelling of horse and unwashed hair, though his breath was sweetened by the lemon stick he had licked through the afternoon; there was a stoneware jar of penny candies hidden in the hutch.

Face buried against my shoulder, Malcolm pronounced, "I ain't going without you an' Sawyer."

I kissed the top of his head and murmured, "I fear there is not another way, unless you and Boyd remain here, as well."

"No, Boyd aims to get north," Malcolm said resignedly, drawing back and knuckling at his eyes. He muttered, "I'm sorry, Lorie-Lorie."

"For what?" I asked, petting his hair, not letting him step completely away.

"For crying like a babe, that's what. I ain't a little kid no more," he said, swiping at his nose, the lump in his throat thickening his voice; he turned his attention back to Juniper.

"You know what?" I asked, with great care. When Malcolm failed to respond, I did not press, and instead quietly answered my own question. "I was glad, just now." He tilted his chin my way, dark eyes curious despite everything. I explained, "I worry there might come a time when you do not wish to seek comfort from me at all, because you will believe yourself too old. And I dread that day." Malcolm's eyebrows lifted and it was apparent this thought had never entered his mind. I finished, "And I do hope that you understand it is quite natural to feel sadness, and weep. Even for grown men."

"I won't never feel that-a-way," he insisted. "I swear, Lorie-Lorie. I love you so."

"I love you, too," I whispered, my throat aching. "And I want for you to write me every day, as I will miss you so very much it already hurts me, and keep Sawyer and me informed about what you are up to in Minnesota. You'll grow this winter, and likely be as tall as Boyd by the time I see you again."

He smiled a little at this, though tears sparkled on his lashes. The last of a red sun struck his face, bathing him in the light of day's end; he squinted at the sudden brilliance and I was overcome with an abrupt flash of deep awareness—as though given a fleeting and unbidden glimpse of him as an adult—and an image blazed through my mind. I saw him bent low over Aces and riding hard, the animal's muscles lathered and rippling with speed, desperate with the intensity of some purpose I could not begin to guess, or understand—

And then as quickly as it assailed, the vision disintegrated.

I blinked. The sun had set, the red glow no longer striking the boy's features.

Malcolm bent and transferred Stormy to the ground, where the cat twined about his ankles. He coaxed, "Go on now, boy. Catch a few mice."

"It's pretty out, ain't it?" Tilson asked, startling me. I had not heard him approach, and he chuckled at my jumpiness. "Beg your pardon, Lorie, I didn't mean to sneak up. Young Malcolm, would you mind fetching an armload of wood? I thought to build a fire. Boyd has promised us music."

Malcolm said, "Yessir," and hurried to do Tilson's bidding.

"Sawyer an' Boyd wish a word with you, honey," Tilson said. His gaze flickered over my shoulder and he observed, "There's Becky with the wagon."

I turned to see the cloud of dust lifted by its wheel revolutions, a good quarter mile out. Impulsively, and because I truly wished his opinion, I asked, "What of Rebecca and Boyd?"

Tilson sighed and laced together his fingers, bracing both hands atop his head in the manner of someone shrugging his shoulders with indecision. He said quietly, "Damn."

"You do not approve?" I pressed, troubled at this notion.

"It ain't that, Lorie. My opinion of Boyd is high, indeed. He is a hell of a man." Tilson sighed again, with a little less gusto, and explained, "It's that Quade requested permission for my niece's hand long ago, an' he has properly courted her since I gave my blessing. He aims to marry Becky, always has."

"You consider Rebecca promised to Quade, then?" I asked, and stirrings of agitation prickled in my blood.

Tilson said quietly, "For all practical purposes, I do."

"You don't believe Rebecca should consider Boyd?" I whispered, even as I understood she could not, no matter how much she might wish otherwise. The wagon was near enough to us that Cort stood and waved, hollering hallo.

Tilson roughed up his hair, scrubbing the base of both palms against his eyes. He said quietly, "Becky won't leave this place, an' Carter aims to head north within the week. He is a man who reaches what he set out to reach, I could tell from the first. An' Leverett has had his eye on Becky for a good year now. In many ways, Leverett is a better match for her. He is older, an' will settle down when they marry, he has promised. He aims to get his territory reduced."

"But he—"

Not unkindly, Tilson cut short my plea. He said, "Darlin', I just come from talking sense into your man. I believe I have had all the talk of sense I can handle, just now."

"Sense," I whispered, with ironic inanity.

Looking up at the stars, Tilson murmured absently through its synonyms, "*Intellect, wisdom, sagacity, logic.*"

"Good judgment," I whispered to conclude, studying him, feeling the warmth of kinship.

"Ouch!" Malcolm yelped, from out by the woodpile. He yelled, "I just got stung by some ol' thing!" As we watched, he jumped to the side and yelped a second time, slapping indignantly at his own forearm.

Tilson snorted a laugh, muttering, "Now if we could just get the boy to demonstrate some, as well. I will sorely miss him around here." He winked at me and said, "I, for one, am right glad to have the pleasure of yours and Sawyer's company a little longer, at least. I would spend these months teaching you to midwife, as I promised."

"I would like that very much," I said sincerely.

Inside, Boyd continued to pace the bedroom, Jacob's most recent letter in his hand. Sawyer had managed, with the aid of a hand crutch, to maneuver to the table for dinner the past week, far and away too restless to remain in the bed. His hair was unruly; he had been short-tempered earlier, and only because I knew his head was aching, I did not press when he was unwilling to let me run a comb through its much-shortened length. Just now, he sat with his back propped against the headboard; at my appearance, he set aside the tin cup of water and reached for me.

Boyd was saying, "Jacob says our stock will be accommodated by his barn for this winter. Especially if we leave Whistler an' Admiral here for you twos to drive north in the spring. I will fill out an application for you at the land office in St. Paul, old friend. An' then, first thing, we'll build a cabin. The acreage Jacob wants us to claim is near his an' Hannah's land, close to Flickertail, Jacob said. Y'all will recall."

Flickertail Lake had been mentioned many times in Jacob's letters; I could see the shape of the words, written by Jacob's hand, even now in my memory. Many hours had I spent as the wagon rumbled along, envisioning the deep-blue lake water flickering beneath the warm sun. I found its picturesque name quite enchanting and often imagined, with new variations each time, the home Sawyer and I would eventually build along its shores.

We will reach this place, I swear this, I thought, sitting near Sawyer on the bed, tenderly smoothing his hair. I could not resist teasing him a little, saying, "Did you let Tilson brush it for you?"

Sawyer grinned despite everything, poking his thumb into my ribs. He said, "No, I've managed it myself."

"What say you, Lorie-girl, to spending the winter here in Iowa?" Boyd asked, joining us on the bed, sitting near Sawyer's knees. In the waning light, no lantern having yet been lit, I studied my brother, the conversation with Tilson circling my mind. Rebecca called to her boys in the dooryard; Boyd's gaze was drawn that direction, as a compass to north, at the sound of her voice.

I looked to Sawyer and said, "I believe it is the only choice, for now. The winter months will pass quickly," though I despised the thought of being parted from Malcolm and Boyd for that length of time.

Sawyer curled one hand about the side of my waist, squeezing gently, and said, "I know it isn't what we planned and I do struggle with the thought of being so indebted, but Tilson is right, I am in no shape to travel. We will winter in Iowa if that suits you, Lorie-love, and continue north as soon as we are able." Sawyer rested his hand upon my thigh, which I slanted towards him.

"It suits me to take care of you," I said, leaning to press a kiss to his jaw. "And it suits me to remain near Rebecca. I care deeply for her."

Boyd's chest lifted with tense, indrawn air at my words. He closed his eyes.

I added quickly, "And Tilson. We are indeed indebted to them, for so many things."

"Tilson said he and Clemens would construct a lean-to alongside this house, for us," Sawyer said, though I could sense his unspoken concern for Boyd. My surprise evident at this statement, Sawyer explained, "Tilson assured me that he's been considering the lean-to since last winter, as they are so crowded with the five of them already." He looked to Boyd and understood somberly, "You and Malcolm will be on your way before too long, I would imagine."

Boyd opened his eyes. He said quietly, "Within the week, now that the decision's been made. I ain't been apart from you for more'n a few days since we was nineteen, old friend. Even during the War, we was always with each other. I reckon I won't know what to do with myself." Sawyer reached and curled his hand over Boyd's. Boyd vowed, "But I aim to finish this journey. I survived the War, I left the place of my birth, an' I mean to get where I set out to get."

"We won't be far behind," Sawyer promised. "The winter will pass quickly."

Malcolm banged inside the front door and then into the bedroom. He was visibly out of breath.

"Hold up, boy, what's got you worked up?"

"Quade just rode in," Malcolm answered his brother. "An' he brung roses for Mrs. Rebecca. Said he found 'em blooming on the prairie."

Boyd covered his face with both hands. Though pain raked his throat, he said only, "It's for the best."

At last he lifted his gaze to Malcolm and his dark eyes burned with determination. He said, "Let's go north, shall we?"

※

The story continues in *Grace of a Hawk*, coming in 2017

T HE CREATION OF a book is an intricate process that is never the solitary work of the writer. I want to thank those of you who contributed to the writing of this book, whether consciously or not, including the incredible musicians, primarily in the stringband and bluegrass genres, whose artistry inspired me during all those late nights (my preferred writing time), and the readers whose spirited emails requesting more about Lorie and Sawyer, Boyd and Malcolm, and of course Whistler, gave me even more reason to continue their journey. I truly love these characters; when the series is complete I will go into a mourning of sorts, likened best perhaps to the way you feel when your child experiences newfound independence in any capacity, whether heading to nursery school or embarking upon his or her own marriage, when you think, I've done my best and I can't look back now.

My husband and three girls, of course, deserve credit for their patience and encouragement, for sharing me with my computer and bearing with me when I can't seem to stop talking about the nineteenth century and all its delectable charms and fascinating horrors; for my middle daughter running inside and shouting, "Mom, come see this sunset! I bet you could write it into your book!" and for my husband, who simply grins when people ask if he's read the "love scenes."

I must thank my publisher, Michelle Halket, for her ideas and suggestions, which have made *Soul of a Crow* into the book it is today. I enjoy her company tremendously, and cannot wait to see where this road we're on will take us—but then, the unexpected is half the fun of any journey. (The journey is the thing, of course).

And finally to my readers—thank you for letting me know how much you've loved reading about Lorie and her menfolk—most especially my dear friend/reader Shannon Daniels, who loves Malcolm as much as I do. And thanks to all the readers who have found Lorie courageous and inspiring, how you've taken it upon yourself to learn more about the realities of prostitution in the nineteenth century. I believe there is a story in every soul on this earth—around every curve in the road and in every stalk of grass growing over the ancient tracks of wagon wheels long since worn away, in the hues of each sunset and every word ever spoken that remains hovering in the air about us—if we only know how to hear them. It is my privilege to tell even a few of those stories–I've compared it to a kind of haunting, but one that I welcome, wholeheartedly. And so thank you for reading; I promise to keep writing.

Printed in the United States
by Baker & Taylor Publisher Services